THE TREGENZA GIRLS

Rosemary Aitken titles available from
Severn House Large Print

Against the Tide
The Granite Cliffs
The Silent Shore
Stormy Waters

THE TREGENZA GIRLS

Rosemary Aitken

Severn House Large Print
London & New York

This first large print edition published in Great Britain 2007 by
SEVERN HOUSE LARGE PRINT BOOKS LTD of
9-15 High Street, Sutton, Surrey, SM1 1DF.
First world regular print edition published 2006 by
Severn House Publishers, London and New York.
This first large print edition published in the USA 2007 by
SEVERN HOUSE PUBLISHERS INC., of
595 Madison Avenue, New York, NY 10022.

British Library Cataloguing in Publication Data

Aitken, Rosemary
  The Tregenza girls. - Large print ed.
  1. Blind - Fiction 2. Sisters - Fiction 3. World War,
  1914-1918 - England - Cornwall (County) - Fiction
  4. Cornwall (England : County) - Social life and customs -
  20th century - Fiction 5. Domestic fiction 6. Large type
  books
  I. Title
  823.9'14[F]

  ISBN-13: 978-0-7278-7612-6

All Severn House titles are printed on acid-free paper.

Printed and bound in Great Britain by
MPG Books Ltd, Bodmin, Cornwall.

To Kay and David

Part One – Spring 1910

Chapter One

It was cold in the garden, that late March afternoon, when the two girls went out after lunch. A gusty little wind was blowing in from the sea, bringing the smell of salt with it, and the first of the primroses and daffodils were obviously out down on the cliffs because if you closed your eyes you could just detect a hint of their delicate fragrance, as well. The smell of Cornish spring. Helena took a long, exultant breath, revelling in the fresh feel of the breeze against her face and hair, but her sister was already tugging at her arm.

'Helena Tregenza, what are you thinking of!' Lucy could sound just like Aunt Edwards when she chose. 'You can't stand about here like a gypsy selling pegs. You'll catch pneumonia and so will I, though I at least had sense enough to put on my cape before I came outside. This easterly is bitter, and you've got a tea gown on. I don't know why you want to come at all. There's nothing out except a few camellias – and they're all brown and withered with the wind. And so will I be, soon. Come on! It's boring out here at this time of year.' She gave another tug.

Helena gave the impatient hand a squeeze.

'We'll go in in a minute. I'd like to go down just as far as my new bower first. I haven't managed to go near the place for weeks.' That was a subtle ploy. The bower had been a present from the family for Helena's nineteenth birthday last July, and it was Lucy herself who had suggested it – a sheltered seat set in the angle of the boundary wall, with an arch and climbing roses over it – and it had been a wonderful success. The bower had quickly become Helena's favourite hiding place and she had spent many contented hours there.

Lucy hesitated. 'Well...'

Helena pressed home her small advantage. 'Oh, come on. It's only for a minute, Lucy, and you know how much I like to come out when I can. A walk around the gardens does me good. I love all this – the lawns, and trees and everything...' She waved a vague hand in the direction of the grounds. 'Especially the scented herbs and flower beds – I don't know how you can be bored with it. I know I never am.' It was true, she thought, though sometimes she felt that she knew every inch of it by heart.

Lucy was still grumbling. 'Oh, very well. Just to the bower, then. But only a moment, mind.' She took her sister's arm in hers and led the way along the gravel path. 'Well, here we are – we're at the bower now. So, now you've had your walk and frozen both of us to death, perhaps you will consent to go inside. You know that Mama's expecting visitors for tea. And – since you insist on walking round the gardens in a gale without a hood – you'll have to go in anyway, to give Maisie time to do your hair again.'

Helena raised an exploratory hand. It was quite true. The exuberant curls were escaping from their restraining pins and threatening to tumble in ringlets round her face, just as they had done when she was young. She tucked in an errant strand and said in her best persuasive voice, 'Can't we sit down, just for a moment? At least we will be sheltered from the wind.' She did not wait for an answer, but had found the seat, and was already sitting down, patting the space next to her invitingly.

Lucy gave a loud, exasperated sigh. 'Well, Lena, you can stay out here and perish if you wish, but I—' She got no further, interrupted by a cheerful voice from the direction of the nearby gate, which led out from the garden to the lane.

'Good afternoon, ladies. What a nice surprise. Miss Tregenza – I am glad to see you here. And Miss Lucy, you are looking well. Turned out a lovely afternoon, although a trifle breezy, I suppose.'

Helena felt the hot flush flood her cheeks. She recognized the voice. And, it seemed, her sister did the same.

'Oh, James, I didn't see you there.' Lucy abandoned Helena on the seat and went running over to the wall, crunching on the gravel as she went. Her voice was gay and playful. 'Yes, Lena decided that she wished to

11

take a turn outside before our guests arrive for tea. Your mother is to join us, I believe. You are going to the mine venturers' meeting with Papa this afternoon, I suppose? Will you be looking in later on yourself?'

Helena found that she was hoping that he would. James Morrison had always been a bright spot in her life. He was not only the son of an ancient family friend, he was a distant cousin – almost like the brother she had never had. They had all played together in the park when they were very young – and he had always had the gift of mischief, with his blond fringe and his laughing bright-blue eyes. He'd even had a pony and had taught her how to ride, on one of those summer picnics long ago. Though of course there could be nothing of that nature any more, and she could not show Lucy's innocent enthusiasm for his presence now. She put on her best adult manners. 'Mr Morrison!' she cried, getting to her feet. 'What a pleasure to encounter you again.'

She took a step towards him as she spoke, and – inevitably – wished that she had not. A trailing rose branch caught her in the face and she let out a startled exclamation. 'Oh!' She clapped her hand to it.

Lucy was at her side in an instant, all concern. 'What is it, Lena? Have you hurt yourself? Here, let me see.' Helena took her hand away, and Lucy caught her breath. 'You have. You've got a nasty scratch – and it's bleeding too. You've got drops of red all over your fichu. You'll have to go inside and see to it – and change your dress as well. Come on, give me your arm.' And then, raising her voice she called aloud, 'I'm sorry, James. Helena has scratched herself. I'll have to take her in. My fault. I should never have left her on her own like that. Well – I'll see you later, perhaps.'

Helena was completely mortified. To make an exhibition of herself like that, in front of James, of all people! She wished she could close her eyes and disappear. And Lucy was so thoughtless. It wasn't that she meant to be unkind – it was simply that in looking after outward things she sometimes forgot that mental things could hurt. It too was a sort of blindness, in its way.

Helena raised her fingers to her face. She could feel the trickle of warm blood against her cheek. Red. She could remember red – just. The colour of a dress that she had worn one Christmas long ago. The colour of hot coals in the big granite fireplace in the drawing room; of apples; of Lucy's hair ribbons when she was very young. The colour of the poppies in the golden field, vivid against the blue of sea and sky, the day she'd caught her foot against the stile and tumbled on her head – almost the last colour she had seen before the world went dark and became a place of shadows evermore.

She sighed. It did no good to dwell on that. Aunt Edwards, Mama's maiden sister, always said that her affliction was a cross to bear, which she could use to bring her close to God. All very well for her, Helena thought, she did not have to put up with it. But the Reverend Flower from St Evan's church had said something once which did reach a chord, 'Raging against fate will not alter things, my dear. Learning to do your best in spite of it will make your misfortune at least easier to bear.'

It was a precept she tried to live by, most of the time – though sometimes she felt that she could scream at the injustice and frustration of it all. She turned now and gave Lucy an apologetic smile. 'I'm sorry if I spoiled your afternoon.'

She was rewarded with a deep offended sniff. 'It doesn't signify. It's only that it makes a change to talk to James – someone of my own age. Who else do I ever meet except Mama's tedious lady friends?'

'Oh, come on Lucy, I'm sure they're very nice. You've always been fond of Mrs Morrison.' Helena did not add that she would have given a great deal to attend this afternoon herself, but of course she was too much of an embarrassment. Not that she would be entirely excluded, naturally. She would be brought in to meet the ladies and to say hello, but then she would be taken to her room – where Maisie would come and serve her with her tea, until the guests came up to say goodbye and make embarrassed observations until they could decently escape. It had been like that ever since – at one of Mama's 'do's' – Helena had forgotten herself enough to jump briskly to her feet, sending the tea table flying, breaking several of the cups and upsetting hot tea across the vicar's knees. Everyone had been very kind, of course, but she had never been invited to a tea party again.

Lucy was obviously still following her former train of thought. 'Aunt Morrison is lovely, but she doesn't count, of course. We see so much of her. But I ask you, who else is likely to be there? Only Aunt Edwards with her pious platitudes, and half a dozen people that I've never met.'

'But surely Mrs Passemore-Jenkins is coming, too? Your friend Anna's mother? I'm sure that I heard Mama mention her.'

A mirthless laugh. 'Mrs Passemore-Jenkins is a colossal bore – on and on about all the balls and dinners that her eldest girl attends and how Anna will be going to all the same things very soon. It doesn't seem to strike her that I won't be going myself. It isn't fair. Sometimes I wish that I were you, and could get out of listening to her prate.'

It was a bitter little outburst and a concealed complaint, but Lucy had a point. Helena's affliction was a blight on both of them. It was not done for a younger sister to go to social functions, if the eldest was not out – and Papa was a stickler for convention on such points.

'Well, wait and see what happens,' Helena said. 'Perhaps Papa will come to change his mind. There's time enough. It's not as though you were old enough to have a beau, just yet.'

'What difference does it make how old I am, since I am never to meet anyone at all?' Lucy retorted. 'I shall end up like Aunt Edwards – just a sour old maid. It isn't fair. It's not my fault that you can't go to things.'

It was not like her sister to be so blunt and unkind. 'Lucy...?' Helena began, but they had reached the house by now and Lucy was already knocking on the door with a fierceness which showed how cross she was, and which brought the maid scuttling to let them in.

'Lor, Miss Elenner' – Maisie's broad local accent always rendered Helena's name that way – 'you're blown to rats. You come away and let me see to you. Idd'n long now before they people come. And you, Miss Lucy, you'd better run along. Your mother'll be wondering where you're to.'

'You'll come and read to me a little later on?' Helena said quickly. She did not want to part from Lucy on that irritated note, and reading was an evening ritual they had. Lucy often skipped whole passages or hurried through chapters in a monotone to get them done. Helena was well aware of that, but she looked forward to their sessions, all the same.

Lucy was not willing to be wooed. 'I doubt if after this I shall have time tonight. And you choose such boring things. No doubt your current story is an improving read – otherwise Papa would not have given it to you

– but there is no fun or excitement in it. Could you not contrive to find us something interesting, like Mr Conan Doyle? Or even a romance from the penny library. But *Adam Bede*? It's so worthy that it's a wonder I don't fall entirely asleep. It's a pity that someone else can't read aloud to you. Maisie could, perhaps. Everyone goes to school these days, and I dare swear even she knows how to read?'

'They learned me when I was at school,' Maisie said proudly, as she helped Helena upstairs. 'But I aren't so good at hard words, like 'part-ick-er-lar' and things with double-yous and zeds in them. But I could try for you, Miss Elenner, if you want me to. I don't like for to think of 'ee not having your bit of read at night.'

'It's all right, Maisie,' Helena said, feeling her way to the dressing table to sit down on the stool, 'Lucy is always threatening things like this, but she's good at heart, and she always comes round in the end. I'm sure she'll do it really. Won't you, Luce?'

But the click of a closing door was all the answer she received. Her sister had already gone downstairs.

Lucy put her teacup down and stole another surreptitious glance at the French clock on the drawing-room mantelpiece, but its turquoise hands seemed as immovable as the gilded cherubs which supported it on either side. She sighed. Surely it was not possible

17

that it was not yet four o'clock?

The afternoon was just as tedious as she thought that it would be. Partly because she was not in the sunniest of moods in any case.

If truth were told, she was inwardly ashamed at being so unpleasant to poor Lena. Of course she hadn't meant to be so horrid and unkind. It was just that – well – sometimes, secretly, she could recall a time, before her sister had that dreadful fall, when she herself had been the darling of the house, 'pretty little Lucy with her bouncing curls', the carefree baby whom everyone adored. Even Aunt Edwards and Papa had indulged her hopelessly, and she had learned exactly how to smile and get her way.

And then, quite suddenly, everything had changed, and now it was Helena who was the centre of everyone's concern. Lucy had been expected to grow up overnight and take responsibility for her sister, instead of the other way about, and to play the grown-up young lady of the house and assist Mama to entertain her friends, when Helena could not. Yet all the fun that should have gone with that – the house parties, the dinners and the balls – looked likely to be unavailable. She could hardly admit it, even to herself, but sometimes it was very hard to bear. Especially on occasions like today, with Mrs Passemore-Jenkins going on and on and on (exactly as predicted) about the balls and parties that Celestine, 'my eldest, such a pretty girl, and so much in demand', had been invited to

18

attend, and how Annabelle would soon be old enough as well – just as though no one else had any feelings to be hurt.

She glanced at the cherub clock again, but there was no comfort there. The hands were still pointing stubbornly at five to four. And there was no sign at all of James. Surely the wretched mine venturers' meeting must be over now?

'Do you not think so, Lucy dear?' The voice cut suddenly across her thoughts.

Lucy was suddenly aware of Mrs Passemore-Jenkins, who leaned forward in her chair so that her stays creaked audibly. She was a short, stout woman with a sloping chest – rather like a pouter pigeon, Lucy thought – who must have been whaleboned within an inch or two of death to be compressed into that beaded purple dress. She wore a dashing feathered hat as well that would have befitted someone half her age, and sported a dreadful folded purple parasol. She was smiling at Lucy now, with an expectant air.

Lucy found herself smiling back, though rather foolishly, as she had not the slightest notion what she was being asked. She had given up listening half an hour ago, halfway through the description of the 'sweetest little muslin dress with self-embroidery' which was apparently being made for Annabelle in preparation for her sister's birthday ball.

'I'm quite sure, Mrs Passemore-Jenkins,' she murmured dutifully, wondering what nonsense she was agreeing to. The superiority of ribbons over lace for trimming a girl's first ball-dress, probably. That's what she had been droning on about before. Annabelle's mother had strong views on that. However, it did not greatly signify. A vague reply and warm smile was usually all that was required.

Not today, it seemed. 'Why, Lucy!' Aunt Edward's voice was sharp. 'Is that all you can say? When your friends have been so kind as well. I'm very sorry, Mrs Passemore-Jenkins, I'm sure I don't know what young girls are coming to, these days!'

Lucy felt the colour rising to her cheeks. 'Of course, it's very good of Mrs Passemore-Jenkins,' she blurted, and then – seeing from their looks that something more was still required from her – she added hastily, 'I'm sure that it would be the very thing.' She attempted to hide her confusion with one of her most winning smiles.

Aunt Edwards was looking daggers still, but Mrs Passemore-Jenkins was mollified. She said, 'That is quite settled, then,' in a triumphant tone of voice, and leaned back against the cushions of her chair, making the whalebone stays protest again. 'I was sure that dear Lucy would welcome it, and Annabelle was hoping she'd say yes. So, if she has your blessing...?' she added, to Mama.

'Dear Lucy' was wishing fervently by now that she had paid a little more attention to what was being said, especially when Mama flashed her a doubtful look and muttered,

'Well, Lucy, if you're sure...?'

But Mrs Passemore-Jenkins was rushing on. She was like a runaway locomotive when she chose to be – dangerous to hinder and impossible to stop. 'There then, Lucy! Your mother says you may. So, it only remains for us to ask permission from your dear Papa and – look! – you will have the opportunity to do so straight away. For here he comes this minute, riding up the lane towards the house! I can see him through the window as I speak. What could be more fortunate?'

Lucy was forced to smile assent again, though really it was not fortunate at all. Matters were swiftly going from bad to worse. She'd intended merely to avoid embarrassment and cover a sticky situation with a smile, but now she was going to have to ask Papa for permission for something – and since she had not the slightest idea what the invitation was, her ignorance would clearly be revealed. She gave an inward groan. She was always being chided for her daydreaming. Inattention to their guests was inexcusable enough, but exposure of her little artifice would be more damning still.

She made a desperate resolve never to let her concentration wander in that way again, but of course it was already far too late. The front door was opening and she could hear Maisie greeting Papa in the hall.

'Why, it's the master, and Mr James as well. Allow me to take your hats and coats,' she began, politely, and then added, in her own inimitable way, which sometimes half drove Mama to despair, 'Dear saints! It's blowing half a hurricane out there. Come in out the draught, the pair of you, before you catch your death.'

Then Papa's voice. 'Thank you, Maisie. I'm sorry if we are a little late. A little mishap at Penvarris mine, though fortunately nobody was seriously hurt. Is my wife about? Still with her ladies at the tea party, perhaps?'

'Oh yes, sir. In the drawing room, they are, all chattering on like Trevenna brook. Though the mistress is expecting you – said to send you in when you arrived, if you'd a mind to it: I'm to bring up fresh tea and sandwiches. There should still be cake, we put out two kinds so they won't have ate it all, and Cook is toasting you some muffins now. Though, course, you could have them in your smoking room, if you'd rather do.'

The smoking room? Lucy found that she had held her breath. Then Papa was laughing. 'No, by all means, we'll go and join the fair sex after all, since we're invited to. Come, James. Put on a public face. That poor fellow is in good hands by now and you know there was nothing we could do to help. They think of us as gentry and we were simply in the way. Come and charm the ladies – it is nothing grand. I believe your mother's here, in any case, and no doubt Lucy will be glad you've come.' And almost before Lucy had time to blush, the door was opening and there they were: Papa splendid in cutaway coat and

22

waistcoat, complete with his gold watch chain and cravat, whilst James looked very young and awkward in his riding clothes.

'...can't you, Lucy? Ah, Paul, my dear brother! There you are,' Aunt Edwards said, and Lucy realized that, once again, she had allowed her attention to go wandering off.

She was spared the embarrassment she feared, however, because – as soon as greetings had been decently exchanged – Mrs Passemore-Jenkins burst out, 'It is so convenient that you should arrive now. I have just invited Lucy to spend Saturday night with us. We are having a small house party, for my eldest, Celestine, and we propose a little ball that evening. Of course, it would not be proper for Lucy to join in, but she might watch the dancers from the upstairs balcony, and come down for supper, do you think? That is what Annabelle always liked to do, and she would so enjoy a little company, and someone of her own age to talk to afterwards. Lucy has said that she would like to come, and her mama consents. So it is up to you. Come, what do you say?'

Lucy felt her spirits plummet to her boots. Of all things guaranteed to make her feel deprived, the sight of other people dancing, when she knew she never might, was fairly high upon the list. Even for supper she would need a dress and she had nothing suitable to wear. Other people's gowns were no delight to her, and besides Helena would feel excluded too. Yet it seemed that she had just

23

agreed to this, by accident, and now she must bear the consequence with as good a grace as possible. She found that she was waiting impatiently for what Papa would say: if he found some objection, as he often did, she was sure she could feign disappointment to a nicety.

He was not, however, in obliging mood. He looked at her and smiled – obviously the venturers' meeting had been a successful one. 'I dare say it would do young Lucy good. She has little enough to entertain her here. So yes, by all means, if she wants to go.'

'Then we'll send the carriage for her. Half-past six perhaps, that will give the coachman time to fetch our other guests. And we will deliver her back to you on Sunday, safe and sound, directly after church.'

Lucy's heart sank lower still at this. Dr Flower, at St Evan's, was acceptable enough – a known, familiar figure who'd begun a choir and had a slightly High Church tendency, but kept his sermons reasonably short. The Passemore-Jenkinses attended the neighbouring parish, where there was a great deal less incense, and long impassioned homilies that went on an hour or more. However, she forced her lips into a smile and said, 'Well, that will be delightful!' in a cheerful voice. After all, she told herself, it could have been much worse. A visit to one of Mrs Passemore-Jenkins's charities or – worse – some trip into Penzance to choose material for 'little Anna's sweetly pretty dress'.

Annabelle had been Lucy's closest chum at school and they had kept up their acquaintance ever since, but recently the friendship had begun to change. Gone were the days of dolls and giggling, and passing notes when teachers couldn't see. Anna was only interested in her appearance now and it seemed that she could talk of nothing else except the stir she hoped to make when she reached eighteen and was old enough to go to balls. Perhaps it was part of growing up, Lucy thought, a little loftily. There were so few people from Penvarris way, at Miss Worthington's Educational Establishment for Young Ladies, that perhaps they had been thrown together, more than anything: certainly there were times when she felt she no longer had much in common with her friend.

'Well, Miss Lucy, here we meet again!' She looked up to see that James Morrison was already in possession of a cup of tea, and had somehow contrived to find a chair near hers. He selected a slice of cake from Maisie's proferred tray. 'So, you are to go to Celestine's birthday ball?'

'Only to the supper,' she muttered, knowing that she spoke with less than perfect grace.

'Then I shall have the pleasure of seeing you, no doubt. I am invited to the ball myself. Perhaps you will permit me to escort you to the buffet table and assist you with your plate?'

And suddenly the afternoon took wings, even when James was commandeered by Mrs

Passemore-Jenkins, who was sitting on the other side of him.

When Lucy went to read to Lena later on – she'd always meant to do that, really, she supposed – she gave her sister such a bright account of everything, and such a humorous account of purple pigeons, feathered hats and creaking stays, that there was very little progress made with *Adam Bede*.

James had intended to ride directly home, after he had extricated himself from Mrs Passemore-Jenkins, but instead he turned his horse around and went out to the mine. He wasn't sure exactly what he was hoping to achieve, but he was still vaguely troubled by that nasty incident.

It was only by accident that he had witnessed it. He had come out from the meeting of the venturers in an elated mood. It was only the second time that he'd attended one of those affairs and the first time that he had ever spoken up. But he had swung the meeting with his speech this afternoon and so he'd been an influence on the future of the place. It made him feel proprietorial and proud, and he'd decided on an impulse to go down and look at it – the 'venture' of which he owned a tiny share.

He had been down the mine before, of course – with Grandfather, who had once worked underground himself. Actually down into the shaft that time, wearing a miner's helmet with a candle on the front, and riding the whim the way the miners did. James could still remember that heart-stopping descent, into what seemed like endless darkness and the noise of hell: the rattle of the chains, the flimsy cage and the feeling of relief which had washed over him when the driver, far above them in the engine house, let out the valves and brought them safely to a stop. That's why he had spoken as he had today, in favour of a new winding engine for the largest pit.

He reined in his horse and sat looking down at it. It still looked much as it had this afternoon, except that the sun was beginning to set and some of the surface workers were packing up and making for the 'dry' to change their clothes. The carpenter's shop, however, was still hard at work – you could see the shapes against the oil lamps through the door, and the blacksmith's forge was still ablaze with light, while the different sounds of hammering issued from them both.

Men were still pushing trams along the tracks, up to the spoil heaps and clanking back again, though they too would shortly turn off for the day. Yet the sound of the stamps and the engines never ceased. It made very little difference to a man deep underground whether it was day or night outside, and as one shift – as now – came 'up to grass', another was already going down to take its place. James recalled a funny story his grandfather had told, about the time the stamps had been stopped for a repair – and the silence had kept the neighbourhood awake!

And over there the processing sheds, where the settling tanks and shaking tables were, washing the tin and other metals from the useless waste after the stone had been smashed small enough. That was where the accident had been this afternoon. James had been sitting pretty much where he was now, when all at once there was a mighty scream, and a complete commotion in the furthest shed. He'd got down from his horse, instinctively, but did not quite like to go running in and see what had occurred.

It was not very long before the mystery was solved. Two men came out half carrying a stocky, fattish lad, and laid him on the ground not far from James. The boy had turned the colour of greengage jam. His eyes were shut and he was giving moaning gasps. It was easy to see why. His shirt and working waistcoat were half-drenched in blood, and his right hand was a twisted mangled pulp.

James went over. 'Anything I can do to help?'

The younger of the two attendants squinted up at him. 'You a doctor, are 'ee?' and – as James shook his head – 'Well, shouldn't think so, then, should you?' He turned to his companion. 'I'll get over to the stores. Bit of carbolic and some rag. We'll bind it up for 'un.' He bent down to the victim and said, quite tenderly, 'Then we'll see if Frank'll take 'ee home.' He gave James a last disdainful look and set off at a gallop.

James shuffled on his feet. 'Won't you get a doctor to him?'

The older man looked up. He was grey and grizzled and up to now he had paid no attention to James at all. 'Capt'n'll come and see to him, and that's the next best thing. He generally d'deal with things like this. Don't have a proper doctor here if we can help. Cost you a guinea, just to have him shake his head. 'Sides, nearest doctor's over to St Just. Have to go and fetch 'un, if you wanted 'un. Be half an hour before he got to we, even if the office would agree to telephone.'

James thought about the doctor, who was a friend of his – or the father of a friend in any case. He'd said that poorer people wouldn't call him when they should, although he very often waived the fee. James wondered what he would have said to this. 'What happened?' he enquired.

'Lad caught his fingers in a pulley-belt somehow – silly bugger – he shouldn't have been there. Very nearly lost that hand, he did. If it hadn't been for Eddie there, pulling the lever and letting it go slack, it would have been some mess. But as it is, the lad will be all right. Look at him, he's coming to himself.'

It was true, up to a fashion. The boy was opening his eyes. He looked at his bleeding fingers, and muttered in distress, 'How am I going to keep my Mary now? And her with a baby on its way as well?' Then he lay back with a moan and closed his eyes again.

James put his fingers in his pocket. There

was a sovereign there. Not quite a guinea, but it had to help. He held it out. 'Get him a doctor.'

The grizzled man got slowly to his feet. 'The welfare fund will help 'im, if it has to do. We don't take charity from strangers 'ere.'

It was said so stoutly that James felt inches high. Nonetheless he held his ground. 'I'm not a stranger. I'm a venturer – a shareholder in the mine. The welfare of my workers is part of my concern. If I want to pay to have this man attended to, then I've a right to do it, I believe.'

The man looked closely at him. 'You, a venturer? You're very young for that. 'Ere – you aren't young Morrison, by any chance?'

'That's right.'

'Well, how didn't you say right away that you was one of we? I knew your grandfather when he was 'ere – only a kiddly-boy then I was, but he was good to me.'

James nodded. 'Left me his shares when I turned twenty-one, a month or two ago.' He had been very fond of his old grandfather. The old man may have struck gold in the end but he'd never forgotten what his background was. That's why he'd come back and put his money in the mines – though Pater thought he was a fool for it, and never made a secret of the fact.

'No future in dwelling on the past,' he'd said a hundred times to James. 'We're as good as gentlefolk, these days, my boy, and don't you forget it.' It was the same thing every

30

time. 'Railway trains and bicycles. That's where the future is. Not blooming tin-mining!'

Which is perhaps why Grandfather had left half of his estate to James, instead of all to Pater as everyone expected him to do.

The grizzled man stuck out a grimy hand. 'Pleased to meet 'ee. Bill Raddle is my name. The old fellow would have known it. He'd be proud of you today. Spoke up for the miners like a good 'un, I believe.'

James found he was grinning. 'How did you hear of that?'

It had been quite an argument, in fact, and he had spoken out although he was by far the youngest there. Some of the old school had not been impressed – made it clear they did not care for 'jack-come-latelys' with too much to say. One in particular, a portly man, with an air of pompous self-importance, had roused James to fury with his ignorance. 'If that damn-fool engineer – Captain Maddern or whatever his name is – won't allow his men to ride to surface on the old machine because the winding-gear is worn, then they can damn well walk up like their fathers did. Maddern can't demand a whole new winding engine 'cause he feels like it. Thousands that would cost us, and he must know that. Tin isn't the commodity it was. Prices are falling all the time. You can't pour good money after bad.' He sat down, and looked around him for approval.

Several people nodded, but James was on

his feet. 'But we can't go on without it. Twice it has only been the skill of the engineman which stopped the winding-gear from running out and causing a nasty accident.' Then inspiration struck him. 'And there'd be benefits for us. Couple the engine to the winding shaft when it's wanted for the men, and use it for the compressor in between. Then we could use those air-compressor drills you gentlemen have just installed at such expense.' He found that he was unconsciously holding his lapels, just as the pompous man had done, and he let go hastily and sat down again, his face burning.

'Young jackanapes,' the pompous man remarked loudly, as if James wasn't there. 'What does he know about venture capital? I've had shares in this mine for years – and paid calls on them too, a dozen times. And I say, no engine. And if Maddern persists in making trouble then we turn him off.'

But Paul Tregenza had supported James. 'Lad's right, you know. Seems like good sense to me,' and Tregenza was an influential man. The proposal for the engine was passed, and several people afterwards had come up to shake James by the hand, though that pompous idiot Robinson had walked past and cut him dead. He had given a good account of himself, he thought.

'How did you hear of that?' he said again. 'The meeting only finished a half an hour ago.'

Raddle laughed. 'You'd be surprised. News

travels fast round here. But we'll take that sovereign, if you're still offering. Different thing if you're a Morrison. I'll see he gets a doctor, if I have to use the damty telephone meself. I'll ask the Cap'n – here he comes with Eddie Purdy now.'

James had no wish to encounter Eddie any more. 'Very good.' He turned back to his horse, and to his surprise saw Paul Tregenza there. The older man was standing on a little wall, watching him, and holding both their mounts.

'I saw that you had come this way, and I came after you. You'd not forgotten that you were expected back to tea?'

He had forgotten, drat it, but he said, 'Not at all,' and quickly gave an outline of events.

Tregenza nodded. 'I saw you give him money. That was kind. Don't let the others see you – there must be an accident of this kind every week.' He climbed into the saddle. 'You can't help all of them, you know.'

James was mounting too. 'Unless I was a doctor, like the fellow said.' He turned to Paul Tregenza. 'I'd thought about it once or twice, you know. Mama's brother is a surgeon – studied up in London, years and years ago. I've often thought I'd like to do the same. Do something useful, instead of frittering my life away. Dr Neill's son, Rupert, is an old friend of mine, and he's going to London later in the year to read medicine himself. He's told me all about it and I must say I am tempted to go up with him. Though Pater wouldn't like it, you could be sure of that.'

Tregenza urged his horse into a walk. 'Haven't you got money of your own these days? Perhaps that is your answer. You'd have no trouble to matriculate, and I'm sure your father would come round in the end.' And they talked of nothing else until they reached the house and attention had turned to Lucy and her ball.

He smiled. He was quite pleased with the way he had handled that. It was obvious that Mrs Passemore-Jenkins had made a set at him, and wanted to make a match for him with Celestine. Thanks to Grandfather's inheritance, again no doubt.

Well, he was not ready for entrapment yet. If he was to wed – and he had no plans at present to do anything of the kind – he would prefer a livelier sort of wife. Someone like Helena, before she had that fall: though of course now it was impossible to think of her that way, and anyway she had always been more of a sister than a potential sweetheart. And Lucy, too.

Lucy! She was getting to be a pretty little thing. Very young, of course, and rather scatter-brained – but charming, certainly. So charming that he wouldn't mind at all escorting her to the supper table at Celestine's ball.

'Evening, young Morrison. You back here again?' Bill Raddle's voice brought James back to the present with a jerk.

'Came out to see the sunset,' James replied. It was a picture too: the dark silhouettes of wheels and ventilation shafts stark against the redness of the sky. 'And to find out how Jethro's getting on.'

Raddle smiled. 'They had the doctor for him, like you said. Stitched it up some 'and-some, and gave him laudanum. Says he might get the movement in his fingers back – and if he does he'll be as right as rain. Thanks to you that will be, if he does. Had a whip-round for the other shilling and a bit more besides, but 'e never would have had it seen to proper if it weren't for you. So thank 'ee, Mr Morrison, I won't forget today. Nor Jethro either, I'll be bound.' And off he went.

James passed him on the road, a tired figure with his grizzled hair.

He thought about it later, when he got home at last, and was joining Pater for a glass of brandy after dinner in the library. Pater had only recently begun this ritual – 'a rite of passage for a gentleman' he said – and it was not an unqualified success. Conversation was always unnaturally stiff. What would he say if James described this afternoon's events? Snort into his brandy glass, no doubt. No, better to talk of safer subjects, like the Passemore-Jenkins' ball. James had became, quite suddenly, 'a catch', positively begged to escort daughters here and there, but the Passemore-Jenkins family were the summit of ambition hereabouts. An invitation from them was a passport to the best society. Even Pater was impressed by that.

James took a gulp of brandy, and wished

that he had not – though he managed not to make a total ass of himself by spluttering. He didn't really care for brandy and cigars: he had a secret preference for beer and cigarettes, which his friend Rupert had recently introduced him to. But he dared not confess to that. They were vices of which Pater would surely disapprove, and he didn't want to scupper the London project straight away.

'Lucy, eh?' his father huffed, sipping his drink with an appraising air. 'Well, you could do worse. Though the Passemore-Jenkins filly would make a splendid match. The family's well connected and there are no sons. Everything will come to those two girls, you know. I am sure you could charm Celestine, if you put your mind to it. Your mother seems to think that you'd have quite a chance with her. Give the matter a little thought, perhaps?'

James forced himself to smile. Celestine Passemore-Jenkins was amiable enough: pretty, in an insipid sort of way, but she had no conversation and a habit of saying, 'Well, I never. Is that so?' to almost everything, which dissuaded a fellow from venturing to talk to her at all. There were a dozen girls that he'd prefer to squire. Much better to escort little Lucy, as he'd planned, though he hastened to make his motives clear, before Pater started jumping to conclusions.

'I shan't be trying to charm anyone,' he said. 'I've made my mind up what I want to do. I want to study medicine in London like Uncle Bertie did, and I've no intention of rushing into things before I leave and breaking anybody's heart.'

He waited for the outburst, but Pater simply said, 'Well, perhaps you're wise. I hear they have young women up there too, these days – special colleges for them and everything. Bluestockings most of them, of course, and no doubt useless when it comes to keeping house, but if there's money, that doesn't signify. Their parents are a decent class of people, I believe, or they wouldn't be sending them at all. Or so Tregenza says. You know he called on me earlier, while you were getting dressed for dinner?'

So that was that. Paul Tregenza had paved the way for him. James found he had the leisure to look forward to the ball.

Chapter Two

Helena was glad when Saturday evening came at last. The whole week seemed to have been a whirl of preparation and Lucy had been quite impossible for days, able to talk of nothing except her dressmaker (the very thing she had complained of in Annabelle's mama!) until Helena thought that she would be relieved never to hear another description of flounces, fittings and ruched sleeves.

'It is to be of cream organza,' Lucy must have told her at least a dozen times, 'With an accordion-pleated overskirt and a pastel sash. After all, I am not really 'out', and anything too modish would not be suitable.' She was obviously trying to be modish all the same, by being fashionably half bored and loftily detached: but when the longed-for evening came at last she was so excited that she forgot herself and came up to whirl around Helen's sitting-room to 'show off' her first long skirt – as if her sister could do more than listen to the swish.

Helena was quite thankful to hear the carriage wheels go clattering away, and know that Lucy was safely on her way, though secretly she felt a little like Cinderella. Except that there was no fairy godmother for her, she thought.

She was sitting at her pianoforte – a present from Papa. She was an accomplished pianist and usually it lifted her spirits when she played, but tonight not even Mozart could assuage her pique. She stopped in the middle of her favourite gavotte, banged out three angry discords and slammed down the lid – just in time to hear a footstep on the stairs.

It was Papa, coming to see her, as he did every night. Helena was embarrassed to recognize his step, but all the same it raised her mood at once. She turned away and said, 'Good evening, Papa!' before he said a word. He crossed to where she was sitting, the floorboards creaking softly under him, and she heard him set down his nightlight on the mantelpiece. She could detect the faint lightening of her gloom the candle gave, and smell his familiar scent: bay rum and brilliantine. She stretched out her hand to him.

'Good evening, Helena.' He took her palm between his own. His touch was reassuring – warm, dry and firm. He pressed her fingers briefly and drew his hand away – Papa was not given to caresses, even fleeting ones. 'I trust this evening has not been too tedious for you,' he said. 'I should have been up to see you earlier, but your mother and I have been entirely occupied in seeing to Lucille.' He gave an ironic little laugh. 'She had such a large portmanteau for a single night you would think she was going away for weeks – and even when the carriage came for her, your mother insisted on fetching an extra cushion so as not to crush the dress. She was almost more excited than your sister. I have had my hands full with the pair of them, I assure you.'

He sounded so wry that Helena found that she was smiling too. 'I'm sure she looked enchanting. It sounds a charming gown.'

Papa chuckled. 'And so it should be, after all the trouble and expense. But certainly she looked a pretty little thing. Quite grown up suddenly, in fact, with her ringlets all piled up and pinned with flowers. Not quite the ugly sister driving to the ball, though it must feel a little bit like that to you.'

It was so exactly what she had been thinking that she felt her colour rise. She struggled to keep her answer whimsical. 'Well, I have not been weeping into the ashes, I'm afraid, as the fairy tale demands. I have amused myself by playing the piano for a little while.'

'So I heard,' he observed, drily. Obviously her peevish thumpings had been clearly audible. 'And your sister did not quite neglect you, after all. She came to read to you this afternoon, I think?'

Helena laughed. 'She did. At least that was her intention, I believe, but she was so full of this trip to Annabelle's – what I thought that she should absolutely take, and whether two Sunday bonnets were a necessity in case it came to rain – that there was very little reading done at all.' She heard his answering murmur of amusement, and was moved to add, 'Actually, it surprised me that she was so keen to go: she has always scoffed at Annabelle for watching her parents' parties through the stairs. She always said that it was childish, and now she wants to do it for herself.'

'I think the offer of young James Morrison to take her down to supper might have played some part in her sudden change of heart.' There was a touch of laughter in his voice.

Despite herself she stiffened. 'James?'

'She didn't tell you about that?'

'No, she didn't mention it.' She kept her tone as light as possible. It was the one part of the proposed evening about which Lucy hadn't said a word. 'She thought that I would tease her, I expect, and so she kept it to herself. Well, I know she likes his company, and I'm not surprised. He's very charming, and of course they've been good friends for years. I'm sure it would be a splendid match for her.'

Papa chuckled. 'I don't think we need to call the marriage banns just yet. This is her debut supper at a grown-up party, that is all. She is a little young for real entanglements. And James hopes to go away to university, I hear.'

Helena said briskly, 'Well, anyway, it doesn't signify. I hope she has a lovely evening.' She forced herself to smile. 'We can't waste all that clever dressmaking.'

He must have realized that she was a little bit upset, because he reached out suddenly and squeezed her hand again. That was unusual. Papa was generally very formal in his dealings with his girls now they were growing up: he always called them by the full versions of their names, for instance, and rose to his feet whenever they came in – just as he did for Mama. He could even seem a little bit severe sometimes, insisting on correctness even when at home. Lucy grumbled that he was a social dinosaur, a stickler for conventions and 'not a bit like Annabelle's papa' – but Helena sensed the real affection behind that stiff facade, and knew that he had secretly spoiled them both when they were young and still indulged them in most material regards.

Even now he was saying, in an altered tone of voice, 'I see that I am thoughtless, Helena. I can read it in your face. Of course you must wish that you could go out yourself, and I'd forgotten that you were great friends with young Morrison when...' He hesitated, and for a moment she thought that he was going to talk about the accident, and say something that would embarrass both of them, but all he said was, 'When you were a little younger. No doubt that's why your sister didn't mention him. Poor Helena. Do you mind so very much?'

And she had sufficient control of her emotions to say, with a little laugh, 'Oh, don't be so absurd, Papa. Of course I'm quite delighted for Lucille. And it gives me something different to look forward to – no doubt she'd tell me all about it when she comes home tomorrow afternoon.'

Her father's visit had been cheering, though, and she was able to turn back to Mozart with a better grace.

Maisie stood out on the doorstep, watching Miss Lucy's carriage drive away. Now that would be something, wouldn't it, she thought – all dressed up like Christmas, to go off to a party, and have nothing else to do but smile and chat. Mind you'd have to watch your step. That gauze organza of Miss Lucy's dress was so dratted fine, you could put your slipper through it if you didn't watch your feet.

Well, it wasn't a problem she was likely to be confronted with herself. She looked down at her own blue worsted skirt – Mrs Tregenza gave the servants new material each Christmas to make their uniforms, and a fresh pair of grey lisle stockings and neat brown button boots. Not like some households that you heard about. There was a great deal to be thankful for. But there was no harm in dreaming, Maisie told herself. After all, she wasn't so much older than Miss Lucille – Maisie was only just nineteen herself – though the difference between them seemed much more than that. Of course, by the time she was Miss Lucy's age, she thought, she had already been in service for three years, pretty well, while everyone still treated Miss Lucy like a child.

Anyway, there was no point standing here all night. There were lots of things to do and it was getting cold. Besides, Miss Lucy wasn't the only one off gadding hereabouts – she was hoping to go out herself a little later on. She closed the door behind her – as gently as she could, to disguise the fact that she'd been loitering – and went hurriedly upstairs to lay the fires and put away the garments still strewn about the bed, where Miss Lucy had been deciding what to pack and take with her.

She was just putting the last of the rejected gowns back on its hanger, and enjoying the music which she could faintly hear, when there were three sudden discords and the

43

piano-playing stopped. She winced. Miss Elenner was in her rare, unhappy mood. Well, who could blame her? You couldn't help feeling jealous of Miss Lucy now and then, but who would want to be in Miss Elenner's shoes? She closed her eyes and walked across the room, trying to imagine what the world must be if you couldn't see what you were at, but barging painfully into the open wardrobe door soon put a stop to that.

Maisie put the dress away, and went downstairs again, rubbing her elbow where she'd barked it on the door. She reached the kitchen where she found the kitchen maid, sitting at the table and already eating tea. ' 'Ello, Rosie,' Maisie said. The two were friends.

'Ah, there you are, at last!' That was Mrs Lovett, the cook-housekeeper, emerging from the scullery to gesture to the range. 'Your supper's on the saucepan keeping hot. I've had it ready nigh on half an hour. Wonder it isn't spoiled, the time you took to come.'

Maisie picked up a knitted oven cloth and fetched the plate, which was too hot to touch. It was a good meal too: if there was anything left over from the table, Mrs Tregenza always allowed the staff to have the 'scraps'. Today it was roast beef and carrots, and a slice of bread as well. Maisie had never eaten half so well at home.

Mrs Lovett came in and scraped chopped cabbage into a waiting pan. 'You'll have to eat up quickly, if you're going to do. I'll be

44

wanting that table in a minute or two, to roll the pastry on. Master has taken a fancy to some apple pie today.'

Maisie sat down quickly and tucked into her meal, while Mrs Lovett waddled over to fetch the teapot from the hearth. She was a short red-faced woman almost as wide as she was high, with her greying hair swept up into a bun and a spotless apron round her ample form. She poked at a bubbling saucepan, and opened the oven door to test the joint of meat, before she came back and put the teapot down, remarking with a sigh, 'You two going out to the chapel lantern-slide show this evening, did I hear?'

Maisie made a final mouthful of the bread and beef. 'Mrs Tregenza has agreed we can. Rosie's got the evening off in any case, and I'm going to come back early on my half-day off, in lieu.'

Mrs Lovett finished pouring out the tea, and added a careful spoon of sugar to each cup. 'Don't know what girls these days are coming to. Never would have dared to ask a thing like that when I was young.' It was only a token protest, though, both the girls knew that. Mrs Lovett was generous enough at heart, but she couldn't let them go without complaint. 'Well, I suppose we'll have to manage. Maisie, you can take Miss Helena her soup up on a tray – she's got a headache, and she's eating in her room – and go up and lay the table before you disappear. And turn back the beds as well. Edgar will serve at

45

table, but he can't do everything.'

Edgar was the lugubrious manservant, who kept himself apart. He had been with the master since he was a boy, and in fact he did peculiarly little, Maisie thought, except prepare his master's bath water and clothes, clean the boots and silver once a week and preside over the wine bottles now and then. However, she knew better than to say as much.

'I will,' she said, placatingly, 'soon as I've finished this. After that there'll only be the supper trays to do – shouldn't be much else until the family go to bed, and I shall be safely home again by then.'

Mrs Lovett gave a mock-affronted sniff. 'Meantime, it will be me who's running up and down every time they ring the bell, I suppose. Why you want to go out in the cold in any case and sit for ages in a draughty hall just to see a lot of heathens in them pictures, I don't know.'

Maisie said nothing. There was a reason, naturally – and not only that it made a change from work, and there would be buns and cocoa afterwards. A reason called Frank Carter – and he was a carter, too. Nice-looking in a homely sort of way, she s'posed, if you had a taste for freckles, grey eyes and heavy boots. His father was a carrier out at Penvarris mine, and – though nothing had ever been exactly *said* – she knew that Frank was putting a few pence by each week, in the hope of buying a wagon of his own and being able to support a wife and family one day.

However, Mrs Lovett didn't know about all this – one reason why Maisie always went out with Rosie when she could. Servants were not encouraged to have followers. The cook was still grumbling gently. 'Well, I don't know, I'm sure. Just as well there's only the two of them eating in the dining room tonight. Miss Helena is going to have hers in her room.'

Rosie – a thin, apologetic girl with mousy hair – was about to make some earnest answer to all this, but Maisie caught her eye and shook her head. Rosie thought better of whatever she had been about to say, and moved off to take the dishes and wash them in the sink, pouring the hot water from the kettle over them, and adding a little soft soap and washing-soda mixture from the enamel bucket on the floor. There were only their two plates and the kitchen knives and forks, but she was taking as much care over them as she might have done if she was washing the best china from upstairs – it was enough to try the patience of a saint.

Maisie rushed up to lay the table and came downstairs again. Rosie was still wiping down the sink. Mrs Lovett must have gone out to the safe, the ventilated zinc box in the yard where things were put to cool.

Maisie said impatiently, 'Oh, come on, Rosie, do, for Heaven's sake. It's getting on for seven, and if we don't get a move on we shall be too late to go.' She was already pulling on her cape and a pair of crochet

47

cotton gloves which Mrs Tregenza had passed down to her – almost as good as new they were, only a very little stained. 'Otherwise Mrs Lovett will be back, and finding other jobs for you to do.'

'All right, then,' Rosie answered, with a grin. She wiped her reddened hands dry on a piece of towelling cloth, and whipped off her apron. 'Just half a minute while I get my shawl.'

And a moment later they were off, laughing and chattering in the lane. Two hours of freedom stretched ahead of them. You didn't have to be Miss Lucy in a fancy gown to have a jolly evening, Maisie thought.

Lucy was having a delightful time – rather to her own surprise, in fact. The birthday ball was in full swing by now. She and Annabelle had not yet come downstairs because there was dancing and they could not join in, but they had taken up a strategic position on the upper landing where they could see and not be seen, to wait for supper time.

Annabelle had found them a splendid vantage point, and had even got the maid to bring out a pair of small upholstered chairs which she carefully positioned in the shadows, commanding a good view of the reception hall below. There was even a glimpse into the big room opposite, where the oriental rugs and tiger skins had been moved away, and the floor polished for the dancers. Lucy found herself leaning forward to peer through the banisters – exactly as though she were a child of six again.

When the two girls were still at school, Annabelle had often talked with glee of doing this and 'spying on the guests', though Lucy had been secretly scornful of such childish goings-on. Tonight, however, she could see the joy of it. Of course, it was not something she could have done at home. There were no parties like this at the Tregenza house these days – it would have been too difficult for Helena.

'Look,' Annabelle whispered, close beside her ear, 'there's Celestine this minute. Do you like the gown? Now if I were her I would have wanted the very latest style – "directoire", they call it – with a narrow skirt and the prettiest little Empire waist high up. It comes from France, but London is in a frenzy over it. It's very flattering, and it is quite the thing – but Celestine said she was too thin for it, and insisted on her pigeon look and those old-fashioned frills.'

'That young man seems to like it,' Lucy said.

Annabelle fetched a long despairing sigh. 'I know. Elder sisters have all the luck, don't they? That's our cousin Simon. Isn't he divine?'

Lucy murmured something meaningless. Divine was not the word. He was quite dark and handsome, she supposed, and Celestine was palely pretty in a frou-frou gown with a sweeping hem and a torrent of little fabric

49

roses at the waist – though that neckline drew attention to her freckles, Lucy thought. But she had no time to spend admiring them. Her eyes were for the young man now striding through the door, his face flushed and his fair hair flopping forward in a most endearing way. James!

She didn't speak his name aloud, but in her head she tried to call to him, willing him to glance towards her. He did not look up.

'Honestly, it isn't fair,' Annabelle was still muttering, in an undertone. 'I would give anything to have a dance with Simon Robinson, and by the time it's my turn, no doubt, he will have left and gone away – or Celestine will have got him, which is worse.'

Lucy dragged her thoughts away from James for long enough to say, 'Robinson? Is he the venturer down at Penvarris mine? I seem to remember that James mentioned him, after the meeting the other afternoon.'

'Gracious! I shouldn't think so!' Annabelle's tone contrived to suggest that such mercenary matters were beneath the notice of a Passemore-Jenkins. 'His father might be, I suppose, he has a finger in lots of local pies. It isn't something I really understand, and I don't imagine Simon takes any part in it. He's too interested in his horses out on their estate. The family have a huge place out Tregenna way.'

'So he has expectations?' Lucy was teasing. 'No wonder your sister is smiling at him so. Though it's no use, if he is your cousin, anyway.'

'Well, we're only second cousins really, so it would be possible.' Annabelle was pink. 'Though I don't think he likes her specially – but I don't suppose that he'd ever look at me. Celestine doesn't help. She calls me "little sister" in a tolerating way and tells me to "run along", whenever he's around, and then of course he treats me like a child. I'm sure she does it on purpose. It really isn't fair.'

She might have gone on talking in this vein if one of the maidservants had not suddenly appeared downstairs and flung open the door of the big dining room, where a sumptuous buffet was set out on trestle tables all around the walls. The servant nodded to Mr Passemore-Jenkins, who climbed part way up the stairs, and clapped his hands. 'Ladies and gentlemen, supper is now served, and we have a special treat tonight. Since this is an informal family gathering, we have two young ladies who are joining us for the buffet. Lucille and Annabelle, if you would care to come downstairs?'

Everyone looked up, and Lucy felt the blood rush to her cheeks, but Annabelle was already moving to the stairs and walking down them with an assurance that took Lucy's breath away. As she reached the lower landing Anna stopped and waited for her friend to catch her up.

'Simon's looking at us. See, he's giving me a smile,' she murmured, without appearing to move her lips at all. She paused, obviously

51

conscious of the picture that she made – tilting her head demurely on one side and smiling sweetly down at the assembled company – and then they walked down the last flight together. There was a little smatter of applause.

Everyone was staring at them so that for a moment Lucy wished the polished floor would open up and swallow her, but then James stepped forward and proferred her his arm. Rupert Neill did the same for Annabelle and the two girls were shepherded into the dining room.

People made way for them and made affable remarks, and soon the pair were sitting in a splendid spot, at one of the little tables by the wall, while their respective escorts fetched a glass for them, and enquired solicitously what they'd like to eat. There was an amazing choice: devilled chicken, sandwiches, canapés and tarts, sliced meats of all descriptions, cheeses, fruit and any number of little toasts and biscuits to eat with potted crab or beetroot mousse and all manner of similar delights – Lucy felt quite baffled just to look at it. In the end she settled for a slice of chicken pie – more because James had recommended it than because she wanted anything to eat. She was too excited to be hungry anyway.

Annabelle, however, was in sparkling form. Rupert was clearly paying court to her, and she was laughing – almost giggling – up at him, while he handed her what should have been a glass of lemonade, like Lucy's own, but looked most suspiciously like real champagne.

Lucy sipped nervously at her own bland, blameless drink and glanced around the room. It was full to overflowing, though some of the dancers were drifting out again by now. The room was a buzz of clinking glass and little laughs, and snatches of murmured conversation came floating to her ears.

'...I had to get the biscuits specially from Biarritz.'

'...and suddenly there were damn Boers everywhere...'

'...all the way in a motor charabanc...'

'...for some dessert?' That was James. Lucy pulled herself together with a jerk. She realized he was volunteering to go and get her some.

She gave him a dazzling smile and – to prove that she'd been listening really – 'A little of that splendid trifle, perhaps? That would be kind of you.'

He moved off in search of it, and she looked round again. Annabelle was still sitting very close to her, and in the absence of Rupert – who was obviously fetching something from the supper table too – was making frantic signals with her eyes. Lucy leaned towards her.

'I'm sure he's looking this way,' Annabelle hissed. 'He's been doing it all night. I daren't look any more. You glance over – as if it's casual – and tell me if I'm right.'

Lucy was about to ask, 'Who...?' but then, of course, she knew.

'Simon? I thought he was with Celestine? I saw her go next door. The musicians are starting up again, and they'll be dancing soon.'

Annabelle shook her head. 'Don't be a little goose,' she muttered, in an impatient undertone. 'Celestine obviously has another partner for this dance. She could hardly dance with Simon all the time, even supposing she wanted to. After all, this is her birthday ball – she'll be expected to partner all the men in turn. Now, he's over by the mirror talking to Mama. Go on, take a look for me, before our two boys get back.'

Lucy laughed but she turned her head as Annabelle had asked, and sure enough Simon Robinson was looking right that way – so much so, in fact, that he caught her eyeing him. There was no pretending that she hadn't: there was no mistaking the direction of her glance. She flashed the young man a swift embarrassed smile.

'You're quite right,' she murmured, turning back to Annabelle. 'He's got his eye on us.'

Annabelle promptly looked that way herself and turned a pretty crimson. 'Gracious! I do believe he's coming over here,' she muttered. 'You talk to him, Lucy, I shan't know what to say.' She leaned away again, affecting to search for Rupert among the supper throng.

So it was Lucy who turned to him, and heard him say, 'Good evening, ladies!' He had

54

a knowing smile and a lift of one eyebrow which gave him – she thought – an arch, sardonic look, as if he were already halfway to teasing one. He was handsome – you could see why Annabelle was struck – with the kind of dark, slightly dangerous good looks that made James's blondness seem tame in comparison. She found that she was blushing almost as much as Annabelle had done.

'What a pleasure to have two such enchanting young ladies here with us tonight.' His voice was pleasant, light and confident. 'Cousin, no wonder they call you Anna-belle – you were always "Anna" and you're certainly a "belle". And won't you introduce me to your charming friend?'

Annabelle, who had been basking in the compliment, recollected herself sufficiently to say, 'Oh, of course, I forgot that you two were not acquainted. Lucille Tregenza, this is my sort-of cousin, Simon Robinson. Simon, this is Lucille Tregenza, from Penvarris – quite my oldest friend.'

Lucy extended a gloved white hand to him, and he bent over it. 'Enchanted, I am sure.' He almost – but not quite – pressed it to his lips. 'How strange that we have not met before – Penwith is not a very crowded place. Yet I am sure we've not. I should remembered that pretty face at once.'

She drew back her hand and felt her colour rise. 'Our fathers are acquainted, I believe.' She tried to make it brisk and businesslike. 'Then I almost know you already, and I shall feel entitled to ask you for this dance. Or the next, perhaps – since this is almost over. Unless you are otherwise engaged?'

It was so unexpected that Lucy was non-plussed. She blurted, 'Well, no, I have a supper escort that is all – but I am not dancing. I am not 'out', you know.' She did not dare to look at Annabelle – though if poisoned glances were strong enough to kill, she had no doubt she would be dead by now.

He was laughing – a conspiratorial sort of laugh. 'But, come, you cannot waste that pretty dress. And this is not a formal society event. This is a family party. Uncle Richard made a point of saying so himself.' He raised his voice. 'What do you say, Uncle Richard? I tell her this is simply Celestine's birthday ball – a purely private gathering – and so there would be no impropriety in asking these young ladies to take a turn around the floor?'

Chapter Three

There was a moment's horrified hush, and then a little murmur round the room. Mrs Passemore-Jenkins looked quite aghast. Even Annabelle's father seemed a little shocked, but instead of scotching the suggestion with a word or two – as Lucy was sure her own Papa would do – he havered for a minute, as if anxious to avoid a scene, and then said with a laugh, 'Well, I suppose, just one little dance, then – before they go upstairs.'

Lucy felt the disapproving stares. She muttered hurriedly, 'But I could not possibly ... and here is James. He escorted me to supper.' She turned to him for support.

Simon did not lower his voice a degree. 'Oh, he'll excuse you for a moment, won't you, old man?' And then, seeing James's startled face, he added, 'I have invited this young lady to take the floor with me – I wanted to make her first proper party a real event for her – and Uncle Richard has agreed to it. But she protests quite properly that she cannot, since you're officially escorting her. However, I'm sure you wouldn't wish to spoil her little treat. You'll spare her for a little while, won't you, James?'

He made the request seem wholly innocent – the sort of indulgence one might afford a child – and James could do nothing except retreat muttering, 'Of course.'

It was an awful moment. Lucy did not know what to do. All eyes were still upon her. She was just about to mumble that she could not leave her friend – and really in decency she could not – when Rupert solved the problem, by declaring ringingly, 'Well, if we are to have a rehearsal for the girls' first proper ball, then I demand the honour, Annabelle,' and leading his partner firmly by the hand into the other room.

There was nothing for it but to follow them. Lucy longed to protest that she could not really dance: there had been lessons at Miss Worthington's establishment, of course, where the girls had practised awkward steps in pairs, but Annabelle had engaged a dancing-master since, and was now floating round the floor as well as anyone. Lucy knew she would look clumsy in comparison. However, it would now be even more embarrassing to retreat, and she allowed Simon Robinson to lead her to the floor.

Mr Passemore-Jenkins had said something to the band, and the progressive Gay Gordons was announced, which was a huge relief. It was a less intimate and adult sort of dance, since there was a constant change of partners: but there was nothing safe and childish in the way that Simon Robinson was

58

looking at her now and sliding a preparatory arm around her waist. It was only for a moment, and then the dance began, but every time she came around to partner him again he did the same and she found that she was blushing pinker than before. The music did not last for very long – deliberately so, she guessed – and on the third round it was over. The other guests all clapped and she and Anna were escorted back into the other room. James was still waiting with her supper plate, and Simon handed her over with a bow.

However, she had no taste for trifle now and she was glad when shortly afterwards Annabelle's mother came across and suggested it was time they said goodnight. James himself seemed equally relieved. He had been silent and withdrawn since she got back, and did nothing more than say, 'Goodnight, then,' in a strangled tone. Anna, though, went tripping out, calling a gay 'goodnight' to everyone.

Lucy joined her on the landing and began to say, 'Well, that was a—' when Anna whirled to face her.

'Don't you dare to speak to me. You have ruined my whole life. How could you make an exhibition of yourself like that?' Her face was a childish mask of anger and despair. 'First you dance with Simon when you know I wanted to, and then you get me sucked into your silly escapade, so now I can never come out properly at all. Everyone will know about tonight.'

Lucy was astounded. 'I'm sorry, Annabelle,

but what was I to do? I had no notion what your cousin was going to say to me.'

'Don't talk to me about him. I hate him,' Annabelle said, though it was clearly not the case. And then, a minute after, 'Imagine singling you out for attention in that way.'

'But it was only the Gay Gordons, don't forget,' Lucy pleaded. 'And I expect he just asked me so that he could dance with you – since it was a progressive dance like that no one would suspect.' It was a feeble argument, and Lucy knew it was. The next dance on the programme was supposed to be a waltz and Simon could not have guessed that Mr Passemore-Jenkins would change it suddenly.

Annabelle seemed to realize that, as well. She said fiercely, 'Oh, don't be silly, Lucy. I don't want to talk about it any more. I wish I'd never—' She broke off. She had been going to say 'invited you', that was as clear as clear – but Annabelle was a Passemore-Jenkins and far too well brought up. 'Never gone downstairs at all,' she finished. 'It's spoiled everything. So that is that. I'm tired, and it's time for bed.' And after that she said nothing more at all and they went to their rooms in silence.

Only, the next morning after breakfast, when they were getting dressed for church and Anna was pinning on her hat, she turned to Lucy, who was standing awkwardly nearby and said in a voice that only she could hear, 'Mama says it might not signify so much, because it was only a family party after all. I suppose that I forgive you.' She turned to face her friend. 'Do you really think that might have been what Simon had in mind?'

Paul Tregenza was playing the piano in the drawing room – the same tune that Helena had been playing earlier. He smiled at the recollection. His little visit to his daughter had clearly cheered her up.

He turned to Gertrude, who was reading by the fire. She, like him, had dressed for dinner – exchanging the floral tea gown she'd been wearing earlier for a sweeping velvet skirt and a lacy high-necked blouse, with a single gold-set ruby at the throat. He looked at her with approval. She was still a fine-looking woman for her age, he thought: the tawny upswept hair had not yet begun to grey, and when she glanced up and smiled at him her cheeks and eyes were as bright and youthful as they had ever been.

'That was very nice, dear. Do play another one. You know how much I like to hear you play, and we don't have Helena to entertain us this evening, since she preferred to stay upstairs. And my sister has gone early off to bed.' She gave a little laugh. 'So there are just the two of us. It does seem strange and quiet, not having Lucy here. To think of it! Our youngest – gone off to a ball. It makes one feel quite aged, does it not?'

He looked up from the pile of music sheets that he was sorting through, and answered gallantly, 'My dear, no one who saw you as you look tonight could possibly suppose that you had a daughter old enough to dance.'

She put aside her book. 'It was kind of Mrs Passemore-Jenkins to ask her, don't you think? They are very well connected – Lord Penrose, you know.'

'Ah yes,' Paul said wryly. 'I know that she is quite the local arbiter of what's acceptable.'

Gertrude gave him her disapproving frown. 'Lots of other people take their lead, it's true. And that is what I mean. Do you think that it is possible that Lucy will be invited here and there, now that the ice is broken, even if she can't formally come out?'

'Invite the younger sister before the older one?' He picked up Beethoven. 'I suppose you'll say it hardly matters nowadays? Well, you may be right. I no longer understand these things at all. Most of the young women that one hears about don't seem to formally come out, as you put it, in any case. They don't go up to London to be presented to the King, the way girls used to do – or hardly any of them, anyway. They just emerge into society.'

'Paul, you are being deliberately absurd. Of course not every young woman hereabouts can be presented at court and spend the season in the capital. Not everyone has the family connections, for a start. But all the same, any girl who is anyone at all will have a formal ball, when they reach eighteen or so, to introduce them to the local scene – and everyone acknowledges that that's their coming out, and feels that it is proper to invite them afterwards. But poor Lucy cannot do it, since Helena could not. I confess, Paul, I have had worries about her on that score. I couldn't see how she would ever meet a suitable young man.'

He flicked up his coat and settled himself on the music stool. 'I don't think you need to have anxieties on that account. She's already quite taken by young Morrison, as it appears to me – and she didn't need the social niceties in order to be introduced to *him*.'

Gertrude gave him another of her smiles. 'There you are, you see! The very first young man she comes across, and she half-imagines she's in love with him.'

He laughed. 'Perhaps she is. He would be admirably suitable.' He twinkled at her. 'And think of the savings in expense!'

She ignored his teasing. 'I'm sure he would be very suitable. But how would she ever know that he's the one, if she has no one to compare him with?'

This piece of female logic left him lost for a reply, and he contented himself with saying, 'Well, we shall see. There's time enough for that. Lucy's very young, of course. But she won't lack for suitors, unless all young men are blind. She looked a picture when she went out tonight.'

'Yes, I thought that I should miss the fun of this, you know – the dresses and the dressmakers and everything. When Helena had that dreadful accident, I thought...' She trailed off.

'That it was the end for both of them?' He nodded. Privately, he had thought so too. But he could not admit that to his wife. The accident had affected her so much – as if Helena's darkened world had taken the light out of her soul, as well. 'In fact Helena has done wonderfully,' he said. 'The scars have healed up so well that one would hardly know.'

His wife nodded. 'Though it is fortunate that she's a patient sort of girl. Not many people of her age would bear it half so well. Of course, she has you to thank for that, my dear. Few girls in her condition have such opportunities – you getting her that little pianoforte of her own and paying for her lessons, even though she couldn't see.'

Paul thought about the thumping discords earlier. Patience had not been any part of that! He smiled. 'I feel a little guilty all the same,' he said. 'Helena has a lively mind, and it can't be much fun for her sometimes, cooped up in that room of hers all day. I had hopes of that woman who came to teach her how to read – that Fry embossed system was supposed to be the best. It won the Edinburgh Prize and everything – but Lena didn't get on with it all.'

'Well, I'm sure you did everything you could. We all do. Her Aunt Edwards and I take her out whenever possible – to Mrs Morrison's, and to the church. And Lucy's very good. She goes and reads to her for hours. Many of our callers go up when they come, or she comes down to them. So she isn't short of company, and she has her music, which she loves.'

'Would that seem a fulfilling life to you?'

Gertrude looked startled, as if she'd never thought of it like that. 'You think we should engage a companion for her, after all?' she said slowly, and then she shook her head. 'I'm not so sure. She might not welcome it. Remember what happened with Mam'zelle?'

He chuckled ruefully. Mam'zelle had been Helena's governess, a sharp little French-woman called Hortense, whom he'd engaged to try to teach his daughter spoken French, after the failure of the Fry home-reading scheme. However, Mam'zelle's methods were of the ancient school, consisting solely of producing rules and long lists of vocabulary to repeat out loud, punctuated by sharp little raps across the knuckles for every 'fault'. Helena had heartily detested her and that experiment had been short-lived as well.

'I was thinking of something more practical than that,' he said. 'One of those new "gramophones", perhaps. You wind them up and you can have music anywhere. It might afford a little pleasure to the rest of us as well. I saw an advertisement about them in a magazine.' He flexed his fingers and began to play the piece that he had chosen from the pile.

Gertrude listened, smiling. 'Bravo,' she said, 'who needs a gramophone? No, I am

65

teasing, Paul! It would be excellent. Helena could listen to the pieces that she learns and Lucy would enjoy it too, I'm sure. One can buy recorded dance music on these things now, can't one? She could whirl around waltzing to her heart's content.'

Helena had been waiting to hear about the ball – though with rather mixed emotions. Lucy's descriptions might be hard to bear (in relation to partnering James Morrison, at least) but they would make a welcome change from everyday routine. Her accounts were always lively – and often a little bit irreverent.

For once, however, her sister seemed less than keen to talk. She answered eagerly enough when asked about the gowns, the flower arrangements and the supper spread, but when Helena asked, 'And did you watch the dancing much? Did James look after you?' Lucy became immediately coy.

'Oh, don't let's talk about the silly party any more,' she cried. 'I've told it all so often that I'm quite tired of it. It was only for one evening and it's all over now. You are the one with the exciting news. Tell me about this gramophone Papa is going to buy. Mother says he's going to send to London, and order one at once! A modern type as well, with big round discs to play, not one of the old cylinder variety. What music shall you want to get for it? I hear there are all sorts of things available. Even pianists and orchestras these days. Wouldn't that be fine? Like having a proper concert without moving from your chair.'

Since Lucy hated concerts as a rule, this was bewildering, until it occurred to Helena that all this enthusiastic burbling was merely an attempt to change the subject and not talk about the ball. That was surprising too. Helena had been expecting to be bored with it for weeks – and here was Lucy, about as communicative as a Trappist monk, while Helena herself was positively anxious to hear a little more, if only to have an excuse to talk of James.

Possibly that was the trouble. She remembered that Lucy had said nothing about James before the ball – not even that he'd promised to escort her to the supper table. Perhaps she really was afraid of being teased. Or did she realize that her sister was a little envious? In either case, it made it difficult for Helena to raise the subject now.

However, there was no need to worry about that. Lucy brought the subject up herself. 'James is to go to London very soon to see about a place at university.' For some reason, she sounded quite surprisingly unmoved. 'If you could decide what record-discs you want, perhaps he could arrange to bring them back.'

Helena forced a smile. 'I've no idea what is available. Anyway, I dare say Papa will choose our discs for us.'

She heard Lucy's little cross, impatient flounce. 'Oh, of course. I might have guessed.

I suppose he will. I had been hoping for a little fun, but no doubt he'll choose something boring and improving – like your wretched *Adam Bede*.'

'I'm sorry you find that so very tedious. Perhaps one day they'll put such things on gramophones as well! Performed by the finest actors in the land. That would save you the necessity of entertaining me.' Helena had intended this to be self-mockery, but it came out as rather a rebuke.

There was a little silence and then Lucy said, 'Well, in the meantime, there is only me. So am I reading it to you tonight, or not?' And then, obviously feeling that she had been ungracious too, she added. 'The weather is turning more agreeable. We could take a turn out to the bower if you prefer.'

Helena didn't hear another word about the ball. And it was the same the next day, and the next. So, when James Morrison called in on Thursday afternoon to see Papa about some business relating to the mine – and came up to visit Helena afterwards in her sitting room – she took the plunge and asked him openly.

'And did you have a lovely evening at the Passemore-Jenkinses?'

She sensed that he had stiffened, just as Lucy had. 'As well as could be expected, I suppose – at least till that oaf Robinson arrived.'

'How so?'

There was a pause. 'Lucy didn't tell you

about what happened, then?'

She shook her head. 'I can't get her to tell me anything at all.' She tried to make a little joke of it.

James laughed. 'That speaks well for her discretion, anyway.'

'I'm not so sure of that. It is so unlike her to be silent that she's made me curious.' She sat sharply forward, suddenly. 'James, what do you mean, "discretion"? She didn't do anything ... reprehensible?'

Another laugh, a half-embarrassed sound. 'Not really. If anything, it was that wretched Simon's fault – thinks that everything becomes him because he's a Robinson. And Passemore-Jenkins is fool enough to go along with it. But I'm surprised. I never saw such wretched manners in my life. I tell you, Lena – Robinson may be well connected and all that sort of thing, but money does not make a gentleman. I hope I know better than he does how I should behave.'

He gave a brief account of what happened, and Helena listened in astonishment. 'I can see that Lucy's actions were a bit unfortunate – leaving her escort in the lurch like that,' she said, sensing that he was genuinely hurt. 'No wonder she wouldn't talk about the ball. But I'm sure she had no intention of being discourteous to you. He put her in a difficult position, it appears, and of course she's very young.' Things could have been so very different, she thought, if it were not for my wretched accident. I would never have left

69

you, if you'd escorted me – but naturally she could not say such things aloud.

'Of course, you're right.' He came across and laid a hand on hers, where it was lying on the arm of the chair. He smelt of bay rum and shaving soap. 'You are such a comfort, Helena. I was a bit affronted, I confess. But when one thinks about it coolly, as you say, obviously nobody could suppose that Lucy was to blame. It was her first proper party, after all – how could she be expected to refuse with grace when confronted with an arrogance like that? Honestly, I'm very glad to have this talk with you. I need your common sense. I should have been sorry to have gone away and not been best of friends with little Lucy when I left.'

'Gone away?' she echoed, a little mournfully. 'Ah, of course. Lucy said that you were leaving us – going up to London to university, I think.'

He laughed. 'Yes, but that won't be immediate, of course. I am to go up for a meeting with them later this week – my father has some business with his shirt-maker and I shall travel up with him – and then I am going to stay on for a day or two. With Rupert Neill, in fact. He's going up to study medicine as well. He has relations who've agreed to put us up – and he's promised to introduce me to the place and show me round. Your father has given me a commission too, while I'm in town. I am to buy a gramophone and bring it back. On your account, I think.'

'And Lucy's,' she replied, and added daringly, 'So we shall both be waiting anxiously for your return.'

'I shan't be away for very long. Not this time, anyway.' He squeezed her hand again. 'Oh, Helena. You are a brick! I don't know what I'd do without your good advice. I'll have a word with Lucy as I leave. I hear she's writing letters in the morning room. You think that she'd be pleased?'

'About the gramophone? I'm sure of it,' she teased, and they were still laughing when he left the room. But once the door had closed behind him the laugh died on her lips. She pressed them hard together and if it hadn't been for Maisie coming in with tea she might have betrayed herself with tears.

Chapter Four

Lucy was indeed writing letters – or one letter, over and over, to be more precise. It was difficult. She had crumpled up half a dozen previous attempts, but the missive was already overdue and she could in conscience no longer put it off.

She picked up her pen and dipped it in the ink. 'Dear Mrs Passemore-Jenkins,' she wrote again. 'This is to thank you for a ... ,' She paused. What could she say now? She had rejected 'interesting evening' and 'delightful supper' in earlier drafts. She had to say something. 'Splendid'. That would do. '...a splendid evening,' she wrote, carefully.

Drat! These new iron nibs got crossed and now she'd made a blot. She turned the paper upside down and dabbed it on the blotter underneath, but the letter was still ruined. She screwed it up and tossed it to join the others in the wastepaper basket on the floor beside the desk. She took another sheet of notepaper.

'Dear Mrs Passemore-Jenkins...'

'Lucy?' That was Papa's voice. She turned to find him standing at the door. 'You have a visitor. He's waiting for you in the drawing room, I've sent for tea. I'll come and join you there.'

She put down the pen at once. So James wanted to see her. She gave a little inward smile. She'd been half expecting this, ever since she had seen him come into the house some little time ago. She'd been at the downstairs window when he first arrived, and as soon as she set eyes on him the embarrassments of Saturday came flooding back to her. Indeed, it was his unexpected appearance which had finally sent her up to start her letterwriting chore – though she could not have said herself whether that was because she hoped to avoid his company, or because it gave her an excuse to be up here alone in case he came to find her. At all events, his visit flurried her. In the nicest way, of course.

She smoothed down her dress, prepared a face to meet him and went to the drawing room.

'James?' she ventured, in her sweetest voice, flinging wide the door.

But the man who was standing at the window staring at the grounds, and who looked up to greet her with a quizzical expression on his face, was not James Morrison at all.

'Why, Simon ... that is ... Mr Robinson!' she cried, in astonishment. 'This is an unlooked-for pleasure, I am sure.' Her voice produced the greeting, but her mind was all a-race. What was he doing here? It was one thing for James to come and ask for her, he was half-family in any case, but this man was a stranger to the house. Indeed, by any normal social standards they had scarcely been introduced – though normal social standards seemed not to weigh with him.

He had no such reservations now, that was clear. He came towards her, saying, as if they were old friends, 'Miss Lucy. I hoped that I would find you in. The maid who let me in told me that you were occupied with correspondence. I'm sorry to disturb you, if that was the case.'

'It doesn't signify. Nothing that cannot wait till later on.' Politeness required that she offered him her hand. He did not merely press it: he captured it in both his own and almost refused to let it go. She had to draw it back and say, with her best official manner, 'To what do we owe the honour? My father said you wished to speak to me.'

He gave a mocking grin. 'Ah yes, your father. I am afraid I used a little subterfuge with him – called on the pretence of asking his advice.'

'Advice?' It was not what she'd expected.

'About the wisdom of buying an interest in the mine – I know that he is a venturer himself. Not that I have any intention of ever doing so – but a man is always flattered when his opinion's sought, especially when he has strong views about a thing. And I know they are looking for more capital – to finance a new winding-engine, or something of the kind. I heard my father grumbling about it only yesterday.'

'But surely, since your own father has an interest himself, it must seem odd to come and ask Papa?'

He gave a chuckle. 'Ah, but they don't see eye to eye – that was the whole design. I knew he'd be doubly delighted to offer me advice, not only because it was a compliment to him, but also to prove my father wrong. And as you see, it obviously worked. I quite won him over, I believe, and when I said I'd met you at the Passemore-Jenkinses' ball, that I was a cousin of young Annabelle's and would like his permission to speak to you again, he was only too happy to agree to it.'

Despite herself, she was a little shocked. 'You mean that you deliberately deceived

74

Papa, simply in order to come and call on me?'

He laughed. 'Is that so dreadful? Who is hurt by it? Not your father – I have paid him a harmless compliment – and certainly not me. I would have gone to greater lengths than that to further our acquaintance, I assure you. Unless you are displeased yourself, and have no wish to speak to me? If so, say the word, and I will leave at once.'

She felt the colour rising to her cheeks. 'No, of course I do not wish to do anything of the kind,' she said, in a confusion. 'In any case, you can't go walking off. Papa will expect to find you here. He has ordered tea and says that he will join us in a little while.'

Simon smiled. 'In that case, who could possibly resist?'

Drat the man, why did he always put her at a disadvantage in this way? And why did she find it so disturbing when he smiled at her like that? She was about to make some perfectly inane remark when there was the sound of footsteps on the stairs. Simon was obviously conscious of them too, because he drew back a little, and said in a completely altered tone, 'Besides, I have a little invitation for you, from Annabelle. They are making up a little party to go into Penzance: Miss Clara Butt is giving a recital there next week. My sister was hoping to attend, but she is indisposed, and now there is a spare ticket and a carriage seat. So it was wondered if you would care to take her place?'

Lucy was really flustered now. 'Well … that is very kind of Annabelle. Obviously, I should have to ask Papa.'

'Well, here he is.' Simon turned to face the doorway, where her father was appearing as he spoke. 'Though I'm sure he'd have no objection, would you, sir? That ticket to the concert that I mentioned earlier? I've taken the liberty of asking Miss Lucille if she would care to take the empty seat. It would all be very proper, and duly chaperoned. Both of my cousins will be going, and Mrs Passemore-Jenkins, and naturally they'll bring her home betimes. In fact, I'll personally undertake to see they do.'

So he had already mentioned the concert to Papa! She wondered how her father would have reacted to the scheme, and in fact he did sound a little dubious at first. 'I have been thinking about that. I wonder that the Passemore-Jenkinses do not write, or at least deliver the invitation in person while they were in the house…' But Simon quickly laughed him out of that.

'Ah, that is my fault, sir, I fear. They regard me as one of the family, more or less. I told them I was coming here to speak to you, and would be pleased to bring the invitation on my aunt's behalf.'

So he was calling Mrs Passemore-Jenkins his aunt, now, Lucy thought. Just as well Anna didn't know of that. She certainly didn't think of Simon in that light and nor – judging by the other night – did Celestine.

Simon was still blandishing Papa. 'I'm sure you will forgive the informality on this occasion, sir. After all, there is not a lot of time. And it is quite an informal outing – no supper party or anything like that. Simply an opportunity to hear the great contralto sing. A pity to waste a ticket, it was thought, when someone might enjoy it in my sister's place: and it would be such company for Annabelle, as well.'

'Well ... Under the circumstances, I suppose...' And – rather to Lucy's astonishment – it was agreed.

Simon murmured the expected thanks, and adroitly turned the conversation on to other things. He began to talk of horses, which he clearly knew a lot about. Her father was obviously charmed, and was soon suggesting that their visitor come out and look at the new bay that he had bought.

It was all so swift and unexpected that she had no time to think, and it was not until the two men had gone to see the horse that it occurred to her to wonder what Annabelle must think – and why her friend had wanted to invite her on this trip, rather than keep Simon's company to herself and Celestine.

She shook her head. Anna would tell her on Saturday, perhaps.

James was rather disappointed not to find Lucy in the morning room after all. It was obvious she had indeed been writing letters there – the impatient crumpled notepaper in

77

the waste basket was sufficient evidence of that – but the chair was pushed back from the desk and there was no sign of her.

She had been there very recently, as a closer examination of the desk made clear. Her abandoned pen was still lying on the ink-stand, dripping ink, and there was a half-finished letter on the blotting pad. For a moment he wondered if he should stay and wait, since it appeared that she was shortly coming back, and he loitered at the door, but then the maidservant came toiling up the stairs with a tray of tea for Helena and saw him standing there.

'I didn't realize that you was still 'ere, Mr James, or I'd've brought up a bit a tea for you, as well. I knew you'd finished with the master – 'e came down a little while ago – and I thought you'd gone. Been up to see Miss Elenner, I 'spect?'

'I have called in on Miss Tregenza, yes. But now I was looking for Miss Lucy. Do you know where she is?'

Maisie balanced the tea tray on the banister and rolled her eyes at him. 'Gone down to the drawing room, I shouldn't be surprised. I was told to bring in tea for three down there, when I'd finished taking this upstairs.'

'For three? So Mrs Tregenza is in after all? In that case, I'd better call in there myself and pay her my respects. I thought she'd gone out with Aunt Edwards to Madron for the day.'

'And so she has.' She leaned a little closer, confidentially. 'And I wouldn't go in there, if

I were you. There's some young man come to see the master – well, I never saw the like. Too stuck up to blow his nose – pardon me, Mr James, but that's the truth of it. When I opened the front door to him, he just walked in without a by-your-leave and handed me 's coat. 'Kindly tell Mr Tregenza that I'm here,' he said and handed me his card. Never looked in my direction once and too grand to bother giving me his name. Well, you was with the master at the time, so I had the greatest pleasure in telling him to wait.'

James found that he was smiling. Of course it was not up to a servant to witter on like this, but he was fond of Maisie. Everybody was. She had been with the Tregenzas for ... what? it must be five years or so by now – and she was what mother called 'a treasure', devoted to her employers and honest as the day was long. But somehow, though she intended no kind of disrespect, she had never learned to mind her place and speak when spoken to. It had been quite embarrassing once or twice when there were guests, and he had heard Aunt Tregenza threaten several times that they would have to let her go, but everybody knew it was an idle threat. Servants were two a penny, but girls as good as Maisie were very hard to find. So Maisie would be formally rebuked, would maintain a gravelike silence for a day or two – and then something would happen and she'd forget herself, and gradually the whole thing would begin again.

She seemed to be aware of what was running through his mind. 'I s'pose I'm talking out of turn again,' she said. 'But honestly, Mr James, if you'd seen him standing there, looking down his nose at everything – more stuck up than sealing wax – you'd have said the same yourself.'

Privately he rather doubted that – although he might have thought it, he supposed. 'Did you get the impression that the visit would take long? Obviously I don't want to interrupt, but I had rather hoped to see Miss Lucy before I left the house.'

She made a little face. 'And you're not the only one, if I am any judge. Of course he made out it was the master that he'd come to see, but before I'd even gone to take the card upstairs Mr Snooty-boots was already asking if Miss Lucille was in. Clear as twopence what he really had in mind. And seems as if he got it in the end. Her father's asked her to go down there, by the look of it.'

Just when he had hoped to make his peace with her! James found that he was unreasonably annoyed. Lucy probably was not aware that he was even in the house, and of course she was expected to take tea with guests – especially if her mother wasn't there to be hostess. But it was particularly galling, when he had come with such magnanimous intent, to find that the lady he was generously condescending to forgive was happily entertaining someone else.

Maisie gave the tea tray another little hoick.

80

'I can see that it is vexing,' she said. 'But I'll have to go. Miss Elenner will be waiting for her tea. But if you don't want to interrupt them all downstairs, why don't you stop here and drop a little note? I'll see Miss Lucy gets it when she comes up again – after that Simon Whatsisface has gone.'

James seized on the idea, and had begun to walk towards the desk and take the pen when Maisie's last words brought him to a halt. He turned to face her. 'Did you say "Simon"? Not Simon Robinson?'

She nodded. 'That's right. Said so on that card. I sneaked a look at it. Though I should not have been surprised if it said his name was God, at least – the way he gave it me. Why? Know him, do you?' She stopped suddenly, and went on in alarm, ' 'Ere, Mr James, I do hope he isn't a friend yours – and me going on like this.'

'It's all right, Maisie,' he replied. 'There's no need to worry on that score. I assure you Simon Robinson is no friend of mine – though perhaps this should be a warning to you, not to speak before you think.' He added the last words, in an admonitory tone, almost automatically.

'Yes, Mr James,' she murmured, quite contrite. 'But what about that note?'

He shook his head, not wishing to explain. 'I think I will not leave one after all. You might just tell Miss Lucy that I was here this afternoon, and that I am to go to London later in the week. Tell her I'll hope to see her when I'm home again.'

'Yes, Mr James,' she said again, 'and when is that to be?'

'I am not altogether sure,' he said. Damned if he was going to be more precise than that. If Lucy didn't like it, then she'd simply have to ask somebody else for information. In some vague way it seemed to serve her right. 'I may be gone some little while,' he went on. 'Now, it's time that I was off. You take that tea tray up. Don't worry about me. I'll see myself out.' He managed to soften his brusqueness with a smile, and strode on past her down the stairs and out.

Maisie leaned over the next banister and watched him go. She'd gone and done it now. Her and her big tongue. She knew from the way that Mr James snatched up his coat and jammed on his hat before he was half through the door that he was in a funny sort of mood. And it was obviously something that she'd said as well. He was perfectly all right until a minute since. He'd even smiled a little bit when she'd described the visitor, so it wasn't that which made him so disturbed – though perhaps she had got rather carried away with that.

Miss Ellener was in a taking, too, when Maisie got that far. Not that she said anything. She was just sitting in her chair, and if she could have stared at anything, you would say that she was staring at the wall. It wasn't like Miss Ellener at all. You could see from her expression that she was all upset, and that for tuppence ha'penny she would start to cry.

Mind, you had to be sorry for the poor thing, Maisie thought. You'd come up here sometimes and find her sitting in the dark, and you'd almost think she wasn't there until she spoke, and there she would be knitting in the dark. Course, it was all the same to her whether there was candlelight or not. Wonder she wasn't crying all the time.

Maisie put the cup out as quietly as a mouse – supposing that a mouse could pour the tea – and placed it where Miss Ellener could put her hand on it. But then her silence failed her and she burst out all at once. 'Here, Miss Elenner, have a piece of sponge. Cook's only made it this afternoon, and it's as light as light. Do you good and cheer you up a bit. Better than they old sandwiches you always have. I brought you up some, shall I put it out?'

'Thank you, Maisie. I may have a little sponge cake by and by, when I have finished my salmon sandwiches. But why do you suppose that I need cheering up? I'm sure I've had a pleasant afternoon. Mr James has been to call on me.'

'Lord, so he 'as. I'd quite forgotten that. Well, I am surprised to find you in the dumps. Generally, he'd perk you up.' As usual, the words were out before she'd thought and Maisie could have bitten off her tongue.

But Miss Elenner had forced a sort of smile.

83

'Of course he does. He's very good to me. And Lucy is coming up a little later on to read to me, I think.' She reached for the teacup and raised it to her lips. Always made Maisie hold her breath, that did – in case it got knocked over, though it never was. Yet it didn't do to help her. Miss Elenner liked to do things for herself.

'Won't be for a few minutes, then. She's downstairs talking to a visitor.'

Did she imagine it, or did Miss Elenner flinch? 'That would be James, I suppose?'

'Oh no, miss, a stranger. Came to see your father, or that's what 'e made out...' and Maisie was launched on a lively description of the visitor which had Miss Elenner smiling in a trice. 'Good-looking sort of fellow, in a flashy sort of way,' she finished. 'Leastways, he thinks so, you can tell that at a glance. Looking in the mirrored bookcase and pretending that he's not.' She edged the plate of sandwiches a little closer to her charge's hand.

Miss Elenner felt for one and picked it up. 'Then you mustn't keep him waiting. I am sure they'll want some tea, You can put out a piece of sponge for me, and then take down the tray. I expect Lucy will tell me all about her mystery visitor when she comes up later on.'

Maisie did as she was bid and hurried off downstairs. Well, that was Miss Elenner sounding more like her cheerful self. But people did seem to be in funny moods today.

Miss Lucy seemed to be out of sorts as well, when Maisie delivered Mr James's message later on – though if she was annoyed at missing him, pity she hadn't thought of that when Simon Snooty came.

But there was no time to dwell on other folks' affairs. If she looked lively with her chores there would just be time to go down to the post: Mr Tregenza had some letters that he wanted mailed, and Miss Lucy had finished hers by now – and Maisie was hoping to be sent with them, instead of Edgar going.

At this time of day you never knew if you might meet a certain freckled carter in the lane.

Chapter Five

It was getting late on Saturday afternoon as Frank Carter trotted his wagon down the lane. Leastwise it wasn't quite his wagon yet – though it was going to be. Farmer Crowdie, who had a bought newer one with springs, had named a reasonable price for it and, in return for the princely deposit of Frank's half a crown, had promised not to sell it on else-where. So Frank was working every hour God sent to put a little by each week, though it would want a lot of care and painting even then. In the meantime he was hiring it:

Crowdie was very good and did not charge him very much, any more than he charged him much for hiring the horse.

At the thought of Brownie, Frank shook a mournful head. The wagon he could see his way to, more or less, but Brownie! That was quite another thing. There was an awful lot of money in a horse.

But there was no time to think of that. He'd come to the address. He pulled up at the cottage and went and rapped the door. 'Ma Jones?' he hollered, peering into the darkness of the hall, and out she came – up to her elbows in flour, which took him by surprise. Saturday didn't belong to be a baking day for most folks hereabouts.

She shook her head at him, wiping her hands in her white pinafore. 'Come for that parcel, 'ave 'ee? Well, I got it 'ere. Wait while I run in and fetch it for 'ee.' She disappeared into the gloom again, and came back tugging a suitcase after her, a battered leather object tied around with string. 'Here 'tis,' she straightened up, puffing with exertion and then stood back and supervised as he hoisted the heavy suitcase on the cart.

When he had stowed it between the other boxes which were his cargo for today, she gave a little grunt – all the approval he was going to get. 'You take that to my sister Edna, down Levant – the address is written on. Mind you take care of 'un, and all. Mother's best china, that is: she wanted for Edna's girl to have it when she wed, and so she shall – if

86

you can get it there before she leaves this afternoon. And tell Edna I'll be down myself a little later on, and bring a few yeast buns. It's miles to walk, but I dare say she'll be glad of a bit of company tonight. Now, ninepence, did you say?' She fiddled in her pocket and brought out the coins. 'Daylight robbery, that's what it is. But don't know how else I should have got it there.'

Frank touched his cap, 'Thank you, Ma,' but made a mental note. He could have asked a shilling and she would still have paid. He sighed. The fees he charged were only just enough to pay the hire and put those precious few pence aside to buy the cart. It was hard work. He swung up to his seat and moved away.

He hadn't gone a hundred before he heard a voice. 'Hey, Frank!' It seemed to be coming from the field path to his left. He slowed and looked around. A plump red face popped up across the stile. 'Be a pal and give a friend a lift!'

Frank grinned. 'Come on then, Jethro!' Jethro, or 'Fatty' as he'd been called at school, had been a friend since they were very small. His family only lived a door or two from Jack's, though they didn't see each other all that much these days, since Jethro had followed his father down the mine. 'Second time within a week or two I've took you home. Though this time I aren't going all the way. Drop you at the crossroads, if you like.'

Jethro lumbered into a run and climbed

87

heavily up into the seat. 'Thanks,' he said, as soon as he had got his breath back. 'Saved my bacon, you have. I'm already late. Stopped into the Tinners' Arms, and stayed a bit too long – Ma and Mary'll won't half give me what for.'

'What you doing here, in any case?' Frank flicked the reins and they were off again. 'Should have thought as you'd be off for weeks. Half-dead, you was, when I took you home.'

Jethro waved a bandaged hand at him. 'Doctor came and stitched it up for me. Good as gold it will be, by and by. Even get some of the movement in my fingers back, perhaps. Wonderful what they doctor chaps can do. Came right to the house, like I was Earl of Muck. One of the owners gave me twenty shillin' for the fee, and the miners' social had a whip-round for the rest. Then Capt'n Maddern sent a message that if I came down today he'd see about finding some light work now and then. Won't be much, but we'll have something coming in. Gave me another shilling, and I'm to start next week. That's how I called in at the Tinners' Arms – to celebrate. Make a big difference that will, the way things are at home, now Mary's had to stop that scrubbing job of hers.'

'Yes, I heard she's in the family way. How is she, anyway?'

'Bit hot and bothered. Ma's looking after her.'

'Lucky your ma and da had room for you at home.'

He had spoken with such feeling that Jethro looked at him. 'Yes, course! I forgot that you were courting, too, and you couldn't ask your folks to take an extra in. Hardly room to turn round in your house as it is.'

Frank snorted. 'If it wasn't for the big girls having jobs where they live in, and me and Lennie sleeping head to tail like we do, there'd hardly be bed-space for everyone – let alone a room! And we can't look to Maisie – both her folks are dead, and you know she was brought up by an auntie who had children of her own. Good as gold to her, but glad to see her into service all the same.'

'So what you going to do?'

Frank sighed. 'Bit more of what I'm doing, I suppose. Working for Fathyer and the tally shop all week, and trying to earn a little extra on the side to set up on my own. Mind, I'll be ninety before I manage it, the rate I'm going.'

'Can't your father help you out a bit? You have two horses, and two wagons then. Stands to reason, you'd have twice the work. Pay for itself in no time.'

'Well, I've talked to him about it, but like he says, what are you going to use for money, boot-buttons? He hasn't got anything to spare – can't feed the family on fillets of fresh air. And who would lend to us? The tally shop don't pay a fortune, anyway, and what there is we have to give to Ma – all but a few pence, anyroad.'

'Trouble with being the eldest of all that lot, I suppose.' Jethro said.

Frank nodded. That was the rub, of course. He was the eldest – damn nearly twenty-one – but there were all the others coming afterwards. 'The trouble was, the next three are just girls – they're in domestic service, course they are, but they aren't earners like a boy would earn, though I s'pose they get their keep.'

'Bring home a few shillings now and then, though?' Jethro said. 'I know my Mary did.'

'Well, course, it all helps out a bit,' Frank was quick to hide his tactlessness, 'but tiddn't much and tiddn't bound to last. Any minute they might all get wed, and then where are we? Course, if those twins had lived, that died when they were four, they would have been coming on by now and they could do a bit – picking up potatoes or something after school. Maybe then I could have seen the end of it – but as it is the smaller boys aren't old enough for that, and little Davy's only toddling now.'

'So you're still working for the tally shop?'

'Got to, really, haven't I? Fayther can't lift and carry like he used to do, but we've got this contract with them and it's got to be fulfilled – though we only fetch the little things, and where's the cash in that? There are days when nothing's wanted, and then when something is it's wanted yesterday, and never mind if it makes up a proper load. Profit hardly stretches to pay the both of us,

90

but it's no good telling Fayther that – he'll never change his ways.'

'Well, perhaps he's sensible. Always be wanting boots and candles, miners will, and someone's got to fetch them from the town. May not pay a fortune, but it's steady work – and clean.'

Frank shook his head. 'Steady work? I aren't so sure of that. Look at all the stoppages there've been this year or two because the miners had to buy things from the blinking tally shop – for more than the shops were asking in the town.'

Jethro looked a little bit uncomfortable at this. Obviously he was thinking about the man who paid his fee. 'The owners backed down in the end, though, Frank. Cut their prices back *and* let the men shop anywhere they liked. My dad always uses the tally shop himself. Says it gives you credit when the town shops won't, and lets you pay off your tallies bit by bit.'

Frank snorted. 'And by the time you've finished paying you forget what it was for! These new unions will never stand for that. The tally shop will have to close one day. And what happens to that famous contract then? It might have been a fine thing once, but times are different now. We're well into the twentieth century. Time for us to strike out on our own. Carting furniture, or fetching parcels from the town – there's plenty we could do. A lot of people haven't got a wagon, and they'd be pleased to pay. You wait till I

91

pay this cart and Brownie off. Be out of that damn contract before you can say knife.'

He was interrupted in his grumbling by Jethro's urgent pulling on his arm. ''Ere, you've just gone past the crossroads!'

'Sorry, boy!' Frank stopped and let his passenger get down. 'But I'm fed up, Jethro, and that's short of it. Give my love to Mary – and love from Maisie too! And don't you go doing anything foolish with that hand!' He trotted Brownie off.

They had turned off down Penvarris lane by now, the narrow lane that led to St Just. Usually Frank loved the view across the moors – the bracken and the massive granite stones close by, then the greener fields towards the coast where lazy cows grazed and cheerful cottages were plumed with chimney smoke and always in the distance the blue-grey of the sea – but today he was so wrapped up in his thoughts he hardly looked at all.

He'd urged Fayther scores of times to start a private round, but Fayther refused to be convinced. He simply stuffed his famous pipe again – the few pence that he kept himself each week always went up in aromatic smoke – and said, 'You think that, boy, then good luck to you. You think you've got time to build up customers – you do that, and welcome. I won't stand in your way. But not in my time, see. The shop comes first. So it'll be Saturday afternoons and weekdays after six, and no requests for extra time, you hear? And don't think you're using my horse and wagon, neither. When my Dobbie's done a whole day in the shafts, tiddn't fair to take her out again. You want a horse and cart, you'll have to buy your own.'

So the arrangement with Crowdie had been made and here he was, using his precious afternoon moving Ma Jones's china, and two crates of books. That would earn him perhaps another sixpence off the cart. Sixpence off two guineas: that left two pounds one and six. He sighed. It was like that blessed tally shop again – by the time you'd paid an item off, it was time to throw the dratted thing away.

He was so wrapped in his calculations that he did not see the sulky coming round the bend until it was almost on top of him. It was being driven by a gentleman – too fast – and it was a wonder it could stop before it hit the cart. Brownie reared up, startled, and Frank got down to soothe and comfort her.

The gentleman had jumped down from the sulky too, but his attention was not on the horse. He stormed towards them, brandishing his whip, in a way which made Brownie skitter sideways in alarm.

'Back up! Back up, do you hear? You're blocking up the road with that damned cart of yours.'

Frank looked around him in surprise. True there was no room for both of them to pass but there was a gate not very far away. The sulky had just passed it by a yard or two. Perhaps the fellow in the fancy clothes had failed to notice it. Driving too fast to see it, probably. 'If you were to put your sulky over there a minute, sir,' he suggested with a deferential smile, 'then I could get past easy, and we could both be on our way. I'll help you with the horse.'

'Pull back over there, to let a cart go past? Damn your impudence! You'll back up, as I say!'

'But...' Frank was about to protest that the nearest gateway to the cart was half a mile away, and there was no room here to turn around. He would have to take Brownie right out of the shafts and edge her past, walk her down, and then come back and push the cart himself. Take him twenty minutes at the least. It was two minutes' work to back the sulky up – you scarcely needed to unhitch the horse.

The sulky driver raised his whip and for a minute Frank thought that he was going to be attacked. It would have been a poor lookout if so. Frank would have laid the fellow flat without a thought – and paid for it in the police courts afterwards. However, all the man did was lay into the hedge, and send small branches flying.

'Do you hear me? Back up, instantly!' The gentleman – if he deserved that name – paused suddenly and looked more closely in Frank's face. 'Wait a minute, I know who you are. You're the son of that carrier up at Penvarris mine – I saw you unloading parcels there just the other day, when I drove my father to a meeting at the purser's house. Well, mind who you obstruct another time.

My family has a major interest in the mine. Now, are you going to get out of my way, or not?'

It was not a threat, exactly, but it was as good as one – and a good deal more frightening than the whip had been. If Fayther lost his contract it would affect them all. Frank still had a strong desire to punch that casually good-looking face, and see those blue eyes fill with something other than contempt, but common sense and twenty years of deference prevailed. 'Yes, sir. On my way to do it.'

And he did – though it made him a good deal later than he had meant to be, and Ma Jones's sister wasn't pleased: and he did not have time to drive past the Tregenzas', as he'd hoped, to see if Maisie had managed to get out for half an hour with the post.

The concert was a tremendous artistic tour de force. The Passemore-Jenkinses said so, and they ought to know. Even Lucy had quite enjoyed it, in a peculiar sort of way – looking around at the gowns and jewellery – and she had joined enthusiastically in the applause at every song.

They were in a box, which perhaps was just as well, since the arrangement of the chairs was flexible. Lucy was able to sit a little to one side and watch the audience without needing to make conversation with her friend. If Annabelle could still be called a friend. She had scarcely addressed a word to anyone all night. Not since she came down to the carriage and found Lucy sitting there.

Simon had sent his coachman round alone to pick her up and Lucy had thought nothing was amiss. In fact she thought it tactful of Simon not to ride with her alone, and to contrive it so the Passemore-Jenkinses did not have to wait. But as he handed his cousin to the stop, Annabelle turned to him and said, 'I thought your sister was to come with us?' It was clear that Lucy's presence was a complete surprise and not a welcome one.

Simon gave that throaty laugh of his. 'Ah, but she couldn't make it in the end, so I asked your friend instead. I thought you would appreciate the thought. You can amuse each other in the interval,' and he bundled her inside, where she flounced and frowned and crossed her arms and stared out of the window on the other side, without even a pretence at civility. Simon cheerfully ignored this exhibition and went back for Celestine, who at any rate was nervously polite and kept up strained conversation until her parents came.

Even then, Lucy formed the distinct impression that the senior Passemore-Jenkinses were not best pleased to find that she was there – though they were far too well mannered to express that openly. It was embarrassing. There was not even a great deal of room inside the chaise. Lucy squashed into a corner and tried to disappear.

Simon seemed oblivious of any atmosphere and prattled happily about the splendid concert programme they were due to hear, and telling an amusing anecdote about meeting a blockage with his sulky in the lane. He had squeezed in between his cousins, and he waved his arms about, though Celestine at least did not appear to mind.

And so the evening had progressed. Stern glances from her parents had made Annabelle behave in a manner more befitting one of Miss Worthington's young ladies, and a period of cool correctness had ensued, though she was still avoiding speaking when she could. Simon did try to talk her out of it – he was sitting just behind them and Lucy saw him whisper something in her ear – but Anna only flushed and turned her head away and maintained a stubborn silence till the end.

It was only when the concert was over, when the standing ovation had finally died down and the gentlemen had gone to find their coats, that Anna finally came over to her friend. 'Why didn't you tell me what you were up to, then? If I'd understood the reason, I wouldn't have been cross – but of course you've made it rather difficult. How am I supposed to explain things to Mama? She can see I hadn't the faintest notion that you were to come.'

She sounded almost normal, like her friendly self, and Lucy turned towards her. 'I don't know what you mean.'

'Oh, don't be silly, Lucy, you don't have to feign with me. Simon's told me all about what

97

he'd explained to you – how he wouldn't have been able to sit with me at all, unless there was somebody to come and take his sister's place because he'd have been expected to pair off with Celestine. Well, of course I understand – and it's nice of you to go along with it, though no doubt you were pleased enough to come in any case. But it would have been so much easier if I'd known before tonight.'

Lucy was too flabbergasted to say anything at all, and after a moment Annabelle went on, 'Simon recommends that we should tell Mama that it was his sister who suggested you should come and use her seat. If that was so, then no one could object, because it looks like a sort of compliment to me. He says I shall have to say I wasn't feeling well – that will explain why I was out of sorts – and then I can lean on his arm as we go out, as well. Here he is now, coming with our coats – so don't say anything to contradict me, will you now?'

Lucy was taken so thoroughly aback that she could think of no reply. Whatever was Simon playing at? It was clear now this invitation had been wholly his idea, and he had put her in an awkward situation with her hosts – people who had been very kind to her as well. On the way back it was her turn to be subdued, but Simon's subterfuge had clearly done the trick and everyone was positively cordial by now. In fact, Mrs Passemore-Jenkins was even good enough to invite 'dear Lucy' in to have a little supper with the girls.

Dear Lucy was too embarrassed to accept. She made some scrambled apology, saying that she had promised to be back betimes, and Simon's coachman took her home again. In fact, if it hadn't been that Simon had already accepted supper for himself, and was being led off in triumph by Celestine and Annabelle, Lucy had the uncomfortable feeling that he would have broken all the rules, and offered to accompany her home in person – all alone.

Though no doubt he would have come up with some plausible excuse.

Helena took off her Sunday gloves and bonnet with a sigh, and sat down at the pianoforte in her sitting room. The new étude she had been learning was dancing round her head.

'Da, da, dee, dah ... no ... da, da, dee, dah-dah ... oh bother!' It wasn't any use. If she could not remember, it would be 'practising' and that was frowned on, on the Sabbath day.

She shut the lid of the piano and turned away. It was so frustrating when you'd begun to learn a piece and the harmonies escaped you in that kind of way. There was nowhere you could look to see which chords were next, and Lucy was worse than useless when it came to things like that – she played with great bravura but she wasn't accurate, you couldn't be convinced she'd got it right. Perhaps Papa would help. She'd ask him later on: 'performing' on a Sunday was all right.

Otherwise the étude would have to wait until her teacher came again. Unfortunately, that was days away.

'Da, da, dahh...' No, singing didn't help.

She was trying to divert her thoughts to other things – sprinkling talcum in her gloves and putting them away – when she heard Maisie coming up the stairs. It was a brisk, distinctive tread: she must have had her boots reheeled and soled, because there was a little metallic tap on every step.

'Why, Miss Elenner, you're up here on yer own,' Maisie burst out, before she was fairly in the room. 'You aren't going walking round the garden with your sister, then? Thought you would've liked it, for a bit of change.'

Helena smiled. 'I've been to church this morning, and that's change enough for me.' Hard to explain the truth of that to anyone – even her family found it hard to understand sometimes. 'I'm no good when I'm out for very long. The trouble is, when I'm outside I don't know where things are. But here, I know exactly where to put my hands on what I want, and where the cupboards and sharp corners are. I manage beautifully.' She said it with some feeling. She could still detect the bruised place on her shin where someone had left the hymn-book cupboard open in the church porch today. 'You see, I've even put away my gloves.'

'Well, I'm here now, so give that bonnet 'ere and I'll put it in its 'at box,' Maisie said. 'It's my job after all. Oh, it's some pretty, isn't it?

Little flowers and all.' And then, hastily – as if she'd realized what she'd said – 'Pity you can't see it for yourself. Now, playing the piano, was you? Want me to put your stool where you can sit?'

Helena shook a rueful head. 'I shan't do any more. I'm having trouble with a piece I like – it's up there on the piano – but if you practise it all wrong it only makes it worse.'

'What you were playing sounded nice to me,' Maisie said stoutly, and made her mistress laugh. 'Though it's a shame there iddn't a way that you could read the notes. Ought to think of something, didn't they?'

Helena laughed again, a little bitterly this time. 'Well, they have – or at least a blind man did in France. He had an accident, like me, when he was very young, and he worked out a way to write it down so you could feel the lumps. M. Braille his name was. It isn't only music, he did the same for books.'

'Like that Fry thing you used to do?'

'Better, from what James was telling me. And simpler than the Moon system that he was on about. That's pretty good to read, but it's so long – an ordinary book takes seventy volumes when it's done in Moon. And it's all set by hand, so it costs no end as well. Papa tried to enquire about it once, in Penzance – but all he could get hold of was the Lord's Prayer in Moon, and that weighed half a ton. And then you have to learn to read it, because it's not the same as print.'

'Pity they haven't got this Braille in English,

then.'

'They're starting to adopt it, so James was telling me. There are so many systems – all quite different – that the English and Foreign Blind Association set up a committee to decide which one was best. It took them two years to make up their minds, but they decided Braille and Moon were best, and now there's lots of books. But they are hard to come by, and expensive too. It's not intended for mere pleasure, I think – it's more for men who need to study, or to read and write for business and that sort of thing. So they can make a living.'

'Not for girls, you mean? Cause they don't have to make a living anyhow. Though – pardon me for saying – you'd had more schooling than most girls, didn't you, before you 'urt yourself? Not just how to read and cipher, but real poetry and that.'

Helena had to laugh. 'I suppose I did. Though James was telling me there is a girl – American, I think – who even went to university and did so well they gave her a degree. She was blind – and deaf and dumb as well! Makes me seem quite useless, doesn't it?'

'You aren't useless – don't you say such things. You play the piano something beautiful.'

This time she did laugh. 'When I know the notes, perhaps! So there you are, I'll wait until my music teacher comes – or James comes back from London with that gramophone. Then I can practise this study to my heart's content, and perhaps I will be some use after all.'

'Know when he's coming, do you Miss Elenner?' Maisie didn't mention James by name, but it was quite clear who she meant.

'No. Papa has had a letter from him from London, I believe. He seems to be having an exciting time. Looking forward to going up there to read for his degree. It's what he always wanted – to study medicine.'

Maisie was rustling tissue in a box. 'Shouldn't like to be a doctor, though, should you? All those sick people round you all the time – you'd be worried you'd catch something 'orrible yourself. Just like those nurses of Miss Nightingale's: now, I ask you – why would young ladies, brought up like yourself, want to go and do a thing like that? All that blood and dirt. I don't understand it. And it wasn't just the Russian war, they've gone on doing it. I 'spect they'll be having women doctors next.'

Helena grinned. 'They already do. It's fifty years since the first woman doctor was allowed – though there hasn't been one anywhere round here so far. As for why they do it – I only wish that I could do something of the sort myself. Make a contribution to the world, instead of sitting up here like an ornament, and playing the piano every now and then. It's all I'm really good for – as you said yourself.'

'I'm sure I never said so for a minute,' Maisie said. 'Besides – that's all your music teacher does, isn't it? And you don't say she's useless. You think a lot of her.'

'She teaches people how to play. That's different.'

There was a little pause, then Maisie said, 'Why couldn't you, if you've a mind to, then?'

Helena laughed. 'It's something I've never thought about. I don't have to earn my living, or anything like that.'

'You could learn me, for instance.'

Helena was startled into sharpness. 'But you don't have a piano. Wherever would you play?'

'I could help out in the Sunday school sometimes,' Maisie retorted, stoutly. 'They've got a piano in the meeting room, where they take the little ones, and old Miss Harper still thumps out all the hymns, though she's deafer than a post and you can't tell what she's playing half the time. They're always saying how she wants some help – and I do get Sunday afternoons sometimes. And there isn't anybody else to take her place. Mr Wylie's wanted for the harmonium next door.'

Helena smiled at the picture that this conjured up. 'Well, in that case – if you would like to bring the music hymn book here, I'll get my teacher to play through the tunes...' She was already thinking of ways it might be done.

'Mind, I couldn't pay you anything, so perhaps that wouldn't work,' Maisie sounded regretful, 'but there must be other folk like me who could. If you got that music from that Mr Braille – you'd have to 'ave it turned to English first, I suppose – I'm sure you could learn anyone to play or sing.'

Helena forbore to laugh aloud at the idea of translating music into English and said, quite gently, 'I'll give you a lesson, sometimes, if you like. And don't worry about paying. It would be helping me. I really think I might enjoy it.'

'Would you really, Miss Elenner? I wouldn't 'alf be thrilled.' And then as if Helena was proposing that they should start at once she added, 'But I can't today. It's Sunday, and I got to help with lunch.'

'Then you'd better run along.' Helena waited till the little boots went tapping off downstairs, then got up and walked – still smiling – to the window. There was still some-one in the garden – Lucy, probably. But there was someone else as well. A man. She could detect the faint sound of voices and the crunch of distant feet upon the gravel path, but it was too indistinct and far away for her to work out who it was. Then a woman's soft, delighted laugh, and quick, light footsteps running up the drive. Yes, Lucy certainly. That was her sister's voice in the vestibule, and her familiar tread upon the stairs. Helena was ready with the question on her lips.

'Who was the gentleman visitor, my dear? Surely not James home from London yet?'

She had not in the least intended a rebuke, but Lucy seemed to find one, all the same,

'Just a friend of Papa's who happened to look in. He didn't even bother to come up to the house. I told him that Papa was out for lunch.' She sounded cross and flustered. 'How did you know he was there, in any case? Has Maisie been spying, and telling tales on me?'

Helena laughed. 'The window was open, and I heard you, that was all.'

There was a silence, then a startled, 'Oh!' And after a few minutes, Lucy muttered in a reluctant voice, 'It isn't ... I didn't mean...' She had flung herself noisily on to the window seat and Helena heard the casement banging shut. 'I forgot you had ears as sharp as oyster-forks. What exactly did you hear him say?'

'I didn't hear anything, in particular,' Helena said, pacifically. 'Just a laugh and then you running in. I wouldn't have thought any more about it if you hadn't come up here a minute afterwards.' And been so desperate to defend yourself, she added, privately.

She didn't have to. Lucy had come to the same conclusion for herself. 'And now I have made you curious, I perceive. Well, I suppose there's no harm in telling you. It was Mr Robinson – Simon – a sort of cousin to the Passemore-Jenkins girls. I'm sure I've mentioned him to you before. He accompanied our party to the concert last weekend. He's thinking of putting capital into Penvarris mine. He comes here to ask Papa for advice.'

'And that's what causes you to laugh so

merrily?'

'Oh, Lena, don't be horrid! Of course he makes me laugh, but there is no cause to use that meaning tone of voice. I was merely being cordial to Papa's visitor. Now, what was that tune you wanted me to play? This étude? I'll hold the chords so you can put your fingers over mine.' She moved to the piano with unwonted eagerness, and Helena heard her pull out the second stool. 'It won't be practising, exactly, so I'm sure Mama won't mind. And Papa isn't here to scold. I'll start from the beginning?'

There was only one explanation for this change of mood that Helena could see. Lucy had lost her heart a little to this Simon Robinson, and didn't want to talk. Perhaps the attachment to James Morrison was not so very great. She found that she was smiling. 'Yes, please do,' she said.

Perhaps she would ask Papa to mention the Braille music when he wrote to James – there would be some in London, if it was anywhere, and she knew that her old friend would find it if he could.

Part Two –
Summer to Winter 1910

Chapter One

The death of the King had stunned everyone, of course, and for a week or two it seemed all normal life had ceased. Then, what with the business meetings for the mine and several birthday dances, including Annabelle's, the summer seemed to pass in one long social whirl. The date of departure for the university was suddenly upon James in a rush.

There was such a lot to do – letters to write, trunks to pack and farewell visits to be made – that the last few days appeared to simply fly. Mother hid a certain tearfulness under a concern for making lists and worrying about his having enough clean socks and under-wear: Pater's after-dinner sessions became occasions for little homilies about the great adventure which lay ahead of him, exhortations about the need to study hard and, on one embarrassing occasion, 'man-to-man advice about the facts of life' (which seemed to consist mostly of cold showers and self-control).

But busy as he was, when another meeting of the venturers for Penvarris mine was called – to discuss transport for the new engine when it came – James felt he had to go. He had been instrumental in voting for the thing: he was convinced that it was needed, and the fact that it would require a special traction engine to bring it to the site was simply a necessary cost and one that he was happy to defend. But that idiot Robinson was there, of course, and with his half-dozen cronies he fought it all the way, raising a host of difficulties, most of them absurd. Between them, they dragged it out for half the afternoon before the arrangement was approved at last.

'Well, that was an unnecessary waste of all our time,' he grumbled afterwards, as he rode back with Paul Tregenza down the lane. It was a brilliant sunny afternoon – seabirds wheeling in a cloudless sky, the sea pinks and foxgloves pink-purple in the hedge, and the distant sea a deep untroubled blue – but it was not enough to lift his mood today. Somehow the memory of the last time he'd come here, and the accident to that poor fellow's hand, made this quibbling over a few pounds seem indefensible. He shifted in his saddle. 'That dratted Robinson! I believe he actually enjoys holding things back as long as possible.'

Tregenza laughed. 'Ah, there perhaps I would agree with you. Robinson sees everything in terms of bank accounts. Though his son seems rather better. I've met him once or twice. Thinking of putting capital into the mine himself and wanted my advice. Seemed quite forward-looking, by what he said to me

– though whether he would really vote against his father in the end, it's hard to say.'

James found that the mention of Simon Robinson was quite enough to make the summer afternoon turn sour. 'So he'll turn up at the venturers' meetings by and by?' He saw Paul's look of mild surprise, and hurried on, 'I ask because, quite clearly, I shall not be there myself – during the term-time anyway. If Simon does support his father in the votes, you might have difficulty getting agreement for any new expenditure at all.'

Another laugh and Paul Tregenza said, 'Then I'll have to send you information about matters coming up, and you can write and let me know your views. I can represent them at the meeting. It's been done before. But don't worry about Simon, I don't believe he's even offered for the shares. I told him to go away and think – pointed out the problems he might face – and he agreed it wasn't wise to rush. His heart's more in horses than in mining anyway. You know him, I assume?'

James muttered, 'Only socially.'

'Seems a pleasant lad, related to the Passemore-Jenkinses, of course. He has a sister too – who has made quite a friend of Lucille, it appears. Speaking of Lucille, are you coming in? She would like to see you, I am sure.' They had arrived outside the side gate of the house, and Tregenza dismounted as he spoke.

James thought for a moment of finding some reason to refuse. If Lucy had been 'taken up' by wretched Simon and his family then she was welcome to their company. He felt distinctly irked. He didn't care for Simon, and if anything he liked the sister even less. He'd once had the misfortune to be introduced to Rachel Robinson, and she had struck him then as disagreeable: 'cutting' people, like himself, that she thought inferior. She had all the makings of embittered spinsterhood, plain, condescending, razor-voiced and vain – though there was some young nincompoop in hot pursuit of her, or at least of the money she would come to have one day. That was some little time ago, when James had just left school. She must have been well in her twenties then – older than Lucy by a good few years. He wondered what the attraction of the friendship was.

'Papa? I heard your voice, and is that James with you?' The voice cut across his thoughts. Helena was in her bower on the far side of the hedge. She had stood up and turned towards them, calling out her welcome with a smile.

'Yes, my dear, we were just coming in,' Tregenza said. 'Where's Lucy? Is she with you in the bower?'

'No, she brought me out, then went inside again – to look at some bonnet trimmings with Mama, I think. I told her I was happy here till tea. I've got my music here.'

'Why don't we have Maisie bring some tea out here, and we can have it in the bower, all of us. I'll get the boy to bring some extra chairs when he puts this horse away. I'll go up and get that sorted out, and I'll be with you in no time at all. James, you go in and talk to Helena.'

There was no question of refusal, after that. James slid down from his horse, tied it to the hitching post outside and followed Paul Tregenza through the gate. But instead of turning down towards the house he took the winding footpath to the bower.

Helena was sitting in the corner, her fingers busy with a book, although her eyes were shut. She looked like an Italian painting, he thought suddenly, framed by the fragrant roses in that soft cream dress, her black hair piled in soft curls on her head. She raised her face and smiled as he approached.

'James?' She said it as lightly as she could, rising and putting down her book. 'What a delight to find you coming here. And on such an afternoon. Just listen to the birds.' She wondered if he could also hear the beating of her heart.

'I know.' He caught her hands and squeezed them in his own. 'And the perfume from the flowers is wonderful. A little bit of heaven you have here. Another thing that I shall miss while I'm away.'

She caught her hands back in a sudden fright. 'Surely you haven't come to say good-bye?'

'Of course not. I don't leave for another day or two. There is to be that dinner party first. I understood that you'd agreed to come.'

She laughed. 'And so I will. For you. Although I don't like dinner parties in a general way.' He couldn't guess how difficult it was. Trying to find the proper knives and forks and being dependent on the servants' whispering to work out what dish was being served, all in a strange room where you didn't know what size your host's expensive dinner plates might be or where the edges of the table were.

'Then we will leave our sad farewells till then. Come, sit beside me,' he said. He took her hands again and drew her down upon the seat. 'Ah, is this the Braille music book I brought for you? I hope it is some use. It took me some time to acquire one at all, and then it was only a hymn book, I'm afraid. Most of the imprints are religious things.'

'But it's been wonderful,' she said, and meant it too. 'It can't offer you all the harmonies at once, but it has given me a lot of confidence. Though it's taken me a long time to learn to read the notes. My fingers weren't sensitive enough to pick them out at first – I think it might be easier when you haven't learnt to read the music any other way – and then you are supposed to keep the memory of that touch when you come to play the piece, and I can't do that. I still turn it into normal music in my head. But I did manage to learn a whole piece by myself last week and play it to my teacher when she came. She didn't know anything about it until I sat down and performed.'

She heard James chuckle. 'What did she say to that?'

Helena pulled a comic, rueful face. 'She said that I had got the fingering all wrong, and I was playing a quaver rest and not a dotted one.' It was not Miss Bell's nature to pay compliments. 'But secretly I know she was impressed.'

'I hear you have a pupil of your own from time to time?'

She was embarrassed. 'Whoever told you that? Oh, Lucy I suppose.' She would have words with her sister for betraying that, she thought. It was supposed to be a secret.

But it seemed it wasn't Lucy after all. 'Maisie mentioned it herself. Told me all about her 'pianner book' and how she had 'a bit of lesson now and then' with you. She sounded absolutely thrilled.'

'But rather less than thrilling, I'm afraid.' She could not resist the little joke, thinking of the tuneless thumpings which marked Maisie's first attempts. 'But, yes, it's true – in a peculiar sort of way. She comes up in the evening for twenty minutes twice a week, when she has finished with her chores. Mama has no objection and Maisie's very keen. In fact, I think she'd stay for hours if I permitted it. She's making progress too. She can manage "Twinkle Twinkle" and nearly "Three Blind Mice".'

He laughed. 'With both hands, I know. She told me. And she's going on to "Now the day is over" soon – she's very proud of that. She

117

wants to play it for the Sunday school.'

'Perhaps she will.' Helena found that she was smiling. 'Though I fear it might take some time to get it right. Poor girl. She tries her very best, but she hasn't got a piano that she can practise on. She can't be permitted to use ours, of course, and she can't ask at the chapel until she's learned to play. But she's extremely keen. She's drawn a keyboard on a piece of wood, and she tells me that she runs through her "pieces" on that every night.'

'And is that any help?'

'She seems to think it is. It's made her familiar with the names of notes, and it's certainly less painful when she makes mistakes! I only wish I had a teaching book for her – the Braille one you gave me is advanced, of course, and isn't suitable. But I have adapted it. And we have used children's songs as well – and all the scales and things. To tell the truth, I've found it rather fun.'

'A change from sitting idly, with not very much to do?'

She turned towards him, filled with gratitude. 'I might have known that you would understand. You always—' She broke off at the sound of footsteps on the gravel path. 'But here are the others coming.'

Perhaps he hadn't heard them, but she was right of course. She even knew exactly who was who. First Papa's stride, purposeful and manly, crunching as he went, then Lucy's lighter footsteps, then Mama's, and last of all the little metal 'clip' of Maisie's mended and steel-toecapped boots.

'James, how nice to see you!' Lucy's voice, playful and girlish, with a little bell-like laugh. (Or 'Bella-like' would be more apposite, perhaps – Helena thought unkindly – since it was an affectation recently copied from Anna Passemore-Jenkins.) Then gushingly, 'It seems a positive eternity since you were here. You haven't even heard my birthday music on that gramophone you brought. Papa sent up to London specially and had three new discs sent down.'

'I am glad to know that the machine has been of some small use.'

'Small?' That was Mother's voice, panting as she lowered herself on to the bower seat. 'My dear James, it has been a wonderful success. Helena loves it – she has learned to turn it on herself – and Lucy has it on for simply hours. Paul and I enjoy it after dinner, for a change, and even my sister asks for it sometimes. It is really quite remarkable, you know. You can change the cylinders and get a different tune each time.'

'They are not cylinders, Mama. These are discs. Really, you're so very out-of-date,' Lucy said, still in her fashionable-young-woman tone of voice.

'And you are forward, Lucille!' Papa said. It was a warning and there might have been a wigging for her, there and then, if Edgar had not come up at that moment with the chairs, and scraped and clunked them into place. The tea tray was set down on the table,

119

Maisie served, and quite a merry tea party ensued.

James was at his most engaging, talking to them all, though it seemed to Helena that he was particularly charmed by Lucy's company. She, in her turn, was very warm to him, prattling guilelessly about some outing with her friends, and springing up to volunteer to walk him round the grounds and show him the new fountain near the summer house. It all sounded very artless, but it occurred to Helena that her sister might be hoping to get James all to herself.

Papa's suggestion put an end to that. 'Perhaps we'll all go over there,' he said, heartily. 'The walk will do us good. Gertrude, may I offer you an arm? And – Helena – you the other one, my dear?'

So Helena's lasting memory of that afternoon was of strolling down the path on Papa's left, making bright conversation to him and to Mama: and of James and Lucy just ahead of them – murmuring to each other in an undertone and laughing now and then at private jokes – while the fountain made little rippling noises on the sill and the heavy scent of roses filled the air. The afternoon sun was making warm patches on her back, but all that Helena could think of was that James was leaving soon and nothing could dispel the chill around her heart.

It was quite late before James took his leave of them at last. Lucy wondered for a moment if he would kiss her cheek – as he had just done to Helena and Mama – but all he did was take her hand and raise it to his lips.

'I'll see you at the farewell dinner party, then. Good afternoon, and thank you for the tea.' And he was down the path and gone.

She raised her hand in a half-wave salute, feeling the prickle of tears behind her lids. It was peculiar. When James was with her, she adored his company. It was only in comparison that he seemed a little dull.

'He is like a brother!' she had said to Simon, once.

And he'd said, 'Boring, humdrum and predictable?' and kissed her on the neck, in a way that poor James would never dare. During one of his sister's fictitious tea parties, no doubt, when the two of them were out walking on the moors.

Lucy had really been to one of these affairs, of course. Rachel Robinson was noted for her charity afternoons, and Lucy had attended with the Passemore-Jenkins girls. Simon had arranged it – she did not quite know how – and had introduced her to Rachel as a friend of Annabelle's.

Lucy had not enjoyed it much, in fact. Simon had spent his time with Celestine – that was an obvious necessity, of course, if his mother and sister were not to be suspicious of Lucy's presence there – and Anna was in a frosty mood because he didn't talk to her, and retired to a corner in a sulk. Lucy had purchased her scones and tea in aid of charity, and spoken to no one much but Rachel Robinson, who thanked her three separate times for having come, and on each occasion asked her for her name.

But it had done the trick, as Simon said it would. She'd talked about the outing in a public sort of way, when Mrs Passemore-Jenkins was visiting Mama. This sparked a little monologue about Miss Robinson, her impeccable connections and her charitable works. Now Lucy had only to mention 'one of Rachel's teas' and she was free to go out for an hour or two at will. Simon even sent his coach to pick her up. Mostly she went to Rachel's for a little while, at least, but eventually she didn't go at all. In fact, she had done that on two occasions now, and no one had done any more than ask when she got back, 'And did you have a pleasant afternoon?'

It had given her a pleasantly naughty thrill to say, 'Very pleasant, thank you very much,' when she had really been walking hand-in-hand with Simon on the cliffs.

She'd been a little nervous of those walks at first. She'd heard – everyone at Miss Worthington's establishment had heard – of dastardly young men who forced their will on you (though she was not altogether certain what it meant). But Simon was nothing but a perfect gentleman. Certainly he didn't force his will on anyone – he was never anything but most agreeable. He was charming, solicitous and he made her laugh. It was just that he had that audacious way with him and did outrageous things – just like the night when he asked her to dance – only now it was planting that wicked kiss upon her neck, or suggesting these imaginary teas. It was obviously daring, but that was half the thrill, especially after Papa's staid old-fashioned ways. And if anybody chided him – as Rachel did one day when they were late – he'd come up with some off-the-cuff excuse and offer it with such angelic earnestness, it was sometimes difficult not to laugh outright.

So why did she suddenly feel bereft this afternoon at the thought of losing James? Well, not exactly losing him, perhaps. When they were by the fountain and could not be overheard, he'd made a point of asking if he might write to her – to her, apart from to the family – and of course she'd said he could. And when she promised that she'd answer him, he said, 'You don't know how much that means to me,' just as though he was her proper beau.

She was looking forward to the farewell dinner night, but when it came she found it rather flat. It was not a large occasion. There was just the family there and she was seated next to Uncle Morrison, who complimented her upon her dress, teased her that she was a lady now and treated her – as usual – as though she were a child, insisting that the choicest titbits should be hers, while making little jokes at her expense. Aunt Morrison looked very wan and sad: she only toyed with the delicious food, and was intently conversational with Mama afterwards. James seemed to spend the evening talking to Aunt Edwards and Papa, and to Helena, who was seated next to him. There was no time for any private words for her.

Only he squeezed her fingers when he said goodbye, in a way that made her blush. More, strangely, than Simon's audacious kiss had done.

Chapter Two

Maisie stood in her little bedroom, looking at herself in the spotted mirror. Best navy skirt, clean blouse and tartan wrap. She looked as good as she was going to do, she thought, though she had stayed too long with her piano lesson and had to wash her hair in a hurry to go out – never easy in cold water in that little bowl. She'd got it clean and it smelt quite nice of soap, but afterwards she'd had to rub it dry and now it looked as if birds had been nesting in it, even though she'd combed it lots of times. Just when she wanted to look her best for Frank!

Well, she'd just have to cover the bird's nest up and hope. She put her bonnet on (the straw one with the ribbons that nearly matched her skirt) and thrust three hatpins through to skewer it in place. That looked a little better, and on an impulse she did a soppy thing – pinched her cheeks and bit her lips to make them slightly pink, the way she'd seen Miss Lucy do.

' 'Ere!' That was Rosie from the bedroom door and obviously she had seen. 'You want to get those liquorice comfits from the sweet shop, like my sister does. Only a ha'penny for an ounce. The red ones make your lips look pink as pink, and you can eat the comfits afterwards. You mind if I come in and use the glass?'

'Course.' Maisie stood back to let her in. Poor Rosie didn't have a glass at all – or a washstand, come to that. Maisie's was an old one which had come up from downstairs – the corner of the marble top was cracked and the jug and washbasin no longer matched, but it was a proper washstand all the same. Poor Rosie had nothing except an enamel jug and basin on the sill, and nothing but bare boards beneath her feet. Maisie had a rag rug, and a chair, and a curtained corner-place to hang her clothes – even a hand-stitched text up on the wall. Much nicer even than the bedroom at her aunt's. She felt quite like a gracious lady as she said, 'Come in and help yourself. I'm off out, anyhow.'

Rosie was scraping her thin hair into a plait and plonking her blue hat on top of it. It was a small old-fashioned one with a round brim like a man's and a row of bright red cherries round the band. It made the poor girl look

125

positively plain. 'You going to the missionary slideshow at the chapel, too?'

'Might do,' Maisie tried to sound off-hand and vague, though of course it was exactly where she and Frank were going. There weren't so many places where the two of you could go – sit together, have a cup of tea and warm – and not have everybody gossiping.

Rosie was still fiddling with her long steel hatpins. 'Might walk down with you then, for company.'

She said it in such a friendly way that Maisie was at a loss for words. Her cheeks were pinker than the pinch had made them, now. 'Well,' she said at last. 'Frank was going to come for me and take me in the cart.'

Rosie wiggled the last pin into place and stood back to admire the effect. 'Oh, good,' she said. 'I'll beg a lift as well. Your Frank won't mind. He's such a lovely chap.'

It was clear she wasn't meaning to be difficult, it simply hadn't occurred to her she might be in the way. Maisie was still wondering how to deal with this when Rosie said suddenly, 'Well, come on, then. We'll have to go. Don't want to keep him waiting, or we'll all be late.' She stood back to let Maisie lead the way downstairs. 'I do like these missionary shows, don't you? Something a bit different – and it's wonderful the way they show the slides. Good as the moving pictures, very near – or so my sister says.'

It was intended as a bit of swank, and Maisie was still fretting about her tryst with

126

Frank, but she said obligingly, 'Seen them, 'as she?' which was obviously what Rosie hoped she'd say.

'Her young man took her there. Paid a penny, took her in the stalls. Some exciting story, too it was. All about a girl and a bad man tried to tie her down in front a train. My sister tore her hankie, twisting it.' She opened the back door and led the way along the path. 'Ah, here's Frank and the cart. Told you he'd be waiting.'

And he was. He raised his eyebrows when he saw them both, and Maisie mouthed an apology to him, but he just smiled and helped them climb aboard.

Rosie was still wittering about the picture show. 'They walked off into the sunset, 'and in 'and,' she finished, with a dreamy sigh, sitting herself beside them in the front. 'I was just telling Maisie about the pictures in Penzance. 'Andsome, must 'ave been. Wish I could've gone and seen un too.'

Frank reached for Maisie's hand beneath her cloak and gave it a surreptitious squeeze. 'Well, better wait until the next one now. Else the story won't be a surprise, will it?' He grinned at Maisie wickedly, and winked.

'It would be nice, though, wouldn't it? Romantic?' Rosie said.

'Walking off into the sunset?' Frank replied. 'I don't know so much. Walk into the sea if you did that round here. Hand in hand, though – that bit sounds all right.' He squeezed Maisie's fingers, underneath the shawl.

Maisie found that she was chuckling. Frank kept up a string of jokes like that the whole way to the hall and even Rosie realized that she was being teased. 'Oh, Frank!' she muttered, with a laugh. 'You are a one!'

'Well,' he said, 'there's two of you, so that makes three of us – and here we are. The chapel. No moving pictures, I'm afraid, tonight. Have to make do with Eli Wallach's slides. But afterwards, when I have driven home, if you don't mind, Rosie, perhaps you'd go inside and leave your friend and me to have a bit of talk.'

Rosie looked from him to Maisie and then back again and turned a shade of pink. 'Oh, 'ere – I'm some sorry if I'm gooseberry. Never thought. Better if I walk home on me own and leave you two in peace.'

Frank gave her arm a friendly pat. 'Don't you do anything so daft. You come on home with us. Only – like I said ... we'd like a bit of talk.'

Rosie only nodded, but all through the missionary show she kept darting little looks in their direction, and giving them shy smiles. Might as well have held a placard up, 'Frank Carter's walking out with Maisie Olds', the way she carried on. She did, however, show a bit of sense when they got home.

She hadn't said a word the whole way back, just sat there humming to herself, but as she was getting off the cart she glanced back up at them and murmured, in an undertone, 'I shan't go straight indoors. I'll wait for Maisie by the back door, in the porch. That way Mrs Lovett won't start asking where she is. Down on you like a ton of bricks if she finds out you're with a fellow in the lane.'

It was embarrassing, of course, because they couldn't be too long, but it was very satisfactory. Frank put a shy, strong arm around her waist, asked her how the piano playing went, and told her he'd paid another shilling off the cart. And then, for a minute, there wasn't a lot of talking done at all.

Rosie was still standing, waiting in the porch when Maisie hurried in. 'Thought you was never coming. I'm frozen half to death. All right for you, out there chatting half the night. Or whatever you were doing.' She looked at Maisie and grinned broadly as she spoke. 'I peeped in the window. Mrs Lovett's in the kitchen gone to sleep. Think we can sneak past without she finds a job for us? The family's not back yet, by the look of it.'

'Shh!' Maisie cautioned, and took off both her boots. Rosie followed suit, and they tip-toed past the housekeeper's retreat with stockinged feet, lit their nightlights from the stove and crept upstairs like naughty children.

Maisie said, 'Good night, then,' and went into her room. As she set the candle down she glimpsed her speckled reflection in the glass. No wonder Rosie had been grinning at her in that way.

Even with the hatpins, her bonnet was awry.

* * *

129

The dinner party was not, after all, the last farewell to James. Mother suddenly decided that the Tregenza family should all go to the station on Saturday and see him on the train. Mrs Morrison would be glad of company, she said, and anyway there were things to do with both the girls in town, so would Papa please ask Edgar to get the carriage out and drive them to Penzance. So that was what they did.

Helena did not enjoy the trip at all. She hated long goodbyes. Besides, she was never very confident in crowds and being in an unfamiliar place was always hard. Papa was very good and took her on his arm, but she still found it difficult. There seemed to be steps and kerbs and railings everywhere, and so many people jostling to and fro that she couldn't listen to his footsteps on the surface of the ground – the difference between wooden floors and paving stones, or the clank of iron grating grilles, for instance – which she generally relied on as a guide to place her feet.

Here there were so many noises crowding in on her. The chattering and clattering of people everywhere, shouts and calls for luggage, sighing steam from trains, the rattling of carriages and the slam of doors, the newsboy's high-pitched holler, 'Tidi-idings. Morning tidi-idings.' And near at hand the family making their farewells.

'You will write, won't you, as you promised me?' That was Lucy, quite high-pitched and strained. Mother added, 'And to all of us?'

'You have got your ticket safely? And your hat and gloves?' Aunt Morrison, while Uncle Morrison muttered, 'Good luck. Proud of you, my boy,' then cleared his throat and hurrumphed in his beard.

Papa said, 'You'll be back before you know it,' and pressed Helena forward too, and then it was her turn to say goodbye.

She said the word. It was inadequate. She wanted to burst out that she would miss him dreadfully. In fact, it began to dawn on her just how much she would. She loved his jokes, his conversation, the way he read the papers and kept her up to date, and never minded if she asked a lot of questions or forgot exactly who was who. But of course she couldn't say that, so she simply said, 'Good luck!' and let it go at that.

James took her free hand in his own smooth grasp and gave it a warm squeeze. 'Take care of yourself, Lena. And keep the music up. I'll see if I can find some more for you.'

And that was it. He was gone. Uncle Morrison went with him to get his luggage stowed, and someone called Rupert, whom she'd never met, came bustling up to them, and said he was travelling as well, and there was a commotion getting him installed. Then there was a whistle from the engine and the guard, and somebody running down the platform who had nearly missed the train, and then the steady huff and clatter as the carriage pulled away.

Lucy said, 'He's waving. Goodbye, James.

131

Goodbye.'

Uncle Morrison cleared his throat again and Aunt Morrison began to talk about the price of silk and the people of the train – anything except James leaving – in a strange flat voice that didn't sound like hers.

Helena stood very still and didn't say a word. But she could never smell that smell again, that mixture of steam-smoke and platform tea, without remembering that moment and the sense of loss she felt.

'Now where have I seen that young lad before?' Aunt Morrison's voice brought her to herself. 'The one with all the parcels over there? Didn't I see him near your gate the other night, Gertrude? He seems to be a carrier, I see. Did he deliver something out to you?'

And Mother answered patiently, 'I don't know, I'm sure. Something Mrs Lovett had, perhaps. But now let's go into town. I know a little tea shop that does lovely scones. I'm sure you'd like some tea, and I know I would myself. Then I must go to White's Emporium and buy these girls some gloves. They've got some lovely kid ones from the Continent. Should you care to come? I don't know what the men are going to do, but I'm sure that they can occupy themselves.'

So then it was Lucy's turn to take her sister by the hand. That meant that Lena needed all her concentration just to move about – Lucy was inclined to forget that you were there and lead you into rather awkward spots when her attention was on other things. But today, for once, Helena didn't mind too much. At least it helped to keep her thoughts off James.

' 'Ere!' Frank said, confidentially. He had contrived – by driving up and down for half an hour – to run into Maisie when she went out with the mail. 'You'll never guess who I saw at the station, up Penzance today.'

Maisie giggled. 'I will then!' She was sitting up against him and he could feel her warmth. 'The family. They all went in to see Mr James go off – 'cepting for Miss Edwards, who stayed home with a cold.' She looked at him sharply. 'Didn't know you knew them, not to recognize.'

He winked at her. 'You'd be surprised what I d'know sometimes.' In fact, he would not have recognized her employers, till today, and even then it was an accident. The pretty girls had been what caught his eye – especially the oldest of the two since, when you came to watch, you realized she couldn't see where she was going – and then a young man had came rushing to the train and Frank caught the name 'Tregenza' as they were introduced. After that it wasn't hard to work out who they were. But he did not say that to Maisie. 'I thought that elder girl looked awful sad. Miss Ethel, is it?'

'Elenner,' she corrected him. 'You've heard me telling about her a hundred times.'

'Elenner, then. Knew it was something starting with an "E". Anyhow, she looked as
133

sad as sin.' He reined in Brownie and they rumbled to a stop. 'Mind you look sharpish with those letters, then. I'll wait for you and drive you back again. Save you a few minutes, and we'll have them to ourselves.'

Maisie was already scrambling down. ''Spect she was sorry that Mr James was off. I think she's rather gone on him, or would be if she could. Though it's Miss Lucy that he's got his eye on, that's as clear as day, and looks as if she's happy to encourage him. She's written to him already, though he only went today. Mind, I can't say I'm sorry – otherwise I wouldn't have an excuse to go to the post.' Maisie flashed him a cheerful smile and disappeared.

She wasn't gone a minute, and she was back again. He helped her up on to the seat beside him, and flicked the reins again. They had gone some way in silence before he plucked up the nerve to say, 'You be sad, would you, if I went away?'

She turned to look at him. 'What d'you mean by that? You aren't going planning to go anywhere, are you, Frank?' She sounded most concerned.

'No, course I'm not. I was only saying – supposing that I went. You'd miss me, wouldn't you?'

She gave his arm a little push. 'Oh, course I would. Don't be so soft. Dunno why you ask. 'Tisn't going to happen anyway.'

He stopped the cart again, just at the corner of the road beside a tree. 'I was just thinking, if I went away like that – not that I'm going to but supposing that I did – I'd have wanted her to promise that she'd wait.'

'Wait? To marry him, you mean?' Maisie seemed to have found something fascinating in the tree, and was staring at it. 'Well, I'm sure that Mr James did nothing of the kind. We servants would've 'eard about it, sure as eggs is eggs.'

'But ... s'posing?' He paused, embarrassed. She went on gazing at the leaves. 'If it was me, I mean.'

She turned to face him then. 'You asking me if I would wait for you?'

He nodded. 'It's only a suppose.' His turn to gaze into the branches now.

'Well, I suppose I would, then.'

He whirled around and took her in his arms. 'You would? You mean it? You would marry me?'

She disengaged herself. 'Frank! Not here, where everyone can see! You'll get me into trouble with the mistress next. What are you thinking of.'

He said, 'I'm sorry,' which he didn't mean, and drove her home again. But he could not help grinning all the way, and when he glanced towards her, she was grinning too.

'Well, here we are!' She clambered down and then looked up at him. 'And Frank, I meant it, what I said. Course I'd wait for you.' She gave a little smile. 'I am doing, aren't I?'

He thought that she would hear the sudden

pounding of his heart. 'So, you're saying that you're willing? When I've paid off the cart?'

'You proposing, Frank Carter? Then the answer's yes.' She gazed at him and for a moment he thought that he saw tears. Then she laughed. 'Silly ha'porth. Who else would have you? Or me either, come to that?'

He was grinning like a flounder. 'I'll have to tell me folks. Though somehow I don't think they'll be all that surprised. They've heard that much about you, they could write a book.'

'In any case, it doesn't change a thing – for now at any rate. Except it's nice to have it said.' She glanced across her shoulder. 'Glory be! There's Rosie coming out to look for me. It's more than time I went. Otherwise Mrs Lovett will have my toes on toast. See you Saturday. And Frank...'

'What?'

'This!' She blew him a big, happy kiss and then she went inside.

Chapter Three

Settling in gave James so much to do that he almost forgot to write to anyone. There were so many lectures and demonstrations to attend that there seemed scarcely time to eat, and the house where he and Rupert had their rooms was itself some little walk from Denmark Street, and then there was the pile of weighty tomes awaiting him that his tutors expected him to study on his own.

He and Rupert had been prepared for this to some extent (warned both by Rupert's father and James's Uncle Bertie), and when they were up in town earlier they had acquired a number of the required volumes, mostly from previous students who were glad to sell them on. But inevitably these proved not to be the books they needed most, because people had hung on to the most important ones. There was a college library and that was very good, but all the students wanted the same titles at the same time, and it was often easier just to buy his own.

So there was no time for the female company his father had foreseen, even if there had been the opportunity. But really there was none. The college had its own teaching hospital, of course, and there were nurses there: but for one thing they were guarded day and night by a formidable senior nursing dragoness, and for another members of the Preliminary Medical Studies Course were – as the regulations pointed out – 'required to study and sit examinations in Physics, Chemistry, General Biology, Anatomy and Physiology' before they were allowed anywhere near the wards.

There was the question of the human skeleton. It was not really necessary to acquire one these days but, since it was obviously a splendid thing to have and the college information indicated where such items might be found, James had determined that he would have his own, as Uncle Bertie had. Grandfather's money would clearly run to it, and once purchased it would last his whole career.

The thing was easily arranged. A visit to the suppliers produced a splendid one – a female, the man said proudly, and it proved that he was right, though at the time neither James and Rupert knew exactly how to tell and they simply had to take his word for it. It – or rather, she – was nattily articulated with a set of wires, and her arms and legs moved most convincingly. She came complete with frame and a hook to hang her on.

It was strange to think that this had been a human being once, and James felt the need to make a nervous joke about how she had not been eating recently.

'She's got no body to dine with,' Rupert said, which made them laugh a lot, but did not amuse the shop-man in the least. On the contrary, he seemed to disapprove. Doubtless he had heard it all before. He enquired, rather curtly, when they should like it sent. James was nettled by his tone and retorted that they would take it now.

Immediately afterwards he wished that he had not. It is one thing to purchase a human skeleton, and quite another thing to take it home with one. The medical supplier's was at some distance from their rooms and it was obviously impractical to carry it through the streets. As soon as they had got it through the doorway of the shop, people were already turning round to stare.

Rupert suggested that it might be wrapped, and even went off and fetched the where-withal, but after a few moments they abandoned the idea. No amount of brown paper and string could disguise the human form, and at the slightest movement all the wrapping moved and left the grisly contents peeping through.

James and Rupert (who had fortified themselves with beer in any case before they came) were almost helpless with the mirth of it, to the disdain of the man who'd served them, who had come outside to watch – though they pretended to ignore him as they struggled with the thing. In the end they took it off the frame and wrapped it up in James's hat and coat and he stayed in a doorway, screening it from view, while Rupert went out to find a cab.

He came back with an old-fashioned hansom cab, which was quite ideal, since the driver did not get down from the front but simply gestured James to get inside. Between them they propped their bony friend upright and bundled her in as quickly as they could, together with her frame, and they bore her home in triumph – although it cost them quite a lot.

'Worth every penny, just to see the driver's face,' Rupert spluttered as they carried the poor creature unceremoniously upstairs. 'I told him that we had a friend who'd had too much to drink – but he happened to turn around when I was paying him, and when he saw the ankles, I thought his eyes would pop.'

James paused at the turning of the stair to lean on the banister and laugh. 'Just as well he didn't see the face. Looks like Mrs Passemore-Jenkins, don't you think? That drop-jawed expression when Lucy dared to dance?'

'Mrs Passemore-Judgement!' Rupert said, and they were off again, laughing like a pair of lunatics. Luckily there was nobody about.

They got the skeleton into James's room at last, and hung her on her frame behind the door, where she caused some consternation later to the maid who came to clean. Rupert's maiden aunt – who was their landlady – was called to look and had a vapour fit. James got a shock himself a time or two but pretty soon they all got used to it, and he and Rupert christened her Miss Judge. They hung their hats and coats on her – and occasionally used her for unkind jokes on unsuspecting friends.

James did not mention any of these things when he wrote home, not even to Lucy, who corresponded every day. He described the splendid friends he'd made among the fellow members of the course, but not their frequent visits to a hostelry nor his own unexpected prowess at billiards. He confined his letters to the more respectable aspects of his new existence here, dwelling on the splendid building, with its imposing great facade, and the equally impressive men who lectured there: all of them large, remote and dignified in old-fashioned formal dress, except for the tutor in Anatomy, who was small, wiry and dishevelled and spluttered quite a lot. (Oddly, his lectures were the most interesting of all.)

He did, however, write about the visit he paid to his Uncle Bertie, who wrote to him as soon as he arrived and invited him to come at teatime one weekend and stay for dinner afterwards. James duly presented himself at the address one Sunday afternoon, though truth to tell he was not looking forward much to the event. He did not know his uncle well and what he knew was not encouraging. Bertie was a bachelor and (on the few occasions he had come down to stay) had always seemed to be extremely brusque, though he could be relied on for a sixpence for an ice cream now and then.

James had visited his uncle in London only

once before – when he came up with Pater a few months earlier – and that had seemed no better. Bertie had entertained his brother-in-law and nephew in a dreary, cold front room, made stiff conversation for perhaps a half an hour and almost seemed anxious to see the back of them.

Today, however, that was not the case. In fact, he could not have been more welcoming. There was a fire burning in the study, where he settled James in one of the deep brown leather chairs and plied him as soon as he arrived with cups of tea, hot buttered toast and vast supplies of cake. After that he sent his manservant away, and looked at James above his spectacles.

'So you've determined on a medical career?' he said, in that booming voice of his. 'What does your precious father think of that?'

So it was Pater who had earned the cool reception earlier? James hitched his trousers up to ease his knees. 'He wasn't very keen on it at first,' he ventured, truthfully.

'Didn't think it was an occupation for a gentleman?'

James gave him a wry smile. 'Something of the kind. I'm sorry, Uncle Hubert, that sounds discourteous.'

The older man hurrumphed, and lit his ancient pipe. 'Hardly your fault if the man's a fool. Cares far too much about appearances. I told your mother that, before she married him. But of course she wouldn't listen –

didn't think she would. Headstrong girl, your mother.' He peered across his spectacles again. 'Seems that you take after her in that. Go your own way, whatever people say?'

James recognized this was a sort of compliment. 'I told him I wanted a profession of some sort – do something useful just as you had done.' That sounded like base flattery, so he added hastily, 'Besides, I was friendly with the doctor's son, and my father knew the parents socially. They're highly thought of in the area. That helped to change his mind. Rupert and I came up together as a matter of fact: he's studying medicine at King's College too.'

Uncle Hubert was still struggling to keep the pipe alive. 'Hmmph! Then you must bring him out to meet me sometime. Now,' he blew a ring of smoke into the air, 'tell me about the course. Is old Whatshisname still there? Used to lecture in Biology?'

And, amazingly, for almost half an hour Uncle Bertie reminisced about his student days. Some of the stories were quite uproarious, and sometimes rather blue – the college had been housed in different buildings then, and the part of town was not salubrious. James, emboldened by all this, ventured an account of the acquiring of Miss Judge. His uncle roared with laughter, and capped it with a story of his own about how one of his contemporaries had gone out to buy a skull and came back with one that had been neatly cut in two.

'Completely pre-dissected by some accident in life. Presumably the reason why its former owner had no more use for it,' the older man finished, with a barking laugh. 'Funny thing. The fellow who bought it specialized in head injuries afterwards.' He leaned forward, suddenly more serious. 'What about you? You going to specialize? Take it from me, that's where the money is.' Hubert himself had a successful practice among the very rich. 'Follow me into obstetrics, perhaps?'

It was not an idea that James had thought about, but he found that he was blurting out, 'If anything, I think that I'd be interested in eyes. There is a girl, I used to know at home...' and he poured out Helena's story. 'Not, I suppose, that there's much that one could do.'

Hubert shook his head. 'Not a lot of future in that area, I think. But they are always making progress, and if you'd done the option you could come back later on. I've got an article here somewhere that might interest you. I'll look it out and send it on to you. And you should meet Samuel Maskins, he's working in that field. Does a lot of cataracts and all that sort of thing. I'll ask him out to meet you, if you like. He wouldn't mind, he's quite a friend of mine. We've even been on holiday together once or twice. His wife had people in the Lake District and they were kind enough to ask me up as well. Mind you, I haven't seen him for a while. His wife died

144

recently and he's immersed himself in work. Pity we can't have a day or two in Cumberland now. Do him good to get away a bit.'

'Then why don't you take him down to Cornwall one weekend?' James said. 'Pater invited you again, when he was here, and Mater would love you to come. She's always regretted that you do so rarely, and now that I'm away, she'd really value it.'

His uncle just said, 'Hmmph,' again, and talked of something else: and by and by the manservant came in, to pour them drinks and show them through to dinner – which was good, if plainly cooked. Altogether it was a splendid evening, and James was rather hoping that he'd be asked again.

But next time that Mater wrote, it was to say that Bertie and a friend of his were coming down to stay, and could James arrange with Fortnum's to send some special marmalade.

Paul Tregenza was eating in the breakfast room, alone. He was finishing his toast before his wife came in. 'And how is Aunt Edwards this morning?' he enquired.

She sat down beside him. 'She's had a better night. Lucy and Helena are with her now.' She looked up at the maid, who had been hovering at the door. 'Maisie, I will just have some scrambled egg today. And you can bring another pot of tea.' She flicked out her napkin, and gestured at the post. 'Anything of interest in the mail?'

He felt a little guilty. He had been looking at it while he ate, a habit of hers which he had been known to publicly deplore. Of course it was different when one ate alone. He had pushed aside the pile of envelopes, in deference to her, but it was obvious that she had noticed them.

'Nothing of much consequence, except a note from James. He's sent me an article – some Czech doctor who's found a way to operate on eyes. Put a new lens in them or something. Thought I'd be interested. For Helena, I suppose.'

She looked at him reproachfully. 'Operate? Oh, Paul, that can't be right. Everybody knows that eyes are watery. How could anybody graft new bits on to them? And don't go saying these things to Helena. There's no chance of doing anything for her – that's what the doctors said.'

'I won't say anything to her, of course, one mustn't raise false hopes, but it is the twentieth century, after all. They do amazing things these days – you should see this magazine. There's general vaccination against smallpox now, and apparently it's almost stamped it out. Think of what that would have meant when you and I were young. And it says that deaths from cholera are cut by more than half since cities put in modern waterworks and drains.'

Gertrude looked affronted. 'Must you talk to me about the drains? And at the table too? I know that you've had breakfast, but I'm still

146

eating mine...'

He laughed. 'I'm sorry, dear. I thought it was very interesting, that's all. Especially that article about the eyes. Though even if there is a new technique, I suppose it will be years before it gets down here, and even more before it's wholly safe. But very nice of James to think of us, I thought. Seems he got his uncle to look out the magazine.'

'That will be Hubert, I suppose. You remember him? Jane's brother? We had him here for supper with the Morrisons.'

Paul nodded. 'Apparently the uncle is coming down to stay again. Perhaps we should invite them one night, supposing that your poor sister is well enough by then. Then I could ask him about this article – he's something senior in the world of medicine. Anyway, it was his magazine. He would be bound to know.'

She looked a little doubtful. 'Well, don't do it over dinner, will you, dear? Hubert is a specialist in...' she hesitated '...subjects that aren't especially delicate. Women's problems, and that sort of thing. I'll invite him here by all means, on Saturday perhaps, so you can talk to him. But wait until the port. Otherwise he'll simply blurt it out and embarrass everyone. All about babies being upside down, and parts of ladies that are quite uncouth.'

'Gertrude! Surely not. The chap's a gentleman.'

She laughed. 'He did the same before. He isn't used to female company, I suppose, and simply talked as if the room were full of men. Didn't modify the subject in the least. I remember, I asked about his work and the way he answered I did not know where to look. And as for poor Jane Morrison! But enough of that for now. Not before the servants. Here's Maisie with my egg.' She dropped her voice and was gesturing to the door where the girl was just arriving with the tray.

He nodded. 'We will invite them, then. I'll just be careful what I say to him, that's all.'

Gertrude had put on the sunniest of smiles. 'Thank you, Maisie,' she said graciously, and leaned back in her chair to let the maid put down the plate. 'That will be all for now, I think, except a little more soft butter for my toast?'

Lucy was rather irritated. 'Visitors for dinner? And on Saturday!' She could not hide her genuine dismay. She had been hoping to find the opportunity of joining Simon at a concert once again, but now that would clearly be impossible. Drat! She had said too much. Lena and Mama were looking startled, so she added piously, 'When poor Aunt Edwards isn't well at all?'

Aunt Edwards, in fact, was rather better now. Doctor O'Neill had been to see her, prescribed a sleeping draught and what his patient called 'a newfangled aspirant', but was actually something called an aspirin. The old lady had recovered quite remarkably.

True, she had elected to take dinner in her room, rather than come down when there were guests ('Oh no, my dears, I couldn't possibly'), but it was clear that she could have joined them, had she chosen to. Aunt Edwards was keen on self-inflicted martyrdoms like that and always announced them in a sweetly injured tone.

Lucy herself, who didn't want to go at all, was obliged to pin up her hair and put on the gown she'd worn to Celestine's. That made her look quite pretty, and she didn't want to be: since she couldn't be with Simon it was just a waste, tonight. There wasn't even James to flatter her and make her laugh, only a pair of ageing doctors, dull as dull could be – and the senior Morrisons, of course, but they didn't really count. They were very nearly family, and one didn't dress like this for them. She went into dinner in a strange, resentful mood.

She found she'd been seated next to Mr Morrison again, with James's uncle on the other side, though he was hardly very talkative. He was a big, balding, red-faced man, impeccably turned out, though in a fashion which had ceased to be a fashion years ago. Lucy made a half-hearted attempt to talk to him, but he just mumbled a few social platitudes and directed his attention fiercely on his soup.

But it was quite impossible to talk to Morrison. Already this evening he had chucked her underneath her chin and told her that she was getting to be a winsome little thing: so, not wishing to be condescended to again, she struck up a conversation with the other visitor, who happened to be sitting opposite. He was a doctor, but they called him 'Mr Maskins', because he was a surgeon, it appeared.

He was even more ugly than James's Uncle Bertie and pretty much as tall. But where Hubert was florid and wore his few remaining strands of hair combed painfully across his high, domed head, Mr Maskins was quite pale, with a big nose and a mop of wispy hair. The most striking thing about him was his protruding pale-blue eyes, which bulged disturbingly at you. They were not unkindly, but they were very shrewd.

She found that they were boring into her. He said, 'You're not the daughter with the vision problems, then?'

'That's Lena,' Lucy said, hurriedly, 'she doesn't care to eat with us when there are visitors. We have to alter all the seats around. She finds it difficult when things are moved.'

He looked at her intently. 'But she wasn't blind from birth, I understand? Some kind of accident?'

Lucy looked up and down the table in dismay. This was not a topic which was often talked about, especially not at dinner and, above all, not with guests. She looked about for rescue – or guidance, anyway – but everyone was otherwise engaged, so in the end she gave him a muttered swift account. 'She's

150

very good,' she finished. 'She plays the piano very well indeed, and she is learning to read Moon and makes the best of it. We don't generally discuss it. There is nothing to be done.'

She had intended this to be small rebuke – the sort of thing Aunt Edwards would have said – but Mr Maskins didn't seem to care. He said, 'Perhaps you should permit me to be the judge of that – or your father should, at least. I deal with ophthalmics – Bertie here will tell you that – and Morrison was asking if I'd take a look at her.'

Lucy looked at Mr Morrison with ill-concealed surprise. He was murmuring to Maisie, who had come to take his plate.

Mr Maskins saw her. 'No, not that Morrison. I meant the younger one. Bertie was good enough to introduce the lad to me. Bright fellow. I should think that he'll do well. Very interested in what I had to say.'

'About op ... tholomy? Was that the word? I don't know what it means.'

James's uncle had finished his assault upon the soup, and put in suddenly, 'It means the study of the eyes, my dear. We're not all general practitioners, you know. Many of us are specialists in our different fields.'

It was so unexpected that Lucy turned to him. He was smiling at her, almost as if he hadn't noticed her before – and looking at her quite approvingly, she thought. She was surprised and flattered by this change of mood.

She opened her mouth to say something in

151

return – glad to change the subject and talk of other things. 'And...?' The words died on her lips.

A sudden hush had fallen in the room. Everyone was gazing at her, all at once. What could be wrong with them? They seemed to be turned to statues suddenly, except that Mama was scowling, and Mrs Morrison was making little shakings of her head.

She gave an inward shrug. If they hoped to warn her not to talk too much, it was far too late by now. She had already told Mr Maskins about Helena's affairs. She turned to James's uncle, with her sweetest smile. Her voice rang out across the silent table like a bell. 'And what exactly is your field?' she said.

Chapter Four

Helena was not certain that she welcomed Samuel Maskins' call. 'I felt like an exhibit at the zoo!' she complained to Lucy, after he had gone. 'Or a performing monkey!'

'Oh, Lena, don't be so absurd.' Lucy had volunteered to brush out her sister's hair, just as she used to do when they were small, a sure sign that she had something she wished to talk about. Usually the hairdressing was one of Maisie's chores. 'I don't know what you mean.' She was gently twisting a curl around her finger as she spoke.

'Of course you do. You heard the way he spoke. First he asked Papa if he could "have a look at me", just as though I wasn't there – I'm accustomed to having doctors speak to me direct. And then he wanted to hear me play the piano, and see me reading Moon.'

The ringlet-twiddling abruptly ceased. 'He talked to you, I heard him. About the plot of *Adam Bede*.'

Helena retorted, 'That wasn't a proper conversation. I got the feeling he was testing me, rather than wanting to discuss the book like you and I'd have done.'

She heard Lucy's little chuckle of embarrassment. 'Yes, I suppose he was a little bit abrupt. But it wasn't just to you. He put me through quite an interrogation too, and poor Mama as well – with him it seems to pass for conversation. And James's uncle has a manner which is rather similar.' She resumed her brushing and Helena leaned back, enjoying the sensation of the long and languid strokes. 'Is it because they're doctors, do you think, and not accustomed to social company?'

'It can't be! London doctors are quite social lions these days – Uncle Morrison was telling me as much. That's why he was happy for James to study medicine. And Dr Neill is not the least that way. He's a most amusing conversationalist, and accepted everywhere – even to Mrs Passemore-Jenkins's.'

' "An asset to any company" ' Lucy did her imitation of Mrs Passemore-Jenkins's voice. 'She told me once that she'd invite him anywhere, if she wanted to seat a table and was rather short of men.'

Helena laughed. 'That doesn't sound especially flattering, do you think? Inviting the poor fellow as an afterthought? But if Mrs Passemore-Jenkins says so, who am I to question it? Isn't she the final arbiter of what is thought to be polite?'

'Oh Lena, don't be such a tease. I know she's rather pompous, but I do owe her quite a lot. People have begun to ask me out to things. Everyone takes notice of what Mrs Passemore-Jenkins says.' She speeded up her brushing. 'I wonder what she'd make of James's uncle and his friend?'

Helena was suddenly impatient with Annabelle's Mama. 'You know exactly what she would make of them. They would be warmly welcome at any of her "do's". They have important friends in London – that's a passport of itself – both are quite succesful in their respective fields. Brusque, unsocial manners are always easy to forgive – or overlooked as "eccentricities" – when they are accompanied by sufficient wealth.' She knew she sounded waspish, and she wished the words undone.

'Anyway,' Lucy was wielding the hairbrush with gusto now, she found a little tangle and made her sister wince, 'You may not have cared for Mr Maskins's manner very much, but it's clear that he was most impressed with you. I heard him afterwards, when he was talking to Papa. He said that he had found you a most interesting case, and asked Papa's permission to call on you again.'

'There you are you see,' Helena moved her head away. 'He's not impressed at all. I am like an exhibit in a museum to him, that's all.'

'No, it isn't. You wouldn't say that if you knew what else I heard. "Your daughter is most charming," those were his very words. "And very talented. I've heard her play the piano, and I know she reads as well. She's just finished *Adam Bede* with her sister, I believe. We talked about it for a little and it was obvious that she had a splendid grasp of it."'

'I told you—' Helena attempted to twist her head around.

Lucy brushed aside the interruption – in more ways than one! – and went on, punctuating every sentence with a little upward flick. 'Sit still! I haven't finished. I am just coming to the most important bit. He said to Papa, 'I like a woman with intelligence. I would like, with your permission, sir, to call on her again.' So there, Helena Tregenza, what do you make of that?' She dropped the brush and put her hands on Lena's shoulders as she spoke. 'So if he does come courting, just remember that I told you so!'

Helena found that she was grinning. 'Well, we have Papa to thank for that. He selected the George Eliot for us. Left to yourself you would have chosen something else, and Mr Maskins would have found me an expert on

155

the works of Aphra Benn, or *The Little Match-girl* or something of the kind. I doubt if that would have impressed him very much.' She was teasing, but she could not disguise a tiny thrill. It was a long time since anyone had chosen to call on her account – just for the pleasure of her company – and longer still since anyone had paid her compliments.

'But aren't you pleased?' Lucy was moving round to sit in front of her, and was gazing at her face. 'He is a widower, you know. No children, though, he said so to Papa. I rather got the feeling that he regretted that. So there you are, Lena, you seem to have a beau.'

Helena laughed. 'Don't be ridiculous. I've hardly spoken to the man.'

Lucy ignored that. 'He said that you were pretty. Don't shake your head at me, he did. "It's fortunate the accident has not destroyed your daughter's looks. There is a little scarring but she's still a lovely looking girl." I heard him saying it.'

It was a rather startling notion. Helena waited for a moment and then said lightly, 'So he approves of me. Would I approve of him? I can tell that he is clever, and I know that he is brusque. What about *his* looks?'

There was a little hesitation, and then Lucy said, 'What a funny question.'

'Why? You tell me that he's asked to visit me again and I can't even imagine what he's like. He could be fat or small or hideous, how am I to know? I presume that he is not exactly handsome – or you would have told me so.'

156

'Of course he isn't hideous. I'm sure he's very nice.'

Helena waited, but her sister said no more, so after a moment she burst out herself, 'Well, tell me! You can't come here and half-suggest that he is courting me and then not help me to make a picture in my mind. Dark hair, or fair?'

There was a silence before Lucy muttered, 'Dark.'

'Straight, curly, wavy? What colour are his eyes? How tall is he? Oh, come on, Luce. You can't work these things out from shaking hands.'

Another hesitation and then Lucy grumbled, 'I don't know what to say.' And then in an altered tone of voice. 'Oh, very well – dark hair, wavy and quite a lot of it. The same height as Papa. Brown eyes, very deep ones: full lips, a handsome nose.' Her voice was growing almost dreamy now. 'Smooth cheeks, broad shoulders and a charming smile. Strong hands, from dealing with his horses I suppose, and—'

Helena interrupted. 'Does he have horses? I thought he lived in town.'

'Oh, he's a doctor, I am sure he must.' Lucy was back to being businesslike and brief.

Lena laughed. 'He sounds quite a paragon. You clearly like him, Luce. Mr Maskins must be younger than I thought, since he has cheeks so smooth that you remark on it. I had pictured him to be of middle age, probably with whiskers and a deeply furrowed brow. Of course, I didn't realize then that I might encounter them, but if you're right and he comes courting me I suppose I might be permitted to explore his face. I almost hope I do. You make him sound a great deal more agreeable than I feared.'

'Smooth for his age, of course, is what I meant.' Lucy had clattered to her feet again, and Helena heard the thumping sound that meant she was plumping cushions on the window seat. 'He does have side-whiskers. But enough of all this chatter. Here's Maisie coming, with your supper tray.'

'Can't be long this evening,' Maisie muttered, the following afternoon, as she climbed up to join Frank on the cart. She liked to think of him as 'her intended' now. Of course it didn't alter how they lived – you couldn't have people talking – but it made a big difference to the way she felt.

Rosie had been told, of course, but sworn to secrecy. Frank had been rather doubtful about that. 'You mind what you do. We don't want you turned out on your ear, because Mrs Lovett learns you've got a follower. She'll think you mean to leave and wed – even if it isn't for a year or two, while I pay off this cart.'

'Oh, Rosie can be trusted,' Maisie said. 'And I had to say to someone, or I would have burst. Anyway,' she snuggled up to him, 'saves her wanting to come with us, everywhere we go. Gives us a few minutes, like tonight. But

158

like I say, I can't be very long. That Mr Maskins is coming round again – just for a sandwich supper this time, but they'll be wanting me to serve.'

Frank frowned. 'Hope they give you another hour, Saturday, in lieu.'

She laughed. ''Tisn't as if I mind it very much. It does a power of good to poor Miss Elenner. Quite comes to life, she does, when he's around. Though Lord knows why. I wouldn't want him, if he came courting me.'

Frank slipped a sly hand around her waist. 'Well, he better hadn't, that's all I can say.' He pulled her to him.

' 'Ere, mind! You'll have somebody see.' She pushed him playfully away, but not before he'd given her a kiss. 'I mean it, though. She seems quite struck on him.'

'Because he takes a bit of notice of her, I suppose. Poor soul can't have hoped that she would ever find a man. Especially not a London doctor, but he's courting her, you say?'

'So Miss Lucy thinks, in any case. She said as much to Miss Elenner, only yesterday. Not that she meant for me to hear, but I had to put the tray down just outside the door, and I couldn't help catching everything she said.'

He turned to look at her. 'You haven't been listening at the keyhole, surely, Mais?'

She knew her cheeks were burning. 'Well, I never meant to. But I couldn't help it, Frank. Lucy was telling about that Dr Maskins, like I said, and ... well, to tell the truth I aren't very sure what I should do. She was saying what he looked like – I'm sure that's what it was – only it didn't sound like him a little bit.'

'We all see things different,' Frank said peaceably.

She snorted. 'Said he had dark hair: well, that's true enough, I suppose, but then she went on about his brown eyes and what a nice-looking chap he was. Well, you'd think that she was blind herself! I know he's very clever and all that sort of thing, but he's nice-looking, I'm a Chinaman. He looks like a piskie – only tall and thin, with hair that looks like Mrs Lovett's mop. Besides, he hasn't got brown eyes. They're blue. And don't say Miss Lucy hadn't noticed them, 'cause you can't help but do. They're very pale, like boiled sweets, and they stick out like a frog's.' She sighed. 'So, why did Miss Lucy want to go and say a thing like that.'

Frank urged Brownie into an ambling trot. 'I suppose she didn't think that it would 'urt, seeing as how her sister couldn't see. Might as well imagine him as nice as possible.'

'I s'pose. But doesn't seem quite right to me, somehow. Think I ought to tell her, do you? I mean, if he's coming round to court her, you'd think she ought to know.'

He thought a moment and then shook his head. 'Shouldn't have been listening, that's the truth of it.'

'I s'pose,' she said again. She pulled her cloak around her. 'But you should have heard Miss Lucy talk. Think he was that Ranolph

160

Vaselino, the film actor, the way that she went on. Or like that Simon Whatsisface, that I was telling you about. I suppose you'd call *him* handsome, if you like them lah-di-dah.'

There was a little pause and then Frank startled her. 'Very like him, I imagine, if it's the same fellow that I saw her with last week. Very dark and flashy and dressed up in fancy tweeds.'

Maisie giggled for a moment and then turned to look at him. 'How do you mean, "the fellow that you saw her with last week"? Miss Lucy hasn't been out anywhere with him, that I know of. The master'd never stand for it – her going out with a man – and anyway she didn't go out at all last week, 'cept to one of those charity teas she goes to with the Passemore-Jenkins girls. Or is that what you mean? Out somewhere all the lot of them, were they? That's different. This Simon is some kind of relative of theirs.'

Frank continued to stare straight ahead. 'Nope. It was just the two of them – no one else in sight. Out walking on the moors, they were, and miles from anywhere. I b'lieve that they were 'olding hands, as well, though I couldn't swear to that. But I knawed at the time they had no business to be there, the way they went skulking behind a wall to let the cart go by.'

Maisie shook her head. 'Oh, Frank, it can't be them. Miss Lucy would never do a thing like that. She's fond of that nice James Morrison – she writes him every day – and Simon

161

Whatsit's going to offer for Miss Celestine. Her mother said so to the mistress, just the other day, when I was pouring tea. He's already been to see her father for his blessing on the match. So how was he out with Lucy? It don't make any sense.'

Frank remained unmoved. 'I can't help it, Maisie. I know what I saw. It was your Miss Lucy, I am sure of that – I saw her at the station and it was her all right. And as for him, I'd know him anywhere. Nasty piece of work – I've run into him before. Remember, I told you about the business in the lane? Damn nearly set about me with his whip. Father is some bigwig, who owns half Penvarris mine.'

'Sounds like him all right. You think he took her to the moors and never said a word? Gives me a strange sensation in my innards, thinking that, like caterpillars crawling.'

Frank was still staring straight ahead as if he didn't want to meet her eyes. 'Didn't look as if she minded, I'll say that for him.'

Maisie tutted. 'Be no end of trouble for Miss Lucy, if anyone found out. We'll have to tell her, won't us? Warn her off. Cause if *you* saw them, anyone could do.'

Frank looked sober. 'I don't know. You were on about you didn't know if you should tell the truth – well no more do I. You can't go charging in and say anything to her, or to her father either. That would make it worse.'

'Well, you can't say nothing, either. Only takes one person, and it'll be all over town.

Upset her parents something dreadful, and Miss Elenner as well. Might even put that Dr Maskins off from courting, if the family's in disgrace. Just when she might have had a bit of chance at happiness. No, I'll have to find a way to let Miss Lucy know we know, and I'd better do it quickly, before more harm is done. She isn't going to like it, mind.'

'Well, maybe it would be for the best.' Frank sounded enormously relieved. 'Now are we going to sit here half the night, or do what they did and go and find somewhere a bit more out of sight?'

Maisie giggled. 'Well, only for a minute, then. I'll be expected back. But if them two can hold hands and have a kiss, I don't see why we shouldn't do the same.'

Paul stood before the dressing table in his room, and looked at his younger daughter in dismay. And in amazement too. He was in his shirtsleeves, without his collar on, with his braces showing and his bow tie in his hand. He'd never imagined in his wildest dreams that she would catch him in this state.

'Lucy, what's the meaning of this shameful pantomime? How dare you come barging in here while I'm getting dressed?' He was really shaken. It was the first time in all her life she'd ever done anything so alarmingly bizarre.

She was not even repentant. 'I didn't barge. You told me to come in.'

That was true, of course, but he went on

muttering. 'Only because I thought that you were Edgar coming back. He went down with my shaving water a few minutes ago, but he was coming back to help me with my studs.' His coat was hanging on the bedstead and he shrugged it on, with some idea of covering his braces up, but he still felt at a disadvantage with his collar loose. 'I hope you have good reason for interrupting me?'

She was looking very pink and pretty, now he had the leisure to observe, dressed for the supper party in a simple gown, but there was a heightened colour in her cheeks which almost made him wonder if she'd been using rouge, the way these modern hussies some-times did. But no, he realized, it was quite natural – just like the unusual glitter of her eyes. She was angry about something, and emotion made her glow.

'Well, I should think I do have reason,' she burst out all at once, flinging herself down upon a chair with a dramatic flounce. 'I've come to tell you Maisie's got to go. She's been unconscionably rude to me tonight. You'll have to send her packing. As soon as pos-sible!'

Paul put down his tie and stared at her. 'Am I hearing you aright? You've come in here to tell me that I should dismiss the maid?'

She nodded, with a vehemence which took him by surprise. 'I know it is unfortunate, but if you heard what she said...'

This was not like Lucy. His anger had evaporated, all at once. 'And what was that, exactly?' He squatted on the dressing stool, rested his elbows on the table and smiled up at her.

Lucy's cheeks flushed pinker. 'She said ... She accused me ... it doesn't matter now. Only that she was impudent, that's all. I won't put up with it. Surely you are not going to sit there and forgive a thing like that?' She was getting more emotional with every word she spoke.

He laced his fingers underneath his chin and said, as calmly as he could, 'I know that Maisie has a tongue that runs away with her, and clearly she has said something ill advised to you. No doubt – since it upsets you – she merits strong rebuke. I cannot imagine that she deserves to be dismissed but if you tell me exactly what she said, I will deal with the matter accordingly.'

Lucy said nothing, just heaved a hefty sigh.

'Well? It must be something very grave indeed, if you want to deprive the poor girl of her livelihood.' He said it gently. Lucy was a kind girl at heart, although she was given to little tantrums now and then and said things which she didn't mean. This was one of those occasions, it appeared. If he could put it into context, it would dissipate itself. 'So what was it that insulted you so much?'

'I ... I can't recall exactly, but it was very impudent. Annabelle's papa has dismissed a girl for less.' His daughter sounded sullen.

'But fortunately I am not Annabelle's papa. I am the father of two lovely girls, one of whom is rather headstrong now and then. And rudeness from the servants is not acceptable, however inadvertent. I will speak to Maisie as soon as I am dressed. You can stay and ensure that she gives me an accurate account.'

Lucy was on her feet again. His rational tone had done its work, it seemed. 'Oh, never mind. It doesn't matter now. No doubt I'm making far too much of it.'

He shook his head. 'No. Maisie has been impertinent – it is a failing, I'm aware. Ask her to wait for me in the drawing room. Now, there's Edgar at the door. Tell him to come in, and I will see you both downstairs in quarter of an hour.'

Chapter Five

'Oh, Simon, it was simply dreadful,' Lucy said. 'You can't possibly imagine how I felt. Having that wretched servant standing there with Papa quizzing her, and expecting every minute that she'd tell him everything.'

He was as upset as she was, she knew that from the way his hand had tightened on his driving whip, and his neck had gone a mottled purple around his collar edge. 'But she didn't? I assume she didn't or you

166

wouldn't be here now.'

'No – she just went all peculiar and pink and admitted that she had spoken out of turn. Even said that she was very sorry and all that sort of thing. Giving me little looks under her eyelids, though, while Father jawed her out like anything. I offered her a pair of stockings when I got her on her own – quite nice worsted ones – but she got all offended and said she didn't want a bribe: she'd held her tongue on my account and she'd only intended to warn me, anyway – that we'd been spotted out together and there was starting to be talk.'

'Must have been that carter – I wondered if he'd seen.' She had expected that Simon would attempt to comfort her, put an arm around her or something of the kind, but all he did was crease his brow, and stare in front of him. 'We shall have to consider what we are to do.'

There was a pause before she ventured, 'I've taken quite a risk by meeting you today – I don't think it will be possible to come out any more.' She looked at him sideways. 'Unless we have a formal understanding of some kind.' She placed her hand where he could grasp it if he chose, but he made no move to take it.

He shook his head and said, as if she hadn't spoken, 'Rachel has another do this afternoon, of course. I'll take you over there. If anybody is asking questions, you will have been seen there alone. Find an excuse to go home early, a headache or something, so you have an explanation for not being there throughout, and after this you can lose interest in her charity affairs. Don't worry about that nosy parker, I will deal with him. And I've thought of something else that I can do to help. I'll make an offer to Celestine tonight, that should put a stop to any gossip straight away.' He reached across and put his left hand on her knee – not as he always used to do before, but in a perfunctory sort of way. He patted it and then withdrew again. 'Anything to get you out of trouble, eh?'

'But you can't just suddenly propose to Celestine!' She could not help it, she was close to tears. 'Supposing she says yes?'

He laughed. 'I rather imagine that she will. Her family are expecting it, I think. But don't look so distraught. It deflects attention from you perfectly – and it will do me a little bit of good in Father's eyes as well. He always hoped I would marry her – keep the fortune in the family – though Celestine herself would have preferred James Morrison, I think, if only he had been inclined to ask. But James has lost his heart elsewhere, as you – my charming rogue – are quite aware, so I don't think there's much danger that I shall be refused.'

'But what about *me*?' Lucy wailed, like a child.

He did that little laugh again. 'It needn't make any difference to the two of us, you goose. We'll have to be more careful for a little

168

while, that's all.'

'But you can't ... we couldn't ... Not when you are engaged to someone else.' Lucy felt as if the solid earth had split and she was spinning through a void.

'But, my sweet, why should it alter things?' He turned his usual charming smile on her. 'After all, I've been escorting her for months – just as you've been writing to your friend James Morrison. A betrothal is a convention for the public world, that's all. But what's that to do with us? We are romantic spirits, aren't we, free as air?'

He had moved the hand to capture hers by now, but she snatched it away. This was Simon in a wholly different light. 'You never really cared for me at all.'

'Of course I cared for you, my dear. You're very pretty and you're very sweet. But you said yourself that this would have to stop. I'm falling in with your suggestion, that is all.' They were driving past their usual stile but Simon did not even slow.

Lucy had heard of heavy hearts, but hers seemed made of lead. She could feel the dragging weight inside her ribs. 'Very well, we'll do as you suggest.' With an effort she kept her voice from quavering. She had her pride. He should not have the satisfaction of seeing her in tears. 'Take me to your sister's. I'll find my own way home.'

She had hoped – she did not know what she had hoped – but he only gave her knee another pat and nodded with a smile. 'That's

169

my good girl, Lucy. I knew that you'd see sense. We'll let the rumours die, and in a month or two...'

'Don't count on me for anything,' she said. Her voice was very high and forced and sounded far away. 'I am glad that you have shown me where my real affections lie. James Morrison has written to ask me to wait for him, and I intend to write back to him tonight and tell him that I shall.'

It was an exaggeration, but she could not sting him even so. He actually smiled. 'Well, congratulations, Lucy. I'm sure that's very wise. I always knew that there were brains inside that pretty head. So, we will both be spoken for. We shall look back on this, in future years, and it will make us smile: a little secret pleasure that only we will share. And if, from time to time, fate puts the chance our way...'

'Take me to Rachel's, Simon,' Lucy said, and those were the last words between them until he dropped her at the gate.

Frank knew there was a problem the moment he got home. Fayther was sitting at the table with his head in his hands, and Mother and the boys were tiptoeing around like a cat in a hen-coop trying not to crack the eggs.

'What...?' he began as he took his wet boots off at the door but Mother shook her head at him and he let the question drop.

Ma didn't say a word. She gestured to a teacup and the plate of bread and jam, then raised her eyebrows and he nodded to show he wanted some.

How long this mimed conversation might have gone on, Heaven knows, but suddenly Fayther raised his head. 'Well, tiddn't no use pretending. The lad'll have to know.' His face was pastier than Ma's baking dough. 'It's over, then. Called me up the purser's shop to tell me, nice as pie. Gave me a fortnight's wages, but where's the use of that? Up the workhouse we shall be, the damty lot of us.'

Frank was so astonished that he dropped his second boot and it fell onto the flagstones with a thud. 'And what about the contract?'

Fayther shook his head. 'Seems they were allowed to. It's in they little awkward bits that's written underneath. I aren't so good at reading fiddling print like that. Never would have put my name to it, if I had 'ave know. "Notwithstanding the above" or something of the sort. Means that they can change their damty minds about it any damty time they like.' He heaved a sigh and glowered furiously at Frank. 'And don't you go saying that you told me so, it's more than I can bear.'

Frank padded to the table in his stockinged feet. 'Wasn't going to,' but it was exactly what he'd thought. He took a big bite of his bread and jam but he hardly tasted it. Shock had deprived him of his appetite. A pity – treats like this would be a rare thing from now on. He gulped a bit of tea. 'So, what we going to do? Can't really let them drive us to the workhouse, can we now?'

Fayther put his head into his hands again. 'What else is there? I'm too old to mine, at my age – I haven't got the strength. Know nothing about fishing – nor farming either, though I could lift a few potatoes when the season comes, I s'pose. But how's that going to pay the rent and feed and clothe us all?'

'I could do a bit of scrubbing,' Ma volunteered. 'There's Mary Trembath, young Jethro's wife – she used to have a job, and she can't do it while she's carrying. I could take her place, if she'd keep an eye on Davy and the little ones for me.' The little ones in question, realizing that she meant to farm them out next door, set up a tearful wail at this but she quelled them by adding, 'Better than us being separated, up the workhouse.'

Fayther shook his head. 'Wouldn't do no good. Couldn't even pay the rent on what you'd earn from that. Just have to sell the blessed horse, that's all. Fetch a few shilling – we could live on that a bit. Eating money otherwise, with the cost of feed and shoeing and my share of the field. Fond of old Dobbin, I'll be sad to see 'un go – but no use to have 'un if there's nothing he can cart.'

Frank put his cup down on the table with a clunk. 'And who says there isn't? What's got into you? You going to lie down like a carpet and let them walk all over you? Where's your spirit? I got customers. I've been telling you for months that we should start up on our own. Well, now's your chance to do it. When you had the contract, you wouldn't think of

172

it, but now perhaps it's damty time you did.'

Fayther got slowly to his feet. 'Don't you swear at me!' He came towards him, and Frank waited for a blow, but his father just stormed out into the rainy night and shut the door.

'Frank!' Ma's face was scandalized and pained. 'Now look what you have done! Don't talk to him like that! He's not a young man – this is hard on him.'

Frank wolfed down the remainder of his supper. He felt strangely powerful and responsible, as if Fayther had abdicated – like a king – and he'd become head of the household suddenly. 'Sorry, Ma. But he wanted swearing at. Ready to give up before he's even tried. I only want to help. I mean it. I can put some customers his way. And if it's hard on him, it's hard on everyone. I know it's damty hard on me. If anyone is going to lose a horse and cart round here, it's me. Here have I been working months and months to pay it off and not only is there no chance now of ever doing that, it's likely I shall lose the damty moncy that I've paid.'

'You watch your tongue, in front of the little ones,' Ma said. 'Though anyway, it's time they went to bed. Go on, the lot of you, get upstairs – and mind you take your shirts and trousers off. Lennie, you help Davy if he can't undo his buttons by 'isself. I want you in your bed before I count to ten. I've put a nightlight up there, and by and by I'll come and tuck you in. Go on. One ... two ... three...' And

173

before she'd got to seven they had all four disappeared.

She listened for a moment to the thumping overhead and then she turned to Frank. 'You mind what you say to your poor fayther, Frank. 'Tisn't his fault we got in this mess. He 'aven't said so to your face, but it's down to you he lost that contract in the first place, I believe. One of the owners grumbling that the carrier was rude, and deliberately blocked the public in the lane. Well, it wasn't your fayther. So who was it, eh?'

Frank felt his face turn beetroot red. 'Wasn't me, neither. If anybody blocked the lane, 'twas 'im. And I'm damty sure I wasn't damty rude.'

His mother picked up his cup and tea plate with a scowl. 'If you spoke to him like that I'm not surprised that he complained.' She put the china in the sink and poured the kettle over it.

'Course I didn't. Any road, that was months and months ago. Why do 'ee want to make a thing about it now?' He stopped. 'Oh, great snakes! I do believe I know.' He picked up a dishcloth and came to wipe the cloam.

She paused in her dishwashing to stare at him. 'What, then?'

He shook his head. 'Not my secret, I can't really say. But nothing in the world to do with blocking up the lane. Just spite, because of something that I saw. Well, I won't forget that in a hurry and nor will other folk, when I've had a quiet word to one or two. You mark my words, Ma – there'll be work for us. And if the railways go on strike again – like they've been threatening – that mine will be begging us to cart their goods for them. Ah – here's Fayther coming now.'

But it wasn't Fayther. It was Jethro standing, dripping, at the door.

'Evening, Mrs Carter, mind if I come in? Only there's something I want to talk about to Frank, and it's raining rats out here.' He was already stripping off his streaming cap and coat and boots.

'Always welcome, Jethro. Now, I've got to go up and see the little ones, so I'll leave you two alone. Put the kettle on, and I'll make a drop of tea for 'ee when I come down again.' She lit another taper from the candle on the side and disappeared upstairs with it.

Jethro sat down on the settle. He fidgeted a little, but he didn't speak.

Frank made a guess at what was in his mind. 'Fayther been round your house, has he?' and, when Jethro nodded, 'So you've heard?'

An even bigger nod. 'That's what I've come to talk about. Your fayther was asking about Mary's scrubbing job, and saying how you were on about a private round again, but he wasn't man enough to do the heavy work these days, though perhaps he could do the bookwork and you could drive the cart.'

'Did he, now? Well, that's something, I suppose. He was talking about selling it when he left here tonight. Like as if he hadn't got a bit of fight in him. When you've got a horse and cart you might as well try and make a living – not just go giving up.'

Jethro turned a plump face towards him. 'That's just it. I thought ... you and Brownie and the wagon ... you were going to pay them off.'

Frank gave a bitter laugh. 'Out of the question, isn't it, with things the way they are? Give up thinking about getting wed, as well. But there you are, can't let the family starve. If Fayther wants me, I shall have to drive for him. I can forget buying Brownie. I haven't got the money to set up on my own.'

His friend had turned a surprising shade of puce. 'That's just it,' he said again. 'I got a bit put by, me and Mary, for buying furniture, supposing we could find a place of our own to rent one day. Tidn't a great lot, but you could have it, Frank – if you'll let me come in with you and drive the other cart. I could do that, even if I have got half a hand. You told me weeks ago that there was work enough for two, and it's clear I aren't going to earn much down Penvarris any more. Cap't Maddern is as good as gold, but it's only boy's work he can put my way and that's never going to pay. We're going to eat that money up, just living day to day, 'less we do something with it. This way we'd be partners in Brownie and the cart, and there's at least a chance that we could make a living out of it. Would you think about it, Frank?'

Think about it? He could not believe his

ears. He got up and grasped his old friend by the hand. 'Jethro, you're sure? I aren't taking charity.'

Jethro's fat face creased into a smile. 'And I aren't offering. I want a proper document – all drawn up and signed – that half of Brownie and the cart belong to me. I suppose that means that I pay 'alf the feed and everything – but I get half the profits. Just that cart, of course, I don't expect to get a share of what your father's wagon earns. Now, what d'you say, before I change my mind?'

Frank was thinking about owning Brownie once and for all, and his eyes were in danger of misting with relief. 'Well, I say yes,' he said. 'I'd be a cloth-ears else. You wait till I tell Ma and Fayther about this.'

'About what?' Ma was coming down the stairs again, her taper in her hand. So they had to tell her, and then Fayther came in too and they had to go all over it again – after Frank had apologized for his language earlier.

Fayther was peculiarly against the plan at first – 'No point in dragging others in our private mire and pouring good money after bad' – but even Ma could see the sense in it and after a little while he bucked up a bit, and when he began to talk about how there wouldn't be many customers at first and they couldn't expect to make a fortune overnight, Frank knew the war was won.

He went up to see Crowdie with the money the next day, taking Jethro with him to explain. Crowdie was more than generous, and threw in the harness too – which Frank hadn't had the sense to think about till now – and said that they could go on grazing Brownie in his field. Wouldn't take a penny extra for the privilege, and what is more he found them their first job – carrying a load of broccoli to the station the next day, to catch the London markets.

So the 'J.J.F. Carriers' were born. (The first J was for Joshua, which was Fayther's given name, though he hadn't been called by it for years.) And if that broccoli load was a kind of charity – Crowdie had his own cart and a boy to drive it too – that did not occur to Frank until much later on: and by that time word had got around the mine, and other jobs were starting to arise.

'Course they are,' Maisie said stoutly, when they got a chance to meet. 'Stands to reason people would put any work your way, once Cap'n Maddern told them what happened to your Pa. Turned off because you wouldn't back your cart, indeed! Folks round here have a way of looking after their own, and they don't like Mr Snooty Robinson no more than I do.' She smiled and snuggled closer up to him. 'Mind, I might forgive him – even for what he did to Miss Lucy – after this. The horse and cart is paid for, and you're working for yourself the way you always wanted, instead of slaving for the tally shop all day. And it never would have 'appened if it weren't for him.'

He put an arm around her. 'Perhaps you're right, things work out for the best. In fact, I've got another bit of news for you. Ma's taken on that scrubbing job of Mary's, so she's earning now, and if things go on the way they've been going, I'll be able to start putting a bit aside again. Then we two'll be able to think of getting wed.' He grinned at her delight. 'In fact I'm damty glad I blocked that beggar in the lane.'

He didn't mention that the real reason that Fayther'd lost his job was most likely simple spite, because Simon Robinson knew that Frank had seen him on the moors. Maisie would only think that it was her fault, if he did, for speaking to Miss Lucy out of turn.

Helena was sitting at her dressing table in corset and chemise, getting ready for the evening with especial care. Lucy was helping her, alive with glee.

'So Mr Maskins is coming to supper yet again. I told you he was eager to court your company – and I believe that you are beginning to enjoy his coming here.'

Helena pretended to ignore this, and busied herself with fiddling in her trinket box. But there was a certain truth in what her sister said. It was not only that he gave her hope (he had told her once that there was an operation now, which might help her see again one day), but the fact that he dealt all the time with people who had problems with their eyes made her feel less of a curiosity, and at the

179

same time she knew that she was interesting to him.

And it was no good dreaming of James Morrison. Lucy had confided, only recently, that he had written asking her to wait for him and marry him – and she had responded saying that she would. So that fantasy was over, and Lena had to face the truth. Samuel Maskins was successful and respectable. She was lucky to have attracted anyone at all, she told herself – let alone so enviable a beau.

So she would try to look her best for him. She was still fiddling with the jewellery – she knew most of the pieces by their shape, and Maisie had told her what colours they all were – and she took out a little string of pearls and laid it to one side.

'Well?' Lucy's voice cut across her thoughts. 'Aren't you flattered that he's coming here again?'

'Don't be absurd. He is spending the weekend with the Morrisons again, and of course he's dining with us – since they always do. He's going back to London on the early morning train.'

'But he'll be back again on some excuse, you wait. Makes you wonder what happens to his patients while he's gone,' Lucy giggled. 'They'll be pleased when you've accepted and he doesn't have to rush.' Her voice was rather muffled, and from the rustling noise Helena could tell that she was rummaging in the wardrobe by the door. 'Now, shall you wear your pink tonight, or do you want the green? If you're coming down to dine with us you must look your very best.' She creaked across the floor, presumably to put the chosen garments on the bed, and then there was the slide and creak as she began to open drawers. 'And your prettiest white silk stockings, where on earth are they?'

'Don't worry, Lucy, Maisie will help me and she'll attend to that. Just be certain that you close the drawers.'

'You can't leave this to Maisie. We must get this right. Anyway, Mama suggested I come and help you choose. I'm practically certain that he will make a move tonight. That's why I'm delighted that you dine with us these days.'

Helena knew that there was colour in her face. 'Mr Maskins – Samuel – is so nearly family now, it hardly seems to signify if I'm a little slow. And you will help me, won't you – choose the easy dishes and that sort of thing? He does encourage me to dine in company. The trouble is, I'm sure he thinks I manage perfectly. He doesn't realize how hard it is sometimes, knowing exactly where the food is on the plate, and where the edge is so you don't push peas onto the tablecloth.'

But Lucy wasn't listening. 'There you are, you see, he wants you to be there. He as good as asked me yesterday if I thought that he would have a chance with you. Of course I told him, yes, that you would welcome it.'

'What did he say to that?' She tried to push the thoughts of James away, and imagine

Samuel the way that Lucy had described – strong, dark and handsome with those deep and burning eyes.

A scrape as Lucy pulled out another drawer. 'He asked what I would think myself – whether he was too old, and all that sort of thing. I said I'd be delighted – and I'm sure Papa would be – because he was a person of distinction. He liked that very much. He even came across and took my hand and kissed my fingertips – shows he's quite romantic when he has a mind to be. Ahh! Here they are, your stockings! I'll put them out for you. And your little white kid shoes to go with them. There's nothing more becoming than a flash of pretty foot.' There was the sound of a returning drawer, and then, 'So what is it to be? The green is prettiest.'

Helena said demurely, 'Whatever you decide. If I'm to join the marriage market, I must be dressed for it.' She reached up her arms and let Lucy put her into her petticoat. Its rustling folds were feminine and suddenly she felt quite beautiful.

'And now your stockings,' Lucy said, 'I've got your garters here. There!' as the silk rolled up against the thigh. 'And now the other one. And last of all the dress. That's it. Sit still while I do up the buttons and arrange the lace fichu. And a spray of pretty perfume, you can do that yourself.'

'Well!' Helena fastened the pearl necklace she had selected from the box. 'It just needs Maisie to come and do my hair, and I shall be

182

ready for whatever Samuel has to say.' She got to her feet and did a clumsy pirouette. 'How do I compare to your Miss Passemore-Jenkins, then? Mama says that she's had an offer for her hand, and has accepted it. They are to be married very soon, as I suppose you know ... Lucy?'

The room had become unnaturally still.

Then Lucy's voice, quite snappish. 'Yes, of course I was aware. Simon told me weeks ago that he was going to ask. And yesterday I had a letter from Annabelle saying so as well. She was to be an attendant to the bride, along with Simon's sister, but I don't know if she will. She's come down with a fever and has taken to her bed – it's doubtful she'll be well enough to stand up to the strain. That's why she wrote and asked me not to call. She isn't eating and she won't see anyone.'

'Oh, poor Lucy. And how awful for your friend.' Helena felt genuinely sympathetic now. 'You will miss her company, I'm sure. I wondered why you hadn't been out much recently – not even to those charity after-noons you used to like.'

Lucy was slamming cupboard doors and shifting chairs with noisy energy, and all the teasing pleasure had vanished from her voice. 'I dare say I shall find other things to do.'

'Luce. Have I upset you? You were fond of Simon – is that what it is? But I thought that you had chosen James...? You said you'd writ-ten...?' She felt a spark of hope.

Lucy quenched it. 'So I have. I told him I

183

was far too young to think of a betrothal yet, but if he'd undertake to wait, I would be willing – when I am twenty-one. Or when he qualified. So, as for Simon, of course I'm not upset. Obviously, I'd made it clear to him that he was free to look elsewhere.' There was a little sniff, a pause and then, 'I know that Papa rather liked him, but he's not the type for me.'

There was something in her tone which made Helena enquire, 'Surely he wasn't ... presumptuous at all?'

Lucy laughed with a gaiety that sounded rather forced, 'Of course not! What do you take me for? But he's so shallow – not like James or Mr Maskins with a proper job to do. He's only interested in concerts, balls and horses, as far as I can see. Anyway, don't let's waste time talking about him any more! Here's Maisie come to do your hair, and I must go and get dressed myself.' She kissed her sister lightly on the cheek. 'Can't have my future brother-in-law not see me at my best.'

She kept up that artificial sparkle all throughout the meal – though she did remember to help Helena – but afterwards, when Mr Maskins asked Helena to play a Chopin waltz for him, Lucy pleaded a headache and went early to her room. It seemed to be a signal, because the older adults slipped away on the excuse of playing cards, and Helena and Mr Maskins were alone.

He listened to her play the chosen piece, and then said awkwardly, 'Miss Tregenza –

Helena – I need to talk to you. I suppose that Lucy has told you how I feel?'

So it had come. She nodded, not knowing what to say.

He cleared his throat. 'I know that I am a good deal older – but she seemed to feel that need not be a bar. What do you think, Helena? It seemed most sensible to ask you outright for your views. I should not wish to rush things and embarrass anyone.'

She forced herself to smile. 'Then if I am honest, I think perhaps you're right. It would be wise to wait. Not that I mean to dash your hopes – the contrary, in fact. Your suit is almost certain to succeed.' No! That had gone too far. She was almost panicking. It seemed unreal, discussing a future with a man she hardly knew. She blundered on. 'But much as I respect you – and grateful as I am for your concern about my eyes – I think it would be better if you'd consent to just be friends, at least at present. Marriage is a serious matter. It would mean such enormous changes of life for all of us.'

He came and put a hand on her shoulder. 'I can see it will be difficult, especially for you – since we should have to move to London. I'm sure you'd miss your sister very much indeed, but obviously we should be able to welcome visitors. I'll ensure that proper arrangements are put in hand for you, so that you don't have too many problems in the house in town – and we can come to Cornwall very often, too, I'm sure.'

'You're very thoughtful, Samuel.' Greatly daring, she reached out and touched his hand. It was sinewy, and more hairy than she'd thought, and despite herself she did recoil a bit. She found that she was saying, 'But I do think it would be better if you'd agree to wait.' That sounded rather horrid, and she went on with a laugh. 'I sound like Lucy – she said just the same. She doesn't want to marry for four years or so, she says.'

'Does she?' His voice was sombre and the hand withdrew. 'Four years is a long time. Anything could happen. People change their minds.'

'Not if they have given a solemn promise that they'll wait, as Lucy has. I would be willing to do just the same.'

She could not have said herself why she was so anxious to delay, but she was aware of huge relief when Samuel said, 'Then of course I shall take heed of what you say and wait before I speak to your papa. Marriage is a considerable step, as you observe, especially where there is such a disparity in age. I should not like to frighten my young bride away – and if I have her promise, I'm content with that.' He paused. 'Helena, I'm grateful that we've managed to have this little talk.'

She lifted her face, half-expecting to be kissed, but all he did was pat her hand again and say, 'Now, should we join the others, do you think? Or shall I ring for Maisie to help you to your room?'

Part Three –
June to August 1914

Chapter One

' 'Ere I am, Miss Lucy, and here's your breakfast too. Sorry how it took so long. First egg we 'ad was addled, and we 'ad to start again.' Maisie came back into the breakfast room and set the tray down on the side.

Lucy looked up from her letters. She was reading James's latest. And the contents were so gratifying she could not restrain a smile. James's training course in London had almost finished now – he still corresponded faithfully with her every week – and since her birthday had just passed and she was now of age, the moment he'd been waiting for had come. Here he was proposing to speak to her Papa, and like several of her friends she would be properly engaged.

She had begun to get impatient for that recently. After that dreadful disappointment over Simon Robinson there had been one or two good-looking fellows she'd allowed to flirt with her – she was invited to all the better houses now – but never anything remotely serious. She had allowed it to be whispered that she had a secret beau – it lent her an air of thrilling mystery – but lately, as the young men in question became betrothed to other girls, this charming situation had begin to pall.

And there wasn't even Annabelle to confide in any more. Shortly after Celestine's wedding (Lucy sighed – the thought still had the capacity to wound), Anna – who had been a bridesmaid after all at her mama's insistence – had been ill and the doctor had apparently prescribed a change of air, so Anna had gone off to an aunt in Yorkshire to recuperate and really she hadn't lived at home since then. When she did come back to visit she'd completely lost her spark. She was pale and listless and not a bit of fun, and gradually the friendship between the two of them had waned.

Lucy found she wasn't sorry, the way things had become. Every time when she was with Anna she was on tenterhooks lest it should somehow unwittingly emerge that they hadn't been together all those Rachel afternoons, and at the Passemore-Jenkins' house there was always the chance of meeting Celestine, and enduring endless stories about 'dear Simon' and his doings. Lucy had found it very hard to bear, though she had rather missed her girlish confidante.

So James's prospective visit was a wholly welcome one. She put aside her letter, beamed broadly at the maid and said, with conscious graciousness, as the girl put fresh toast and scrambled egg in front of her, 'Thank you, Maisie. I'll have some tea as well, and then I think that will be all for now.

Mother and Father have finished theirs, I see?'

'Through here like a dose of salts today, and straight out to Penzance. In fine spirits too.' The girl was busying herself with pouring Lucy's tea. 'Everyone's cock-a-hoop today! Must be this picnic that they're planning for the weekend, I suppose. Miss Elenner was up before I got there with her tray, standing at the window so she could feel the breeze and grinning like a witnick at the thought of this here jaunt. Even your poor auntie's roused herself a bit and says that she will go.'

Lucy nodded. Poor Aunt Edwards was becoming very frail and rarely ventured past the doorstep now, though she was as firm as ever when she lectured you. 'Well, let's hope the weather continues to be warm. It will be a lovely outing if it's as fine as this. Papa has spoken to a farmer, and he's set aside a field that looks across the sea. There's a rocky outcrop and some grass where we can sit, and shelter from the trees in case there's too much wind. I'm sure that James and Samuel Maskins will enjoy it too. It will be such a change from London, where the streets are always grey.' She could not resist gesturing to the letter as she said, 'You heard that they were coming down again?'

'Lor', yes,' Maisie muttered. 'Been baking for a fortnight, Mrs Lovett has, on account of all the extra. Not that those two are strangers, not by any means. Mr James has been coming here since he was just a tot, and Dr Maskins visits quite a lot, these days.'

'He comes to see my sister,' Lucy said. Samuel Maskins had become a regular visitor to the Morrisons, and always came to visit and spend time with Helena. 'He's taken an interest in her eyes.'

Maisie nodded. 'She told me that he says that Mr James was right, and there's a possibility in a year or two of an operation that might 'elp her eyes a bit, poor soul. Quite bucked her up, it did. Thinks a lot of Mr Samuel, in a funny sort of way.'

'I should hope she does, indeed.' Lucy paused, torn between a desire to work round to her news and the knowledge one shouldn't chat to servants in this way. Temptation won. 'In fact, I shouldn't be surprised if there was an engagement very soon. She wanted him to wait, while I was still at home, but James is coming back for good in just a month or so, and then I'll be betrothed myself. James is hoping to ask permission of Papa when he is down this weekend.' There, the gleeful words were out – and straightaway she wished them back again. 'Though obviously this is all a secret until it is announced,' she added hastily. 'We don't want gossip in the servants' hall.'

No use. The girl was clattering the breakfast things away. 'You could 'ave a double wedding,' she ventured eagerly. 'I've heard o' that before. Be some romantic, wouldn't it – all the four of you at once?'

'Maisie, don't be preposterous! Of course

we shan't do anything of the kind.' Lucy's voice was sharper than she meant. She had planned her wedding day a hundred different ways since she had promised James that she would wait, but none of them included Helena. That wasn't selfishness, she told herself. Her sister would need another sort of thing – a quiet wedding with not many guests at all: Lena would hardly wear a fancy gown when she couldn't see it anyway and Maskins was so old. A smart tailored skirt and jacket perhaps, with Lucy as a bridesmaid in a toning shade and James as attendant to the groom. Then, with her sister safely married, it would be Lucy's turn and that would be something very different, crêpe de chine and embroidered boleros – even better than Celestine Robinson's elaborate affair.

That memory was enough to sour her mood again. So when Maisie said, 'I didn't mean to cross you, speaking out of turn. And of course you won't do it, if you aren't minded to. But I allus thought it sounded very nice. Wouldn't cost so much, neither, cause you could share the feast,' Lucy was furious at her impudence.

She very pointedly left her scrambled egg untouched. 'Well, you're not getting married, are you, so it hardly signifies. Now will you take those dirty plates away and bring me some fresh tea?' She was about to spurn the toast as well, when she remembered that she was reliant – once again – on Maisie's willingness to hold her tongue. So she took a slice and spread it, and forced a little smile, 'All this talk of addled eggs has spoiled my appetite. But tell Mrs Lovett that the marmalade is good. As for the other matter – keep it to yourself.' She patted Maisie's skinny forearm through the blouse. 'I know you can keep a secret, from that other time. I can rely on you.'

'Yes, Miss Lucy.' But she didn't sound as flattered as Lucy hoped she would. Perhaps she was still smarting about that incident.

It was an uncomfortable memory, in all sorts of ways. Lucy was not unkind as a rule, and she was a bit ashamed of how she'd acted then, threatening to have Maisie turned away. Besides, it reminded her of Simon Robinson – much as she wanted to forget. She took a cross little bite out of her unwanted piece of toast, and turned her attention to the unopened envelope.

Two close-written pages, in a hand she recognized. 'Good gracious, it's from Anna!' she exclaimed aloud.

It was the old Anna, warm and full of news. 'I am sorry that I haven't been in touch for such an age. But now I am recovered and am home again, and I have some thrilling news – which I am simply dying to impart. Do write and let me know when you can come. It will be like old times, with just two of us, since Mother isn't here. She's gone to stay with Celly, who (between ourselves) is in the family way. "An interesting condition," Mother says, though it doesn't seem very interesting to me – Celly can talk of nothing but how unwell she feels – and of course it can't be whispered outside the family.' And then a lot of chatter about a brand-new hat – as if the coolness of the last few years had never been.

For a moment Lucy was tempted to refuse to go, but a second reading made her change her mind. Who could refuse the lure of that 'thrilling news'? Besides, she had her own exciting information to impart: she had never had a chance to tell Annabelle about her secret pact with James, and after this weekend there would be a formal proposal to confide. She gulped down the remainder of the tea and all the toast, then went upstairs and wrote a friendly letter in return, saying that she would be pleased to come on Wednesday afternoon.

'So the master asked you to do the carting, then?' Maisie was grinning like a maniac. 'I said to master they ought to get a cart, take all the extras to the picnic place. Never get it all into just two carriages, with all the Tregenzas and the Morrisons as well. Nine of them there's going to be, and never mind the staff, though you can bet your life they'll want me there, at least. Not that I shall mind – make a change to be outside in the sun, instead of cleaning silver half the afternoon, like I belong to do on Saturday when there are guests to tea. 'Sides, you never know who you might meet!'

Frank laughed. 'Well, looks like I'll be there all right, and paid for handsome, too. You want to mind it, though. Doesn't do to have you mentioning my name – they'll think there's something brewing between the pair of us.'

She gave him a playful push. 'Don't be so soft. I made out I had to go and ask the chapel for your name. Mind, wouldn't 'urt if they did think something of the kind. We got to tell them sometime, 'aven't we?'

Frank gave a long, despairing sigh. 'Maisie, lover, don't go on again. You know I'm doing everything I can. But Fayther isn't up to things these days. Like as if losing that contract knocked the stuffing out of him. Worse than a baby, he is, when it comes to carrying – and that cough is something awful. Right down on his chest.'

She shook her head. 'But when will it be different, Frank? That's what I want to know. Doesn't seem to be no end to it at all. There's Jethro, he's married, with a nipper and another on the way – and two of your sisters fixing to be wed. When is it going to be your turn?'

He reached out and twined his fingers into hers. 'I know, my lover, but what's a man to do? The business did brilliant when the trains were out on strike – managed to pay our way, and some to spare. But things are harder now the railways are back, especially seeing Fayther's not much help: I still got to meet the rent and keep the little ones in food and

196

shoe leather. Mother's out scrubbing every hour God sends, but she got to pay for Mary to mind Davy out of that. Different when we can get him into school.'

'Couldn't you go and ask them if they'd take him young? I remember when I was in class they had a little one – exceptionable circumstances or something, they d'call it – 'cause her ma was ill. You could say your fayther was, it comes to be the same.'

Frank shook his head. 'He would 'ave to ask them, and he never would. You suggest he isn't up to working and he blows his cork – like a shook-up bottle full of ginger beer. And they teachers wouldn't take no heed of me.' He gave a little laugh. 'We aren't so very popular with them as it is. Sent a letter home with our Will the other day, asking why our Lenny hadn't been at school. Well, course, Fayther thought he had, and gave him no end of a leathering when he got hold of him.'

'I'm not surprised, if he was missing school.'

Frank made a doubtful face. 'Really, you can't rightly blame the boy. He's gone eleven – near old enough to leave – and he isn't a scholar, like the rest of them: born upside down he was, and always has been slow. He'd been out picking winkles and making a few pence, then coming home with sprats and things for tea. Wanting to make a contribution, see. But when Fayther heard what he'd been at, he leathered him again – for making out we couldn't manage how we were. Mind you, I noticed that he ate the sprats, all right.' He squeezed her fingers. 'But you see how 'tis. Can't rightly ask them down the school to take an extra one, when the top one isn't going there when he should.'

Maisie gently took her hand away. 'Pity we can't get Miss Elenner to help a bit on this. That schoolmistress d'come to see her now and then, wanting a bit of help with playing tunes. There's two or three that come to her, since she'd been teaching me.'

'That's 'cause you tell everybody at the Sunday school how she learned you 'ow to play the hymns.'

' 'Tidn't that – her piano teacher's sent her one or two. Says she ought to charge for it, though I don't think she will. But don't you change the subject! I meant what I said. I'm sure she'd speak for Davy, if you think that it would help. But, here, there isn't any time to talk about it now. We're coming up to your house, and they'll be waiting tea. Am I looking halfway decent? Can't have your mother thinking I'm a tramp.'

He made a face at her. 'You look just grand to me. And don't you worry, they'll take to you no end. Been telling me for months I should bring you home, but it hasn't been easy to find a day to suit.'

Maisie said nothing. It had crossed her mind to wonder sometimes if he was ashamed, it had taken so long to ask her home like this. Or perhaps it really was because there wasn't any room – which was what he always told her when she suggested it. Until now, suddenly, he'd seem to change his mind.

Obviously it was a little tense at first, all crammed round the table in the tiny kitchen space. Frank's mother had put on a welcome spread – bread and cake and different kinds of jam – but there was hardly room to reach it with elbows jammed so tight. And this when three older girls were missing and Fayther was out too. Maisie wondered how on earth they ever coped if everyone was there.

Maisie took some 'wild salad' (dandelion leaves) and a little piece of cheese. She almost wished she didn't know how tight the budget was, and how the family were holding back so that there was enough. There were a few remarks about the weather and then a silence fell, while the younger children stared at her and the older ones looked anywhere but at the visitor.

It was little Davy who broke the awkwardness at last. 'How can't I have a proper piece of cake? I knaw it's for the visitor, but she idn't going to eat all that lot, is she, Ma? It's my favourite, and I'll only have a crumb, 'cause there isn't enough pieces to go round.'

Frank's ma looked mortified at this. 'You have a slice, Miss Maisie, don't pay no heed to them.'

Maisie laughed. She took the very largest slice of cake, and – before the children's jealous, unbelieving eyes – cut it into several little bits. Then, instead of eating it, she gave each one a piece, saving the largest one for Davy, who giggled with delight.

' 'Ere,' he said to Frank, his mouth still full, 'she's nice, your Maisie.'

'Course she is,' Frank answered, 'but not as nice as cake!'

Everybody laughed, and after that it was much easier. After tea (which did not take very long) Davy brought his toys for her to see – a whittled whistle and a wooden dog – and after she'd admired them she took him on her knee and told him a story about beanstalks she'd once heard at school. She couldn't recall it rightly and had to make bits up, but Davy seemed to like it and several of the other children crowded round as well.

'Sorry if the little ones were climbing over you,' Frank said, when it was time to take her home, and he was helping her to step up on the cart. 'Gets a bit boisterous with all the lot of them.'

Maisie shook her head. 'Handsome, I call it. I don't mind at all. Never had a family like that when I was small – it was all sit up and mind your manners, keep your elbows clean. No laughing and jostling and talking all at once.' She took her seat and tied her bonnet as she spoke.

Frank laughed. 'Fighting and squabbling half the time, more like.'

'No, I mean it, Frank. You can tell the way it is, as soon as you walk in. All of you together, like a sort of team.'

Frank's grin faded suddenly, and he said

soberly. ' 'Tidn't always like that Maisie. Not when Fayther's there. Time was...' He trailed off. You could tell he was upset, the way he jerked the horse. 'Anyway, you see the way it is. Isn't room to bring a kitten home, let alone a wife. Still, I'm glad you've met them, it's been long enough. But it's set me thinking. Since you're so fond of families, perhaps it could be done. Not setting up our own house, we couldn't run to that. But, maybe, in a little while when Davy goes to school – if Len and Mother can bring something in and the carting goes on paying like it has – perhaps we could find a bigger house to rent, and you and me could have a room in it. So now then, Maisie Olds, what d'you think of that?'

But she couldn't tell him because her eyes were full of tears.

The picnic day had dawned quite beautiful. Helena was aware of it as soon as she awoke, and she pulled the curtains back to feel the sunshine on her face. Even now, in the carriage, as they bounced along the lanes she could still detect the warmth, and the scent of summer flowers in the hedges as they passed.

She put her face beside the open window space, delighting in the breeze which brought the sound of seagulls and the distant crash of waves. It was a long time since she had ventured on an outing such as this – a proper picnic with a hamper, taken to the sea – and she was foolishly excited at the novelty: usually she had to be content with a tray of cake and tea and sandwiches in her private bower. She pushed her head out further, to enjoy the feeling more.

'Helena, do sit back properly!' Aunt Edwards' voice was sharp. 'Your face is getting dusty, and as for your poor hair! You'll look like a gypsy before we've half arrived.' She plied a handkerchief with force on the offending smears and the cloth was slightly damp, as if she'd licked it first. 'Can't you feel that it's all gritty when it blows on you like that? Just as well your mother's closed her eyes and is having forty winks. She'd be horrified. There, that's a little better. I should think so too. Whatever would James Morrison and Mr Maskins say?'

Nothing whatever, since they are polite, Helena thought, but of course she didn't say the words aloud. Instead she leaned obediently back, and permitted Aunt Edwards to close the window up and shut out the glories of the summer day. There was enough enjoyment to be derived simply from the contemplation of the afternoon ahead.

No doubt it was Samuel who'd suggested she should come. He was encouraging her, more and more, to venture from the house. Well, she was very grateful – as she always was. He was entitled to her affection and respect, not only for his care, but for the way he'd kept his word, and never once alluded to that little tête-à-tête in all the visits that he'd paid to her. In fact, he had been a good deal better than his word. Even the presents that

202

he brought for her were not romantic ones: Braille music books, or eyedrops, or something of the kind. Not a word was ever said about his private thoughts and hopes or the promise that she'd made to him that night. Sometimes she thought that she'd imagined it.

There were times when – almost – she rather wished she had. She had become attached to him – dependent on him almost – as a doctor and a friend, but the thought of marriage was another thing. The recollection of the time she'd touched his skin remained uncomfortably vivid in her memory. Yet surely a hairy hand and stringy wrist were trivial things to cause one to recoil?

She put the thought determinedly away, and spoke aloud. 'The horse is stopping. Are we nearly there?' She kept the question gay.

'Edgar's got down and is opening the gate.' Lucy had been unnaturally quiet all the way, as if she was suppressing something.

Even Mama had roused herself and murmured sleepily, 'Tell him to take us in across the field, and stop right over there beside the wall, where Papa is. I told him to ride on ahead and choose the best place to spread the picnic cloth. Ah, splendid, here are the others coming now.'

Helena had already heard the wheels, coming up the lane. Two lots of horses. First the Morrisons' – which would have James and Samuel on board – and then a heavier sound, no doubt the carter that Papa had hired, to bring the assortment of necessities like hampers, umbrellas, tables, rugs and chairs. That drew up a moment later, and they all went bumping in, over what seemed to Helena like miles of lumpy grass, until there was a 'Whoa there!' and they stopped again.

She would remember snippets of that golden afternoon, like little pictures, ever afterwards.

Sitting on a rug, as though she was a child, and feeling the sharp grass blades pricking through her skirt. The wind that threatened to blow her bonnet off, and sent soft ruffles through her hair when she removed it and held it on her knee. The salty taste of salmon sandwiches, and the freedom to pick things up and eat them in her hands: and James's voice, quite close to her, telling her – and Lucy – all about his life.

'The subjects that you study sound so impressive now. Because you are a senior student, I suppose!' Lucy was being her flirtatious self again. '*Materia medica*, Pathology and I don't know what. And that study about eyes. I'm sure I shouldn't understand above of a half of it – even the names are double Dutch to me.' She gave a girlish giggle.

'No doubt you enjoy the work in the hospital?' Maskins sounded almost envious and sharp. 'So many pretty nurses, as I seem to recall?'

James laughed. 'Not much chance of talking very much to them, I fear, with the clinical professors looking on. We're only there by their arrangement and they take us round the wards – usually ask us questions about the patients, too. Or sometimes the problems are theoretical and they're the tricky ones, because you don't have the evidence of what's in front of you. You have to answer on your feet, so you always hope the glance won't fall on you.'

'And does it?' Lucy sounded positively rapt.

'Oh, I've always got away with it,' James muttered modestly. 'But I remember one occasion when poor old Rupert was the one. Got asked a theoretical question about an earlier case – a child who'd swallowed sixpence and was brought in turning blue. "So, what would you have done in such an instance, Mr Neill?" Well, of course Rupert thought of all the things that we'd been taught – choroform the patient and sterilize the skin – but the old man gave him an awful bawling out. "Well, you'd better call the undertaker if you're going to do all that. Whip out your penknife and make a hole so he can breathe, then you can worry about getting back the coin"!'

Lucy gave a little yelp of pretended horror. 'James, don't talk of such disgusting things. Making a hole in the poor child, indeed!' It made James laugh aloud.

Helena laughed with him, but Maskins sounded sour 'So the old man's still asking the same trick questions, then? Still trying to prove that the best surgeon is the quickest one? That might have been true, last century, when the patient was awake – but surely that went out once we had chloroform?'

James said politely, 'It would still be valid in a choking case, I suppose. Though I felt for Rupert. I'd have made the same mistake.'

'James!' There was the sound of Lucy jumping to her feet. 'I quite forbid you to talk about these gruesome things on such a sunny day. I declare I can't abide another word of it. Now, shall we take a walk? Maisie is packing up the food, and it will soon be time to go. I have a fancy to go over there and look down on the sea. And Helena would like it, if we could help her too. Dr Maskins – Samuel – could you take her other arm?'

It was difficult – and worrying – on the uneven grass, even when her guides were leading her. Lucy, in particular, wasn't guiding very well. She was too busy talking confidentially to James, who was walking on the other side of her – and even Samuel seemed preoccupied. Several times Lena caught her foot and almost tripped, but it was worth the effort in the end when they stood together on a ledge of rock, where she could hear the surge of surf, the cry of gulls and feel the blown spray on her skin.

But Lucy decided she did not like it after all. She said it made her dizzy and she went tripping back, calling to the others that they should follow her. Helena was reluctant, 'Let me stay a little more,' and the two men remained with her to support her either side.

It was an exhilarating moment and terrifying too. She knew that she was standing safe – and yet there was nothing beneath her but the cliffs and sea. Was it because James had taken Lucy's place – and was therefore standing on her right – that Helena found that she was leaning most on him?

Chapter Two

Paul Tregenza was a troubled man. He looked at Maskins. 'Lucy, did you say?'

The doctor's thin and whiskered face was wreathed in smiles. 'That's right. I presume there is no problem? I intimated to you some long time ago that I was interested in your daughter and asked for your permission to call on her, with the idea of asking for her hand one day – which you were pleased to give, as I recall.'

Paul looked down at his empty brandy glass and didn't say a word. Not even a mouthful, when he needed it! He didn't wait to ring for Edgar. He went straight to the decanter and poured another drink, remembering just in time to offer Maskins some.

Maskins looked at the amber liquid with delight. 'Then I take it I may drink a toast to the prospect of success?' He was not, in general, an expressive man, but he was wearing one of his most expansive smiles.

How could Paul have failed to perceive how astonishingly unprepossessing Samuel Maskins was? Of course the man did have a certain air about him deriving from his age and status: and his clothes – although old-fashioned – were immaculately cut. Even the bulging eyes and forehead could be seen as attributes, being well-known indicators of intelligence. But the rest – the large head with its pointed nose, the fringe of whiskers and mop of thinning hair, the gangling arms and legs and awkward lanky frame – would have been thought ugly in another sort of man.

He swallowed the brandy in a single gulp, but did not drink the toast. Maskins, who had been sitting in the big chair by the fire, seemed to realize that something was amiss. The smile vanished abruptly from his lips and he rose and went to stare disconsolately at the flames.

'You think she will not have me? That I'm still rushing her too much? But, dammit, man, how long am I to wait? She has her, life before her, but I'll soon be forty-six. I have tried hard to be patient, heaven knows.'

Paul was not fifty yet himself. It seemed bizarre to find this man appealing to him for his youngest daughter's hand. But he could not help a certain sympathy: he realized that he'd played an unwitting part in this. He put down his glass and joined the doctor by the hearth – almost tempted to reach out and pat

Maskins on the arm. But at the last moment he felt that was impossible and he settled for leaning on the mantelpiece instead.

'It's ... ah...' The words abandoned him. 'I thought ... I'm sure we all thought...' He began to fiddle with one of the china ornaments – a strange lopsided cat with eyelashes that Lucy had once brought home from Corpus Christi fair – 'I understood you wished to speak to Helena,' he finished, in a rush.

Maskins seemed to brighten. 'I have done so, indeed. In fact, it was Lucy's own suggestion that I should – and I think you also mentioned something of the kind. I do appreciate it would be difficult for Helena at first without her sister's aid, but she's doing well in both Moon and Braille and young James Morrison has done some training in ophthalmology and I know he's keen to help. And obviously I'll continue to monitor her sight. I have told her that I am willing to have her visit us as often as she chooses, and naturally we'll come here from time to time.' He took a sip of brandy. 'Provided that you are happy to welcome us of course and we aren't prevented by...' he paused, '...happy accidents. I shouldn't be prepared to put Lucy's health at risk.'

It took Paul an instant to work out what he meant. The image was so shocking that he dropped the ornament and it smashed into a thousand pieces on the hearth. He was almost grateful for the incident, it gave him the excuse to go and ring the bell and turn his back to Maskins while he composed himself. After all the man was talking – as he supposed – about the woman that he hoped to make his wife.

'My dear fellow.' He toyed with a cigar – one couldn't have a third brandy, not in company. He grasped the nettle. 'I fear there has been a misunderstanding here. Of course you have my blessing to propose to whom you wish' – magnanimous, that was the tone to strike – 'but I had always thought – presumed – that it was my elder daughter you hoped to offer for.'

'Helena?' Maskin's cheeks had turned quite mottled, under the side-whiskers. 'Of course, Tregenza, she is quite a gem, and I am genuinely interested in her case. But – surely – you could not imagine...? As a wife? How could you possibly have concluded that?'

In fact, looking back, it was hard to see how he had formed the impression with such certainty. Lucy had contributed, beyond a doubt, by prattling about how 'Samuel Maskins is keen on Helena' and Paul had continued to suppose it was the case. Yet Maskins hadn't said so, when you thought back carefully. He had expressed an interest in 'your daughter' in his usual awkward way – Maskins always had a tendency to be oblique and vague – but when you reviewed it closely he hadn't said which one. Paul had drawn his own conclusions, hearing what he hoped to hear, perhaps. Poor Helena!

210

'I'm afraid she may have derived the same impression.' It pained him to have to frame the words. 'And little Lucille, too.'

Maskins gave him a rigid little smile. 'I don't see how they can have done. You needn't worry there, Tregenza. As I said, I spoke to Helena – some little time ago. I asked if she thought I had a chance, and she said yes I did, but she thought it would be better if I delayed until Lucy was of age. However, she did give me cause to hope – she told me that Lucille had privately agreed to wait and consider my proposal kindly when it came. I hope that, under the circumstances, you will not withdraw consent and will permit me at least to take my chance with her?'

Why did Maskins seem suddenly grotesque? If he was a match for Helena, why not for Lucy too? Paul was forced to face the answer – not an honourable one: Helena would be lucky to find any man at all, but for Lucy the fellow did not seem good enough – too old, too ugly and too humourless. Surely she had not really undertaken to consider him? Maskins was wealthy and she was fond of luxuries, but she could hardly be so desperate as to marry him for that? There had been other boys. There was a time when Paul had wondered if she wasn't rather keen on that Simon Robinson who married the Passemore-Jenkins girl – but obviously that hadn't come to much. These days, if anything, she seemed attached to James.

He glanced at his companion. The doctor

was wearing a complacent smile again. Well, Paul thought, let him speak to Lucy – what else was there to do? The man was obviously convinced that she would welcome it, and if he was mistaken she could tell him so herself. It was Helena's feelings which concerned him most. He had teased her many times about Maskins wanting her – her dreams would be as shattered as the china cat had been.

He forced himself to smile at his visitor. 'Then, Maskins, you may speak to Lucy with my blessing, though naturally I can't answer for what she'll have to say—' He was interrupted by a tapping at the door. Edgar had come, in answer to the bell.

Paul gestured to the fireplace – 'Can you deal with that?' – and the boy withdrew again, to be replaced a moment later by the little serving maid who got down on her knees and swept the pieces up. Neither Paul nor Maskins said a single word until she'd finished. One didn't talk of personal matters in front of the servants.

'There now.' The girl was on her feet again. 'I think I got the last of it. Be careful where you tread.' She addressed her master with a cheerful grin. 'Sorry if I've interrupted, 'aving to do that.' She glanced sidelong at Maskins. 'I wouldn't spoil Miss Elenner's 'appiness for the world.'

So even Maisie thought that Maskins wished to sue for Helena? Now where would she get an idea like that?

From Lucy, almost certainly – she'd never

learned to hold her tongue when servants were nearby, and no one else would ever have hinted such a thing. But why should Lucy have spread such a rumour if she knew it wasn't true? She was capable of playing foolish tricks, but she was not deliberately cruel. No, there had been a genuine misunderstanding, Paul was sure of it. No doubt Maskins mumbled something vague and awkward, the way he always did, and Lucy – as usual – wasn't listening very hard. Perhaps she had simply failed to believe that anyone so dull could have an interest in herself. She'd complained a hundred times that Maskins was a bore. Well, there was only one thing to be done.

'Thank you, Maisie,' he murmured to the maid. 'Could you find Miss Lucy before she goes to bed? Ask her to come and see me if you would. There's something I would like to hear her views about, and then Dr Maskins also wants to speak to her.'

'She's listening to Miss Elenner, in the music room – playing something beautiful, like she always does. I'll go and fetch her, soon as I've thrown these china bits away.' She was still holding the dustpan carefully on end so as not to spill the contents on the floor. 'I suppose you want me to do it right away?' she asked. 'Only the mistress says to tell you that when you've finished here, there's Mr James would like a word with you.'

Lucy had clearly been on tenterhooks all

through dinner, and afterwards it went from bad to worse. She refused to join the Morrisons and Mama at cards, and insisted on 'Waiting here with Lena, until Papa comes back.' But she was not listening to Chopin, though she'd requested it, she kept fidgeting and moving in her seat, and when Helena asked her what the matter was she just said, 'Nothing,' in a funny voice and scraped her chair across the floor again.

Helena attempted to ignore it and hoped that it would pass, but she was in the midst of playing a favourite polonaise when her sister came over and closed the piano lid – not hard, but enough to interrupt the flow.

'Lucy!' Helena protested, drawing back her hands.

'Oh, I'm sorry, but I can't bear any more. If I hear another crotchet I believe I shall burst.' Lucy sounded halfway between giggling and tears. 'What on earth is taking the men-folk such an age? Samuel has been closeted with Papa for half an hour, and poor James has been waiting to go in all that while.' She must have taken special pains tonight, she smelt delightfully of roses and cream soap.

Helena tried the sensible approach. 'Well, perhaps it's not surprising. You heard the table talk – if the railway workers all come out on strike, like the builders and the electricians and the coal miners have done, there might not be any train to London for him and James to catch. And it isn't just in England, so Samuel Maskins says. It's all over the Empire.

There are strikes and riots in South Africa, and in Ulster it's so bad there could be civil war. And there's Germany re-arming at a terrific pace – we'll be lucky if there isn't trouble there.'

Lucy made a noise that might have been a 'Hmmph!'

'You needn't be so scornful. There was that archduke somebody who was shot in Bosnia last week – that's going to lead to problems, Samuel's sure of it. Mind you, he thinks we need a war to buck the nation up. Traditional society is breaking down, he said, what with these new trade unions and the lady suffragists throwing stones and behaving in such a shocking way. Of course, Mama thought that wasn't a suitable topic for dinner-table talk, and changed the subject on to other things, but it was clear that Papa was very interested. Perhaps they are still discussing it over cigars.'

Lucy made a small impatient noise. 'They're not talking about what's happening in the world, you goose! They're talking about us! Much more important than all those silly things! Maskins has gone to ask for you, I'm sure – he murmured to me when we were out today that he proposed to speak to Papa tonight – and once he's done that James will ask for me.' She giggled. 'I told him that he ought to wait till you were spoken for.'

Helena placed both hands in her lap and twined the finger-ends, squeezing her eyelids tight as though that would somehow help.

'Spoken for'! So it had come at last. She thought of Maskins, always so formal and so ponderous and – even at the picnic in the open air – smelling of mothballs and strong carbolic soap. She should be grateful to him, honestly she should, but the thought of his caresses made her shrink! Yet, what would become of her if she should refuse? End up in a blind asylum or – at best – an unwanted dependant in James and Lucy's home: a sort of sad, blind Aunt Edwards hanging on the fringes of other people's lives.

Something of her inner struggle must have shown on her face because Lucy came and gave her arm a squeeze. 'Don't look so downcast, Lena! I won't spoil your news. I don't propose to marry James for at least another year – long after you and Samuel are wed. But it would be something to be formally engaged. It gives a girl such cachet, when that is announced and people know that you are to be married soon.' She laughed. 'I wonder what Annabelle will say? I dare say she'll be quite envious – of the pair of us. You know I'm going to see her later in the week?'

Helena guessed that Lucy was looking forward to the chance to preen, artlessly discussing bridal outfits with her friend who (judging by the gossip from Mama's tea parties) had no immediate marriage prospects herself. The idea made her feel untypically severe, and she was about to say something rather tart when Maisie's distinctive footsteps interrupted them.

'Wasn't sure if you was in 'ere, seeing how the pianner-playing'd stopped, but I'm sent to fetch Miss Lucy. The master'd like to see her, in his library, soon as ever Mr James comes out,' and she tip-tapped off again.

'Well!' Lucy got up with a clatter. 'Didn't I tell you something was afoot? He'll want to talk to you next, see if I'm not right!' She came and gave her sister a fluttering little kiss. 'Imagine! Dr and Mrs James Morrison. It sounds immensely grand!'

Helena could still hear her giggling as she closed the door.

'Ah, Lucy!'

Whatever was the matter with Papa? She had expected to find him expansive and relaxed – even to offer one of his rare caresses, possibly. But he was standing by the fire-place, not sitting in his chair, and he was running a finger round the inside of his collar as he did when he was vexed.

She tried to look receptive. 'You wanted me, Papa?'

He didn't answer. He folded his arms and stared into the fire, as if it might tell him what he ought to say. She could hear the clock tick, and the crackle of the flames, but still her father didn't look at her.

She could bear the wait no longer. 'I presume that James has come and asked you – as he said he would – for your permission to offer for my hand?'

He did look at her then, stroking his side-whiskers with a thoughtful hand. 'Permission which normally I would be pleased to grant.'

She beamed at him. 'Papa, that's simply wonderf—' and then she stopped. 'Normally? You mean you haven't granted it?'

There was another pause before he said, 'It was rather a formality in any case, I understand, since you have already given him an undertaking without seeking my consent.'

She knew that she was scarlet. 'Well, of course we meant to ask you – as indeed he did tonight. We supposed that you would be delighted. And his family, too. Perhaps I should not have made a promise without telling you, but I never dreamt that you would disapprove. You knew that we'd been writing, ever since he went away – I thought the way I felt was clear to everyone.'

Her father sat down in his big brown leather chair, leaned back and stretched his feet out on the hearthrug, staring at them as if he had a sudden interest in his boots.

'Not absolutely clear to everyone, I fear. I've had Maskins here this evening, to ask me the same thing.'

'Ah!' She saw – or thought she saw – the problem now. She sat down on the matching chair and looked across at him, tipping her head in the way she knew was her most captivating pose. 'You think James should have waited for another day? That was entirely my fault, I'm afraid. I knew that Samuel was going to speak to you tonight...'

'Lucille! You're not listening. Did you hear

what I said? Samuel Maskins asked me the same thing.'

She arched her brows and gave him her most winning puzzled look. 'But of course he did, and I'm delighted for Helena, of course. I'm sure he'll be a splendid husband, in all sorts of ways...'

'Then you will treat his proposal with a certain courtesy, even if you refuse it in the end – as I presume you intend, from the other things you say. However, it will come as a surprise to him, I think. He believes he has your promise, and has done for some years.'

She found that she was staring. 'Samuel? My promise? But that's absurd.' She laughed, though it was certainly more from nervousness than mirth. 'He told me that he wanted Helena.'

This time he did look at her. 'So what, exactly, did he say to you?'

'He said ... oh, I can't remember. Something about how pretty we both were, and how attentive I was to Helena.' She gulped. 'Oh dear! Perhaps he did intend his compliments for me. I thought ... well, you know what I thought!'

'It's what he thought that's more significant! He tells me that you actively encouraged his advance.'

'Well, I did try to be charming to him, I suppose. Pretended to be interested in what he said and even did my best to flatter him – but it was just for Lena's sake.' That wasn't altogether true, in fact. There had been occasions when she had flirted shamelessly, simply to make James feel jealous when they'd had a tiff. A small hot shiver coursed up her neck. 'But he's grotesque. He's old and stuffy. Surely you haven't given him consent?'

'We are in the twentieth century, Lucille. I am hardly likely to trade you like a slave. However, I have given him permission to ask you for your hand. I tried to warn him that you might not accept, but he is confident that he knows otherwise. He believes that he's been patient until you gave him leave to speak. He is waiting for you in the downstairs parlour, where I suggested he should go.'

'But, Papa! You must call him back and tell him...'

He shook his head. 'On the contrary, I will do nothing of the kind. If you wish to disabuse him, you must do so for yourself – though I insist you treat his proposal with due civility. It seems quite clear that you've encouraged him, whether deliberately or not, and you'll have certainly caused your sister unnecessary pain. To say nothing of a measure of embarrassment to me.'

Her mind was conjuring unpleasant visions of the coming interview. 'And what about James Morrison?' she pleaded, urgently.

'I could hardly give my blessing for his proposal on the very same occasion. I have told him that you have received another offer for your hand, but that if you refuse, he may propose to you himself – and with my blessing – though at some other time. When he has finished his training, I suggest. That, I think, is the most that I can do.' He shook his head again. 'Lucy, I do not blame you for the awkward situation in which we find ourselves, but I do think that you have contributed to it. Your Aunt Edwards says that you lack judgement and decorum in your behaviour sometimes, and it seems that she is right – both in your over-friendliness to Maskins and your clandestine undertakings to young James Morrison.' He sounded more sorrowful than angry, which doubled the rebuke.

She could only stand and stammer and feel her cheeks turn red. 'But, Papa...'

He sighed and rose slowly to his feet, as though he suddenly felt old. 'Your suitor will be wondering what is delaying you. It is time you went and faced him and told him where he stands – and I must go and tell Helena what has happened, I suppose.'

He went to the door and opened it, and she had no option but to go to downstairs where Samuel Maskins was awaiting her.

Chapter Three

The next half hour was the most difficult that she had ever spent. She tried to do it gently – assure him that she was flattered but he'd misinterpreted – but Maskins was simply incredulous and hurt.

He did not withdraw in silence, as she had hoped he would, but bombarded her with arguments and rationality. How could she possibly have mistaken him? He had given her the clearest possible indication as to what his feelings were, and she had given him to understand quite clearly that she returned and welcomed them. It was not only her smiles and demeanour which had convinced him of her very warm regard, hadn't she actually told him once that she was fond of him?

It was true, she recognized with some chagrin. 'As a brother – or a brother-in-law – I meant!'

But how could she have supposed that he was courting Helena? His amazement and dismay at the idea were quite as great as Lucy's own in discovering what his real intentions were!

In the end she had to put it bluntly. It had

all been a mistake. She didn't love him and she never would.

Even then he still persisted. 'And is that the only basis for a marriage, in your view? Does reliability and mutual regard not count for something? The fact that I can offer you a house and way of life which most people would find enviable? And even – should you wish it – interesting company? I am not much of a lover of dinner parties myself, but such things are expected of a married man, and I have many professional colleagues who would provide you with a wide circle of acquaintance if you find the business of managing a house a too constraining one, at least until a family comes along. I believe solid affection may be earned, and learned – better than the romantic "love" we hear so much about.'

'I have made a promise. To wait for someone else.'

That silenced him a moment and then he said, in a different tone of voice, 'Ah yes, your promise! Your sister mentioned it – and of course I thought it applied to me. In that case it is fortunate that I am disabused, I have bestowed too much affection on you as it is. As for your sister, I am sorry to disappoint her hopes but clearly she was in no hurry for my hand. She asked me to delay my suit till you were twenty-one – I thought for your sake – and I imagine therefore she'll be consolable. I flatter myself that I did not prolong her pain. Now, I will not wait for the carriage

– it is a fine night and the Morrisons' is not far to walk – and I shall be in London tomorrow if there is a train. Pray pardon me for having imposed my sentiments on you for so long.' He gave an old-fashioned bow, in which he clicked his heels, and left the room without another word.

But worse was to come. When a chastened Lucy crept upstairs again, it was to find Helena still in the music room, playing the same Chopin polonaise with controlled intensity. Her sister hesitated for a moment at the door.

'It's all right, Lucy,' Lena said. 'Come in, I know you're there. Papa has been here and told me what occurred.'

Lucy stole in, ignoring the sofa and the padded stool nearby, and deliberately sat on one of the uncomfortable gilt, high-backed chairs against the wall, as if the lack of cushioning was a penance for her sins.

'I'm sorry, Lena...' Lucy said – she had to raise her voice over the vibrating chords. 'I thought ... I really thought...'

'So did I,' said Helena. She stopped abruptly and brought down the piano lid, then turned her sightless face to Lucy. 'I thought there was a chance that I might lead a normal sort of life – to have a home and husband – but I see that I was wrong.'

'I know,' Lucy murmured, in misery. 'It is all my fault. I—'

'Let me finish, Lucy. The strange thing is, it's rather a relief. Maskins is a respected, wealthy man, and I know you tell me he is a good-looking one, but there is something awkward in his presence now and then ... I can't explain it ... but I don't find him in the least attractive, in the way a woman ought.'

'But I thought you told me you were fond of him?' Stupid! She was making a bad situation worse, but her sister's reply was strangely dignified.

'I respect him, certainly – and I owe him such a lot that I can't help feeling a certain affectionate regard. He has earned that much from me.' Helena could not guess how much she'd echoed Maskins' words, and how discomfited it made Lucy feel. 'I have tried to persuade myself that it would be enough. A good many marriages are built on less than that.'

'But, Helena.' This glimpse into her sister's feelings was so desolate that Lucy had sprung to her feet before she checked herself. 'Surely you couldn't think of that? To tie yourself forever to a man you did not love? Why, I would rather...' She trailed off and sat disconsolately down again.

Helena was wearing a most peculiar smile. 'Not marry anyone at all? Indeed. When you told me earlier tonight that he was speaking to Papa, it actually crossed my mind that I might refuse his hand – but I doubt I should have found the courage when it came to it. Why is it that a woman's life depends on being wed? A spinster is pitied if she has to earn her keep – such cruel words, aren't they, "spinster" and "old maid"? – whereas a bachelor like Hubert Morrison can live respectably alone, while people admire him for devotion to his work?'

Lucy had never considered matters in that light – the thought of a career had never crossed her mind – but she knew the arguments. She had heard them all rehearsed a hundred times. 'Most women have homes and children which require their care, and anyway they're not as strong as men. Our minds and natures don't equip us for grappling with such things.'

She got up and began to tidy up the chairs and plump up the velvet pillows on the big settee. It was not a job she often did but she felt the need for some activity, and she thumped the cushions with some vigour as she said, 'That's why we're called the gentler sex, I suppose – except those dreadful suffragists, of course. Though they hardly count as feminine at all, chaining themselves to railings like human bicycles.'

It was an attempt to change the subject. Lena was rather surprisingly in favour of some of Mrs Pankhurst's views and though Lucy did not usually enjoy an argument, she felt that one would be a useful thing just now.

But her sister was not willing to be drawn. 'Then as a representative of the gentler sex, you will oblige me by not punching that cushion any more. I rather think that if anyone has the right to punch anything, it's me. Whatever my feelings towards Samuel, the

226

prospect of a blind asylum in my later life is not a very happy one, I fear.'

'There's no need for you to worry on that score, I'm sure.' Lucy paused in mid-thump to utter her reply. 'You know that Papa has put aside a special sum for you, so you can always have enough to live on – with a nurse or anyone you need. Besides, James has promised me that you can have a room of your very own with us if anything should happen to Mama and Papa – once he finally gets Papa's permission to marry me, of course.'

She meant it kindly, so why did Lena laugh in that strange way?

'I'm sure that is extremely kind of you. However, I have thought it over, and I know what I must do. I am a woman, and since it seems I am not to wed there is only one honourable solution that I can see. Doubtless everyone will be upset by it, but I'm confident Papa will come to understand, in time. I refuse to be a burden, like poor Aunt Edwards is.'

Lucy was so horrified, she almost couldn't speak. There had been a famous incident when she was still at school – one of Miss Worthington's former protégés had tried to hang herself after her father lost his fortune and her beau deserted her. The woman had recovered but she'd been pronounced a lunatic and shut away for life. The scandal and disgrace had been quite terrible, and the memory had remained with Lucy ever since.

She dropped the pillow she'd been pummelling and rushed over to seize her sister by the hands. 'Helena, you mustn't even talk of such a thing. It's a mortal sin to think of suicide.'

Helena pulled her hands away, and laughed. A proper laugh, that flooded Lucy with relief and at the same time made her feel a little daft. 'Suicide? I wasn't talking about suicide, you goose. I was talking about earning my own living, if I could.'

Relief gave way to outrage. 'But, Helena! You couldn't! Earn your living as though we had no money at all?' Lucy was appalled. It was almost as dreadful as the idea of suicide had been.

'Why not? I believe that I could manage it: I could teach singing, piano even – if only to little ones at first. Certainly Miss Thompson thinks so – she's even offered to send me pupils if I like. And I'm sure that Maisie would agree with me – when she has finished hovering at the door.'

'My lor',' Maisie said afterwards to Frank. 'That was some awful evening. I've never known the like.' It was a lovely afternoon, and they were sitting together on a granite stile, looking out across the farmlands and the moor.

Maisie swung her legs, looking at the darn where her stockings met her boots. 'First that Dr Maskins stalking off like that and walking all the way back to the Morrisons' – in the

228

rain as well. And then they didn't know how to conduct themselves, whether to wait their carriage, or to ask for ours and go home to their guest – with the poor mistress trying to pretend that everything was just as usual.'

'Don't sound as if they'll be wanting me to cart for picnics any more.' Frank was busy with his penknife and a piece of wood. He was always clever with anything like that.

She threw him an apologetic glance. She knew she did witter on about her job a bit. 'Sorry, my lover. Don't know any of these people, do 'ee, any road? Or only to look at, if you do. And you were telling me about this railway strike. Make a big difference, will it, to the money coming in?'

Frank stopped whittling the piece of wood he was working on. He was making a little letter rack for her. Beautiful it was, with their initials on the top, and a little bird and leaves around the front: they'd stand it on the mantelpiece when they were wed, he said, though Heaven knew what letters they would get to put in it.

'Make all the difference in the world,' he answered her, 'if it goes on a bit. Last time there was no end of business for any waggoner – long as you could get the hay and feed. Course, being with Crowdie, we should have no problem there – but there were some, up London, couldn't keep their horse. Though even Crowdie's going to feel the pinch, this time, if he can't get his broccoli and swede and flowers up to the city markets on the train. It seems to be the way the world is, nowadays – one little change and it puts everything about – just like your pianner playing for the hymns.'

Maisie wasn't sure this was a compliment. 'I told you Miss Elenner was going to teach?' she said. 'Properly, for money, I mean. Her piano teacher says she's got some pupils she can send, cause she's got too many beginners as it is. Thought the master and the mistress would burst their buttons when she said, but in the end she got them to agree. Not that she'd going to charge me anything. She promised I could go on like before.' She had picked up some wood-shavings and was fiddling with them. 'Without I leave their service and get wed, of course. We might be able to, you think, if things go right? Only I got to give them six weeks' notice, when we do.'

There was a slender ash tree growing near the stile, and Frank thrust his penknife deep into the trunk. 'Ready to do that, are 'ee? I think my family would be pleased to have you come – 'cepting for my father – that's the truth of it. There isn't anything that pleases him these days. And I aren't sure it's fair to let you in for that.'

'Still fretting for that contract?' Maisie said, winding the sliver of wood around her finger like a ring.

He didn't seem to notice. 'I wonder sometimes if it's something more – he's gone to nothing but a pile of aches. No energy for

230

anything but finding fault. Only thing that seems to give him pleasure these days is his pipe – and even then it's like as if it's too much bother to light it half the time.'

Maisie nodded. 'That's just 'ow poor Miss Edwards is, up at the house. Only with her, it's her embroidery. Texts and chairs and all sorts, used to be – never an idle moment – and now she doesn't hardly touch it. And she doesn't eat enough to feed a fly. If I was the mistress, I'd ask that nice young Mr James to come and take a look when he gets back from London. After all, he'll be a doctor soon.'

Frank was struggling to retrieve the knife – he'd thrust it in with so much force it was defeating him. 'Still hoping to court Miss Lucy, is he, then?'

Maisie shook her head. 'I'm not so sure, after this last weekend. He was in some taking after Maskins went. I found him in the drawing room, staring in the fire – all by himself and mad as anything. 'Lucy must have led that Maskins on,' he said to me, 'I've seen her doing it. And other people, too. Makes me wonder if she really wants me after all.' Well, what on earth was I to say to that? Course, it wasn't really meant for me at all – he was that hurt he was worrying aloud.'

Frank glanced round from his tussle with the knife. 'So, what did you say?'

'Just told him that his father wanted him upstairs, and he went stomping up. I b'lieve he made a four at cards until the carriage came – though it was clear he didn't want to in the least. And even then Mr Tregenza and the girls didn't come and join them till I brought the supper in. Ooh, it was a dreadful evening. Everybody pretending there was nothing wrong – but all of them gone peculiar and withdrawn and Miss Lucy looking like she'd burst into tears if you offered her a ha'penny for her pains. Worse than Newlyn ice-works for a chilly atmosphere. I didn't know where to put myself.'

'Well, I know where to put you.' Frank had rescued his pocket knife by now, and suddenly he slid down from the stile and looked teasingly at her. 'I'll roll you in that patch of stickle-back over there – like we used to do when we were small!' He nodded to a corner of the field, where the sticky weed was making a soft green blanket on the ground. It was a game that children often played – to pull the strands and throw them so they stuck on to your clothes, or better still to roll you in the softness of the plant.

She caught his mood, and playfully evaded him as she jumped down from her perch. 'You'll have to catch me first,' she cried, and set off running helter-skelter in the grass, with Frank flapping after her in hot pursuit. His cap fell off, but he just came laughing on, and when she stopped breathlessly beside the wall, he caught her round the shoulders and the waist and carried her laughing and squealing back across the field, kicking her feet and giggling like a six-year-old. 'Oh, don't, Frank, don't!' She was laughing so much that she could scarcely speak. 'What ever are you like?'

He held her half-suspended over the chosen spot, and she clung to his neck. 'Don't drop me!'

He pulled her tight, and showered kisses on her laughing face. 'That better?'

'Much!'

And then he dropped her in the stickle-back. Gently, of course, but dropped her all the same.

She struggled to her feet. 'You...! Now look what you've done.' She was still laughing, and was picking burrs and sticky-backs from her skirt and hems. 'All over bits I'll be when I get in. And Mrs Lovett frowning at me like a thunder cloud.'

'Well, I can't help it. You needed cheering up.' Frank tugged at a strand or two himself. 'But, talking about thunder clouds, look out across the sea. We'd best be getting 'ome. Be here in quarter of an hour, that will, and you haven't got a shawl.'

'Oh darnie!' Maisie muttered, and she didn't mean the stocking-mend. (It was a strong expletive for a chapel girl, and Frank looked quite surprised.) 'How does that always 'appen, out of a clear blue sky – just when I got an unexpected hour or two with you?'

Frank was already hurrying to fetch Brownie and the cart, which had been tethered underneath a tree beside the lane. The old horse had been patiently chomping at the grass, and seemed as reluctant as Maisie was to go. But 'Come on,' Frank was calling, 'no good lingering. The wind is blowing up.'

It was. It was blowing half a gale before they got back to the house, and the first hard spots of rain were falling so they stung. She had to snatch a hasty kiss and hurry off inside.

'See you Sunday, then, as usual?' Frank called after her. 'Did you say you're free? With it being Bank Holiday weekend and all?'

She hunched her shoulders up, as if to guard her ears. 'Have to be next week, my 'andsome, I'm wanted all weekend. Like I said, I had this afternoon in lieu: Miss Lucy's off to see Miss Annabelle today, and the master and the mistress have gone in to Penzance, so it's only Miss Elenner's and Miss Edwards's trays to do for tea, and Rosie can manage that for once. Good thing you had that delivery out Nanvedra way – I'm some glad I managed to run into you and make the most of it.'

He nodded, and turned his jacket collar up. She stood and watched him, from the shelter of the porch until the cart had vanished round the bend. She oughtn't to have done it – Mrs Lovett came out with a pail, and made a song and dance to find her there. Then when she got inside she had to go and change her blouse and skirt, because the ones she had were soaking with the rain.

The tea party with Annabelle was not a lot of

234

fun. There was no prospect now of sharing wedding plans, and although she made as much of Maskins as she could ... 'I did have a proposal – such a dreary man – though of course he was quite wealthy and a doctor too but, my dear, one cannot be too careful whom one weds...' it did not have at all the same effect.

So when Anna gave her a conspiratorial grin, and said, 'Well, I did tell you I had exciting news. Actually I am betrothed myself – though you are not to whisper it to anyone, until Papa has put the announcement in the newspapers and written to everyone in the family,' Lucy was hard put to it to smile.

'And who is the lucky fellow?' She put down her cup.

Anna laughed. 'You'll never guess. It's someone you know. Someone who was with us at Celestine's birthday ball.' She looked at Lucy with a quizzical air.

It could not be Simon. Lucy shook her head.

Anna had that secret glow that came from confidence. 'Strangely enough, he is a doctor too – or will be by the time he comes back. He's been away for several years at University.'

Lucy found her mouth had gone unaccountably dry. 'Not ... not ... surely not James Morrison?' She had brought her new bonnet up to show and she was fiddling with the strings.

Annabelle gave her dreadful little laugh.

(Strange to remember how Lucy had copied it.) 'Oh, no, not *him*. There was a time, when I was very young, when Celestine was keen on him, but I have always thought him rather – I don't know – ordinary and a little dull. No, this is Rupert – you remember him? His father is a doctor over at St Just. Papa was rather scornful when Rupert asked him first, but in the end he changed his mind. It may not be an ancient family but there are good connections on his mother's side, and doctors are regarded as quite respectable these days. Rupert has good prospects, that's another thing – and as the only son he stands to do quite nicely when his father dies.'

Lucy looked at her friend in disbelief. 'You make it sound like making a bargain in a shop. You must be a little bit in love with him?'

Some of the sparkle went from Anna's face. 'Well, naturally. I mean – I'm very fond of him. But family and financial matters are important, too. I could never be one of these people that you hear about in songs, who run off with a gypsy, or anything like that. No, Rupert is eminently sensible for me, and we shall be very happy, I am sure. We propose to have the wedding at St Evan church and I want you to be an attendant for me, if you will, along with cousin Rachel – whom I suppose I have to ask.'

Lucy swallowed once or twice at this, but Anna didn't wait for a response. 'Celestine had crêpe de chine and swansdown, so I shan't be wearing that, but I thought perhaps Chantilly lace and figured silk? I've found the dearest little pattern, with a matching bolero...' and on she went, for what seemed like hours and hours while Lucy could only nod and smile.

'I shall not have a wedding bonnet but just a circle of fresh flowers and a net headdress trimmed with lace – it is quite the thing these days.' Anna produced a copy of a ladies' magazine and showed a picture of the sort of thing she meant.

Lucy found something admiring to say, though she had to grit her teeth. This should have been her conversation, she thought bitterly.

'And when I'm married, you shall come and visit us. We won't be far away. Rupert will join his father in the practice at St Just, and of course he will be coming home in just a week or two. He's coming down with your old friend James Morrison, I think. He writes they are bringing a Miss Judge with them, as well. I wondered if you'd ever heard of her.'

Lucy frowned. 'Miss Judge?' One of Rupert's London relations perhaps, though James had never mentioned this projected trip. 'I don't believe I have.'

'Nor have I.' Anna leaned forward confidentially. 'Some friend of James's as I understand, and not all that respectable, from the sound of it. Rupert says he's often seen her hanging round his rooms – though he won't tell me anything much else about her, even when I ask. He seems to think it's a terrific joke.'

Lucy was scarcely listening. 'A friend of James's, you say? Hanging round his rooms?' There was a horrid cold tingle running down her spine and the world seemed to have slowed. Everything – the long-case clock, the stuffed birds in the case beside the window, even the tree-branch on the other side – seemed to be stopping as if to hold its breath.

Anna broke the silence with another of her laughs. 'I know, intriguing isn't it? And it's been going on for years. I thought that you might know about her, since your families are such friends.'

Lucy could only shake her head. 'Perhaps she is an older maiden lady, after all. I'm sure I should have heard...'

'No, a young lady, – Rupert told me that. Though it seems she's not a pretty one – I asked him and it made him laugh out loud. She's very thin and bony and has no accomplishments, but James has spent a lot of time with her. Perhaps she is one of these bluestockings you hear about these days – she's helped them with their studies, Rupert says. But it's most mysterious. He wouldn't tell me who her family was, just said she had nobody living in the world, then slapped his leg and hooted as if that was the funniest thing he'd ever heard. And when I tried to chide him for being so unkind, he just laughed again and said he'd introduce me when James brought her down – but he refused to promise to bring her here for tea. Said it would not be suitable, and when I saw her, I would understand. Can you imagine?'

Lucy didn't wish to imagine anything. She felt she would burst if she was forced to stay another minute in that room, and it was with undisguised relief that she heard the merciful rumble of a carriage in the drive. Edgar was a little early – she had told him four o'clock and the long-case in the corner was still showing quarter to – but it offered her the opportunity she sought. She had already risen to her feet and was tying her bonnet ribbons underneath her chin. 'Yes, I'm truly sorry, Annabelle, I think my carriage is here. It has been such fun, as well. We must get together very, very soon and make plans for the dresses. Thank you for the tea.'

'Oh, but surely you can stay a little longer. Just another slice of cake?'

Lucy looked around her for a plausible excuse, and found one through the window. 'There's a horrid black cloud coming, and I'll have to hurry home. Don't bother with the bell-pull, I can see myself out.' But her friend had already rung for the maid, and a few minutes later Lucy found herself outside.

There was no sign of the carriage. It couldn't have been hers – most likely someone delivering something to the house. But she was so disturbed she hardly cared. She was simply glad to be in the open air again. She would start to walk, that was the thing to do, although her pretty boots and bonnet were not made for that. She wanted to be alone and have some time to think, and she would be bound to cross Edgar and the carriage on the road.

But as she walked she found that thinking was impossible. Her mind refused to contemplate the truth of what she'd heard. Miss Judge and James? James, with whom she'd had an understanding all this time? To whom, if it had not been for Maskins, she would now be formally engaged?

Had she after all had a remarkable escape?

She was tramping through the muddy margins, oblivious of her hems, but a sudden gust of icy cold forced her to pay attention to the rising storm. Soon she was struggling to keep her bonnet on, and having to lean forward to walk at all against the wind. She glanced up. Soon there would be heavy raindrops and her bonnet would be spoiled, and she would arrive home drowned and dripping like a rat – even if Edgar came past in a little while and picked her up. Questions would undoubtedly be asked.

Why had she been such an idiot? And now there was something coming – not Edgar, this was a lighter vehicle coming from behind and very quickly too. Doubtless it would splash her as it passed. She huddled in a gateway, wishing most heartily that she had stayed at Annabelle's and waited for her carriage after all.

'Lucy Tregenza, as I am alive.' The trotting hooves had stopped.

She looked up. Simon Robinson was sitting in his gig, grinning at her as he always had. He leaned over and reached out a hand. 'Come on. There's going to be a storm.' He saw her hesitate. 'What are you waiting for? You'll get drenched, and spoil your pretty dress. And that would never do. I'd better take you home.'

Somehow – because of the stories of Miss Judge, perhaps – she didn't hesitate for very long.

Chapter Four

Mother was having another of her ladies' tea parties, and this time Helena had decided to be there. It was one thing Samuel Maskins had done for her, she thought – given her the confidence to handle things like this. She would not attempt the cake and sandwiches, but Maisie had instructions to just half-fill the cup, and by having the little table placed exactly on her right Lena could manage a social drink of tea. She still found it demanding, and she would not stay down long, but it made a refreshing change from all those afternoons upstairs.

She was startled to feel a firm hand on her arm, which almost caused her to overturn the cup. Small plump fingers took a determined grip, and the smell of Mrs Passemore-Jenkins' wafted over her: lavender, mothballs and sal volatile.

'I hear you are to do some music teaching, then?' There was no mistaking the condescending tone. 'I'm sure that's really very brave of you, and how far-sighted of your father to permit it, too.' The fingers gave another, unexpected squeeze.

Helena felt discreetly for the table edge and put the imperilled teacup safely down. 'He wasn't very pleased at first,' she said. 'But he's come round to it.'

In fact, the decision had been greeted with dismay by both her parents when she first mooted it: Mama pretended that she thought it was a joke – though she clearly didn't, from her tone of voice – while Papa got very formal and tried for several hours to talk her out of it. It was Lucy in the end who changed his mind, by saying tactlessly, 'Oh, Papa, what does it matter now? I thought the same as you did, when I first heard of it, but you can see that Lena's set her heart on this – and thanks to Mr Maskins she's already been disappointed quite enough this week. Besides, it will help to take her mind off things.' It was so clumsy that it had made Lena go hot with embarrassment, but it had done the trick.

However, she could scarcely say this to Mrs Passemore-Jenkins, who was now leaning forward so confidentially that Helena could feel the flutter of the feather in her hat. 'I'm sure that Celestine would be glad to have you come and teach her little one in a year or two – you know that they are thinking of moving back this way? Celestine does miss her family so. In fact I got Simon to bring her back with me the other day, because I'd heard about a property nearby that might have suited them – but Simon took a look at it and decided not to buy. We only missed your sister by a whisker, I believe. I was hoping I might see her here this afternoon, but I am to be disappointed, I perceive.'

Helena frowned. 'But surely she's gone out with Annabelle?'

Mrs Passemore-Jenkins gave a laugh. 'Oh, I don't think so, dear. Anna is entertaining Simon's sister, I believe. Talking about wedding outfits I expect. I imagine Lucy told you about dear Annabelle? We're announcing her engagement to that young Rupert Neill. Such a very nice and sensible young man. Lucy is to be an attendant to the bride.'

Lucy had said very little about that afternoon, in fact, except that she had found it a rather dull affair – though that verdict was delivered in the tone of voice which usually meant that she was secretly extremely pleased with things. 'Ah, that explains it,' Helena observed. 'I guessed there was a secret, but I did not know what it was!'

Mrs Passemore-Jenkins relinquished Lena's arm. 'It is very good of dear Lucille to have been so discreet.' The woman sounded like a cat, oleaginous with cream. 'But it's in the papers and the banns will soon be read. Of course, one would have preferred a fellow with money of his own, someone who didn't need to have a trade – or a profession, as I suppose I ought to say – but in the circumstance...'

'The circumstance?' Surprise upon surprise! First that Lucy should have held her tongue, when she must have been bursting with excitement at her news: and now that Mrs Passemore-Jenkins spoke as if Annabelle was almost on the shelf and lucky to get an offer from anyone at all – instead of being only twenty-one and likely to inherit half her father's wealth. 'The circumstance?'

The feather had retreated suddenly, and Anna's mother gave a dismissive little laugh. 'The circumstance of his being such a splendid chap, I mean, and Anna being so very fond of him. Now, it has been delightful seeing you again – I'm so pleased you feel able to join us now and then, but there is your Aunt Edwards over there, and I really must go and have a word with her. She's sitting all alone and looks so very frail.' There was a creak – Helena remembered Lucy's description of the stays – and the mothballs and lavender retreated hastily.

Helena reached tentatively for the saucer edge, in the way that Samuel Maskins had shown her how, and was about to venture on another sip, when there was a disturbance from over by the door.

''Ere!' It was Maisie stumbling in, and

blurting out the words to the astonished guests. 'Madam, you'll never guess what's gone and 'appened now. The dairyman's just been 'ere – and 'e 'eard it in Penzance.'

'What is it, Maisie?' Mama's voice was crisp.

'Everybody's talking about it, in the town he says, and Mrs Lovett says you ought to know. And the master iddn't here, or I'd of told he first.' Emotion had made her quite forget to modify her speech.

'What is it, Maisie?' Mama said again.

Maisie didn't answer, except to sniff and gulp. It was clear that she was very close to tears.

'I think you'd better tell us.' Mama was gentle now.

'Well, madam, I'm some sorry, but it's them Germans, see. Gone and made us go to war, they have. And they foolish hooligans of men are cheering in the street!'

'Don't know what you're so worked up about, my girl.' Mrs Lovett put the rabbit on the table with a slap, and set about it with a skinning knife. 'Not as if you're going to have to fight. Be all over before Christmas, that's what the milkman said – and serve the jolly blighters right. I don't care if he is a cousin to the King – I don't trust that old Kaiser. Anyway, he doesn't seem to care: he's already declared war on the poor Tsar and Tsarina, as if they hadn't enough trials, poor things, what with losing to the Japanese and all those riots that they've had at home – and they are his blood relatives as well.' Snick, the knife made a slit beside each foot, and then ran up inside the skin, so that Mrs Lovett could peel it off the legs and then in one smooth motion right up to the head. 'Here, fetch me that big saucepan and put it on the range, so I can blanch the pieces and get on with this ragout. All this excitement's put me back no end, and I won't have it on the table if I don't look sharp.'

Maisie did as she was bid, filling the heavy saucepan and setting it to boil. She wasn't asked to help out in the kitchen as a rule, but after her outburst at the tea party she had been glad when all the visitors had gone and she was able to come down and escape. She'd made an exhibition of herself, she knew, and doubtless madam would have some words to say about the way she'd managed to startle all the guests. After her announcement they hadn't stayed for long.

'And now that bowl, so I can wash the carcass clean,' Mrs Lovett said, and so there was another struggle with the pump, and a big enamel basin to put on the tabletop – without spilling a drop of water on the way.

Maisie went through the motions like a wind-up toy. She couldn't say exactly why this war distressed her so: it wasn't likely to affect them here, and as Mrs Lovett said, it would hardly be for long. Britain was the strongest country in the world. It was only that the dairyman had brought her news of

Frank, who had apparently been cheering with all the rest of them. 'Must have had something to deliver to the railway, I suppose – but the news had spread like wildfire all around the town,' he said. 'The passengers on the trains were telling everyone. It'll be in the evening papers, but it hardly needs to be. Everybody's heard. Anyone who's got a telephone had been rung to say, and people were rushing out into the street. Surging up Market Jew Street like a school of fish, they were – all singing the national anthem and swearing to enlist. And there was your Frank Carter in the midst of it.'

Enlist to be a soldier and go overseas to fight? Frank? But he wouldn't, would he? Couldn't. He had his family to support – and there was her to think about as well. Course he never would. She shrugged the thought away. It was only a bit of silliness. Carried away with all the crowds and that – and it wasn't as if they'd want a carter when it came to it. If England really needed him, it would be another thing – you had to serve your country if you were wanted to – but it wasn't going to come to that.

She let herself be comforted by this idea and fetched the cloth for Mrs Lovett to dry the rabbit with before the housekeeper had even asked.

Mrs Lovett cocked an eye at her. 'Well, if you've stopped looking like a mourner at a funeral, you can go upstairs again and take Miss Helena her bit of sandwich tea. The egg-mimosa ones are on the plate – and there's a bit of her favourite cake as well which I've put by for her.'

Maisie nodded. 'Poor soul never had a bite to eat all mortal afternoon. Looking beautiful, she was, in that new lilac dress, but she can't see it to appreciate, and people get embarrassed when they talk to her and don't know what to say, so I can't see how it's any fun for her. Don't know what the pleasure is, but she seems keen to try. I suppose it makes her feel a bit more normal, that's the thing.'

'Well, get that tray up, quickly as you can, and you can come and give me a hand down here.' Mrs Lovett was cutting the rabbit into pieces now. 'I sent Rosie down to Crowdie's to get some extra eggs a half an hour ago. I don't know why she's taking all day to get back.'

Maisie smiled. She had a good idea. Rosie had got very friendly with one of Crowdie's sons. But all she said was, 'Thought we had a dozen in the pantry in a bowl?'

The housekeeper fetched a little sigh. 'Well, I'll be needing eight for breakfast, and with all them sandwiches, I'd only left enough. Then mistress came down when you were showing out the guests and asked me if I'd bake another cake first thing, for tea tomorrow afternoon. The Morrisons are calling in, straight after they've picked Mr James up from the railway train. Don't know what the hurry is, since he's coming home for good. All afire to see Miss Lucy, I suppose.'

She dropped the last of the rabbit pieces in to blanch, and picked up the slotted spoon to take the first ones out again. She was unusually chatty for a change. 'I hear they've got to take the carriage down, just to carry all the stuff he's bringing home. Great pile of bones and everything, the mistress said. Well, I hope he doesn't bring them here and terrify Miss Lucy, that's all I can say.'

Maisie laughed. 'I won't be here to see it, even if he does. You haven't forgotten it's my free afternoon?'

'Now would I be likely to forget a thing like that? Never here when wanted, that's the thing with you. Though I dare say wc shall cope. Edgar can serve at tea time for a change. Now are you going to take that tray upstairs or not? Otherwise the poor lady won't have chance to eat them before it's dinner time.'

Maisie took the sandwiches and scuttled off with them. By this time she had forgotten all about the war.

Lucy heard the news as she was walking home. Walking! It must be better than a mile, and her best new button boots were pinching her. But she refused to get back up into the gig, even when Simon drew up next to her and begged and teased and wouldn't go away. And when he dared to lay a hand on her, as if to compel her to climb up with him again, she tore herself away and clambered over a stile into a field. There were people pulling broccoli close beside the path, so he could not follow her without making a public spectacle of them both.

Or course, she should never have agreed to have him pick her up at all, but he had made it sound so charming and innocuous. A little ride out in the carriage, just for old times' sake, to one of Rachel's charity affairs. And then, when she had done it – excused herself from Mama's tea party as well! – just when she was smiling ruefully and offering him her fingertips to kiss, as a sort of wistful talisman of what might have been – he had sprung it on her that there was no charity afternoon at all.

'Simon!' She knew her voice was very sharp. 'But you said that Celestine and Annabelle were there! I told the family so. And Mrs Passemore-Jenkins will be at Mother's now. What if it comes out that I've been telling lies?'

He flicked a disrespectful finger underneath her chin. 'Oh, you'll think of something, Lucy. You're a clever girl. Anyway, why should it come to that? My mother-in-law will be too busy telling everyone about "dear Anna's wedding plans", I'm sure.'

She jerked her head away. 'But, Simon, that's the point. If they're talking about Anna it will come around to me, and the fact that I'm supposed to be out with her this afternoon. At Rachel's charity. That is what you told me, you can't pretend it's not.'

He didn't look repentant. 'I didn't tell you

anything of the kind. I said that Annabelle was going to be with Rachel all this afternoon, and that's absolutely true. She and Celestine have asked my sister to come and have some tea, and talk about what kind of wedding outfit she will consent to wear. That is why I took the carriage out – I picked her up and I was driving her, though I did not go in myself.' He gave her the smile she used to find so irresistible. 'I try to avoid my estimable sister-in-law as much as possible these days – she's never really forgiven me for choosing Celestine – and I thought you would appreciate the chance to be with me.'

Lucy was furious. 'You deliberately misled me, that is what you mean! You didn't give a thought to me at all – how I was to manage when I got back home and it was clear that I had not been where I said I was.'

He had pulled the carriage up beside a field gate now. It was a place where they had often stopped before, a pretty spot, with a long view down across the fields towards the sea. But he didn't even glance at it today; he was leaning back and looking at her with his head on one side and a peculiar mocking expression on his face. 'Perhaps you'll have to tell them you were out with me?'

She was quite appalled. 'Well, of course I can't tell them. What would people think?'

'They would think that you wanted to be with me. And that was what I supposed as well. You always used to be quite eager for my company, I recall.'

'That was different. You're a married man.'
'All the same, you seemed quite keen to come.' He tipped her face back and grinned down at her. 'Tell them that I offered to take you for a spin. I don't mind if you don't.'

He was teasing, surely. 'You're not being serious. Of course I mind.' Lucy was very close to tears. 'Don't you care anything about me at all?'

He reached out and pulled her to him – holding her, although she fought away. 'Of course I care. I like you very much. You're very pretty, and a lot of fun. What have I ever done to make you think that I don't care?' He was – she blushed even now as she remembered it – trying to undo her bodice buttons as he spoke, and putting his hand in underneath her dress.

She struggled upright, and a button burst. (How was she ever going to explain that to Mama?) 'How dare you, sir!' Like something in a melodrama. She almost smacked his face.

He laughed. 'Come on, you like it really. Everybody does.' He tried to take her in his arms again.

'Well, I'm not everyone!' He wouldn't let her go.

'I love it when you pretend to struggle, you enchanting thing.' And he was pressing his lips against her neck and throat. 'But I know you like it. I can feel your heart beat fast.'

It was fear, not excitement, that made it thud like that. She managed to twist her head away from him and take a long deep breath, and with it a kind of inspiration came to her.

'Well, not here, Simon,' she muttered. 'Anyone might come. Drive further down near Crowdie's farm, there's that copse of trees down in the valley there.' Anything to make him take her a little nearer home. He'd have to get down from the cart to hitch the horse somewhere, and that would give her an opportunity.

He did permit her to sit up, at that, and urged the horses to walk on again. 'That's more like it, Lucy. I knew you'd come around. You won't regret it, I can promise you – you know I always wanted you that way. And life's so dreary nowaways, with blessed Celestine. Always feeling sickly, and won't let a fellow near.'

So this was a makeshift because he could not have his wife? Lucy felt she could have murdered him at that moment, but she forced herself to smile. 'And you can help me to think of what to say to my mama. You are so clever at finding an excuse. What am I to say when I get in?' Flattery would put him off his guard and make it easier when the moment came.

It seemed to be successful. Simon smiled. 'As near the truth as possible, that's what I'd advise,' he said. 'Annabelle is entertaining Rachel to tea this afternoon, and I supposed you were invited too – since you are to be the other bride's attendant as I understand. I volunteered to come and pick you up. You

253

weren't paying attention – as you often don't you know – and thought it was one of Rachel's charity affairs until we took the lane up to the Passemore-Jenkins's house.'

'But I've been out for half an hour at least. I would have gone back straight away if I'd found that was the case.' She would pretend to do him the courtesy of considering his words – in fact she found that she was doing so. She really would have to offer some excuse, and she could think of no plausible alternative herself.

He laughed again. 'But of course, you decided that you'd prefer to walk. You were a bit embarrassed by your own mistake and it was such a lovely day. After all, you set off to walk from there the other day – and would have done, if I hadn't happened to come by and pick you up.'

The effrontery of it took her breath away. She was to be embarrassed by her own mistake, was she? But she controlled her temper long enough to say, 'Well, you can stop here, Simon, over by those trees.'

He did so eagerly enough, and got down – as she knew he would – to tie the horses to a makeshift hitching post. 'Now then, little Lucy, we should have time enough...' Too quick! He was already turning back to her, his arms outstretched to jump her down.

She swung her legs around as if to drop into his grasp, but as he came to catch her she aimed her foot at him and caught him a nasty blow beneath the chin.

He staggered back and clapped a palm to it. 'What the...? You little vixen, you've made me bleed.' But she had seized the instant and had slithered down, and while he was still fumbling for a handkerchief, she ducked away from him, and was running wildly down the lane towards the stile. He took a pace or two in vague pursuit and then he changed his mind. He went back to get the sulky and followed her in that.

It did not take him long to catch up with her, of course, and after that he had tried every trick he knew – threats, cajoling, teasing – everything. 'Lucy, little Lucy, let's forget all this. Obviously I misunderstood your intentions. Just let me drive you home, and we can still be friends.'

And she had found the breath from somewhere to retort, 'I'll never go anywhere with you again. I can't believe it! You, a married man? What sort of girl do you suppose I am?'

He was driving close beside her as she said all this, forcing her to walk up on the verge along the wall so the nettles stung her legs beneath her skirts, but she refused to turn around and look at him. Instead she kept her eyes fixed straight in front of her, and addressed her answer to the empty air.

'The sort of girl who likes me – and you know you did. Would you have made such a scene when we were driving out before?'

This time she did whirl angrily about. 'You never behaved in such a dreadful way!'

'But I was often tempted, and you must know I was. And you encouraged me. Wanted me to kiss you and all that sort of thing. What was I to think? You'd go out walking on the moors with me, without a chaperone, and tell your family you were somewhere else. And never mind what people might have thought.'

That was uncomfortably true, she knew, and the knowledge didn't improve her present state of mind. She didn't answer. He looked her in the eyes and smiled.

'Two kindred spirits, free as air – that's what we used to say.' He leaned down from the sulky and tried to seize her arm, saying knowingly, 'Of course I would have made a play for you. Come on, little Lucy, you are not a fool. You must have realized how I felt for you. You're a damn attractive little filly when you try.'

'I realize what a total fool I *was*.' She snatched herself away. 'And anyway, it's all quite different now. You are married, and I'm to be betrothed. No, don't look at me like that. It's true.'

He was still smiling in that infuriating, disbelieving way. 'Strange that neither Anna nor her mother seem to know.'

'It has not yet been announced, but it will be very soon. James Morrison has asked me, and I've told him that I will. Now you have had your answer, kindly go away, before I call some passer-by to help. And mind I don't tell Papa about all this when I get home –

256

and Celestine and Annabelle as well. Or James! He would come and punch your nose for you.'

He laughed, but he did withdraw his grasp, and drive a little further from the wall. 'I do not really think that you'll do that, my dear. I'd have to tell them what good friends we'd been. Doubtless your little maid could bear out what I said, and what would happen to your reputation if people learned about our little private walks? Your precious James would never have you then!'

She was about to say 'You wouldn't!' but she realized that he would. She looked up towards him and he leaned down again and tried to make another grab for her. That was the moment she had snatched away to climb the stile and take this path across the broccoli field. She was still pink and troubled, and she slowed herself, trying to compose herself and look more ladylike.

The pickers straightened up to watch her come, a motley group in boots and dusty clothes. She prepared to walk past them with her head held high, but as she approached the oldest man stepped out to bar her way.

He was a grizzled fellow with a tattered kerchief tied around his neck, stripped to his shirtsleeves so that his ancient braces were on view. He smiled, and for a moment Lucy feared she'd walked from the frying pan straight into the fire, but he simply waved a broccoli head at her and said, before dropped it into the great wicker basket at his feet,

'Heared the news, 'ave 'ee, my maid? Some awful iddn't uh?'

''S all right, my lover, don't you pay no 'eed to him.' Another of the pickers flung a scornful look at him. 'Going to teach they Germans a thing or two, we are, and serve them right.'

The old man shook his head. 'Never so easy as they think it is – you mark my words, my maid. Going to be five minutes when we fought the Boers, they said – and of course it never was. But there's no help for it. We're in with the French and Ruskies – that's one good thing, I s'pose. Government announced this morning, seemingly – Crowdie stopped to tell us when he came back from Penzance. In all the London papers – you'll 'ear when you get home.'

Lucy had stopped, despite herself. 'You mean there's really going to be a war?' She'd heard the rumours that it might come to that, but she'd not believed a word.

The fat woman with the headscarf showed her snaggled teeth. 'No "going to be" about it, my bird. It's already 'appening. Crowdie says there's been a run on all the banks in town – people wanting to get their money out and turn it into gold.' She laughed, plunging her hands into the pockets of her ample overall – it was "over" several jumpers and a ragged woollen skirt – and pulled out a brass halfpenny. 'I got mine, you see?'

There was a general laugh at this, in which Lucy briefly joined, and then they turned back to their work and Lucy hurried on. It took her quite a half an hour to get back home again, and by that time her hems were dusty and her feet were killing her. She was tired, limping and bedraggled when Maisie let her in.

But there was one advantage of this wretched war. The whole house was abuzz with it when she got home. The rest of the family was together in the drawing room. Papa had all the papers and was looking serious, and reading little bits to Mama and Helena. Lucy looked in for a minute, to say, 'I'll be down in just a minute, when I've had time to change,' and Papa just nodded and went on with *The Times*, all about how the Empire was rallying to the call.

Nobody asked any questions about where she might have been, or noticed the missing button on her dress.

Chapter Five

James had been planning what to say since Exeter. He wondered how Lucy and his family would react. It seemed a huge adventure – and of course it was a big responsibility as well – but after thinking about it overnight he'd made his mind up now.

It was Rupert Neill who'd brought things to a head. They were sitting in a first-class carriage, just the two of them. Miss Judge, with all the other baggage, was in the luggage van, wrapped and crated so the porters didn't stare. The portly vicar who'd been sitting opposite had got off at Newton Abbot and now the two boys had the compartment to themselves.

They had a hamper of refreshments, and when they'd emptied it Rupert moved over to the seat opposite and took out his faithful Woodbines. James lit up his pipe. (It was an affectation he had taken up quite recently, in fact. It made him feel more manly and judicious, puffing it, though he often found it difficult to keep the thing alight.) They puffed in companionable silence for a bit.

'The vicar's left his paper in the luggage rack.' Rupert took it down and glanced at it.

He made a little face. 'Nothing but the war. The Germans have got a million men already mobilized – makes you wonder where they get them from.' He put the sheets aside. 'You know, if it wasn't that I've promised to marry Annabelle, I'd have gone out and volunteered myself. A lot of fellows did. Says here they've already had thousands signing on.'

'And what about the miners and their families you used to talk about?' James lit the pipe again, looking at his friend, and cradling the match.

Rupert was blowing fresh smoke clouds in the air. 'A month or two won't make much difference, in the scheme of things. One can always come back to do those things afterwards. Father will still be there, like he always was – he's managed very well without me there for years and years. He doesn't really need me, not yet at any rate, though obviously the practice will come to me when he retires.' He pursed his lips and formed a perfect smoke ring, then watched it wafting till it reached the roof. 'All the fellows were talking about it in the bar last night – when you were packing Miss Judge into her box – and most of them were thinking that they ought to volunteer.'

James nodded. 'Uncle Bertie came to say goodbye, and he was saying very much the same, that if he was younger he'd volunteer himself. Though there isn't much call for obstetrics in a war, I suppose.'

'That's what you think.' Rupert laughed.

261

'My father says that, last time, even in St
Just the birth rate rose quite sharply nine
months after the Cornish regiments went off
– though they were going all the way to South
Africa, of course, and nobody could tell when
they'd be back. This time...' He stubbed out
the cigarette and began to stare out of the
window fixedly, as though the sight of sheep
and cows was fascinating him. He was
struggling with some emotion, James realized
with surprise

James squinted at him with one eye as he
inhaled. 'A penny for them?' he murmured,
when his friend said nothing more.

Rupert got up and turned to face him,
leaning on the door. 'Fact is, I'm not to marry
until well into the New Year, old chap. You
think I should offer my services to the army,
anyway? Shouldn't feel that I was doing my
duty otherwise.' He took another cigarette
and bounced the end against his palm. 'I
don't suppose you'd...?'

'Go with you? Is that what you mean?' He
found that he'd stopped sucking and let the
pipe go out.

Rupert turned back from the window and
picked the paper up. 'I'm sorry, old chap, I
had no right to ask. Of course, it's different
for you. You wouldn't just be signing on like I
would have to do, and take your chances
where the army sent you to. You've got
connections – if you want to go, you'd find
someone to put in a good word for you.'

James laughed. 'That's just what I was

talking to Uncle Bertie for. They've got hundreds – thousands – signing up to fight, but they'll be wanting doctors in a little while, you see if they don't. Where there is fighting there are always wounded, that's the way of things. Bertie says one ought to make an approach to the Medical Corps direct. He knows one or two people at the top, he says – trained with one of the senior officers – and might be able to pull a string or two. We've only got our practical papers to complete. He might persuade them to rush us through. After all there is a war on.' The pipe was dead as Dido. He struck another match and tried again. 'I could ask him, I suppose. You're quite serious? About going in for it?'

'If they'll have me, yes. It's been on my mind all night.' Rupert riffled papers, and put them down again. 'Several of the others are already signing up, and one wants to do one's bit. But you don't have to feel obliged, of course, and I wasn't asking favours. I ought not to have said. Forgive me, old chap, it was most colossal cheek.'

James got his pipe to draw at last, and sat back in his seat. 'Funny thing is,' he said at last, 'I was going to ask you the very same, but I didn't have the nerve to do it, when it came to it – since you were recently engaged, you know.'

Rupert was staring at him, like a startled fish. 'You were?' He jumped up and stretched out his hand to James, who rose and shook it, rather formally. 'Then we're agreed. My dear old fellow!' He slapped James on the back. 'This is marvellous! Calls for some bubbly. Could we arrange to get some, do you think? I'll find the guard. The dining car, perhaps?' And he rushed out into the corridor and disappeared from view.

They had rumbled into Plymouth before Rupert came back, flushed with triumph, and brandishing two glasses and a bottle of champagne. He brushed aside James's questions about where he'd got it from, and poured two hefty servings. 'A toast!' He was drunk already, with the idea of it. 'To comrades in arms, and to Uncle Bertie too. And damnation to the Germans!' He raised his glass on high.

James was more thoughtful. 'What about the girls? Annabelle and Lucy, they are bound to be upset. Lucy has already waited several years for me. I have been thinking very carefully about what to say to her.'

'They'll be proud of us, what else? Going to serve our country!' Rupert was recharging his already-empty glass. 'To the ladies, then, God bless them.'

James drank the toast, with pleasure, but he said musingly, 'In any case, I don't suppose the army will want us straight away. Uncle Bertie said it could take months and months before they realize how much they need our services – though they are already planning how they'll handle volunteers.'

Rupert put his glass down on the armrest and leaned back. 'Months and months? It will all be over by that time, in any case.'

'Well, that's what he seems to think. And if they need us, they can call on us. Make you an acting officer, he thinks that's what they'll do – give you a rank, so there isn't any doubt about your authority and who you have to take your orders from.'

Rupert was nodding. 'It would be a disappointment, though, if we didn't get to it. But I suppose you're right. Better to offer them our skills than just go out and try to man the guns. Perhaps it's a good thing if they take the time to plan. It was a shambles last time, so my father says. He had an old patient who was wounded at Sebastopol – still had a piece of metal in his leg, and he was ninety-three. Kept him awake at night until he died – just because it wasn't attended to in time. Never enough doctors when you wanted them, he said, and often not even enough beds to put the wounded in. People lying in the open, and left to bleed to death. And apparently it happened in South Africa as well, and in Egypt in General Gordon's day.' He sighed. 'Thank Heaven it won't ever be like that again. They've got those proper nurses now, thanks to Miss Nightingale, and ether and chloroform and all sorts of things.'

James said nothing. He was thinking about how different it would be, performing surgery on a living man, instead of the corpses they had practised on. How messy, how alarming, and how much more worthwhile!

'Still thinking about young Lucy, then?'

Rupert's cheerful question cut across his thoughts. 'I'm sure she'll only think the more of you. And so will everyone.'

And oddly, it seemed that he was right. His mother was quite tearful at the station, when she first heard of it, before she hugged him and said he must do what he felt best, and his father coughed and muttered, 'Quite right too, my boy,' in a strangled voice. But they were proud of him, and were so ready to boast of him to the Tregenzas that he had to silence them, so that he could tell Lucy for himself.

He told her in the garden, where the fountain was, the same place where she had made her promise long ago. She was in a strange mood, clinging to his arm but being otherwise standoffish, in a way that made him quite disturbed about what he had to say.

He said it. 'Lucy, you will agree to marry me?'

She tossed her head. Her answer startled him. 'That would depend on what you have to say. About the friend that you brought down with you.'

'Rupert?' He was puzzled.

'Not Rupert, no. Your lady friend. Miss Judge.'

It made him laugh. 'Who told you about that? Oh, Annabelle, I suppose. No doubt Rupert thought it was a jape to mention it.'

'So you admit it?'

'Lucy, there is nothing to admit. Miss Judge is nothing but a silly joke – a name I gave a skeleton, that's all. My study skeleton, the kind that doctors have – I told you I'd bought one years ago. Rupert thought it funny that she should have a name. If you don't believe me, come and see. She's packed up in a crate on top of Pater's carriage now.'

She looked from underneath her lashes. 'You're telling me the truth?'

'Of course I am. How could we have romantic secrets, you and I? Dear, silly darling, have you been doubting me?' She must have been embarrassed, because she turned a rosy pink, which made him say with sudden fervour. 'Lucy, there is nobody but you. Do say you'll marry me. Your papa has agreed.'

'You know I will.' She hugged his arm. 'Even if he hadn't given his blessing, I'd decided that I'd run away with you.'

'Well, there'll be no need for that.' He laughed, and kissed her on the nose. And then the words he practised all those miles in his head: 'But, Lucy, before we tell our families, there is something quite serious that I need ask. Could you bear it if I went away again?' He saw her face fall and he hastened to explain. 'I mean offer my services to the army, as a surgeon if I can. My Uncle Bertie says he'll speak for me. They'll probably make me Lieutenant – that seems to be the way, and it's likely that I won't have to go for months. In fact, if it's over quickly, I might not go at all. But I felt that you should know in any case.'

He need not have worried. She hugged him even more. 'Mrs Lieutenant Morrison – I like the sound of that. Oh, James, you are so brave and wonderful.' She tipped her head on one side and looked coquettishly at him. 'Well, officer, you may give a kiss to your prospective bride and I shall start thinking about wedding outfits from this very day.' She hugged his arm again. 'Do you think you'll be able to wear your uniform?'

Helena was sitting in the music room – not playing, but sitting at the piano quietly – and she heard the two young people come chattering up the stairs. They sounded so happy with each other, she thought – James laughing and Lucy gaily kittenish. She waited until she heard the footsteps stop, and was already rising when they came into the room.

'Lena, you simply have to be the first.' Lucy came pattering over, and held her sister tight. She took Helena's hand and guided it to touch a dainty ring – two little stones and a bigger one between. 'Rubies and a diamond,' Lucy said. 'James brought it down from London specially.'

Helena tried to picture it. 'I'm sure it's beautiful.' She was going through the motions better than she'd feared: she had known that this was going to happen, and she'd braced herself for it, but a sort of cold numbness had taken hold of her. She found that she could smile and say the proper things. 'Best wishes then.' She raised the hand

and pressed it to her lips. 'And you too, James, of course.'

He had crossed to be beside her, she could smell the scent of him, and he briefly pressed her to him and kissed her on the cheek. 'Thank you, Helena. I shall be proud to be your brother.'

'I have always wanted one.' How did she manage to keep her voice so light? 'Though it is a little too late to take me birds-nesting, I fear.'

He chuckled. 'But you shall be my dearest sister, all the same. And any eggs I ever steal shall be for you.' But then the joke was over, and he moved away.

'Perhaps he'll bring some birds' eggs back from Germany for you.' Lucy's laugh was trilling. 'Did you know he plans to join the army when he can? He will be an officer and everything, he says.'

'I felt it was my duty,' James said, carefully. 'The army will need doctors, at least when we invade.'

'You know he won a prize for surgery?' Lucy was as proud as any mother. 'For being the best student in his year?'

'A gold medal and a certificate – it isn't quite a prize.' James was laughing but you could tell that he was flattered, too. 'And I did make a special study of trauma to the eye – not that I suppose that expertise will be much good to them. Much more likely to be pulling bullets out of wounded legs.'

'Oooh!' Lucy made her little-girl squeal of

horror and dismay. 'Do we have to talk of such awful things today? Almost as bad as that terrible Miss Judge that you tell me is wrapped up on your carriage in a crate.' She giggled.

The words meant nothing at all to Helena, and she must have looked perplexed because James said quickly, 'Don't be such a tease. I bought a skeleton in London and I've brought it down with me – that's all – but Lucy heard about it and thought I'd brought a girl.'

'It wasn't my fault,' Lucy protested, 'it was Annabelle. Rupert told her that you'd brought Miss Judge – and what was I to think of that?' She sniggered. 'Only do let's take her over, when I go to visit next. It would be such a jape to see her face.'

Something stirred in Helena's memory. 'So you did see Annabelle the other afternoon? I thought you said you did. Only her mother seemed to think that she was doing something else.'

There was a very awkward little pause. Then Lucy said, in a funny tone of voice. 'Oh, sometimes Annabelle hardly seems to know what's what these days. She asked me over just last week – on purpose for us two to be alone, she said – and all the time her sister and her mother were coming home that day. Excited about her wedding plans, I suppose.' She did the trilling laugh. 'Which I can understand! That reminds me – I suppose that I can't ask her to be attendant now –

270

because she will be married by that time.'

Lena began to say, 'It's not impossible...' but Lucy was already opening the door.

'Anyway, it's time we went and told our families the news. They will be wondering what's happening.'

Helena laughed. 'I think they'll have a very good idea. They were talking about it when I came in here, but I had a lady come to see me – wants me to teach her son – so I had to leave them to it. Oh, and on that subject, I've got something here for you.' She reached beneath the music on the piano top, felt for her leather purse and opened it.

'A sovereign?' James sounded startled.

'It's my own. My very own. Not given to me by Papa, like the money that you put in the collection plate at church, but the first money that I ever earned. It is not a fortune, I'm aware of that, but I want you to buy something as an engagement gift.' She sat down abruptly. She'd surprised herself. She hadn't planned to do that in the least, but suddenly it seemed important that she should.

'Oh, Lena, don't be silly, I shall have things from Papa. I can see that's rather special. You keep it for yourself.'

But James understood, as always. 'That's probably the nicest gift that we shall ever have, though I'm not sure that I want to spend it. More like a lucky talisman that we should always keep.' He came back to the piano and she felt the soft brush of his kiss upon her hair. 'Are you coming with us, when

271

we face the crowd? After all, your visitor has gone?'

So she allowed herself to be cajoled, and went to join the rest: toasted their health while Papa made a speech, laughed at the jokes from Mr Morrison, and listened to the mothers cooing with delight. Perhaps it was just as well she did, she had no time to brood, and by the time the Morrisons had piled into the carriage to go home at last, Helena had forgotten what she'd half-noticed at the time – how Lucy had evaded her question about meeting Annabelle.

'Well?' She was on the cart beside him, but he wasn't getting down. He had drawn up outside the house and was just sitting there, the reins hanging limply in his lap. 'What you waiting for? Your ma will have tea waiting, and we don't want it to spoil. The little ones will want to see you, 'sides.'

He nodded, but he didn't budge at all, just pulled his cap a little lower on his eyes.

She hadn't mentioned what the dairyman had said, but now she ventured it. 'Got something to tell me, have you? You've been strange all afternoon.' A pause. 'I heard about you in the town the other day.'

He pushed the cap up with his thumb and looked at her at last. 'What's that supposed to mean?'

'Marching up and down and threatening to enlist. 'Ere' – with sudden panic – 'You haven't gone and done it, and not said a word

272

to me?'

He swivelled his cap round back to front then, before he answered. 'Don't be so soft! Of course I 'aven't. Not that I wouldn't like to. Might have done it too – prove myself a man, defend my home and country like you're supposed to do. Lots of others went to send their name off, straight away. But how could Frank Carter do a thing like that? He's got a wife and house and family to support. Only they're not his, cause he can't afford to have his own. So no, I didn't. I'd have said so if I had.' He snatched his headgear off again and put it on his knee.

'Yes,' she said simply, 'I suppose you would. But you've been that grim and silent that there must be something up. Frank, what is it, lover? I can't bear for you to be cast down like this. Frowning blacker than a shaft, and nothing right since I set eyes on you.' She looked at him: he was still tugging morosely at his cap after that bitter outburst, as though it was the source of all his woes. 'Look, I know you don't want fussing, but you'd better out with it. Shouldn't have secrets, we two, if I'm to be your wife.'

He slapped his cap down on the seat so hard it made her start. It was the first time that she'd ever seen him do a thing like that. 'That's just it, Maisie. I don't see how it's ever going to be. No sooner do I put a bit aside – think I got it managed so we two can wed at last – than something else turns up and spoils it all.'

This was a worry she could understand. She almost felt relieved. 'What is it this time? Something wrong with Dobbin? I know he'd got a limp.'

'Oh, that was just because he'd cast a shoe. Got the blacksmith to 'un, and now he's right as rain. Doesn't help, of course, when you're putting money by – fellow wants paying and it isn't cheap – but that's just a pebble to the rest of it.' He sighed. 'No, it's Fayther – when was it ever anything but him? You know I was putting a little bit aside, under my mattress in an envelope?'

Maisie nodded. He had mentioned this before.

'When I got home Tuesday, the damty thing was gone. Could only have been Fayther, the children were at school. I tackled him about it, and do you know what he said? Said it was his carting business, when it came down to it – and if that was profit, it was due to him. Well, that made me madder'n a bull. I told him it was Brownie and my cart did half the work, and I'd only saved the money from my share, but he didn't care a hang. In any case it was too late by then. Turns out a neighbour told him about the damty war, and he'd gone off down the Tinners' and drank the lot of it. Came home impossible as well – like he belongs to do. Whoa, Brownie!' This last because the horse was getting restless as she stood, and he touched the reins to calm her – but he still did not get down. 'I'm sorry, Maisie. It iddn't fair on you.'

274

Maisie stretched out a hand and touched him on the knee. ' 'Tisn't your fault, Frankie. You never meant for that. 'Ere, I've thought of something. I'll tell 'ee what we'll do. I got a little box at home, it's got a key and all. Miss Lucy gave it to me years ago when someone broke the spring: used to have a tiny ballerina stood up and turned around – ever so pretty, though it lost its head – and you can still get a note or two of tune if you shake the box a bit. Thing is, it's got this space inside – supposed to be for beads and things, I think, she gave it me to put my hairpins in. So if you got a bit extra that you want to put aside, you give it me and we can lock it up. Your Fayther can't find it, if I've got it home.'

Some of the cloud had lifted from Frank's face at this. 'Sounds like a good idea to me. I s'pose it will be safe?'

She poked her tongue at him. 'Safer than your mattress, from the sound of it.'

It made him smile, a little ruefully, and he did get down at last and began to hitch the reins around the gatepost. 'Well, I suppose we'd better get inside. Davy's at the window and he's seen we're here. We'll try it your way, see how we get on.' He reached up to help her down and she dropped into his arms. He squeezed her briefly. 'Thing is, my 'andsome, it'll take us years, especially if we 'ave to start again. We got to get enough saved up to rent a room somewhere. Otherwise it's the same old problem as it ever was. If we got married, where are we to live? Can't hardly ask you to come home 'ere and sleep in an armchair.' He shook his head. 'Honestly, Maisie. Sometimes I despair. Better off if I did go in the army, probably. At least they pay you something and you get your keep.'

'Extra, if you're married.' She leant against him. 'Frank, we ought to have a plan. Set a date – let's say a year from now – and we'll get married then, whatever happens. Lenny will be old enough to get a job by then: perhaps he could even get somewhere living in, and then there would be a room for us – we could even share with Davy if we have to, for a bit. Or if the war's not over, perhaps Len could use the cart and you could go for a soldier like you wanted to.' She sighed. 'Pity Edgar doesn't decide he wants to volunteer. There'd be a vacancy at the Tregenzas' then. There's room enough in my bed for the pair of us, I'm sure, and it's not unknown for married couples to be taken on. Sometimes they even get a cottage of their own.'

'I couldn't do what Edgar does!'

So he was considering what she was saying, then? She rearranged her bonnet which he'd crushed in his embrace, and waved to Davy at the window pane. 'Of course you could! He mostly tends the horses – you'd be good at that – and drives the carriage when it's needed. You could do that in your sleep. Apart from that, it's only seeing to the master's drinks, putting out his clothes and things to wear and serving at the table now and then. I could soon learn you what to do

276

with that. I don't suppose Edgar knew when he began.'

'Well, he hasn't volunteered and isn't likely to, I s'pose.' He was taking up the reins again, ready to lead Brownie round and unhitch her from the cart – at least until it was time to take Maisie home again. 'And nothing's any use while Lennie's still at school, and Fayther's as useless as a wheelbarrow at sea. Here. Don't go in without me – it's likely he'll be there. It looks as if this damty war has shook him up a bit, or perhaps it was that argument that got him stirred like that. Any road, this morning he's like a different man. Did his boots and started making lists – took a sudden interest in the cart.' He grinned. 'Aren't sure it's an improvement, cause of course he knows what's best and never mind what me and Jethro have been doing all along. Anyway, you hang on there. I shan't be very long.'

And he wasn't really, but it was long enough for all the children to come bursting out of doors and tug her to the doorway by her skirts, demanding songs and stories. By the time she had admired the drawings on Davy's slate and heard how well the girls had learned their poetry by heart, Frank was already finished and coming up the path.

Tea was the usual cheerful chaos, and they went out for a walk – or a scamper, rather, dropping flower stalks in the tin-stream and racing them downhill, to the loud delight of all the little ones. It was a golden evening, and

Frank was happier, even when they got back to find his fayther in.

Mr Carter was perfectly polite – even when Frank spelled out their wedding plans, 'A year today, whatever,' which made the youngest children squeal with glee.

Fayther just smiled vaguely and finished up his tea. 'Job to do,' he muttered, and disappeared upstairs.

Ma Carter wiped her fingers in her pinafore. 'I don't know, my lovers,' she muttered, with a sigh. 'Something queer about him. I don't know what it is. Got a bee, now, about this damty war and thinks he should enlist. Found him polishing his buttons, when I went up before – said he was getting ready for when inspection came. Only his old overall, he used to wear to work.'

'Ought to get Dr James to have a look at him,' Maisie said.

Ma shook her head. 'Can't afford to call a doctor when he iddn't ill. Leastways he isn't drinking – that's one blessing anyway. Not when he's on duty, that's what he said tonight. I thought he was gone off with the piskies for a bit, but then a minute later he was as right as rain. Even helped me clear away the cloam, and he hasn't done that since we were newly weds. Better when he's peculiar and that's the truth of it.' Ma Carter was smiling, but her eyes were tired. 'Some funny family you'll be wedding into, Maisie dear.'

'I'll manage,' Maisie answered. And she meant it too.

Part Four – Summer 1915

Chapter One

Uncle Bertie had been right in what he said; it took several months before the letter came. James was beginning to despair of ever hearing anything at all.

He and Rupert had written off – to Bertie's friend in person, as they'd been advised – almost as soon as they came home, but singularly little had seemed to come of it. Embarrassing, when so many men were enlisting every day. When the news about the defeat at Amiens was printed in *The Times*, there were so many volunteers in just a week that the army could hardly process them. Advertisements were appearing daily in the press, urging all young men to serve their country, and people began looking at you strangely in the street if you were old enough to go and weren't in uniform. James was expecting a white feather any day.

It was all right for Rupert, he had a practical post at once – his father had agreed to let him help with patients until the summons came – but there was little James could do but cool his heels. He applied for every position he could find, and even offered his services to Penzance Hospital, but to no avail. No one wanted a brand-new doctor who had no experience and might be about to leave at any time. 'Fit young man like you, ought to be fighting at the front,' seemed to be the unspoken message everywhere he went.

The only offer of appointment he could find was as a temporary stand-in at the Railway Workers' Hospital and Recuperation Home at Hayle, when the usual doctor was indisposed. It was a very unfulfilling post, and inconvenient too. His time, apart from a lot of travelling to and fro, seemed to be spent in filling in forms and listening to complaints – mostly about the sanitary arrangements or the quality of food – and hardly any chance to use his skills.

As one of the old fellows put it when James looked in on him, 'It's all right, Doctor, kind of you to call, but I won't bother you. I'll wait till the proper fellow comes, if you don't mind. He knows my chest and the kind of medicine I generally have. Green stuff in a bottle – you can see it does you good – not these modern powders that you wanted me to have. I know you mean it kindly, but I'm not used to it.' And nothing James could say would change his attitude.

'Worse than useless, that's how it makes me feel,' James complained to Mater over tea that night. 'I've got a good mind to write up to the army again – perhaps the first letter got lost or misdirected. Or perhaps you could write to Bertie, like you did before, and ask him to find out if it arrived.'

'I'm sure they'll call you if they need you, dear.'

James put his cup down impolitely hard. 'It can't be that they don't need us, I see by the paper that they're calling back some of the senior students who volunteered for France, because the army is so short of doctors now-aways.' He sighed. 'Perhaps I ought to give up writing private letters of that kind, just go as an officer like other people do. I hear that Simon Robinson has volunteered and gone.'

'Well, I'll write to Bertie, if you want me to,' Mater said, and she must have done it too, because a few days afterwards the communication came, enclosing a railway travel warrant and inviting him to report to London on the nineteenth of the month.

'The nineteenth – poor Rupert!' Mater said at once. 'He'll barely be back from his wedding trip by then. I'm surprised that he was so anxious to sign up at all – nobody expects a married man to go.' She was inclined to be severe, he noticed with surprise, especially when she added, 'I don't know what your own prospective bride is going to say.'

He smiled. 'Lucy will be delighted that I've heard at last.' It was the truth, he knew. She had been asking him with some impatience when it was going to be, mostly because she wanted a bridegroom in dashing uniform. 'It's not as if we're going to put ourselves in danger, after all. We're only going to help the wounded – not to add to them.'

283

Mater turned away and took up her stitching. 'I suppose you'll be wanting to ride out over there and see if Rupert has got a letter too?'

'I will. And I will call in and see Lucy on the way.' He saw that his mother was still distressed and added, 'Mater, you might at least be pleased for me, I've waited long enough. We were afraid at one stage that we would miss the war.'

His mother sighed. 'Not much chance of that, from what the papers say. Well, I'm sure I'm pleased if you are. And your father will be proud of you, I know.' She was unhappy, though. (It wasn't until months afterwards, when he was out in France, that it occurred to James to wonder if she had been responsible for the original delay.)

Lucy, however, quite made up for it. She seemed as thrilled for him as he was for himself. She took him into the garden, where they could not be seen, and gave him a warm kiss to tell him so. 'James, that is simply wonderful. I shall boast to all my friends. My fiancé, the gallant officer! When do you get your lieutenant's uniform?'

He had to limit her enthusiasm, in fact. 'It's all conditional on this interview, you know. There's nothing certain yet.'

She picked a rose and put it in his buttonhole. 'Oh, don't be silly. Of course they'll snap you up. And Rupert, come to that. I suppose he's had a letter too?'

'I imagine so. I was just going down to ask

284

him, but I thought I'd see you first.' He held her at arm's length and looked at her. 'And very pretty too. Though it will be hard for him to leave on the nineteenth. He will have a wife by that time, as Mater pointed out, though that may mean they give him a posting nearer home. There are plenty of base hospitals in England that they can use him in. I might get Uncle Bertie to have a word again.'

Lucy looked suddenly a little tremulous. 'But they won't send you into danger, will they? I mean, you won't get shot?'

He laughed down at her. 'Not if I have anything to do with it, I won't. They don't put hospitals in the line of fire.'

She nodded. 'Anyway, you're soon to be a married man yourself – though we have not decided on a date.'

'I've been thinking about that. I could get a special licence, the first leave I get. People are starting to do that, with the war and everything. You read about it in the papers all the time.'

He thought she might be horrified, but she didn't seem to be. She opened her big eyes very wide at him. 'That would be so romantic, don't you think? Besides, big affairs like the one that Annabelle has planned are not so fashionable as they used to be.'

He nodded. 'People think it's unpatriotic, I suppose, when men are out there dying in the field. Spending all that money on food and wedding gowns when the army is short of funds for armaments and men are fighting on tins of bully beef.'

Lucy turned away and pulled off another rosebud for herself. 'Well, it wouldn't mean I shouldn't have a proper wedding dress, I've already picked out the material. I don't suppose the army needs white silk taffeta. And I'm sure that we should have a wedding tea at least, and go to Falmouth for a night or two if you have leave enough. But not a formal ball the night before, and choirs and bells and bishops and the whole church full of flowers, as Annabelle intends to have next week.'

He was about to remark that – given Helena's difficulties in a public place – it was not likely that they would have had these things in any case, but he realized that this was not what Lucy wanted him to say. 'It sounds as if it's going to be a very sumptuous affair. I'm not sure that Rupert really welcomes that. I'm to be his attendant, as I'm sure you are aware, so there will be one advantage anyway. You and I shall be together. There's to be an orchestra and dancing, once the bride and groom have gone, and this time I demand to dance with you. You can't be snatched away by Simon Robinson this time – his regiment's in Belgium, and he won't be coming home: I hear he's making a reputation for himself, and has been mentioned in dispatches more than once.'

She had turned crimson. He felt a pang of tenderness: her modesty became her, and he

286

was unkind to tease. But she dimpled, covering her evident embarrassment with forced gaiety, 'Then I shall have to dance with you. Shall I look charming in my ice-blue, do you suppose, with a band of little rosebuds in my hair?' She tucked the flower in behind her ear and struck a pose.

He leaned forward and kissed the tempting little lobe. 'Much prettier than Rachel Robinson, I'm sure. And now, my dearest, I must tear myself away. I hope to call on Rupert, as I said before, and I should call in before I go and tell Helena my news. If she has finished with her pupil by this time.' She had been busy teaching when he first arrived and he hadn't had a chance to speak to her.

Lucy made a little face at him. 'Oh, Lena won't be finished till four o'clock at least. She's always teaching, these days. It's getting quite a bore. She's got one little girl who doesn't see too well, and she's made a mission out of helping her – and she's getting enquiries from other people now. But it seems to keep her happy, and she won't miss me so much when we are married and I have to move away. I suppose we shall have our own establishment, even if you are working in the war? You do have a cottage in your grounds, I think.'

'Or you could move in with my parents – they've got room enough,' It was an obvious solution, as it seemed to him. 'They would like it, and the house will come to us one day. And you wouldn't be so very far from Helena

287

– you could pay a visit every afternoon.'

She nodded. 'I suppose so ... only...'

'What?'

'Oh, nothing.' She shook her head at him. The rosebud dislodged itself and tumbled to the ground. 'I'm sure I should get used to it in time – living in someone else's household in that way. But don't let's quarrel over trifles. You will soon be gone. Though you will come to see me as often as you can? And I can come to London sometimes? I should like that very much.'

He smiled at her. 'Of course you shall.' And then, at last, he tore himself away. He called in on Miss Edwards, who was looking very frail. She was confined to bed, and not eating much these days: though if she were his patient, he thought privately, he would prescribe sea air and mutton chops.

He did contrive to have a word to Helena as well. She was encouraging, as she always was, and then he rode down to Rupert – who'd had a letter too.

'Broke the news to Annabelle this afternoon, old chap. Can't say she was very pleased with me – but what's a man to do? Dratted nuisance that it comes right now, but I shall be quite pleased to feel I'm doing something for the war effort, shan't you?'

Annabelle's wedding was as spectacular as Lucy had foreseen. Several carriages pulled by matching greys, all bedecked with flowers, and Mrs Passemore-Jenkins in a silver dress

288

and coat that made her look a little like a huge upholstered fish. Annabelle herself looked lovely, if a little pale, and even Rachel Robinson looked handsome in her senior bridesmaid's role, but Lucy knew secretly that she herself was the prettiest of all.

Rupert and James were waiting at the church, where there were more banks of flowers and the promised choir, and half an hour later it was over, and Annabelle was Mrs Rupert Neill. The bridal party and a large number of the guests were invited to the house, where naturally a sumptuous wedding breakfast had been prepared: all kinds of dainties which had been getting scarce – fresh nectarines, asparagus and out-of season fruits as well as the lobster, salmon, roast meats and galantines – and a gigantic wedding cake so huge it took two serving-men from the con-fectioner's to carry it inside.

There was an awkward moment – there was almost bound to be, when she was forced into Rachel's company like this. It happened when the new bride and groom came up to cut the cake. The two confectioner's men appeared again, and bore the topmost tiers away, leaving only the bottom layer, which was half a yard across, and covered with a wreath of sugar flowers. It was so monstrous that they could hardly make the knife cut into it. Rupert made a quip about sending for a scalpel 'to make the first incision' as he said. It was a struggle, but at last they did succeed, just as Mrs Passemore-Jenkins – more like a stout fish than ever – came swimming up to supervise.

'We shall keep the top layer for a christening cake one day, exactly as we did with Celestine.' She turned to Lucy's mother, who had accompanied her. 'I expect you remember when we were very young: the bridesmaids used to come back to the house the next day and box up and address the cake themselves – but it was such a chore. I'm sure that Lucy and Rachel would not have cared for it.'

Mamma smiled. 'It was not the fashion for them to wear such pretty dresses then. When I was married my sister wore a *vieux rose* ensemble, I recall. And I had a bonnet, not a wreath and veil. Though you all look enchanting, I must say.' And then, a dreadful moment as she turned to the senior bridesmaid with a smile. 'Rachel, I'm so pleased to meet you and know you properly. You've been such a friend to Lucy.'

'And to Annabelle, of course,' Mrs Passemore-Jenkins boomed. 'With all those afternoons you asked them to.'

Lucy almost choked. What on earth could possibly have prompted that remark? Simon had confessed to Celestine, perhaps, and Mrs Passemore-Jenkins had stumbled on the truth? Or had Maisie after all let something slip?

She knew that she had turned 'vieux rose' herself, and she kept her eyes fixed firmly on her plate. Annabelle was obviously startled, too. She actually dropped the silver cake knife on the floor, and when Lucy stole a sideways look at her, she was looking positively shocked. Rachel, for her part, was frowning in surprise.

There was an awful pause. The dropped knife had caught everyone's attention, and all the bridal party and the guests were staring at them now.

Rachel broke the silence. 'Well, since you mention it, I suppose I do recall...'

She was going to say that it was only once or twice! Lucy closed her eyes and waited for the guillotine to fall.

It was Annabelle herself who saved the moment. She had fixed her eyes on Lucy, and was now saying with a rush, 'Oh, Rachel is too modest. She was quite famous for her charity affairs, before the war. Quite everyone was there. And I understand she does have plans to host another one quite soon, in support of wounded sailors, is that right, sister-in-law?'

Rachel was preening at the flattery. Yes, she was proposing to have a little do: 'Just three-penny teas and sandwiches.' She'd thought about making it a knitting bee this time, where people could bring their needles and make comforts for the troops – and anyone was welcome to come along and join.

So the moment passed, without an incident, but Annabelle had clearly not forgotten it. She kept looking at Lucy in a most peculiar way, and when she went upstairs to change for going away – and Lucy went to help her

291

into her travelling costume – Annabelle seized a moment to take her on one side.

'About that business of Rachel's afternoons...'

Lucy couldn't think of anything to say. 'I know,' she stumbled, 'it must seem very odd...'

But Anna wasn't listening. 'I'm sorry, Lucy, I ought to have explained. But it's embarrassing. It's just ... you see, I used them as a bit of an excuse. I told my family that I'd gone over there with you, when really I was out with someone else – someone they would not have approved of, specially.'

Lucy said nothing, she was too surprised.

Annabelle sat down at the mirror and looked back at her friend, as if she couldn't bear to look her directly in the eyes. 'Promise you won't tell? I swear that it was someone quite respectable, it doesn't matter who – anyway it was all over long ago and nothing came of it. I'm just sorry it all emerged like that today and I embarrassed you.' She shook her head. 'You must have wondered what it was about. You are looking shocked! Lucy, forgive me – I was foolish to engage in such impropriety at all, but I never should have used your name and friendship in that way. Thank you, in any case, for not betraying me.' She sounded humble and quite close to tears.

Lucy made a little strangled noise. She could hardly believe what she had heard. There was only one possible interpretation she could make, and the implications were quite staggering. She was on the verge of blurting out the truth to Annabelle, when Rachel, the other bridesmaid, came back into the room.

'Here, I have fetched your bonnet and your travelling coat. Rupert and the coachman are awaiting you downstairs.'

Lucy met Annabelle's anguished glance, still in the looking-glass, and managed to hide her feelings with a businesslike remark, although she could not bring herself to smile. 'Then it is time you went to join them, Mrs Neill,' she said.

Anna kissed her cheek. 'I won't forget this, ever,' and they went downstairs. Lucy knew that she'd had a merciful escape and earned a gratitude she did not deserve.

Then there were kisses and flowers and farewells, and then the newly weds were duly waved and driven off – for three days in Plymouth, before Rupert's interview. The rest of the party went inside again, with the strange sense of flatness that always follows such events. But the dramas of the day were not over yet. Just as the orchestra was making ready to begin, one of the servants came in breathlessly.

'I'm very sorry, Mrs Passemore-Jenkins, madam, but there is someone at the door. Wants to talk urgently to the Tregenza family. I said she should wait, but she insisted it was urgent, and she had to see them now. Quite a common sort of person, madam. Shall I show her in?'

But the 'common person' had already followed her, because there was Maisie in her pinafore, pink-eyed and breathless but not at all abashed – although an entire roomful of people, all immaculately dressed, was staring at her as though she was an exhibit at a fair.

It was Lucy's Papa who went across to her, saying warningly, 'Maisie? I trust you have a reason for bursting in like this?'

She looked at him. 'Yes, sir. I'm afraid so, sir. It's poor Miss Edwards, see. Taken all peculiar and fallen on the floor. Thing is, Mr Tregenza, I can't feel her breath. You'd better come. I think she might be dead.'

Mr James was good as gold, she told Frank afterwards. Came and put his arm around her – as if she was a lady, like the rest of them. Led her over to one of the fancy chairs, never mind her pinny, and sat her gently down, and then took over organizing things.

She had come there in the carriage – it was all arranged for Edgar to go a little later on and pick the family up in any case – so she had brought it forward and driven down in state. Leather seats, and little mirrors – like a queen she was – but obviously the family would use it to go back. But Maisie didn't have to walk home in the dark at all. Mr James arranged it beautifully. He borrowed a horse and sulky from old Dr Neill himself.

'This is your son's wedding, don't tear yourself away. And the rest of you – continue with the dance. Miss Edwards was acquaint-

294

ed with some of you, I know, and the last thing she'd have wished is to spoil the day for you. I'll just slip back with Maisie – she's had a nasty shock – and see what's to be done to help Miss Edwards, if it's not too late. Meantime, her own doctor should be informed and asked to call – perhaps the Tregenzas could do that on their way – if only as a matter of professional courtesy.'

It wasn't the same party afterwards – of course, it couldn't be – but when Mr James said that people did turn away and start to talk a bit, instead of staring like a lot of barn owls in the dark: and the band – orchestra, they called it – went next door and played a bit of a tune, though no one seemed to have much heart to dance.

Miss Lucy, seeing as she was bridesmaid perhaps, was told to stay behind.

'It's no use your coming with us, there's nothing you can do. We'll send Edgar for you later,' Mr Tregenza said, 'and don't worry about contacting Miss Edwards' doctor, James, we'll get in touch with him.' And he and his wife took Miss Helena and went home in their coach.

James drove Maisie back with him. She was more or less recovered now, although he was right – it had given her a shock. 'Went into her bedroom, I did, with her tray as usual and there she was just lying on the floor. Well, not exactly lying – she'd fallen out of bed, and gone all sideways with her feet caught up. And turned some funny colour.' She stopped apologetically and gulped. 'Sorry, Mr James. I aren't meaning to run on. Talking too much, as usual, I 'spect.'

'No, it's very useful. Gives me a clear picture of what I'm going to find. You couldn't feel her breathing, I believe you said?'

'Well, I had an idea what you had to do. Read about it in a mission story once. Hold a mirror up in front of her, right up by her lips, and see if it gets misty. But it never did. And her chest – I put my hand on her just here' – she demonstrated on her own anatomy – 'but it wasn't going in and out that I could see.'

He nodded grimly. 'You did very well. Lots of women couldn't do as much. Not without someone to tell them what to do. Now,' they were stopping at the side gate to the Tregenza house, 'you go and warn them that I've come, and you can take me up and show me where Miss Edwards is. Fortunately Rupert has left his medical bag with me, to guard while he's away. I'll bring it with me, just in case it is of any use.'

But of course it wasn't. Maisie already knew it, in her heart, and it was clear that from the expression on Mr James's face that there was nothing anyone could do for poor Miss Edwards any more. Not in this life, anyway. He settled the poor lady back in bed again, made her decent where her night dress had tucked up round her waist, and pulled the blanket up across her face.

'We'll leave her to her doctor,' he said

soberly. 'Though it's pretty clear what's happened to her heart. And perhaps they'd like
the vicar to come round and say a prayer.
But, my dear young lady, it is you I'm thinking of. You're still whiter than the bedsheets.
I'll take you to the kitchen, and you're to have
a cup of tea and sit down for a half an hour.'
He raised his hand. 'Don't argue. I'll tell Mrs
Lovett so. Doctor's orders. It's the living we
have got to care for – the dead are past our
help. Come on, downstairs – before the
family come.'

He was so kind and understanding that
Maisie took a chance. She paused at the first
landing, and turned and looked at him.
'Here, Mr James, I'll be all right. Don't worry
about me. But there is something you could
do for me, perhaps. You won't tell the master
or the family that I asked you this?'

He looked at her from underneath his
eyebrows. 'That depends, I think.'

She shook her head. 'It's nothing terrible.
Not to do with them. It's only private, see.'

'Then I promise.'

She made a rush at it. 'I know I'm being
forward and I'm speaking out of turn, but
I've got a bit of money and I'd pay you for
your time. Only...' Her courage failed her and
she just shook her head.

'What is it, Maisie? Out with it.' She still
said nothing and he said suddenly, 'You're
not ... you haven't got yourself in trouble?
That might be difficult.'

She was horrified. 'Of course I 'aven't. What

a thing to say! No, it's about the father of a friend of mine. Got ever so peculiar, this last year or so.' There! She'd blurted it out. But better that than what he'd thought before!

He was standing on the turn of the stair, looking at her so the light from the window was falling on his face, like something in a chapel painting. Ever so serious and kind. 'Peculiar? In what sort of way?'

'Started when he lost his contract with Penvarris mine – used to be a carter for the tally shop.'

Mr James frowned. 'I heard about that incident, I think. Wasn't there some kind of a complaint about the son – deliberate insolence to a shareholder? Refused point-blank to follow orders, or something of the kind?'

Maisie was too concerned about her narrative. 'I never heard the rights and wrongs of it. Anyway, they stopped the contract, and he hasn't been the same. Gets all dark and moody, and gone from bad to worse – like it was too much effort to do anything, and there was no point in living any more.'

'Drinking?'

She nodded. 'Down the Tinners', that's what started it. And it's gone on from there. Stole all Frank's savings once, to pay for drink he did. We put a stop to that, but several times the last few months we've caught him pawning things – things that weren't his to pawn. Neighbours' things he's taken off the line, and Crowdie's wheelbarrow – all sorts of bits, whatever he can find. And that's not the worst. Half the time he doesn't seem to know he's doing it.'

Mr James was nodding sympathetically. 'How's his memory?'

'Funny you should say that, it seems to come and go. One minute he'll be talking about years ago, as good as anyone, and the next he can't remember who you are or where he is. Frank found him in his nightshirt the other night, out walking down the street – thought he was in uniform enlisting for the war. And he is forever making lists of things – like he used to, I suppose – but when you come to look at them it's only gibberish.' She sighed. 'I'm sorry, Mr James, it isn't fair, I know. I don't know what I think you can do for him. Only something isn't right. One day he's shouting and bawling all the time, and the next he's right as rain again and anyone would think that he was nice as pie. Makes the family's life an awful misery.'

'Well,' Mr James said. He took her by the arm. 'We'll deal with first things first. A cup of sugared tea, and rest for you, I think.' He marched her down the stairs. 'It sounds as if it might be a fever of the brain, and there isn't much that doctors can do for that, I fear. But if you like I'll come and take a look at him before I go away. I might be able to advise you what's the best to do. If you are quite sure his family wouldn't mind?'

She hadn't dared to ask them, but she said, 'I'm sure they wouldn't,' as firmly as she could. She'd simply have to talk Frank round to it, she thought. They were never going to get to marry otherwise.

The resolution cheered her, and she walked obediently downstairs and allowed herself to be sat down on a chair and plied with sugared tea by an affronted Mrs Lovett, who poured it with a sigh and maintained an aggrieved silence while Maisie swallowed it. She didn't even dare protest when she heard the carriage come, and Mr James went up himself to let them in.

'That's the family and they must have brought their doctor in the coach,' the house-keeper observed, as soon as he was gone. 'I recognize the voice. Anyway, finish up that tea. You will be needed soon. Master's taken them all upstairs, and they'll be wanting things sent up.'

Mr Tregenza rang down shortly afterwards – for brandy, tea and sal volatile. Miss Edwards' doctor had pronounced her dead, and it was feared that the mistress might be taken faint.

Chapter Two

Helena was walking unaccompanied upstairs. It was a skill that Samuel had taught her, and she was proud of it – running her hand along the banisters and counting the steps and paces as she went, though of course Maisie was standing by downstairs in case she needed help.

Thirty-seven, thirty-eight. A doorway – to what had been Aunt Edwards' room. She paused and listened, without really knowing why. It seemed oddly empty in the house without Aunt Edwards there. Not that her aunt had ever been a noisy resident and in the last few months she'd scarcely ventured from her bedroom – but she had left a space. Even now Lena half expected to hear the sharp voice raised in some rebuke – for loitering in the passageway, perhaps. But there was only silence.

Thirty-nine. Forty. Bookcase, whatnot, windowsill and she had reached the corner of the upper flight. She was about to place her foot upon the bottom stair, and start to count again, when she heard the doorbell far below. Not her next pupil, surely? He was not due for half an hour, and she had not yet got

Maisie to help her with the books – finding the ordinary copy for the child, so Helena could follow with the Braille. It was a system that worked nicely, and Maisie was so thrilled to be involved at all that Lena had even thought of asking her to play accompaniments: there was another blind girl now, who wanted Helena to teach her how to sing and follow the Braille manuscripts herself. Lucy did not have the patience to be of any help, and clearly Papa did not have the time, but Maisie was quite capable of playing simple hymns and songs – if only she wasn't wanted for other things elsewhere.

Like now, for instance. Helena called down, 'It's all right, Maisie, you may answer it. I'm all right where I am,' and a moment later the little boots went tap-tapping to the door. Lena could hear the sound of voices faintly up the stairs.

'I'm some sorry, sir, the master isn't in, and the mistress and Miss Lucy have gone out to Penzance. Would you like to leave your card?'

And a man's voice – one she didn't recognize. 'Tell him a Major Palmer called. About the horses. We have authority to requisition them – pay a valuation price for them, of course – but I'd prefer not to do that without discussing it. I presume you do have other horses – apart from those two in stable block?'

'You been round there looking?' Maisie was obviously scandalized, and forgot to be polite.

'Answer, please. The family keeps other horses?' The voice was not amused.

'Well, how do you think they've gone out otherwise? The master's riding his cob this afternoon, and I suppose the mistress has got the carriage pair. How they going to manage if you ring-quisition them – I suppose that is just fancy talk for taking them away?'

'Now look here, young woman.' He was blustering. 'This is not a matter for discussion, especially with you. The government's decided and that's the end of it. Horses are needed to help to win the war, and everyone will have to make some sort of sacrifice. We are combing this whole area this afternoon. Farms, shops, businesses, it's all the same – we're taking all the useful horses that can possibly be spared. People will have to share them, or use donkey carts instead.'

Maisie said something indeterminate. It sounded like 'Browning!' which did not make any sense. And then, 'Well, you can't have the horses, can you, if they aren't here to take?'

Helena decided it was time to intervene, before the major lost his temper and Maisie made things worse. She raised her voice. 'Maisie, tell the Major I am coming down. Show him into the ground-floor drawing room, and I will join him there.'

She turned round carefully, feeling with her hands. Windowsill, what not, bookcase, two steps to the door. And then very cautiously she counted down the stairs.

The major was quite charming, when she

spoke to him, though obviously embarrassed when she explained she couldn't see – especially when Maisie was so concerned about the way she'd come downstairs alone.

'My dear young lady, I had no idea! I am sorry to have caused you such inconvenience. And when I see that you're in mourning, too.' His voice was solicitous with sympathy. 'A family member, was it?'

'My aunt was buried yesterday.' She had quite forgotten that her dress was black. Maisie, presumably, wore an armband too.

'I thought perhaps you'd lost somebody in this dreadful war. So many people are in mourning nowadays.' He coughed. 'But speaking of the army, that is why I've come.' He explained the purpose of his visit once again, 'Though I am sure, in the circumstance, that you can keep the carriage pair, at least until a donkey cart is found. We cannot have you being a prisoner in the house. We do have discretion to make exceptions now and then.' He promised to come back that evening when her father – and the horses – would be home.

Maisie came back quite breathless when she'd showed him out. 'My dear Miss Elenner, what are you thinking of? Coming all the way downstairs like that, and without me even there to make sure you didn't fall? How didn't you stop up there and wait for me to come? Suppose you'd lost your footing, what would the mistress say? Have me dismissed before you could say knife.'

Helena was genuinely repentant. 'I'm sorry, Maisie, I hadn't thought of that. I was just delighted at having managed it – the first time that I've ever come downstairs unaccompanied since I had that fall. But of course you're right, it would have got you into trouble if I'd had an accident. And we can't have that. How should I manage without you? I couldn't possibly.'

She had expected Maisie to be giggly and pleased, perhaps a little embarrassed by the flattery but all the girl said, rather soberly, was, 'Well, let's hope that you don't have to – though it looks as if you might.'

Helena was on her feet again, and allowing Maisie to lead her towards the door, but she stopped abruptly. 'What do you mean by that? We aren't to lose you, surely? You're not thinking of packing up and working in a shop or factory – the way that Lucy tells me that girls are doing now?'

Maisie guided her towards the stairs. She sounded miserable. 'No, Miss Elenner, it isn't that at all, though they do say the pay for that is very good. It's just – well, I was going to have to tell you some time, I suppose. I was fixing to get married next September time, and of course I couldn't live in after that. Now here's the staircase – mind the carpet. Careful how you go.'

Helena felt for the banister like an automaton. It had not occurred to her to think of Maisie having a romance, or any kind of private life elsewhere. Her first thought was that it was inconvenient – that Maisie's place was working where she was – though she immediately regretted the selfishness of that. Getting like Lucy, she thought bitterly, and forced herself to smile and say aloud, 'Well, of course I'm very glad for you, if that is what you want. But wouldn't you be able to come in anyway? Lots of people only have daily servants nowadays, with women taking over men's jobs everywhere.'

'I know.' Maisie sounded glummer than before. 'I was going to suggest that I could do that, if the mistress didn't mind. Servants are getting very hard to find, I understand, and we would have been glad of the extra money, too. But it won't be any good, you see, if they take away the 'orse. Shan't be able to get here – it's too far to walk – and the Dear knows how we're going to live in any case. My Frank's a carter – what will 'appen if they ring-quisition us?'

'The army has "discretion", so the Major said. Perhaps I could put in a word for you when he comes here again tonight?'

Maisie laughed, a bitter little sound. 'That's some nice of you, Miss Elenner, but it won't work like that. It isn't like you helping to get our Davy into school. That Major'll break the rules for you perhaps – you are a wealthy lady after all – but he never will for us. If the army want our horses, and I 'spect they will, they'd be a sight more use for pulling guns than half the fancy animals you see, they'll take the damty things, and there isn't a blind thing

306

anyone can do. There's no use your wasting time and breath on it. So give me your arm and concentrate on getting up the stairs – any minute your pupil will be here and we haven't even sorted out the books.'

James was at the Carters' house when the army came, in fact. He'd promised Maisie that he'd go and he was fulfilling that – although he wasn't very sanguine that he'd be any help.

It had taken him a little while to get around to it. There'd been the interview in London, which had taken up two days – though, as Lucy had predicted, it was a mere formality. He'd gone up with Rupert in the train, as soon as the Neills got back from honeymoon, and talked to a dusty officer in a dusty room for half an hour, and come out with a commission and a ten days' leave to go home and pack, and buy a uniform, before reporting back for 'training', whatever that might mean.

There had been a 'medical', a cursory affair, and a visit to the military tailor in the town. 'We met another fellow there,' he wrote to Lucy faithfully that night, 'buying himself a greatcoat. Said he hadn't got one first time round, and that was a mistake. Rupert and I both ordered one at once, and they also managed to sell both of us a sword, though I don't imagine we'll be using it. Might come in useful for a scalpel, I suppose.' He didn't tell her the rest of it – that the lieutenant with the greatcoat was a volunteer who'd paid entrance fee to the Artillery in the first days of the war: paid three guineas for it, and confided now that he'd 'pay three thousand guineas to relinquish it and not have to go back to the war' – he thought the anecdote would worry her.

It worried him a bit.

Then when they had come home there was the funeral, and Lucy, and a hundred other things he had to do, so it was more than a week before he found the opportunity to go out to the house – it had to be at a moment when Maisie had time off and was in a position to accompany him.

'They'll never let you in, without I'm there,' she said. 'I've had some job to talk them into it. Frank's ma keeps saying that he isn't ill enough – isn't dying, that's what she means. She's afraid of doctors. Well, I used to be. Would be now, excepting that it's you.'

James realized this was a kind of compliment.

'She's worried about your fee as well, but I will see to that. No, don't you shake your head – you come out here, you've earned it. And you've been some good keeping this between ourselves,' she added. 'I'd have died if Mr Tregenza found out what I'd done.'

So they had met around the corner, like conspirators, and he had driven her out here in his father's pony trap – which was the only transport that was left to him. The army had taken the other animals.

'Over there. That cottage on the end.' He reined the pony and got down to help her off, but before she was fairly on the ground there were half a dozen children swarming over her.

'Davy, Poppy, Susie, mind your manners now. This here is a doctor, Mr James. He's come to see your fayther, if he's in the house.'

James swallowed. It had not occurred to him that his patient might not be there when he called.

Maisie turned to him. 'We told him you was coming, though we didn't say what for – thinks you're from the army, come to see if he is fit. Once he got hold of that idea he was quite keen to see you, but you never know with him. Could have forgotten all about it and gone wandering off – though most likely we can find him down the Tinners' if he has. Always supposing that he hasn't had a funny fit and gone off in his underwear again, 'cause in that case there's no knowing where he might have gone.'

The boy she had called Davy rubbed a hand across a runny nose. 'He's 'ere. Leastways, he's out there in the shed. You can't get no sense from him. Looks as if he's locked the door and isn't answering. Ma's been at her wits' end with him, ever since she got back home.'

James got his bag down from the trap. It made him feel important, and it must have looked it too, because the children gave him startled looks and ran inside. 'I'd better take a look,' he said, and Maisie led the way.

He had dreamed of helping the miners and their families, but the cramped conditions shocked him all the same. He was taken down a wretched dingy passage to the 'kitchen' – a modest little room, crowded with the cooking fire and all the family, where there was hardly room to walk between the table and the wall. It was clean and cheerful, though, despite the washing dangling on long strings above the fire, and the strips of sticky flypaper that festooned the beams. There were herbs and candles, too, he noticed, on bare nails hammered haphazardly in the wall, and a half a side of bacon curing in the smoke.

The mother was sitting on a stool beside the fire, peeling potatoes by the look of it – she had a pailful of them, and a knife. She got up when she saw them, and wiped her hands politely on her apron-front. 'You Dr James, are you?'

He nodded.

'He's out the back. Been out there since breakfast by the look of it. I put his crowst out before I went to work, but he hasn't touched a crumb. Mind, I said to Maisie we shouldn't trouble you. He isn't poorly, 'zactly.'

'There are different kinds of illness, Mrs Carter,' James replied. He thought he sounded pompous, but it seemed to reassure.

'Well, if you're certain. Davy, you can show the doctor where.'

It was a scrap of a back yard, but there were cabbages and swedes and, right at the bottom, beyond a tiny patch of grass and an apple tree with a clothesline tied to it, there was the famous shed. It was hardly big enough to take a full-sized man, but James went up to it and knocked on the door.

'Captain Morrison, from the Royal Army Medical Corps.' They'd given him rank. It was the first time he had ever used the words. 'I've come to take a little look at you.'

A pause, and then a small suspicious voice. 'You a doctor?'

'That's right.'

'I've been expecting you.' And the inner bolt was opened. A haggard, unshaven face appeared around the jamb. 'Don't let them see you. You'd better come inside.'

James did so. The smell was horrible. Old cheese and the odour of latrines. The apparition handed him a notebook.

'I've been writing down my details, so I don't forget. And a list of things – you'd better see if there is anything I've missed.' There was nothing on the paper but a lot of random lines. James felt a sudden huge surge of sympathy. It was clear there was nothing that his medicine could do.

He was about to say something about examining the man, when Carter said suddenly, 'Who are you, anyway? What are you doing here? This is army property, get out!' And he might have attacked him if James hadn't fled. He was almost relieved to hear the bolt shoot to.

It was a thoughtful young doctor who went

311

back to the house. There was no sign of the children. Maisie, presumably had taken them somewhere. Mrs Carter was putting her potatoes on to boil. 'Is there something you can give him? Is it serious?'

James went over and took her gently by the shoulderblades. 'You'll have to have him committed, you know that, don't you?'

She paused, a lone potato still in her hand. 'Not the madhouse?'

'The asylum, yes. You know I'm right. He could be dangerous. To himself, if not to anybody else.'

She was stifling a sob. 'But the children...?'

'It will be safer for them than if you keep him here. Now, I can arrange it. Will you leave this to me?'

She shook her head. 'You'd better talk to Frank. He'll be home directly. I'll leave it up to him.'

Which is how James came to be standing in the lane when the army came to take the animals. He was just explaining that the pony trap was his, when Frank and his cart came trotting down the lane.

'Mr Frank Carter?' The major had his notebook out. 'We've come to tell you—'

'Let me hear about my father first,' he said, with such feeling that the other man withdrew. He listened carefully to what James had to say, then turned to face the major. 'Take the bloody horses, then, and be damned to you. I know that's what you've come for – they told me in Penzance. I might have

312

argued – tried to make a case – but what does it matter now?' He sounded like a man whose world had crumbled round his feet.

Then Maisie came rushing from further down the road, a raggle-taggle group of children at her heels. 'Frank, I saw them coming and I heard what's happening. You can't just stand by and let them ring-quistion everything.'

The major looked at her with some surprise. 'You again?'

'Yes, it's me. And I remember what you said. The army doesn't have to take from everyone the same. Well, these two horses are his living – and the next-door family's too.'

The major was stony-faced. 'He should be in the army. Fit young man like him.'

'And how is he to manage that? His father's so poorly that we've brought the doctor here, and it doesn't look as if he'll ever work again. So what does the army want to do, let all the children starve?'

'Don't be absurd,' the major said. 'We do our duty – and this fellow should do his. We're offering a decent price for animals. You say there are two horses, and we won't take both, of course, if a family's whole livelihood depends on them.' He looked at the animal Frank had between the shafts. 'That one looks too old to serve in any case.'

James saw Frank's face, and thanked the powers above. One more blow tonight might have finished the poor lad, but as it was he was looking quite relieved – as if one family member had been reprieved, at least. Which, perhaps, was effectively the case.

It was quite shaming, in the light of all of this, to climb up in his own smart pony cart, especially when little Davy was shouting at the major, through his tears, 'How don't you take that pony and leave our Dobbin be?'

James flicked the reins and would have driven off, but Maisie came running after him. 'Oh, Mr James, don't go without your fee. I got a guinea put aside for 'ee.'

He looked down at her, too distressed to smile. He had done nothing but bring bad news to this little family. 'You put that in your wedding-chest,' he said. 'Save me remembering, nearer to the time.'

Her look of astonished gratitude was balm to him. He felt less of a selfish monster as he drove down the lanes, though home – when he got back to it – had never seemed so large and welcoming. The Tragenzas were invited to dine again tonight and Mater was fretting about shortages of things – but he noticed there was plenty on the table, and to spare.

They did get paid for Dobbin, though the army decided on the price. It was quite a wrench to see the faithful creature led away, but somehow – compared to Fayther yesterday – it didn't seem too bad.

That was an awful business. First Dr James Morrison came again and then two men in a sort of motor ambulance, and they took Fayther off. They brought a straitjacket to put

314

him in, but they hadn't used it – Frank didn't think they could have borne it if they had. Mr James had told them not to, and it turned out he was right. Fayther had taken it in his head to think it was the army come for him at last, and he'd gone with them good as gold. So that hadn't been a problem, though it might easily have been.

Ma had wept buckets half the afternoon, and none of them had slept, but now at last a kind of calm prevailed. They were all of them sitting round the kitchen fire again. Ma was knitting socks for somebody, and the younger girls were darning the ones with holes in them – while Davy was sitting on the stool beside the fire practising his writing on a piece of broken slate.

Frank took a sip of the tea his mother had poured for him. 'Where's Lenny to?' he murmured.

Ma looked up from her needles. 'Gone to see about a job. Little workshop somewhere near Penzance was looking for a boy. That fellow at the recruiting office put him on to it.'

Frank nodded. Lenny had gone yesterday to try to volunteer – perhaps because he'd taken Fayther's fate as hard as anyone. Might have done it too, for all he was so small, except the fellow asked what age he was and Lenny told the truth. 'You know they told him to come back again next week, see if he couldn't manage to be nineteen by then?'

Ma nodded. 'But the sergeant outside

writing down the names used to go to chapel and knew who Lenny was – said he wasn't going to let him get away with telling lies. Lenny was fed up about it at the time, but it turned out to be a blessing in the end. Chap said he knew the owner and he'd put in a word for Len. Good money for an errand boy and they'll train him if he suits.'

'Supposing that they'll have him.' Frank pushed away his tea. 'There must be dozens looking – and it's some long way to come and go each day.' He didn't mean to sound a pessimist, but if Lenny was bringing steady money home it would be such a help that he hardly dared permit himself to hope.

Ma said nothing for a minute – she was turning the heel and had to concentrate – and then she raised her head. 'Well, if he doesn't get that, he could get a place up the dairy factory, I 'spect. I hear they're quite short-handed, with all the men away. Course they always took a lot of girls, but there's so many vacancies they're glad of anybody able they can get.' She finished the row and got out another skein. 'I did wonder about going up there myself – more hours, but it pays as much as scrubbing, and it can't be half so hard. Here, Davy, put that down a minute and come and hold this wool for me. I need another ball.'

Davy came, reluctantly, and did as he was told, putting his two hands up at shoulder height. Ma looped the skein around them and began to wind. But he had been listening. 'I aren't too small to help a little bit, Crowdie's paying pennies to people to go down after school and help pick up potatoes – I could manage that. The girls could take me down there and pick me up again, and you wouldn't have to pay Mary next door to keep an eye on me.' He was dipping his hands from side to side to help release the wool.

Ma met Frank's eyes and smiled. 'Don't 'spect you'll make a fortune. But the child's right, of course. There's getting to be lots of little jobs about, cause there aren't the men to do them, like there used to be. Funny, isn't it? We've lost Dobbin, so we can't use both the carts, but we've still got Brownie so in the end we might be better off. And course, I could move in with Davy, if it came to it – you and Maisie could have the bedroom now. Won't seem the same in any case without your fayther here...'

She might have said more but there was a noise outside, and an excited Lenny came tumbling through the door. He was mud and dust from head to toe and he had scuffed his knees, but he was grinning like a frog. 'I got 'un!' he declared. 'Going to start next Monday, and you'll never guess. Given me a bicycle to use, they have – so I can ride to work and use it for deliveries and all. I can have it if I want it – pay it from my wages, just like you did, Frank.' He looked down at his dishevelled clothing, unabashed. 'Took me a minute, but I got the hang of it. Good job I didn't sign up yesterday. Here, what's the matter, Frank? Why are you looking at me in that tone of voice?'

Frank was smiling broadly, a smile of pure relief. 'It's true, isn't it?' he said. 'If anyone should be signing up, it's me. They pay, when you're a soldier – or they pay your wife. And if anything happens, they pay your widow, too. I've wished a score of times that I could go. I've had young women give me white feathers in the street when I've been collecting parcels – you don't know what it's like. Feeling that everybody round you is doing what they can, and you are only half a man because you can't. Well, now perhaps I can. I know you'll feel it, Ma, but you'll have Maisie here. We've already talked about putting up the banns now that there isn't Fayther to be thinking of – and anyway you can get them special licences these days. We could be married before so very long.'

Ma was looking stricken, but nodded just the same. 'They let you have embarkation leave before you go, I think. Be hard for Maisie, naturally, to have you leave as soon as you get wed, but perhaps she could get work up the dairy factory, with me. Keep her mind off worrying, and help her put a little bit aside for later on. Only a pity she can't stay on where she is. She said the Tregenzas would be willing to keep her on, even if she came in every day, but it's too far for her to walk and there's no horse-bus out that way.'

'I could get a bicycle for her, and she could ride,' Len said. 'Though I suppose you'll have to see what Maisie says to that.'

What she said was very simple, when it came to it. She was thrilled to bits about the marrying part of it, and would gladly ride a bicycle to hell and back for that – though she didn't share his pleasure about him joining up.

The recruiting office was enthusiastic, though. They nearly snatched Frank's hand off when he went in to volunteer. They told him how his King and country appreciated him and two women on the pavement, who saw him walking in, actually applauded when he came out again. He went home feeling like a hero, proud as billy-oh, though he had to wait a fortnight till his papers came.

Chapter Three

Lucy was in her petticoats completing her toilette: 'a simple regimen for brides-to-be'. She had read about it in a lady's magazine, and she had undertaken to try their recommendations every morning until she should be married, in order to look as radiant as possible on the day. She had already 'steamed' her face most carefully – Maisie brought up water as hot as possible so that she could lean over it with a towel forming a

319

sort of tent around her head. Now, having sent the cooled water off downstairs again, she dabbed the skin with rosewater and cold cream, as instructed in the article, dusted on 'the merest film of purest powder with a brush' and was preparing to smooth it off again with a chamois-leather piece when Maisie came tapping at the door again.

'Excuse me, Miss Lucy, but the mistress says will you be wanting proper breakfast with the rest of them?'

Lucy looked at her reflection and considered this. The same authority advised a morning diet of thin brown bread and butter and watercress, and though that had been interestingly self-denying for a day or two she was already jolly bored with it.

'Perhaps I might permit myself a lightly boiled egg,' she said, as though bestowing favours on Cook by doing so. After all, her wedding could not be for months. It would have to be in the autumn now, even if James came home several times between – she was still in mourning for Aunt Edwards, and Papa would never have permitted such a breach of etiquette.

'Then I'll go down and let Mrs Lovett know.' Maisie bobbed away, then popped her head around the door again. 'And I'm to tell you there's another letter come. From Mr James in London, by the look of it.'

'In that case, tell them that I'll be down at once.' Lucy put the unused piece of chamois down. She didn't even pause to pinch her cheeks – 'between the first joint of the fore-finger and thumb and always working upwards from below' – which was the final requisite for 'loveliness'. Instead she pulled her day-dress on and quickly buttoned it (a horrid dreary thing it was, in half-mourning colours of lavender and black) then tugged a hasty hairbrush through her locks and hurried to the breakfast room without delay.

The letter was on a salver by her plate when she got down, and she needed no permission to open it at once. Mama offered her own letter knife to slit the envelope, and even Papa looked at her above *The Times* and said, 'Any news, then?' in a friendly way.

There was. The news that they had all been waiting for, in fact. The training weeks were over – James had been ever so amusing about them – and he was to be posted to a proper hospital.

'He doesn't tell me where, though.' Lucy turned the pages over, scanning them in vain. 'I do hope he's in London, so I can visit him. He told me it was likely, the last time that he wrote. Lots of the old hospitals are setting wards aside and making them into military units now, he says.'

'Won't be allowed to tell you, I expect. Military secret and all that sort of thing,' Papa harrumphed, behind the headlines. 'And it might not be London. Be prepared for that. They are opening base hospitals all over the south coast – and I expect they've got some overseas as well. And there are a few convalescent homes run by the army, too, though most are operated by volunteers. There's talk of one opening in Penzance, in fact. Little Manor at Trevanon has been offered for wounded officers. I was talking to Dr Neill the other day and he was telling me – he might be asked to help them, they'll need a doctor there.'

Lucy said pertly, 'They need doctors everywhere.' She was a little needled at her father's last remark. Information about doctors and the war was her prerogative. She vented her slight irritation on the egg, beheading it neatly with one slice of the knife. 'The army are very short of people like my James.'

'And shall we be seeing him again before he goes?' Mama helped herself to a spoonful of Mrs Lovett's blackcurrant jam. Lucy made a face. It was perfectly agreeable, but it wasn't marmalade – some things were getting very hard to find these days.

'I think he says so, somewhere.' She polished off the egg. It was hardly more sustaining than the watercress. A couple of slices of buttered toast looked most enticing now, and Lucy wished she hadn't made such a point of telling everyone about her new abstemious regime. But she had announced her choice for breakfast and she must make the best of it – perhaps she would go to the kitchen for a little something later on. That thought was cheering and she picked the letter up and read it through, more carefully this time. 'Yes, here we are, in the last paragraph. He is to be given five days' leave before he … oh!'

Papa lowered his paper and looked over it at her. 'What is it, Lucille? Something up?'

She was staring at the writing as though by doing so she could somehow persuade it to be saying something else. 'Before he goes overseas.' She put the pages down. It was ridiculous to feel betrayed like this. But she had been counting on a London visit to buy her bridal things. And what about the wedding? That was something else. If James was in England it was easily arranged, but if he was sent abroad who knew when he'd be back? 'Overseas?'

Papa gave her a sympathetic smile. 'Poor Lucille. You're right to be thoughtful, but don't be too concerned. Of course he will be nearer to the fighting, over there, but they won't put the hospital in the front line, you know. Don't worry over that. Think of it another way. He's gone where he's really needed – that's why he volunteered.'

'That's just what he would say.' She could hardly admit that her sighs were for herself. Lucy folded up the letter. 'I suppose you're right.'

'Well,' Mama said brightly, 'I don't expect you are the only one. Perhaps you should get in touch with Annabelle and see if she has heard? I suppose, if James is posted overseas, it's likely that Rupert will be sent as well.'

Bother! Lucy squirmed a little, inwardly. That would mean a visit to the Passemore-Jenkins' house, where Annabelle was living while her husband was away. And that was awkward. The friendship between them had never been the same since Anna had confessed her duplicity about the charity afternoons. Of course, Lucy had been guilty of just the same herself, but in a way that only made it worse. The thought that Simon had been courting both of them, using the same excuses, made her furious – though of course she had never breathed a word of that, to Anna or anybody else.

But the two of them were thrown together more than ever now. As a result of what Annabelle had said at her wedding about Rachel's knitting bees, both girls had found themselves more or less obliged to go to them. Lucy found it a kind of purgatory: she hated knitting even more than she hated Rachel's wretched teas, with the endless stories of Simon and his military career, and how he was singlehandedly about to win the war.

'Mentioned in dispatches last week and put up for a gong – I think that means a medal "For outstanding gallantry and fearless conduct in the field". We are all so very proud of him, Celestine especially,' Rachel had proclaimed, casting off a pair of socks that would have suited a giraffe.

Lucy could believe it – Simon would be brave. He had always been daring and gone rushing into things. But as for his 'conduct in the field'...!

She jerked her thoughts back to the present.

'Perhaps I'll send over to Anna later on,' she said. 'In the meantime, I'll go up and read this to Helena. She always wants to know when I have heard from James, and he's written about some funny incidents, as usual. Someone asked him what his number was, and he said 'Chloroform' – because it numbs you, do you see? So, if you'll please excuse me...?'

She was already pushing back her chair and – rather impolitely – making her escape. She wanted to nurse her discontent alone. The day was not turning out to be a good one after all – and Helena must have felt something of the same, because she didn't even smile at James's funny anecdotes.

They sent them to a stationary hospital, first of all. A day and night of tossing in a wretched ship, and then they were disembarked on to a dismal train. Thank God for Rupert's company, because the landscape which must once have been verdant, with poplars and green fields, grew steadily as dreary as the rain. Ruins of buildings and shattered trees loomed past the windows, solitary markers in a sea of grey. By the time the two young men arrived at their destination those last few days of leave at home seemed half a year away.

The major who received them was affable enough but did not seem to have expected anyone, and they had to wait for ages while a tent was found for them. A meal, however, was a welcome sight and after the rigours of the journey James slept as well on his camp bed as he had ever done on feather mattresses at home

Rupert, however, had been restless ever since they left. Twice James woke to find him standing at the door, staring out into the dark and rain, but he knew better than to ask. Previous enquiries as to what the matter was had brought a furious 'Nothing!' and made matters worse.

It was an enormous camp, as they discovered the next day when daylight came. Six separate hospitals were sited there, which between them could deal with about a thousand men, and each with its own half-dozen medical officers – including themselves, in one instance now. A wilderness of sheds and tents, and – very much to James's astonishment – only a scattering of patients. Barely fifty in the whole establishment.

They looked in on the morning round – their hospital had recently been relocated here and boasted only a number of minor ailments. Influenza, rheumatism and frostbite seemed to account for most of them, and although there were some wounded they were not serious. It was the major who explained the system, over lunch. The RAMC – as they had learned to call the Royal Army Medical Corps (everything had abbreviations in the army, it appeared) – possessed a mess for officers, and the food was a good deal better than they feared it might have been.

'I had thought we would be busier than

this,' James ventured, over a concoction of tinned ham and rice.

The major looked quizzically at him. 'It's true not all our medicals are fully occupied, but we have to be ready for emergencies. There was a time not long ago when we had hundreds in – sent down from the dressing stations nearer to the front – but if they were seriously wounded we sent them home again. Nobody really stays here more than three days or so – we shall need the beds if there is a new attack. Now, have some coffee – it is very good. And I warn you, if you do find yourself going down the line at all – don't drink the water, unless you dilute it with a lot of whisky first.' He laughed immoderately at his little jest. 'Or you'll end up coming back here as a patient yourself.'

In the afternoon there wasn't much to do, but the evening brought a horse ambulance and a stretcher case or two – one with a painful abscess in the groin and another a young soldier with half his leg shot off. The foot had been amputated at the clearing hospital, further up the line, but it was suppurating and it was clear that he'd have to lose the rest as well. It was the first time James had seen an injury like that, a tangled mess of bone and tissue, and it sobered him, especially since the boy was crying like a child.

He wrote to Lucy, though he knew they'd censor it of course. It was maddening not to be able to tell her where he was, though he gave her as many hints as possible. Rupert had decided not to write to Annabelle, he had gone down to the mess, where they had yesterday's *Daily Telegraph* and *Mail*. 'Think I'll look at the papers for a little while, old man.'

James nodded, but when he followed later on, Rupert was drinking, rather heavily. James took him by the elbow. 'Come on, old chap. This will never do. You'd better tell me, hadn't you? What is it? The same thing that made you volunteer for overseas, instead of the easy billet they might have offered you?'

Rupert said nothing. Then, 'It's very well for you. Your Lucy is a sterling sort.'

James led him gently back towards the tent. 'And so is Annabelle. Or...? Is that the trouble? Something has gone wrong?'

Rupert looked at him, his face a white mask in the darkness. 'I don't believe she ever cared for me, you know. I wondered why a girl like that would have me, at the time. With all that money, and her family connections – what did I have to offer her? I should have known.'

James shook him by the elbows. 'Known what, for Heaven's sake?'

Rupert had been drinking or he might not have said, 'I'm a doctor, that's the trouble. She didn't think of that.'

James blinked. 'You mean she wasn't ... You were not the first? Oh, come, old man. You can't be sure of that. There are all kinds of things that can cause that effect.'

Rupert was stumbling stupidly. 'Riding a horse, or bicycle? If only it was that. I know

... I think ... that she has had a child. Or worse still aborted one. There were ... suggestions, certain signs ... and her behaviour too.'

'You must be mistaken. Annabelle? You're misinterpreting.'

'I taxed her with it.' He was sober now. 'She wouldn't let me touch her, and I confronted her. And in the end she broke down crying and admitted it. You know, I could have forgiven her, even then. There are occasions – people breaking in – when some poor girl may have an awful time and be ashamed to own it afterwards. I would have found him, punched his head for him. But she would not tell me who it was, or how. But I do know when. You remember she went to Yorkshire all that time ago?'

'To stay with some elderly relation, I heard. To have a change of air.'

'It was put about that her doctor had recommended it. But it was not my father who attended her. It was your Uncle Bertie, were you aware of that? Agreed that carrying a child to term would be injurious to her health, and disgrace would tempt her to try to end her life – that is grounds enough for legal termination, you're aware. If you can afford the private fees, of course, but Annabelle would have no problem there. And of course she would have the best attention possible. Though I'm not sure that she mightn't have tried some other ways as well. She was very frightened ... of any contact in that area.

329

James, old man, I'm sorry. This is a frightful mess.'

'So what will you do? Apply for a divorce?'

'And create a scandal? How can I do that? Besides, I was genuinely proud and fond of her, you know. No, I have made my marriage vows, and I – at least – will keep them. Though it's not what I had hoped. She was obviously desperate to marry somebody and I almost think that anyone would have done. I can't pretend that she has chosen me.' He turned away. 'I should not have told you. I came here to forget – I should be obliged if you would pretend to do the same.'

It wasn't difficult, in fact. The next day brought orders that moved them up the line. The attack the major had been half warning them about had come. For twenty hours at a stretch they assisted the MO's at a clearing hospital, operating in relays where they stood.

And still the wounded came: men with shattered arms and legs, men with half a head, men so badly wounded there was nothing one could do but tie a tag around them and leave them there to die, and save one's skill and time for those who had some hope.

So when, at last James staggered to his bed – too exhausted to remove his clothes and with the prospect of accompanying a motor ambulance at dawn to collect still further casualties – Annabelle and her troubles seemed very far away. And scarcely important, compared to other things.

★ ★ ★

The day of Maisie's wedding it came on to rain, but honestly she didn't mind a bit. She knew that she looked smart as paint in her pretty borrowed blouse and a brand-new skirt and jacket in a useful navy blue – though Miss Lucy had thought it was a funny choice, when she showed it off the day before.

'Come in for working later, Miss Lucy,' she had replied. 'And it's some lovely material, it will wear and wear. I bought it with the money that Mr James gave back to me. And Miss Elenner gave me five shillings to get myself an 'at.'

It was a lovely bonnet in navy plaited straw, with a bunch of purple grapes and adorned with white ribbons for the day, to cheer it up. 'Like a maypole,' Mrs Lovett said, but she was smiling all the same. Maisie could see her now, sitting in the front seat of the chapel and singing lustily.

And there, on the other side beside the wall, were Ma and Davy and two of the little ones, dressed in their Sunday clothes – though Lenny wasn't there. Off working with his bicycle of course: they would have docked his pay if he had wanted time. There was a smattering of people from the chapel, though, and Mrs Harris thumping out a hymn – all the wrong tempo, and sometimes out of tune, but it only made Maisie feel secretly quite pleased, because she knew she could have done it better, if she had not been the bride.

It was only a pity Miss Elenner wasn't there, not that she could have seen the bonnet if she came. She said she would have liked to, but obviously she couldn't manage it alone and Miss Lucy was doing something else that afternoon – and you couldn't expect the Master and Mistress to be there.

Mind, they'd been very generous in all kinds of ways – sent down an iced cake, like Christmas, and a side of ham, so together with Ma Carter's offering of splits and sandwiches there would be quite a little feast in the back hall afterwards. And that had been a worry: things were hard to get, and what they did have in the shops was twice the price it was, even if the shopkeeper would let you buy it anyway. Some of the grocers in the town were rationing their customers with things – so many ounces of this and half a pound of that – to make stocks go around.

Jethro, buttoned to death in his collar and a huge cravat, was waiting at the front with Frank and turned around to wink at her to say he had the ring. Mrs Harris thumped the wedding anthem and Maisie set off down towards them, with Rosie beside her to take her bunch of flowers, dressed up in her best and suddenly weeping buckets into her pocket handkerchief.

'There's nothing wrong,' she whispered, in answer to Maisie's muttered question. 'Only, I'm so happy for you. And Frank looks so handsome in his uniform,' and she started off again.

Altogether it was the most satisfying wedding anyone could wish. It was only a pity that after a dampish honeymoon picnic out to Gurnard's Head and a romantic walk home underneath the stars to a bed that was everything they had dreamed and more, the groom was forced to leave next morning on the early train, because his unit was posted overseas.

Chapter Four

It was strange not to have Maisie living in the house, and stranger still to think that she was Mrs Carter now.

'Oh, call me Maisie, same as always!' the little maid exclaimed when Helena raised the question of how she wanted to be addressed. 'I'm that used to it, I shouldn't answer else. Now this pink figured muslin's got a tear in it. Do you want me to mend it for this afternoon, or are you going to wear your cream – the heavy one with frills around the sleeves?'

Helena reached out a hand and identified the garments by their feel. 'If I wear the cream one, will it match my wrap?' Lucy had given it to her for her birthday recently, and she had promised to wear it to the Morrisons' to tea.

'Go with it lovely. Cream goes with anything. And if we put your hair up with that ivory comb, you'll look just beautiful.'

Helena smiled. It was to be hoped that Lucy thought so – Maisie's taste did not always accord with hers. In the matter of wedding bonnets, for example. 'You mean you gave her money, and that is what she chose? My dear Lena, you should have seen it – or perhaps it is as well that you could not. Like a navy coal scuttle with a bunch of grapes attached!'

But Maisie had clearly loved it. She'd said so more than once. Helena had been given a minute description of every aspect of the wedding day – and even a special piece of her mother's cake, wrapped up in a doily and brought back purposely for her.

The maid said briskly, 'Well, wear the cream then and I'll take the muslin home and mend it there. Might as well do something as sit idly by. 'Tisn't as if my husband's waiting, for his tea or anything.'

'Of course you must be missing him. It must be such a wrench.'

There was a silence. Maisie was making herself deliberately busy – Helena could hear her moving things about. Then she said. 'No worse for me than anybody else, I s'pose. There were that many women seeing off their men when I went down with Frank, you could hardly get near the train to say goodbye. You hardly see a young man now that's not in uniform, without he's got something wrong with him – like Jethro, my Frank's partner in the cart. They wouldn't have him anyway, cause he's got a half a hand, although I know he tried. Wouldn't know what to say to his children else, when they grew up, he said.'

Helena tried to change the subject. 'You've heard from Frank since he was overseas?'

More busy scrambling noises. 'I've had a line or two, though he isn't a great hand at writing much, and half of what he did write had been all blocked out in black.' Even the phlegmatic Maisie sounded close to tears, and Helena wished she hadn't raised the question after all.

It was a relief, then, to hear Lucy on the stairs and a moment later her footsteps bounding in.

'Aren't you getting ready? We should be leaving soon. And I wanted to have time to read you James's latest letter before we went. It's quite exciting, it's so full of news. They've moved him to another hospital, though he can't say where of course. Sounds as if he's moved up nearer to HQ.'

Unfortunate, after what Maisie had just been complaining of, but Helena said, 'They probably have better facilities, if that is the case. Senior officers like their comfort, and they will have made the best of what's available.' She didn't add that it was probably also nearer to the front, although to her the implication was quite obvious.

Lucy giggled. 'You're quite right, you know. He says the quarters are palatial there – the army's taken over a row of cottages and he and Rupert have a room apiece. He seems to be delighted because he has a proper bed. Do you suppose he didn't have one up to now?'

Helena wasn't quite sure how to answer this, but Maisie chirped up, 'Lucky to have a blanket and a bit of straw, from what I hear, if he's anywhere near where the fighting is. That's what Rosie's young man was telling me – I saw him in the lane the other day. And he should know, he's been there for months. Had a piece of metal cut right through his thigh and then it got infected and he's been in hospital. Come to see his family before they send him back. Jethro and me gave him a lift over in the cart.' She paused. 'Sorry if I'm talking out of turn again. My tongue is running away with me as usual, I suppose.'

Lucy maintained a frosty silence by way of a rebuke. Even if maids were becoming hard to get, the silence said, they were not expected to contribute remarks into private conversations that they chanced to overhear.

Helena eased the moment with a sympathetic word. 'Poor fellow. I expect his family are glad to see him, though.'

Maisie took this as encouragement. 'I aren't so sure of that, even. You wouldn't hardly know him. Gone from being a strapping sort of lad to white and pale and shaky as a leaf. Having nightmares about going back to it he says, but of course he'll have to by and by. He says men in the trenches just have hollows in the wall, and sleep wrapped up in their overcoats – if they can sleep at all, what with sound of shells and bullets screaming overhead all blessed day and night. Thank Heaven Frank is only in the transport sections, moving things about. I don't think I could have bore it, to think of Frank in a trench like that. After Rosie's fellow told me, I wished I'd never asked.'

There was an awkward silence this time, which Maisie broke herself, by clattering hangers in the cupboard as she hung things on the rail. 'So you just be grateful on Mr James' behalf. Though I'm glad he's comfy. I aren't meaning that. I shouldn't like to think of him in trouble any more 'n' Frank – your Mr James has been some good to me. You know he gave me money for my wedding navy blue?'

Lucy said, with heavy irony, 'Yes, Maisie. You've mentioned it at least a dozen times. I'm glad you appreciate the gift. But really I was not addressing you. I was telling my sister the latest news of James, since she is always anxious to hear it when it comes.'

'Go on, then.' Helena knew her sister well enough to urge. 'You say he's happy and he's living very well.'

'He doesn't say very much about his work at all. But he's eating in a mess with the other officers and he is quite hilarious about the food. He talks about a regimental dinner which they held, and really it's delightfully absurd. A dozen courses, which all look very grand, until you work out that the same tinned ham and fruit appear in different guises throughout most of it.' She read the menu out, and made her sister laugh.

'It was moderately delicious,' James had written, 'in the circumstance, and we did our best to make a night of it, with everyone talking and laughing as much as possible to cover the quarter of an hour or so that elapsed between each course, while the kitchen hastily washed up the plates and forks in order to bring them out again with the next offering.' Lucy laughed. 'Isn't that just like James, to see the funny side? I wonder if Aunt Morrison has had a letter too?'

Aunt Morrison had. A later one, at that: mail from France tended to come in batches nowadays. And in the cool shade of a tree, in a garden heavy with the scent of late flowers and the dull drone of bees, she read them extracts as they sipped their tea.

Helena was a little bit preoccupied, of course, dealing with china teacups in a place she didn't know, and having to grope discreetly for her plate of sandwiches which Lucy had placed beside her on the grass, but she was more interested in what was happening to James and she abandoned her picnic to give her full attention to the words.

This was a more sober letter. James had been out with the field ambulance to collect the wounded from the dressing stations once or twice. He didn't dwell a great deal on what that had entailed, but the impression was more vivid for only being brief.

For a moment, no one spoke at all.

'And then there's a PS. "I am moving a bit

338

further up the line next week – just for a few days, to take the place of an MO at an RAP who is due for some relief."' Aunt Morrison paused. 'MO stands for medical officer, as I'm sure you know. But an RAP? It sounds important. I wonder what it means.'

What it meant on that particular Thursday afternoon was a draughty wood-lined dugout shelter close to the front line. It wasn't sunny here. The air was heavy with impending rain and the smoke of guns.

The acting regimental medical officer (or RMO for short) jumped down the steps into the regimental aid post with relief. For five of the last ten days they had been out of range, but today the shelling seemed right on top of them, and he was glad of the protection of the sandbags at the door.

One of his orderlies was lying on the floor, wrapped in his greatcoat and obviously asleep. He snapped awake as James stepped over him, and clambered to his feet, full of contrition and apologies.

James shook his head. He would have been happy to let him snatch some rest. They had been on duty for thirty hours without a break after the last attack. Thirty hours of bringing in the dying and the dead, the stretcher-bearers' faces grey with mud and greyer with fatigue; and there was likely to be another onslaught tomorrow at first light.

'Coffee, sir?' The orderly tried to make amends. He was holding up a billy can and

339

the army issue tin, and was obviously offering to heat it over the camp stove on the table where the oil light was.

James nodded. The stuff didn't taste like coffee, but it wasn't bad, and certainly it was better than the boiled-up leaves and sugar which the army thought was tea.

'The new straw has been delivered, then?' He glanced at the wooden slatted spaces in the walls, and the straw-covered pallets on the floor that was all they boasted in the way of mattresses and beds.

The orderly was spooning extract into the billy can. 'Last of the old consignment from the stores, but there's more expected. And we're ready when it comes. All cleared up and' – he flinched instinctively as something whistled overhead and landed with a crump that shook the walls – 'and waiting, sir!' he finished, as though it had been nothing untoward.

James nodded. Cleared up and waited for the next appalling wounds. They would soon be here, no doubt. Already there were shouts and cries and the sound of running feet – the result of that last explosion, probably. This was the front line in another kind of war – the place where every casualty was brought, to be patched up where possible and sent further down the line.

He said, with the pretended nonchalance that he had learned in ten days of being in this post, 'Reminds me of shopping with my mother in White's Emporium, you know. Big

340

shop in Penzance. You gave your money to the shop assistant and he passed it on – put it in a container with the bill and sent it down the tube to someone in the office, and they put it into a cash register. Then someone transferred it from there to a safe, and then into a briefcase, and so into the bank. Same system, isn't it? Except that the commodity here is wounded human flesh.'

Passed step by painful step back down the line, he meant, just like the money in the vacuum tube – to the casualty dressing stations first, then through the clearing stations to the mobile field hospitals a little further back, on to the stationary hospitals like the one where he had been, and at last (if they 'caught a blighty') across the sea to peaceful wards at home. But, however hopeless, they had to move from here. Some made a shorter journey, straight into a hole, with a bugler and the chaplain muttering a prayer. Even so, he thought, they were the lucky ones – a good many of those who fell out in the field didn't even make it underground. There was not much time for burying in the face of a barrage.

'Like an emporium, sir?' the orderly obviously didn't comprehend. 'Oh, you mean the paperwork. The way we pin the notice to them as we send them on? Saying what is wrong with them and what we've done so far? I see, sir. Very droll.'

It wasn't what he'd meant at all, but it was good enough. 'Supposing we've managed to do anything at all.' James took the mug from him, and took a welcome sip. 'Hello! What's this?'

'Sir?' His other orderly came trotting down the trench. 'There's a fellow wants to see you sir, if you've got time for him. Walking wounded, but a beastly thing. Boiling some milk and tea up when that shell went off nearby, and scalded both his hands.'

James nodded. It was almost a pleasure. Between the carnage, little jobs like this, when there was a chance that you could really help. Splinters, strains, even diseases, like pneumonia. 'Show him in.'

His assistant was already opening the disinfectant, and the precious laudanum. It was a sort of understanding in a case like this – better to give a man relief when there was a chance that they could patch him up and he could fight again.

The patient was an officer, James saw to his surprise. Most captains, like himself, had an orderly to make their tea for them, but this one was clearly of an independent breed. He was walking unaided, but he was shocked and staggering. The shell had obviously fallen very near – the uniform was torn to tatters and like the hair was thick with spattered dust, the eyes and mouth pink circles in a mask of grey. No trivial scald either, the skin was badly seared.

James treated this as best he could, coating both hands in cooling paraffin ointment and then binding them in lint and bandages from the man's own field-dressing pack. 'Ought to send you down the line a bit, and let this heal,' he said.

Most men would have embraced the opportunity with relief, but this one shook his head. 'We're due to be relieved. I'll manage till tomorrow, and go back with the men.' He looked at James intently for a minute, his eyes peculiarly pink-rimmed and dark against the dust, then turned and gave his details to the orderly, and left – still upright, if a little unsteady on his feet.

James was staring after him. 'I meant that as an order. I should have made him go.' He frowned. 'Who is he anyway? Looks a bit familiar, though I don't know why.'

The orderly laughed. 'You know who that is, don't you, sir? He's quite a legend here. Totally fearless, so the stories say – or reckless, depending on how you look at it. But a proper man, if you take my meaning, especially where the drink and ladies are concerned. They call him Captain Hotspur – though never to his face. Taken some appalling risks and got away with it. Charmed life, you might say. His men would follow him almost anywhere.' He consulted the piece of paper on the desk. 'Yes, here we are. Proper name is Robinson, Simon Arthur George. Comes from your neck of the woods, in fact. You're from near Penvarris in Cornwall, aren't you, sir?'

Frank was struggling up the road, and

343

cursing inwardly. Damn lorries. They had been so delighted when he'd volunteered, to learn that he was good with horses – and what had the army done? Given him a month delivering sides of meat by cart, and then transferred him to a special 'training course' to drive a motor van. The army was getting more and more of them – three times the number they'd had a year ago.

So here he was, up to his axles in confounded mud. And not even winter yet. The road ploughed up with passing vehicles, and turned to mire with the first hint of rain. Even horses would have a time of it, though there had been plenty past here, judging by the tracks. He'd seen a few. A motor veterinary ambulance had passed him on the road – if that featureless mud track deserved the name – with several lame and wounded animals on board. Taking them off to shoot them, probably – as if there wasn't enough shooting in this wretched war.

The lorry took another lurch into a ditch and stopped. Frank sighed. Now what was he to do? Supplies to the advance depot was what his orders said, so it could be transferred forward on limbers after dark. He had been part of a small convoy, but a problem with his fuel line had delayed him half an hour, and now the landmarks he'd been given seemed to have disappeared. It was drizzling, too, a damp persistent drizzle that got into your bones.

He got down and put his shoulder to the

wheel, just as he would have done if this had been a cart. No use. His companion in the lorry was far too small to help. There seemed to be a fellow kneeling by the road – a Scottish soldier, by the uniform – and Frank called out to him. No answer. Frank had heard how people were half-deafened by the shells so he went across to ask the man for help.

A moment later he was back again, and retching in the grass. Who would have believed that Death could kneel like that? There had been other corpses – neat parcels by the road awaiting burial, or sprawled in ditches with their boots still on – but this was something grotesque and different. He was still spluttering and heaving when a hand fell on his arm.

'That wagon yours?'

He turned. A corporal. A live one, sprung from nowhere in the mist. He nodded thankfully. 'Rations and fodder for the reserve trench, Sector C,' he said.

The corporal looked at him. 'You've missed your way,' he said. 'I'll get some men to turn your lorry round. You'd better come with me. And your companion, too.'

The companion was a small, slight, nervous lad named Sam, who had said nothing much all journey, and who said nothing now. Underage and clearly terrified, he was more hindrance than help when it came to doing anything. However, he obeyed Frank's orders and did as he was told.

345

'Keep your head down,' said the corporal, and they followed him along a ditch, half-stooping as they ran. 'Don't know how you missed the sentries. You've come right up the line. I'll take you to my officer, he'll tell you what to do.' He led the way to a communications trench.

Frank straightened up and took a look around. He had somehow expected the trenches to be roofed, but this was merely a deeper extension of the ditch. However, since it was shored up with timbers and had sandbags on the parapet, it was certainly a good deal more secure, while duckboards made it slightly drier underfoot. There was a man with a machine gun, too, keeping watch in a sort of platform halfway up the wall, behind a shield of sandbags which looked none too strong.

'At least it's relatively quie—' Frank began, but the words were lost in an almighty bang that seemed to rock the walls. It was followed by another, and another still until the whole world seemed to be exploding round their ears.

The man on lookout raised his head again. 'Blessed Minnie Wafers, again, sir. They seem to have our range.'

'Mini-waters?' Frank enquired.

'Minenwerfen,' the corporal explained. 'Nasty German things.'

Sam's eyes were like pickled onions, and he was trembling. Frank had to take him by the arm and steady him as they made their way

346

along the trench – closer and closer to the thudding guns.

The trench led into another, narrower this time, and flanked by little dugout crevices, where crouching men were huddled from the rain. Some, Frank noticed, seemed to be asleep despite the dreadful barrage that was going on overhead. More thuds. More sandbags. More sentries on lookout with binoculars. Further along there was a grander dugout space that even had a roof, a sort of room with a flattened floor and wattles propping up the sides, and a proper fire-step leading out of it. However, there was a pile of debris by the outer wall, which looked as if it had been hastily repaired with wooden planks.

There was a table in this area, and a lamp as well, and a man was sitting at it with his jacket off poring over some papers in the flickering light. He looked up as they entered.

'Well?' A sharp voice, half-amused. He was in the shadows. Frank could not see his face.

The corporal saluted. 'Convoy lorry for the depot, sir. Seems to have taken the wrong turn somewhere, and ended up with us. Permission to send an escort to lead it back again?'

A laugh. 'Better to unload it, don't you think? Save the trouble of bringing it all back up, since I imagine it's intended for the front line anyway.'

'But, sir, my orders—' Frank protested, though he knew it was a foregone conclusion anyway. By the time he got back to his lorry, if he ever did, it would be stripped of anything of value to the men. Seeing the conditions that they were living in he did not personally begrudge them, but he would have to answer for his cargo in the end. 'If you could write a requisition order, perhaps?'

The man laughed. 'To save your wretched hide?' His voice changed. 'Wait a minute! Don't I know you, though?' He picked the lamp up in one bandaged hand, and for the first time Frank saw who he was talking to. 'Dammit, it's that spying fellow with the cart. Can't keep his mouth shut when he sees me on the moors.' He turned towards the corporal, who was looking mystified. 'This man is known to me. Father was a carter at a mine my family has a business interest in.' He grinned unpleasantly. 'Not any more, though, I believe.'

A sudden fury coursed through Frank's veins. 'That was your doing, Mr Robinson?'

'Major Robinson to you.' The words were almost drowned out by a screeching shell nearly. Sam moaned, and even the corporal flinched a bit. Robinson however merely laughed again, even when the sickening crump was heard nearby.

Somehow, that laugh made Frank forget himself. This was a superior officer and he should not have done it, whatever his grievances from civvy life. But he found himself saying, in a quiet monotone, 'Do you know what you've done to him? You've turned him

348

mad, that's what. Made him a drunkard and a laughing stock, and as for what it did to Ma...' He took a step towards the smiling man, who was holding his bandaged hands up as if in self-defence.

Whether he would actually have struck him, goodness knows, but Robinson made a sudden lunge for him. And before Frank could properly react at all, he found himself pinned face down on the floor with Major Robinson on top of him. Then there was a thump that made the world go black, and half the roof came tumbling in on them.

It all got even more confusing after that. There was the sound of screaming, which he thought was Sam, but realized a little later was himself. No pain, but a terrific pressure, and waves and waves of rolling green which carried him away.

Then voices, 'Moaning. Listen. There's someone here alive,' before the pressure lifted and the pain began. Someone forced something burning down his throat and he noticed a strangely disembodied boot beside his face, before he drifted into merciful unconsciousness again.

When he came to agonizing wakefulness at last, and found Mr James was bending over him, he thought it was another of his dreams. 'Don't worry, old chap, we'll pull you through this yet and get you back to Maisie. You're going down to the clearing hospital and I'll be with you to keep an eye on you. My relief has come and I'm going down the line, so I'll be travelling as an escort to the wounded on the way. Your young companion and the corporal are not among them, I'm afraid.'

Frank forced his mouth to move. He managed, 'Robinson?'

The doctor shook his head. 'Give him a medal, I shouldn't be surprised. He must have flung himself to shield you when he heard the shell. His body took the shock and saved your life.'

Was that what he'd intended? Frank would never know. But he was far too weary to think about it now. He closed his eyes and went to sleep again.

Chapter Five

'Wounded. Visit possible.' Lucy read the telegram several times, but somehow the words refused to reach her brain.

'We were as shocked as you were, Lucy dear.' Aunt Morrison's voice was full of tears. 'We had a letter, just the day before, to say that he was travelling on the train, accompanying the wounded back to somewhere safe, and then, the next thing – this! They've taken him to the hospital where Rupert Neill is, and he arranged a telegram to let us know

350

at once. But it's possible to visit, as you see. We thought, perhaps, that you would like to come.'

Lucy swallowed. 'Go over there? To France?' She had a vision of a place of guns; fire and blood and all kinds of dreadful things. She shook her head. 'I couldn't possibly.'

It was abrupt and Aunt Morrison looked hurt.

Lucy said, 'Perhaps when he is back in England.' It still sounded heartless and she tried to find something to offer as excuse. 'Only, they are starting classes for young women to train as nursing volunteers. I thought – with James, it was the least that I could do.' It wasn't total nonsense, she had thought of it before – even read the paragraph from the paper to Papa. Several of her friends were already doing it. The uniform was very flattering and earned the wearers approving glances in the street. She really had considered signing up.

'I think I've seen it in the paper, haven't I? First-aid classes at the Educational Hall, leading to the Red Cross certificates.'

'That's right. It's quite respectable. Tamsin Beswetherick began it months ago. Little Manor has been recognized as an auxiliary hospital, so with a month's probation you can be a proper VAD.'

It was lame, but Aunt Morrison looked quite mollified. 'I think that's rather noble of you, Lucy dear,' she said. 'And I'm sure that

351

James would say so too – you'll be following in his footsteps, in a minor way. Besides, when he comes home again you will know what to do. So many wives would not begin to have the least idea. They may even bring him back to Little Manor at Trevarnon, I suppose.' She turned towards Papa, who had just brought Helena and her mother to hear the telegram. 'It's a splendid notion, don't you think so, Paul?'

After that, of course, there was no escaping it, and Lucy found herself attending in a draughty hall, practising tourniquets and splints and bandaging on ageing bank clerks and spotty farmers' sons. Still, it was quite engaging in a way. She was deft, her efforts won her praise and she found to her surprise that she was quite enjoying it. And it did avoid the embarrassment of her having to go across to France, and the nameless hazards which she felt that would entail.

James's parents went, of course, and came back chastened by the experience. 'Perhaps it's just as well you didn't come, my dear. I think they only suggest a visit if they don't expect the patient to survive. James has clearly been very, very ill, though Rupert says he's turned the corner now. I found it impossible to judge. The Germans hit the train, apparently, and there was a dreadful fire. His hair and uniform were alight it seems, and he was pretty badly burned. It's hard to see him for the bandages. But they will send him back to England in a week or two if he goes on recovering, and of course you will be able to go and see him then.'

Lucy applied herself with special care to the first-aid lessons about the care of burns, so much so that she came second in that particular exam, but until the moment came to visit him she found it very difficult to imagine what it meant. He was taken to a London hospital, the same one where he had been a student and she went up with his parents in a train. It was a long journey, hours and hours, but there was little conversation: his parents were anxious and withdrawn, while she tried to imagine red and blistered flesh and braced herself for what awaited her.

They took a motor taxi from the station, the first that Lucy had ever travelled in, and as they drew up Mr Morrison leaned across and patted her gently on the knee. 'You mustn't let him see it, if you are very shocked. Bad enough for him, poor devil, as it is.'

They went in. Hard to think that this was where James trained for all those years – though of course it must be very different now. Rows and rows of metal beds, and men in all of them. Some had their legs strung up on slings, or had amputated stumps for arms, others were frightfully disfigured round the head. One poor fellow had a shrivelled scar where half his face should be, his left eye was an empty socket and his shoulder was a brown and blackened mess above the bandages bound round his chest. God knew what further horrors they concealed. She attempted not to stare.

'Lucy?'

Even then she did not recognize him. Not until Aunt Morrison burst out in happy tears, 'James. How wonderful. You've come back to yourself!' She would have flung her arms around him, you could see, but in his state it was impossible. Instead she grasped his one uninjured hand and squeezed it very tight. 'Oh, James, I was so very worried about you. But now, you're clearly going to be all right. Oh, thank Heaven! My darling, darling boy.'

All right? Lucy was watching in a kind of daze. How could anyone give thanks for this? It was almost impossible to believe that this was James. She could feel nothing but a stricken grief. But even James's father seemed relieved and pleased. He actually bent over and gave his son a kiss.

'And look who we have brought you,' Aunt Morrison went on. 'She's training how to be a nurse to help you, later on. Come on, Lucy, come and say hello.'

Lucy came forward. She tried to wrest her eyes away from staring at those scars and concentrate on the bits of James that she could recognize, but her voice betrayed her. 'Hello, James!' she said, and even she could hear the shock in it.

James had heard it too. He turned his one remaining eye on her, and gave her one half of a painful grin. 'Bit of a facer, isn't it, old thing? Or an unfacer, perhaps?'

She gasped. How could he make feeble

354

jokes about it at a time like this?

He gave a tiny nod. 'I know. I can hardly bear to look at it myself. But it can only get better, so the doctor says. And they will provide me with another eye, even if just a glass one. That won't be so bad.'

She managed to say, 'No.' Pause. 'Of course.' Then, 'How are you feeling, James?'

'He's making splendid progress. Much better than we hoped.'

She turned at the familiar voice. 'Mr Maskins!'

He gave her that peculiar, intellectual smile. 'Miss Lucille. And Mrs Morrison.' He was shaking hands. 'And Mr Morrison, of course. I am glad to say that I have splendid news. We have saved the sight in James's other eye – though it was a question whether we should be able to or not, he had burning chips in it. But as you see, we met with good success and he is able to use the eye quite well – though not to read and write, perhaps. Not yet, at any rate.'

Lucy was still reeling. 'But his work? However will he...?'

'That is a question for another day. He is a long way from working yet. I had thought of sending him over to St Dunstan's House, they have begun a system there for helping blinded soldiers and sailors. Train them to read and write in Braille, and teach them skills – to be typists, or piano tuners, or how to care for hens – so they can make a living in society instead of being locked away in blind asylums. They are talking about a course for medical masseurs – teaching people how to exercise their joints, and manipulating them after injury – with James's training he'd be good at that. But it may be that he won't need it after all. He made a special study of diseases of the eye. Appearance isn't so important in that field.' He laughed self-mockingly. 'Look at me, for instance.'

'And Lucy can help him,' James's mother said. 'She is training to be a VAD, you know.'

'Are you?' Maskins looked at her – with new respect, she thought. 'My dear Miss Tregenza, I had no idea. I thought you interested in ... more social things, you know. Though you have always been careful for your sister, I'm aware.'

She found that she was blushing prettily. She stammered, 'When I heard that James was very ill...'

'Of course.' He turned away. He was still a little ... wounded, was it? As if he'd really cared for her.

She managed her best smile. 'Thank you, Mr Maskins. We could talk again, perhaps?'

And she turned back to the travesty that had once been James.

She kept up a frantic conversation for a quarter of an hour – about everything she could think of, which was nothing very much – until he was clearly tiring with the effort and she could decently suggest that they might leave.

★ ★ ★

The transfer to Little Manor took a little time. James had put in for it as soon as he knew that it was possible, but it took other people to pull some strings for him. It was Maskins who signed the papers in the end, of course, but Pater thought the Robinsons had had a hand in it. It was James's written report and commendation, after all, which had resulted in a posthumous medal for their son.

'Strange that you should have made an ally there,' his father went on, on his parents' second visit to the London ward. 'But no doubt it will make matters a good deal easier at the mine. Tregenza tells me that Robinson used to vote against you every time, almost on principle by the sound of it.'

James by this time was able to sit up sometimes in a chair, and even to feed and shave himself – or what was left of him. But the shock of what met him in the mirror was beginning to sink in. He said glumly, 'Supposing I ever get to vote again.' Strange, when he was first injured it had not seemed so bad. It was enough that his burns were healing and the pain had stopped and he was getting stronger every day, But now he was haunted by a black despair. 'You've seen my face. I am a monster now. How can I ever walk the streets again?'

His mother came to sit beside him. 'Maskins said it's possible that surgery can help. They are learning new methods all the time. And even if not, they can fit you with a mask that will hide the worse of it. You're not the only one. There are hundreds of men around with injuries, some much worse than yours. People will understand you got wounded in the war – and recognize you for the hero that you are.'

It was churlish to be stubborn, but he said pettishly. 'And Lucy? What does Lucy think? I can hardly ask her to stand by me, now.' He sighed. 'She would not say so, she is far too sweet, but I could see when she visited what her reaction was. And I notice that she has not come up with you this time.'

His mother looked evasive. 'Lucy is working at Little Manor now, expecting your return. When you come down, she'll see you often there. And of course your appearance makes no difference to her – she promised me as much.'

James thought, 'I wonder!' and they talked of other things. There was news of Frank Carter, who was back at home again. Invalided from the army because he had a limp, but back to driving his horse and cart again.

'Though I understand he has been asking round for little jobs to do – in family gardens and that sort of thing,' his mother said. 'Of course, there isn't so much work for carters nowadays, People don't move around the way they used to do.'

James frowned. 'Anyway, he and his partner have only got one horse. The army requisitioned the other one, I think.'

Mother shrugged. 'I haven't the least idea, my dear. Not really the sort of people I know a lot about. I wouldn't know anything at all, except that his wife is still working for Tregenza and she mentioned you to me. Her husband was very grateful for your care, she said. It's thanks to you he kept his leg at all. She was terribly sorry to hear that you were hurt.'

James managed a wry smile. 'Yes. Ironic, really. I left him at the dressing station nearer to the front, and I was on a train escorting others back to base. If I had stayed on with him, this wouldn't have occurred.'

His mother gave him a little pat, as if to reassure him. 'The Carters sent best wishes for your recovery. They asked if they might visit when you got back to Little Manor, and I said they could. I hope you don't object. Now, here's your father coming, he's brought some books for you – mostly pictures, so you can look at them without straining your eyes.'

His eye, she meant – although now that the glass one had been fitted you didn't notice the absence of the other quite so much. That was Maskins' doing, too. One had to hand it to the man. He'd done his very best for James, as though there had never been rivalry between them at all.

James had cause to think the same again the morning that he was to be transferred to the train. Maskins came to see him, and wish him bon voyage. 'I may even come to see you while you're there. Neill has been appointed to Little Manor as you know, and he has invited me to give my opinion on a case or two. And if Tregenza has no objection, I might possibly look in and see that future sister-in-law of yours again as well. That operation that I talked to her about is having good results. She might wish to contemplate it, a little later on. After the war, perhaps. Methods are getting better all the time. In fact, you might be interested to hear what is involved.' And he outlined the procedures, for all the world as if professional concerns had no connection with his private life.

Then it was Paddington, and the special carriage set aside for them – five of them going to Little Manor all at once.

It was strange to be travelling on a train again, and even stranger to be going homeward. He was on a stretcher – everybody was – but he managed to look out and recognize the landmarks as they passed. The Mount, the bay, the station in Penzance. There was an ambulance to meet them and a girl in uniform together with an older woman, obviously in charge. James was possibly the least ill of the company, but they made a fuss of him, and saw him gently into the ambulance as though he was made of china and might break. He was glad, in fact. The journey had tired him much more than he ever would have guessed.

Then the sweetness of clean sheets and quiet wards. There were professional nurses as well as volunteers and his dressings were soaked off and changed quite expertly and he was even given a sort of blanket bath. He had been hoping to see Lucy but there was no sign of her. There was tea, however, and fresh eggs and he fell asleep content.

Lucy came to see him, before lunch the next day. She was in the uniform of the Little Manor Volunteers with a big red cross on her apron-front to show she'd passed the test, and very smart she looked. She sat beside him, just a little prim, and asked him very brightly how he was.

'Better for seeing you, my Lucy,' but she hardly smiled.

'Well, that's splendid, then. I'm glad you're on the mend. And when you're better and you're out of here, we'll...' Her voice faltered, and he heard the tears in it. She swallowed and jumped quickly to her feet. 'Now, I'm on duty in the other ward. I'll see you later, then.'

Lucy was not the only visitor. His parents came again, of course, and so did Helena, leaning on her father and looking, he thought, immensely beautiful – though the peach colour of her wrap and dress only served to accentuate the paleness of her face.

They fetched a chair from somewhere and she sat down beside him. 'James! Are you very hurt? Lucy says it's bad.'

'Bad enough.' He took her hand in his un-damaged one. 'It's made a mess of me.'

She squeezed his fingers. 'Yes, I know. It's very difficult. People forget that you're the same inside, whatever may have happened to your face.'

361

He nodded, forgetting that she couldn't see, then added, 'I understand that now. They talk to you as though you were a child, or weren't there at all, sometimes.' He looked at the blind, lovely face. 'You must have felt that, too.'

She laughed. 'You never treated me like that, James. It is one of the reasons why I loved your company.'

It wasn't true. He knew it wasn't true. He had been as guilty as the rest. He'd thought of her as just unfortunate – pleasant, pretty and intelligent, but not a girl with feelings like anybody else.

But then Tregenza came and talked to him instead. He was telling him about the business of the mine – treating him like a proper man – but it took all James's effort to concentrate on that. 'There's been quite a rush on tin, you know – all those canned rations for the troops – and the mine is doing better now than it has done for some years. It's that new engine of yours, partly. It's been a great success – increased our capacity to mine the tin, even when a good proportion of the men have signed up and gone to war. So you can feel that you've done something for the war effort in that. Robinson is predicting gloom, of course, says he has it on the best authority that the government is going to introduce conscription very soon and we shall lose the men.'

It was as much as James could do to bring his mind to bear on this, but it was a matter he'd talked about to Rupert many times. 'They won't take so many that we'll have to close the mine. No point in having soldiers if they've got no guns or food.' It was quite an effort but he'd made a valid point and shown his brain still worked, whatever people thought.

Helena seemed to know what he was feeling. She laughed. 'A pity you weren't there to argue for Papa.' She squeezed the fingers that were still in hers.

Then James really was exhausted, so they left and let him sleep. Lucy must have known that, because she didn't come.

'Oh, there you are Miss Elenner.' Maisie sounded out of breath. 'Been looking for you everywhere. Never expected to find you in the garden all alone.'

Helena nodded. 'I asked Mrs Lovett to walk me out here for a bit. I wanted to be outside in the open air.' She wanted to be alone, with time to think in fact, the visit to James had moved her very much. She could hear, from his voice, how very ill he'd been although he tried to be cheerful and grateful when he spoke. One sentence was travelling round and round inside her head. 'I understand ... You must have felt that too.' Affectionate and with feeling – as if there was a special bond between them. If only that were true.

She shook off the recollection. 'Why were you wanting me?'

'It's Lucy's friend Miss Annabelle – or Mrs

Neill, I suppose I ought to say. Come with some flowers and grapes for Mr James, seeing as how he was her 'usband's friend. What should I tell her to do with them, and should I give her tea? Only the mistress is out with that ladies' meeting for the war, your father's driving her, and Miss Lucy isn't back yet from the hospital.'

Helena got slowly to her feet. 'Take me to the house, and I will speak to her. And perhaps some tea and toast, if that is possible.' Things like muffins had vanished with the war.

'I believe we've got some biscuits and a loaf of bread.' Maisie had placed a guiding hand under her arm. 'Not that it's up to much these days, with what they use for flour. But we are short of butter, though I think there's jam – if that isn't too difficult for you.'

'Whatever Mrs Lovett can organize,' Helena said, and was led indoors. Oddly, she was anxious. She had heard a great deal about Annabelle, of course – since she and Lucy were such friends and Mrs Passemore-Jenkins was a frequent visitor – and had even been to her wedding, but she had never actually exchanged private words with her.

She went into the drawing room, and heard the rustle of silk skirts which meant that their guest was rising to her feet.

'Miss Tregenza!'

'Mrs Neill?' There was an awkward silence. Lena guessed that Annabelle was holding out her hand, so she extended her own, saying,

'You are very welcome. My sister will have told you that I cannot see.'

'Oh, of course, I'm sorry,' and a dry little glove clasped her fingers briefly. 'I brought some things for James – some late grapes from the greenhouse and a few hothouse flowers. Rupert suggested that Lucy might be prepared to take them in – I hardly feel I know him well enough to call myself, and it might be awkward, with his … disfigurement.'

Helena said, 'I see!' And then, 'Your husband told you about that, no doubt?'

An embarrassed twitching. 'I spoke to Lucy, and she mentioned it. It must be very difficult, when you're engaged like that. She can hardly wound him further by asking for release, but as she says, how can she marry him? Of course, I know that you have been to visit him yourself, so you will know exactly what she means.'

Helena found that she was saying, frostily, 'In my condition, appearances don't matter very much. James is still James, as far as I'm concerned. But I will see that your gifts are delivered, naturally.'

However, quite a different conversation was going on in her head, and when Lucy came in to see her after work – complaining, as usual about aching feet and legs, and how her hands were rubbed red raw with soap – Helena raised the topic very soon.

'Annabelle Neill was here this afternoon, after my singing pupil had gone home.'

'Yes,' in a vague tone, 'Maisie told me so. I

understand she brought some things for James.' Lucy was moving restlessly around, and had halted over by the dressing table now. 'Are you using all these hairpins, or can I have a few? I seem to lose them like confetti when I'm working on the wards, and of course one has to keep one's hair pinned up. It's very unhygienic otherwise, so Matron says.'

'Have as many as you need. You're welcome, as you know. But don't change the subject, Lucy. We're talking about James. Are you going to take these presents when you see him next? You do intend to visit him properly some time? He says you drop in for a minute and that's all he sees of you.'

Silence, except for the ticking of the clock. Then the sliding of a dressing-table drawer. 'There's a whole new packet of the long ones here. Could I have those? I'll try and get some new ones, when I next have time to shop – but it isn't always easy, and these things are getting scarce.'

'Lucy! You can't ignore this. It isn't going away.'

She heard Lucy pull out the dressing-table stool, and fling herself impetuously down on it. 'Surgery might help him, Samuel Maskins said. Did I tell you Samuel was coming down today? Such a splendid surgeon – it's amazing what he's done. Everyone at Little Manor has the highest praise for him.' She was speaking very fast.

'Lucy!' Helena said again, and this time she

366

was rewarded with a sob.

'I can't, Lena, I can't. You can't see him, you don't know what it's like. How can I marry a man who looks like that? Every time I see his face it makes me...' She didn't finish, but the meaning was quite clear.

Helena felt as though she was in a kind of trance, where nothing was quite real. 'Have you told him how you feel?'

'How can I, Lena? I am not altogether heartless. But...' Lucy rushed over to her sister and buried her head, sobbing, in her lap. 'Oh, Lena! What am I to do?'

Lena ran gentle fingers through her hair. 'You'll have to tell him. It isn't fair to keep him...' she hesitated, 'hoping in this way, if you have decided that you can't marry him.'

She heard her sister's sniffle from somewhere in her skirts. 'You think so, honestly?'

'I believe I'm being honest,' Helena said, trying to still her raging thoughts and speaking very quietly indeed. 'I'm not entirely neutral about James Morrison, you know. I never have been.'

She was aware that Lucy had sat up at this. 'Of course, you were always very fond of him, and he thinks a lot of you.' Another sniff and then she burst out plaintively, 'Oh, Lena, you couldn't ... wouldn't ... talk to him for me? I'm such a coward, I can't bear to do it for myself.' Lucy got up, abruptly. 'No, of course I shouldn't ask you. It's impossible. But suppose I wrote a letter ... could you take him that? I shall put it badly. You'll know what to say. I don't want to hurt him. I loved him, after all.'

It was the past tense that made Helena say at last, 'I'll take the things from Annabelle, and if you write to him, I suppose I could deliver it as well. And yes, I'll try to moderate the blow. Now pull yourself together, there's Maisie on the stair.' She adopted a more formal tone of voice and added, 'I'd like to visit James again, in any case, if Papa will drive me to the hospital – I know he's very busy for the next few days, and it's so difficult now Edgar's gone away and volunteered.'

'Well,' that was Maisie, from somewhere near the door, 'I'm sure my Frank would take you, if you didn't mind the cart. He wanted to see Mr James himself, to thank him for what he did for him. And I could come with you as well, if you would like. Give you an 'and to get up and down the steps and help you find your way.'

'That might be splendid, if Papa can't help. I'm sure I shouldn't mind the cart a bit.'

But she didn't have to. Papa had a counter-proposal, when she asked. He would take the carriage to the venturers' meeting first, and Frank could drive it back again and take Helena and her mother to Little Manor later on. 'Fellow's rather good with horses, isn't he?' he said. 'And mine are very placid and obedient. Too old to cause him trouble. Would he do that, do you think? I'd give him a shilling for doing it, of course.'

'He'd be pleased to help, for Mr James's

sake.' Maisie was taking up the soup but she answered fervently. 'Wouldn't be sorry to earn an honest bob, either. It's not so easy with a twisted leg. He was thinking of trying to get a job down with our Lenny in Penzance – it would be hard to get there, and it's no fun besides, being junior to your little brother, but he might do it yet.'

'That will be all, then, Maisie,' Mama said, in the tone of voice that meant the maid had said too much. And then to Papa, 'But if he's to drive the carriage, I don't think I shall go. Maisie can look after Helena, so it will be quite all right.'

And so it was arranged. Frank arrived back with the carriage ('Smart as paint, Miss Elenner, you'd be some proud of him. Put his Sunday shirt and trousers on, specially, he has. And I've guv him Edgar's green tailcoat and top hat to put on, so he looks like a proper coachman – though the hat's a little roomy, like, and the coat's a bit too small.')

The picture Maisie painted was enough to make her laugh, and so did the breezy commentary on everything they passed. It hardly left Helena time to worry much about the painful interview ahead. She had Lucy's note with her, an anguished message which her sister had read aloud to her last night – it had gone through several drafts, since then and was as little hurtful as the pair of them jointly could contrive.

All the same – and despite the fact that it gave her an excuse to come and visit James –

it was not a mission she was looking forward to. And after that there would be Mama and Papa to confront, and all the disappointment from the Morrisons. Why, then, did she not entirely regret the circumstance?

'I said, we're 'ere, Miss Elenner.' Maisie cut across her thoughts. 'I'll help you out the carriage, and Frank'll take it round the back, and he can come and find us in the ward. I don't know where Mr James is, I suppose we'll have to ask.' She was assisting her mistress to get down as she spoke.

A brisk, brusque female gave them the information that they sought inside the house. Down a corridor, and over to the right. Then James's voice: 'Helena, how wonderful, and Maisie too. And half a florist's by the look of it.'

'Can't have them in the wards. I'll find you a pot and you can put them in the patients' sitting room,' the brisk voice said. 'This way!' and off she went, with Maisie's little heel-plates tapping after her.

'It's wonderful to see you.'

She was alone with James. She felt her way across, and found a chair. 'Perhaps you won't think so, when you hear my news. I'm sorry, James, I'm truly sorry, but I have brought a note...'

'From Lucy?'

She nodded. 'Not what you might think. She feels ... she wants ... You'll have to read it, perhaps.'

His voice was gentle. 'It isn't very easy for

370

me to read things yet. But I think that I can guess. She wants me to release her ... no, don't look like that. I knew it from the moment she first came to visit me. And I can't really blame her, when I search my heart. I think she was always more in love with an idea.'

He sounded wounded and she said at once, 'Try not to think too harshly of her, James.'

He gave a little laugh. 'You might as well think harshly of a butterfly. But I'll not trap her in a net. Lucy is sweet and charming, but she is shallow, too. I have always known that, but I hoped that she would change. If she was able to be true to me, I thought, and keep her promise over all those years, then there was every chance that she would settle down. And she was faithful, I cannot fault her there – other chaps that I have known were not so fortunate. So if she's written to ask me to release her, I do so, willingly. Though, naturally, not without regret. I would not force her to a marriage that she did not want. And with my face, what kind of girl would want to marry me?'

Helena said nothing. She felt two tears run down beside her nose, but she did not stir to wipe them. She sat very still.

He took her hand in his. She felt the ridge of scars. 'Helena? What is it...?'

'It's what you were saying to me just the other day. People forget that when you've had an accident you're just the person that you always were, inside. And I've always ... valued your friendship. I don't want to lose it, I suppose.'

'And I have valued yours. No – more than that. I've loved you as a sister … Loved you, I suppose. Though I did not dream of courting you. I don't know why.' He sounded as if the thought surprised him as he spoke. 'I don't think it occurred to me that it was possible. But I have thought about you, all the time.'

She found her voice. 'I know. You have been very kind. Bringing me music and books that I could read. I don't know how I would have managed without your kindness there.'

'It's more than that, you silly goose,' he said impatiently. 'Give me your hand.'

She put it into his, and he pressed something round and metal into it.

'What is it?' She rubbed it. 'It feels like a coin.'

'The sovereign you gave me. I've always carried it. That shows you how I felt. You were a kind of yardstick to measure girls beside. I think I partly fell for Lucy because she was like you. Though you might not think that altogether quite a compliment.'

Perhaps it wasn't, but she didn't care. The force of what he was saying had just come home to her. He had always loved her. Is that what he had said? She shook her head. 'This is ridiculous. I can see you're hurt. You mustn't go rushing into saying things that you'll regret someday.'

'You know that I am not. I've had a long time to get used to this – Lucy's reaction has

372

been clear for weeks. I am a fool not to have realized earlier and simply let her go.'

'There will be other chances. You'll build your life again.' Then, greatly daring, 'I could help you, even. I would love to try.'

'Perhaps.' He took her hand again. 'No, I can't expect it. It's quite impossible. How could we manage – me with one eye, and you with none at all? Besides, my dear Helena, you can't see my scars. You've no idea what you'd be taking on.'

She said, very quietly, but full of sudden hope. 'I know what I'd be taking on. I don't know what the world sees, that is all.'

He took her hand and raised it to his face. 'It wouldn't be remotely fair to you. You can't imagine it. Touch me. Feel it. I look a monster now.'

She ran her fingers down the rucks of damaged face and skin, and it was terrible. The force of pity made her almost sob. She stroked him, very tenderly, lest she should cause him hurt. 'But it is still you underneath it, isn't it? That hasn't changed at all. And Maskins says he can improve things – perhaps for both of us.'

He held her hand against his damaged cheek. 'Perhaps we'd learn to manage. You had to, after all. You know I had my eyes bound up for just a week, and for all my studies I'd never imagined what a dreadful handicap it was to lose one's sight. I thought about you then, and how admirably you coped.' He paused. 'We could have your

373

Maisie to come and work for us, she knows how you like things done. And perhaps her husband too, since I gather he is looking for a job. He could help me with my side of things. What do you think?'

'I think they would be thrilled, and so would I, if you are really asking what I think you are.'

He laughed. One of his open, glad old-fashioned laughs that warmed her heart to hear. 'We shall scandalize our parents, but they'll come around to it. In fact, I think that in the long run they'll be very glad. And so will Maisie, judging by the look upon her face. She's just come round the corner with that jug of flowers and seen us sitting here like this, and she's grinning like Mr Lewis Carroll's Cheshire Cat. Like everyone in the ward who is well enough to look.'

Helena felt her cheeks flush red and she tried to take her hand away, but he restrained it, saying, 'Helena, my dearest Helena, I'm not much of a catch, and it will be months before I'm out of here. But I suppose you wouldn't care to marry me?'

'Oh yes, I would,' she said.

And ward or no ward, she felt him raise himself and lean towards her lips. She closed her eyes: a sort of instinct, she thought afterwards. He didn't kiss her though – not then at any rate. Just as she felt the warm breath on her face there was a crash as Maisie dropped the jug and then the sound of running footsteps, heavy like a man.

374

'My dear life, Frank, now what have I gone and done! Still, never mind. Smashing to see them two look so happy, isn't it? Go together like a pair of china pigs – like as if they always knew it, and they never knew they knew.'

Helena could not have put it better if she tried.

Epilogue – April 1918

The marriage of Miss Lucille Tregenza to Mr Samuel Maskins was not a grand affair, though it was attended by many of the Little Manor staff – those who could be spared from duty, anyway, and a few of the patients from the convalescent wing came and made a surprise guard of honour at the door. Quite touching, and striking in their blue hospital uniforms.

Mrs Lovett had done wonders with what little one could get – saved up enough butter, fruit and flour to make a proper cake. There were jellies and there were trifles and there were plates of cheese and smoked fish and dainty sandwiches, which she'd somehow made delicious, in spite of 'national flour'. There was even a leg of cold roast beef to carve, enough for everyone to have a slice – though even the best restaurants had to be meatless several times a week these days. More like a children's tea before the war than a wedding banquet, but people were delighted with it, especially the bride.

She had not, as everyone expected, worn her uniform, though that was getting to be quite the fashion now. She looked a picture in a wedding dress of white silk taffeta and lace – apparently she'd put aside the material long ago. The groom was a peculiar-looking sort of man, of course, but he was handsomely turned out and looking proud as Punch. It was the respect that those two had for each other, everybody said, which made them such a match. Nurse Tregenza – Mrs Maskins now – was going to go to London and help him in his work. That had caused a few raised eyebrows when it was first announced – from Mrs Passemore-Jenkins in particular – but more and more married women were working nowadays. Somebody had to do things – until the war was won, at least.

Supposing that it ever was! It didn't look like it. There had been terrible defeats in this last fortnight, even though the Americans had come into the war, and now that Russia had turned Bolshevik and left its Allies in the lurch – signing that humiliating peace treaty that gave half its lands away – things were looking particularly grim. Haig was calling for the army to keep 'our backs against the wall' and that had got into the papers and people caught the mood, so there was little cause for celebration apart from wedding days like this.

And births, as well, of course. It was lucky the bride's sister had been well enough to come, only a week or two after lying in. But she was getting back her colour and her son was doing well, and there she was leaning on her husband's arm, poor soul.

Good thing she couldn't see him, everybody said – though apparently he'd been quite good-looking once, and their baby boy was said to be as pretty as could be. Still, they were happy with each other, that was plain to see, and you had to hand it to James Morrison. The minute he was released from Little Manor as a patient, a year or more ago, he'd arranged to come in once or twice a week, helping Maskins with the men with damaged eyes. He'd offered to assist with other things as well, but they had turned him down. Well, it would never do. It would make a patient poorly just to look at him. Though it was rumoured that he was attending some families out at Penvarris mine – perhaps they couldn't afford to call in anybody else.

Now here was Maisie Carter, handing plates around. That wasn't a surprise. Wherever Helena Morrison went, you were sure to find her maid. It was well known that the Tregenzas had spoiled the girl, of course, and put up with her chattering and speaking out of turn when most employers would have turned her off. But perhaps they had been clever to do so, in the end. It was almost impossible to get staff nowadays, the men had gone to war and the servant class got better wages in the factories. But the Tregenzas had kept their servants when others had lost theirs.

Just as well, perhaps, with James and Helena also in the house, especially now the baby had arrived. Everyone had expected them to move into the cottage on the Morrison estate, or at least move in with his parents. But Paul Tregenza had suggested this arrangement and they'd seized it eagerly. It was easier for Helena to manage where she knew her way about, and James and his father had never quite seen eye to eye – though the Morrisons came to see their grandson nearly every day. Still, it had turned out for the best. Now that the other daughter was leaving home and Paul had offered his services to the War Office, Gertrude Tregenza would have been rattling round in that great house alone and have to close up part of it, like so many others did.

The bride had gone upstairs 'in that great house' to change, and now here she was coming down again in a smart dark blue ensemble, positively glowing as she went round and said goodbye, with her new husband looking patient at her side. And there was Frank Carter, in his coachman's uniform, smiling with pride until you'd think he'd burst, waiting with the carriage to take them to the train.

There were cheers as the newly-weds got up into it and waves as they were driven briskly down the drive. Even Baby Morrison was brought to see them off, carried by Rosie, who was in floods of happy tears. Then the Little Manor crowd began drifting off. Most of them were wanted on duty, later on.

'Some lovely wedding, wasn't it, Missus Elenner?' It was Maisie's new form of address for Helena, and nothing would persuade her to abandon it. She was standing beside her mistress at the front door steps, ready to guide her back inside again. 'Nearly as good as they had for Frank and me, though I'm surprised Miss Lucy was wearing navy blue. She thought I was some funny for doing that, myself, and she doesn't have to wear it for working afterwards. Though I suppose dark colours are more the fashion now – too many folk in mourning to wear pinks and blues. But she won't regret it after. Mine's done me handsome, I'm wearing it today. Still looks good as new.'

'I'm sure it does. And if Mr Maskins does that operation in a year or two, perhaps I will be able to see it for myself.'

'Well, I'm sure you deserve it,' was Maisie's stout reply. 'You've been that good to us. How we'd have managed, if it hadn't been for you, I don't know. Talking the master into giving Frank a job, and seeing that his fayther's looked after properly. Course it's easier now the little ones are growing up a bit, and bringing money home – but we couldn't repay you and Mr James for what you've done if we was millionaires. About time you had a bit of luck yourselves.'

Rosie's footsteps joined them. Helena reached out her arms and took her little boy. He was waking and she could hear him gurgling. James was laughing with their parents – his voice was close nearby, and she could feel spring sunshine falling on her back.

All this, and Maisie to look after her. And one day, perhaps, the war would end and Samuel Maskins would help her see again. But even if he couldn't ... Helena smiled.

'I think I'm very lucky as it is.'